THE SHADOW WAR

THE
SHADOW
WAR

LINDSAY SMITH

For Saana, Katie, Meghan, and Steph

Hamaan tappiin saaka

SEPTEMBER 1942

CHAPTER ONE

LIAM

Liam staggered through the storybook village with a fistful of shadows and a mouthful of lies. The whitewashed cottages glowed in the darkness, weak lamplight seeping around the boarded-up windows, and tire tracks carved the dirt road like scars. Trucks rumbled in the distance, but no one came here on purpose unless they were on their way to somewhere better. Or unless they were like him: more monsters in his head than sense.

The shadows buzzed as he stepped onto the tavern's porch. His palm still stung, blood drying; he should be better at this by now. It had seemed so easy in Princeton's labs five thousand miles away, once he'd figured out the key. The right frequency to dip into the shadows, draw out what he needed, and retreat, the rift closing behind him. He'd balanced every equation in his plan, rehearsed his approach a dozen times—he hadn't gotten where he was by doing anything halfway. But in most of his experiments, he'd controlled every variable, calculated every possible result. This time felt more like crossing himself, amen, getting ready to jump.

Now or never. Liam let the shadowy energy rush through him and steeled his nerves as he recited his cover story one last time. No sense facing these monsters unarmed.

"We're closed," the barkeep called in German from behind the dark oak counter as Liam entered. "Private party."

Liam smiled, his dimples popping, and raked dirty fingers through his crew cut. His face was perfect for this mission—honey-blond hair, light skin, eyes that shifted from gray to blue, depending on the time of day. He was more than a little rumpled from his journey, but it only added to his ruse.

"Oh. Sorry about that." Liam didn't even try to hide his American accent as he answered in German. "It's just—I've been on the road for a while and need some food."

A clutch of senior Schutzstaffel officers looked up from their drinks and turned his way.

Liam worried his tongue over his teeth as he surveyed the cramped dining room. Five officers. One bartender, almost certainly hiding a shotgun or hunting rifle beneath the bar. Two SS guards were posted against the back wall. The tavern barely fit three tables; the rest of the squat Bavarian building must have belonged to the inn. Only one of the electric lights was turned on, unevenly painting the peeling brocade wallpaper and heavy wood paneling with a greasy glow.

"You are American?" one of the officers asked, his English sharp as glass.

Liam's blood froze. SS-Sturmbannführer Junker. His puckered expression and needlelike stare were even more severe in person. But Hans Friedrich Junker and his friends were why Liam had come here, why he was thousands of miles from Graduate Celestial Mechanics and Chancellor Green's stacks and New York's endless spread of noise, that blanket he wanted to wrap himself in every night.

The buzzing shadows in his head became a steady pulse under Liam's skin, goading him as he lowered his gaze obediently. "Ja, mein Herr."

"You are quite far from home." Junker tipped his head toward an empty chair at his table, waving off the bartender's protests. "I should very much like to know why."

Before, Liam never would have called himself a thrill seeker. He'd spent most of his eighteen years buried in one textbook or another, or scrawling equations across onionskin paper like a boy possessed. But the past few years had revealed in him a desperate hunger. *Control,* his mother called it, back when she could, before he learned just how little power he really held. *You want to be in control of things. Dangerous things. You think it'll keep you safe.*

He hadn't been in control then. He would be now.

Liam settled into the empty chair beside Junker and hoisted his bookbag into his lap. Nothing important was in it. If they searched it, all they'd find was a change of clothes, a water canteen, a German-English dictionary, and a journal with asinine entries he'd forged. All he really needed for this mission was tucked safely away inside his head.

He suspected, though, that Junker was more interested in playing with his food.

"Liam." He stuck his hand out. "Liam Doyle. Originally from Manhattan, though I live in Frankfurt now."

"You live here? And your accent is still so atrocious?" Junker laughed loudly, quickly echoed by the other officers. Alcohol and cigarette smoke whetted the sound as it sliced through the dim tavern fug. Junker didn't so much as glance at Liam's outstretched palm, or the red grooves pressed into it from his nails. He just shoved the communal tray of greasy schnitzel and soft pretzels his way.

Liam dropped his hand. It had been a risk, naming a city he'd never visited, but he always did his homework. "Everyone wants to practice their English on me."

Junker eased back, picking up his glass of brandy and watching Liam over its lip as he drank. The other officers, though, were still on guard. Most were at least twice Liam's age—late thirties, early forties—and wore the ravages of battle in their scowls and flinty eyes. One held a cigarette like a pointer, the tip turning to ash. Another clasped his hands before him like Liam was a curious specimen he couldn't wait to dissect.

"And what is it you are doing in Frankfurt, Mr. Doyle?"

He shrugged genially. "I'm a student."

"Your President Roosevelt recalled all the American students from our country," Junker countered.

"Well, maybe I wasn't ready to leave."

Junker considered him, eyes steely. Even if Junker believed him, Liam still had a long way to go—but it would be something. All he needed was an opening. If Junker didn't, though—

Well. Liam flexed one hand beneath the table and let the shadows thicken around it. He had other options, even if they'd make a bigger mess.

"It is dangerous for you to be traveling alone," Junker finally said.

He motioned to the bartender. "Someone might think you're a spy."

Liam smiled, watched the bartender scurry over to refill the Sturmbannführer's brandy. "Sorry to disappoint."

Junker shared another laugh with his officers, this one tinged with malice. The lightning-bolt patches on their collars flashed silver in the grimy light. As Junker tipped his glass toward Liam in a toast, Liam let the darkness stored inside him thread through his thoughts. Might as well let it feed on his terror, keep it awake and ready. It could savor its host for now, but he was always in control of it.

"We are playing a card game." Junker gestured to the strange mix of cards, drinks, and betting chips on the table. They were using everything from bottle caps and Reichsmarks to spent bullet casings and Death's Head rings to wager. Junker's ring, though, stayed firmly fixed on his right hand. "Doppelkopf. Do you know it?"

"I think my classmates tried to teach me." Liam rubbed his chin, the lie flowing easily. "We'd been drinking a lot, though."

Junker collected the cards from the other officers, shuffled them once, then handed the deck to Liam. "Let's see what you remember."

Liam smiled back at him, letting his dimples shine. He'd always been a master at scraping by.

"I think I deal . . . twelve cards each, right?" He shuffled again, then started passing out cards to all of the officers, three at a time. "And then the point value . . ."

Liam let his mouth go on autopilot. Inside his head, the darkness was throbbing, leaching into the air around him, warping and twisting emotions, feelings, fears. It was intoxicating. He couldn't blame Pitr for craving it. The shadows' promises were sweeter than the milkshakes at

Lexington's soda counter—the power to right so many wrongs. All they needed was a suitable conduit.

Einstein's general theory of relativity spoke of gravity, folding time and space, gliding across them uninterrupted. That was how Liam first made sense of it—he hadn't graduated from high school at fifteen by believing in magic. He was a man of science. But now he recognized this force as something far more primitive: harnessing untamed energies, clutching them tight, feeling them shiver as they awaited his command. The whispers turned sharp, pricking him like barbed wire, but he fed the pain right back into them. A positive feedback loop growing into something even greater.

"Not bad," Junker said. "Shall we begin?"

Liam smiled as the darkness inside him sat up straight.

Junker gestured to the piles of betting chips beside each officer. "Now, you must understand, we 'play for keeps,'" he said in English. "Isn't that how you Americans say? You are going to bet with us, yes?"

Liam motioned to his bookbag. "I'm afraid I don't have much."

"That's all right. Perhaps we can barter something else."

"Maybe we can bet with secrets," one of the men offered, revealing a nicotine-stained grin.

Junker nodded at him, but it was strained, like he resented him for jumping ahead in Junker's game. "A promising idea."

"I don't know what secrets I have you could possibly want to know," Liam said.

Junker picked up his cards and began to organize them. "I'm sure you'll think of something."

First round. They placed their bets. Liam bet one secret; the bartender brought fresh drinks while they played their hands. Liam's came in lowest by far, his Ober card badly outranked, but he could barely feel the prickle of fear over the roar inside his skull, the adrenaline pumping through him full-throttle now. The longer he held on to the shadows, the more they weighed on him, sinking sharp teeth into his thoughts and tinging his sight with red. Just a little longer. He had to hold on.

"First secret, then. You are far from Frankfurt, Mr. Doyle." Junker drummed his fingers on his holstered Walther P38. Liam didn't miss the warning. "What brings you to Westphalia? It is very curious, after all"—here he looked around at his fellow officers—"that we should find you so close to France's border."

So they were concerned about the French Resistance at least as much as American infiltrators—Liam filed that bit away for later use. "I'm a historical researcher," he replied coolly. "I've heard there are many interesting archives out here. Besides—" Liam smiled in turn. "Isn't France part of Germany now?"

One of the officers snorted. "Hardly seems like a good time for sightseeing."

"Well, the autumn trees are lovely. Or don't you think your Führer has this war under control?"

One of the officers balked, but Junker held up one hand. "Now, now. For a secret like that, you'll have to win the next round."

While they made their bets and played their hands, Liam's gaze roved the tavern. So much more cramped than he would have liked, and there was little chance he would get Junker alone. Even if things went so sour that Junker decided to shoot him, he seemed like the kind of bastard who would do it right here, in front of everyone.

Liam forced himself to breathe steadily. He couldn't worry about being found out. He was getting by on his wits alone so far, but he needed a backup plan. This was too important to let his only chance slip away—he needed to set things right, he needed to stay in *control*.

He studied the two guards behind Junker, who were doing their best to blend in with the ugly brocade walls. One, his dark eyes gleaming, caught Liam staring and stared right back.

Liam's throat tightened. He suddenly felt very exposed, as if this man—boy, really, probably his same age—could see exactly what he was playing at, the shadows pooling around him and the darkness consuming his thoughts. Liam shrank back, not wanting to look away first.

Then the guard shifted his weight, and Liam caught it: the rip and stain on the guard's jacket beneath his right arm, though he held it stiffly at his side to cover it.

The whispers in his head turned into a warning roar.

"Mr. Doyle?" Junker asked. "Your hand?"

Shit. Liam swallowed, a new terror prickling at his scalp. He hurriedly spread his cards out as his mind whirred. His cards weren't the highest or lowest this time. The rotten-mouthed officer, Stauffen, asked one of the other men for a secret about a secretary at headquarters. But Liam wasn't listening. He was trying to catch another glimpse of the guard's jacket from the corner of his eye, trying to add up numbers that refused to sum.

He saw more clearly now: the way it pulled too tight at the guard's broad shoulders. The cuffs that didn't reach his wrists, his long, slender fingers.

The knife tear.

The hasty bleach stain turning the fabric pale green around it.

Stauffen started dealing their hands for round three. The guard was watching Liam, eyes narrowed in warning. Dark eyes, darker hair, a single curl draping down his forehead. Liam gripped his cards to anchor himself—the shadows were getting impatient along with him, anxious to be unleashed.

"Congratulations, Mr. Doyle." Junker held his hands up in defeat. "What secret would you like to claim?"

He couldn't waste another round buttering the Sturmbannführer up. Not with the guard watching him, the guard who might be something else entirely. He had to cut right to the chase before it was too late and the manuscript was out of his grasp again.

"Your base at Siegen." Liam tapped the rim of his refilled glass. "I've heard your commander, Himmler, has a tremendous collection of artifacts there—old manuscripts and historical records."

"And you would like to see these treasures," Junker said in a singsong tone. "For completely innocent purposes, I am certain, Amerikaner."

The other officers erupted with laughter. Liam stewed, darkness throbbing behind his eyes. What was so damned funny? He was finally so close—and they were taking him for a joke.

He'd let himself get sloppy because of that damned guard—who probably wasn't even a threat, just some poor sap who got stuck with a dead man's uniform. And that stare, that wayward curl—

Liam made a fist underneath the table and let the shadows build further. Coalescing. Festering.

"I don't see what's so funny." Liam cocked his head at Junker. Just a few more seconds.

"Oh, Mr. Doyle. Whoever you really are." Junker wiped a tear from the corner of his eye. "If you honestly think we would let an *American spy* onto our military base—"

The gunshot silenced him. A fine mist of brain and skull splashed Liam's face as Junker slumped forward, eyes wide.

Liam leapt back, cards and brandy and bottle caps flying as the table tilted and dumped the Sturmbannführer onto the floor.

"Shit—"

"Hands in the air, Amerikaner! Hands in the air!"

All around him, the officers jumped to their feet, fumbling drunkenly for their sidearms. Liam raised his hands, keeping one fist closed, as what sounded like thousands of pistols were cocked.

But they were all turning on the young guard who now stood behind Junker's chair, his sidearm still spewing smoke.

"For my family," he snarled, chest heaving as he glared at Junker's corpse.

"Arrest him!"

"Shoot him!"

Liam and the guard locked eyes, and the guard's mouth twisted with unrepentant hatred, his eyes coal black.

"You bastard," Liam said.

Then he opened his hand, spilling darkness all around them. Thick as tar, hungry as acid. As the officers screamed, Liam lunged forward, humming the right frequency, and dragged the guard—the *assassin*—with him into the roaring black.

CHAPTER TWO
DANIEL

Darkness like a swarm of locusts devoured the tavern as the idiot American tackled Daniel. He tried to pull away, but the harder he thrashed, the thicker the shadows grew. It was like trying to swim through oil. At least it sounded like the Nazis were suffering even more. Their screams, sweet as a Schubert ballad, were the screams of men being eaten alive, and for a moment, Daniel felt the old hitch in his breath from when he played, finding the rhythm in their melody before remembering he might be the next course.

The American—Liam, if that was his real name—wrenched Daniel to his feet. He glanced where Junker's body had fallen, but instead of a corpse, there was only a seeping lump of blackness like charred flesh. The whole world was bathed in indigo, and everything in it—the tavern, the Nazis, the chairs and tables and bottles—were only echoes of themselves, like images projected onto smoke. It was as if they'd stepped through a tarnished mirror into a forgery of the room where they'd just stood. The sweat running down Daniel's spine turned icy.

"You can stare later," Liam said. "We need to leave. *Now.*"

Liam tried to yank him through the tavern door—actually *through* it, the wood evaporating around him—but Daniel tugged back, hard as he could. Bad enough he'd almost ruined Daniel's shot at Junker. Staring at him like he knew him, that little twist of sympathy and confusion on his lips. He'd been bound to expose Daniel as a fraud at any second. But now there was this—this darkness. It had come *from* Liam somehow, poured out of his hand and from all around him to swallow them both in its inky net.

Rebeka. If any Nazis survived this, they were sure to search the woods. He had to get back. He broke free from Liam's grasp and barreled through the door.

"Wait!" Liam shouted. "It isn't safe—"

Daniel stepped out of the tavern and into a world on fire.

Deep violet embers smoldered where the buildings should have been; instead of squat Bavarian homes, there were only battered, vine-choked ruins. The air itself was burning, sparking inside his lungs and stinging his eyes. A low rumble drowned out the hungry crackle of flames. Had the Brits firebombed the town? Surely they would've heard it. He turned back around, only to find the tavern completely gone, a thicket of brambles and gnarled trees in its place.

The buzzing grew louder. Closer. It sounded like their uncle's farm when the drought hit, the fields full of swarms and rot. He staggered in the direction of the hiking trail, but the ground shifted beneath him like cinders. Stone columns jutted from the earth at odd angles, forcing him to dart around them. He pitched forward and caught himself on a low branch—it felt like a skeletal hand grabbing him back.

The buzzing was following him. But he'd outrun a squadron of Einsatzgruppen SS—surely he could escape this. Daniel suppressed a hiccup in his chest. He couldn't surrender to fear and panic now. He wasn't ready to give up just yet.

He crested the first hill and found himself in the shattered remnants of a fortress, one curved wall hinting at where a tower once stood. Daniel pressed a hand to the cool stone and risked a glance over his shoulder. If even one Nazi had survived that *evil*, that darkness the American wrought, then he didn't dare head straight for safety—they'd follow him right to Rebeka. And the last thing he needed was the American tailing him. But where the village should have been were only more ruins and figures threading through the eerie flames. Not quite human, limbs too long, fingers too sharp—

Daniel launched himself down the trail and ran. Nazis or not, he had to get back to the barn.

The dead guard's too-tight boots strangled his toes as he flew through the forest. Dry leaves cracked like bones; bird calls sounded like screams. Something was writhing, slithering through the underbrush, and through the leafless tree branches, he could see no stars. Nothing to guide his way but that faint wash of indigo all around. Just a few more kilometers to the barn. He could make it—

A muffled shout somewhere close. He flattened against a tree trunk, heartbeat shrieking in his ears. Would they be coming through with their dogs? Worse, had they already found her? Light shimmered between the trees, and for a fleeting second, he saw the outline of a man—but then it evaporated, leaving only black.

He was losing his damned mind. That had to be it. He'd been so hell-bent on his mission that he'd lost all sense of reality, just as Rebeka had warned.

Daniel forced himself to take a steadying breath. He'd killed Sturmbannführer Junker! He couldn't fall apart now. If he could hold it together for another week, maybe two—then he could surrender. Let the exhaustion and hunger eat him up, let the bone-deep grief swallow him whole. Until then, there were more SS officers to kill.

The tree trunk he was pressed against moved.

Daniel swallowed. *I really have gone mad.* It rose and fell beneath his back. Like a *breath.* Daniel pulled away from the thick sap that coated the trunk—

No. No, that was definitely not sap—

"GET DOWN."

Arms wrapped around him from behind, wrenching him away from the breathing tree, and tackled him to the ground. Daniel jammed his elbow back, directly into Liam's sternum, and Liam wheezed. But when Daniel tried to push himself to his knees, Liam wrestled him down.

"Damn you!" Daniel scrabbled for purchase in the ashen earth as Liam pinned him. "You almost ruined everything—"

"Quiet!" Liam hissed. "Shut up and listen for a goddamn minute. The rules are different here."

That flustered Daniel enough to stop his squirming. He spat out a mouthful of bitter dirt. "What do you mean, *here*—"

"Stay still!"

The earth rumbled around them, like tanks rolling by. But those slow, ponderous footsteps were no Panzer.

Heart lurching into his throat, Daniel went still.

The buzzing sound was back, thickening the air into something noxious. Daniel stifled a cough. Closer now, footsteps ricocheted through the woods. Then the trees parted with a fierce snap as something massive pushed through them.

Daniel turned his head toward the noise, but Liam, still on top of him, moved his lips toward Daniel's ear, his breath heated. "Whatever you do, don't look."

Daniel looked.

The creature must have been the size of an elephant herd, with about as many limbs. In the dull light, its skin glistened like a raw wound. Insects swarmed around it with a buzzing as sharp as radio static, like there were fragments of words trying to break free. And then the creature's face—

As soon as he saw it, the awful images sprang up in his mind, reflected at him from that blankness. Every nightmare that had dogged him across the forests of Poland and Germany. Dr. Kreutzer, pacing the muddy ghetto streets as he eyed the prisoners, measuring, assessing, the ones he studied sure to disappear overnight. Rebeka's hand in Daniel's as they snuck underneath the fence, guards shouting, lights sweeping through Łódź's alleyways. An idling van, hundreds of bodies pressed inside. The smell of corpses burning as the train Daniel and Rebeka had hidden aboard rolled safely past.

Other images seeped in as well, and it felt like claws were digging into his mind. A circular hall, the same sandstone as the ruins he'd stumbled through, filled with shadowy figures. An elongated, eyeless face speaking to him inside his mind. He was being judged, considered. His sins, his value weighed. Every failure ripped out of him, his secrets pulled out, inch by inch, like his insides were unspooling, but still the torture dragged on—

"Let go of your fear. Push it away." Liam's voice, low and steady, cut through the nightmares. "The worst thing you can do is be afraid."

Unafraid. Wasn't he? He'd killed Junker and dozens more. He'd carved his way down the path of vengeance and feared nothing any longer, not even death itself. Hell, maybe he *was* ready for it to end. He could fall to his knees, he could drop his knife—anything to fill that aching hole the Nazis had ripped in him when they'd taken his family. Once Rebeka was off to safety, there was nothing left for him to lose. Maybe then he'd have earned his survival. Maybe then he could rest.

The images dissipated like drifting smoke; the presence in his mind retreated with a tug, a needle pulling a stitch tight. The creature issued a low, wet exhale—the noise the guard's lung had made when Daniel's knife went between his ribs. The reminder he needed—that he, too, could be something to fear.

On top of him, Liam carefully let out his breath.

"Did I do it?" Daniel whispered. "Is it gone?"

Liam's chest rumbled with a suppressed laugh. "I guess it doesn't like the taste of your fear."

"The *taste*—" Daniel started, but Liam shushed him once more.

Finally, the behemoth resumed its heavy crawl. With each thundering step, it retreated deeper and deeper into the woods. Liam waited until the earth stopped shaking and its footsteps faded, then eased off of Daniel with a groan.

Daniel sat up hastily, his skin cooling where Liam had pressed against him. "What was that—what did you—"

"You killed my Sturmbannführer," Liam snapped.

"Are you crazy? He had to die!"

"But I needed him first! Besides, you oughta thank me for saving your ass." Liam looked him over, his scowl deepened by thick shadows. "You didn't have any kind of escape plan, did you?"

Like he was one to talk. "I would've been fine if you hadn't showed up. I had to act quickly before you ruined my chance."

Daniel tried to stand, but as soon as he was upright, his head spun. Buzzing shadows, faceless beings, soldiers dripping with darkness—he gritted his teeth and tried to clear the images away. When Liam rushed forward to catch his arm, Daniel threw him off with a snarl.

"What *was* that creature? And what happened to the town?"

Liam hoisted his bookbag onto his shoulder. For a moment, his eyes looked black, his face badly veined as if inked—but it must have been a trick of the light. "Doesn't matter now, does it? Junker was my best chance at getting into the archives at Siegen, and you ruined it."

"Get out of my way. I don't have time for Nazi sympathizers," said Daniel.

Shadows swirled around Liam, and the forest went still. He seemed to swell, looming over Daniel, that violet fire crackling in his eyes. "Don't you dare call me that."

Daniel's breath caught in his throat, but he stood up straight, curling his lip. "Why else were you cozying up to Junker?"

"I'll kill every last Nazi if I have to." Liam's voice thickened into a chorus. "I will tear the Third Reich apart. But I need to get into the Siegen archives to do it."

Daniel huffed. If the American thought he could intimidate him, he was badly mistaken. His country had barely even stumbled into the war, had only glimpsed a sliver of the horror Daniel had lived with for most of his life. Horror was a real, beating thing, bloody and raw. It was a glower nurtured into a whisper, goaded into a shout, hardened into fists and long knives. Horror was law, a way of life, an unfeeling iron cage. And becoming a horror himself was the only way to tear it down.

"Do what you want," Daniel said. "But stay out of my way."

He turned and trudged deeper into the woods, trying to snuff out the weariness and sorrow that *thing* had stoked in his thoughts. Nothing about the terrain was familiar; none of these shattered ruins had been here when he'd made his way to the town before. He had no idea if he was heading the right way; he was too angry and exhausted to care. So what if Liam had saved Daniel's life? He didn't need saving. He'd been prepared to slaughter the whole tavern, the whole village, if that's what it took. He'd been prepared to die.

He choked back a sob. *The worst thing you can do is be afraid.* What bullshit. Fighting—feeding his fears, nurturing them like parasites in his heart—that was the only thing keeping him alive. Even if it got him in the end, he'd kill every last Nazi he could along the way.

He trudged to the top of the ridgeline—and nearly stumbled back down at the sight of the valley below.

Fires raged, purple and blue and savage, flowing like liquid through the trees. The sky glowed with unnatural light against a swallowing gulp of darkness. And in the distance, a column of flaming stones soared skyward—a pillar. Shadows circled it like giant bats, impossibly long wings scraping against one another in their jagged dance.

Liam appeared behind him. "As I was going to say . . ."

Daniel shrank back, pulse racing. What had happened to his world, his life? The wings beat louder, threatening to drown out his thoughts. "What have you done to me?"

"To you? Not a damn thing. In fact, I think we might be able to help each other."

Daniel turned toward him. Liam smiled so easily, as if his earlier black rage had never happened. He'd said the rules were different here, without explaining, yet, where *here* was—the forest should have been the one outside the tavern, but with so much wrongness, it couldn't be the same.

Liam appeared to be in total control. He was confident—calm, even—despite the strangeness surrounding them. He was just an ordinary college student, a little disheveled, though nothing that couldn't be fixed by a hot bath. His tweed jacket, his satchel, his tidy leather loafers—nothing about him hinted he could unleash hell from his palm.

But Daniel was used to monsters that wore the plainest faces.

"If it means keeping Nazis alive," Daniel said, "then I want nothing to do with it."

"Far from it. I promise you that much."

In the distance, something howled, slavering and cruel.

"What is this place?" Daniel asked again, though he wasn't entirely sure he wanted to know the answer.

"This," Liam said, "is how we're going to win the war."

CHAPTER THREE
REBEKA

Rebeka kept company with darkness, even as she dreamed of starlight.

Instinct, insight, a short circuit in her brain—she couldn't explain the things she saw, or the foreboding they lodged in her throat, rusty like cheap Shabbat wine. It struck whenever it liked, and never when she asked it to: as she walked down the street, she found herself peering inside a building on the other side of town, an argument raging there, smelling of anger and pain. She could be laughing and joking with Ari when suddenly she saw the fires far away.

Sometimes it felt like a dream. Always it was like peering through a burial shroud, everything blurred and washed with darkness. One night, trying to fall asleep on her lumpy pallet, she found herself standing in a graveyard, watching the brownshirts smash headstones, vandalize them—*Only Jewish deaths will save Germany*—and they were all wrapped in a hateful black fog. She wanted it to be a nightmare, but the next morning, she visited the cemetery and saw it was all too true.

Sometimes she could use her sixth sense to her advantage. When the streetcar rolled toward her stop, she could sense the darkness clinging to the other riders, warning that the ride might end with her being spat on or scratched or worse. And worst of all, that night when the officers whispered. Reviewed ledgers. Drew up charts. Prepared to round them up.

But mostly, she couldn't control it. If she could, she would've used it to follow Daniel even as he left her for tonight's strike. Instead, the only vision that taunted her was a stone tower, crumbling, shadows circling it like wolves as a coppery charge filled the air. It was nowhere she recognized, nowhere she'd seen on their long trek west. All she knew was the stench of blood and suffering that clung to it—it was nothing Daniel could resist.

Tonight, though, she could keep it at bay. He was only going one village over—no towers in sight. He'd chosen the tavern because it was small; the cadre passing through, smaller still. Yet as he'd scrubbed the blood from the dead guard's uniform, the stone tower loomed large in Rebeka's mind.

"Six officers of the SS," Daniel had said, a curl flopping down over his brow. "And Junker—he's near the top. We're getting close now."

Close—as if there was an end in sight. As if he wouldn't want to go after Kreutzer next, or Gerstein, or any of the countless men they'd encountered in Łódź. She hated the sight of her brother in that uniform, but said nothing as she helped him button the collar, the cuffs. What more could she say that she hadn't screamed at him a thousand times? None of it would bring their family back. She didn't need a vision to tell her that.

Eight months now they'd been crawling, starving, clawing their way across Germany, but Daniel was further from her than ever. All he wanted was to dwell on what had happened and drown himself in the blood of anyone responsible. There was already more than enough blood on her hands.

Sometimes, it was the only thing she could see.

She wanted to dream of what lived on the other side of their grief. She wanted to believe they might someday leave this purgatory of stolen clothes and cold barns and blood forever staining their hands. But grief turned the world into a stranger—nothing worked quite right in it, none of the old rules applied. Grief lied and lied and lied; it swore things could be fixed, with the right sacrifice, the right exchange. Grief held you in an in-between, kept you from moving forward or back. She feared what would happen to Daniel when there was no more revenge to serve.

The sheep bleated restlessly below her. Did they sense a wolf in the woods? Soldiers and their dogs? She burrowed deeper into the hay. If Daniel was caught, they might just shoot him on sight. But if they took him alive; if they had any sense of what he'd been responsible for—she'd be next.

Rebeka looked up sharply. The sheep had gone silent. The shadows in the barn thickened, starlight lost behind a sheet of clouds. She stared into the darkened corners of the loft, and the stone tower stared back at her from her thoughts.

And then the shadows moved.

They spilled toward her like ink spreading across the hay. Rebeka stifled a yelp as she scrambled back. They twisted upward, gathering into shapes. Rebeka dug one hand into the hay to fish out her Walther P38—

But then the shadows melted, as quickly as they'd come, leaving behind two men.

Rebeka opened her mouth to scream.

"Shh." One of them clamped a hand over her mouth until she relaxed. He smelled fetid, cold. "It's all right. It's me."

Rebeka blinked as her mind tried to make sense of what she was seeing, as her eyes focused on her brother and another boy. But they'd appeared out of nothingness, just the thick darkness and silence—

"You're safe," she breathed. "Did—did you kill him?" Her heart was fluttering frantically, but she willed herself to calm. Her gaze slid toward the other boy, lean and smug and blond. "Who the hell—"

"Liam Doyle. Pleasure to meet you, miss." He crouched down and held his hand out to her.

She stared at the hand, then him. "Are you with the Americans?" she asked in English.

His eyebrows furrowed. "I, uh— You could say I represent myself."

Even smugger than he looked. She whirled back toward Daniel. "What idiotic thing have you done now?"

"Junker's dead. The rest of his cadre, too." Daniel looked toward Liam, who nodded confirmation. She didn't miss how pleased they seemed with themselves. "We're safe for now."

Rebeka pinched the bridge of her nose. A headache was roaring to life behind her eyes. "You can't kill an entire cadre of SS officers and not expect them to come looking for us."

"Well," Liam countered, "in fairness, no one knows they're dead just yet."

Rebeka glared at him so hard she could swear he started to smoke.

"What? What'd I do?" Liam turned to her brother. "Come on. I thought you both wanted to kill Nazis."

Rebeka shrank back into the hay. That was Daniel's quest. Hers was only to try to keep him alive.

"I want them gone," Rebeka said quietly. "Don't much care how."

Liam's smile had faded. What replaced it was far more chilling: the solemn, predatory stare her brother got when he planned his next kill. Just what Daniel needed—a coconspirator. "Then I think we can help each other."

Rebeka glanced toward Daniel, but he was busy staring at the toes of his stolen boots, refusing to meet her gaze. He'd already decided for both of them, then. Whoever this boy was, her brother had sided with him and, whether he meant to or not, against her.

"I assume you have a price," she said.

"The town of Siegen isn't far from here." Liam situated himself on a bag of sheared wool. He was all lean sinew, exuding the confidence of a wild cat waiting for its prey to tire. "Heinrich Himmler's snapping up historical texts from all over Europe. There's something I need from his collection—and I need to get it soon, before he realizes what he has." His mouth scrunched with displeasure. "Unfortunately, the compound's heavily guarded, so I can't get into it alone. I need someone to help me slip past the guards and keep watch while I try to find this book."

An SS outpost. Rebeka's stomach turned. No wonder her brother had been so willing to hear this boy out. Hundreds, if not thousands, of highly trained death squad soldiers would be stationed there.

"This is nonsense. Daniel, we don't have time for this. We should continue on—"

"Kreutzer," Daniel said softly. "Tell her about Kreutzer."

A chill raced up Rebeka's neck. A phantom touch, like the kiss of a scalpel's blade.

Liam clasped his hands in front of him. "Dr. Kreutzer's written several papers about this book I'm after. Some of them using *my* research." His knuckles whitened as he tightened his grip. "Daniel said he was on your list. Of Nazis to kill."

Daniel's list, she corrected silently. "He used to torment our neighbors in Łódź. Make them disappear. People said it was experiments, something unnatural."

There was more to Kreutzer, more she didn't dare voice. The fiery hate that clung to him, smelling like burning meat. The glimpses she saw of a darkness he craved—whispers in the dead of night. He'd stared at her once in the streets, assessing, weighing. Her heart had pounded with a certainty of what he planned for her. She'd made sure to hide herself away that night, curled up in a friend's cupboard. But she couldn't explain it. Not without explaining so much worse.

"Well, if you want him dead, then Siegen's the place to find him."

"But that isn't why you want us to go with you." Her voice shook as she tried to push back those memories. "You think three of us stand a better chance storming it than one."

"Even I can only do so much."

She studied him carefully. He wasn't dressed richly, but neither did he look like he'd been ravaged by the war and everything that came before it: tweed jacket, navy sweater, comfortable slacks over leather shoes. He'd probably even washed his hair recently.

She and Daniel both looked frightful, and she knew it. She'd plucked the dress she'd been wearing for the past week from a clothesline; what had started as a cheerful teal wool was now a dingy corpsegray. Daniel had stolen hiking boots for her from God only knew where when the straps broke on her flats, and she wore them over torn wool stockings. She'd lopped off most of her dark waves and tucked what remained under a driving cap.

Eight months of scavenged meals and terror and grief had whittled her curves into hard, stubborn planes. Before, she'd routinely lugged cow carcasses around their parents' shop, then sacks of grain at their uncle's farm. Now she woke up tired and weak and went to sleep feeling like a shadow of a person, the silk stocking a stronger girl had peeled off and cast aside.

"I'm not interested in getting my brother and me killed. We've survived too much for that. One or three—it doesn't matter. We can't stand against a hundred SS."

Daniel laid his hand on her shoulder. "Please. Just hear him out."

She recoiled from the uniform he wore; the scent of blood covering him was both repulsive and yet—in spite of herself—intoxicating. She couldn't regret the confirmation of vengeance served. "Your—your clothes are in the corner," she managed, throat tight, before turning away.

Daniel sighed, then went to change.

Liam had been studying her, his gaze hollowed out. It was the gaze of loss, the gaze of envy, and it didn't sit well with Rebeka. He had no idea what it had cost her to keep her brother safe.

"You don't know us," she said, arms wrapping tight.

He winced, an acknowledgment. At least he understood that

much. "I grew up in Hell's Kitchen in New York." He perched on a bale of hay. "Saw plenty of unfair fights. Was on the wrong end of more than a few. I know what it's like to feel powerless."

"And you're here to keep up the streak?"

"Rebeka," Daniel scolded from the other side of the loft.

She made a face at him. "You're asking an awful lot of people you've just met, is all."

"You don't have to do this. I've told you that." Daniel stepped out of the shadows, buttoning his shirt up to his throat. "We'll find a train depot, somewhere headed west, get you to safety. This doesn't have to be your fight."

How did he not understand? Someone had to be with him to care whether he lived or died. She swallowed back the same tears she'd been swallowing for months. "Luxembourg won't save us. We've tried that already."

"You're from Luxembourg?" Liam asked. "What the hell brought you here?"

Rebeka tucked her knees under her chin. Autumn was young still, but the night was growing colder by the minute. "No. We're from Berlin. Originally." She closed her eyes. "I don't even know where to begin."

That was true. She'd been six when the National Socialist Party took control, but it wasn't some dramatic change. The rest of Berlin already hated them. They already talked openly about the diseases Jews supposedly carried, the babies whose blood they surely drank. She could see the hate oozing from them, a tangible thing. Vast lacework conspiracies alleging they controlled every nation, every bank, every newspaper—Rebeka always thought, *If that were true, then maybe the papers might not run so many articles blaming everything on the Jews.*

But things did change, so seamlessly she couldn't be sure it was the world changing around her or her becoming more aware of the world her parents had always known. Signs in the shop windows. Stars on their clothes, bright as bull's-eyes. A slow peeling away of every basic right, like peeling away strips of flesh.

Rebeka was ashamed to admit it, but she didn't blame their parents for what they did: the ways they tried to conceal what they were, renounce it. She and Daniel and Ari had continued to attend German schools until the government barred them, and they stopped observing Shabbat, even though their previous observance had been more an excuse to socialize with their friends. But it was far too late to pretend. *They're going to send you away soon,* their neighbors leered, under breaths, on streetcars, in the stores. *Germany will be great once more.*

"I'm sorry," Liam said. "I can't even begin to understand what you've been through."

"You don't even know what you're sorry for," Rebeka said.

Daniel clenched his jaw, shooting her a look. "We—we left Berlin after they smashed our parents' shop. Burned our synagogue. Dragged our friends through the streets and took them away."

Rebeka shrank deeper into her coat. She hadn't needed her strange sense to see that night coming. It was written in the sneer on every German's face, every headline in *Der Stürmer*, every band of brownshirted boys trouncing through the streets. All the night of glass did was smash that fragile belief they all held that this could ever go away.

The Jews are our misfortune. They were the Judenfrage—the Jewish question. Not fellow Germans, not people, but a question to answer, a problem to solve.

"Our parents tried to get us into a youth program so we could emigrate to Palestine. But they were so crowded already, and we weren't Zionists, anyway. We mostly went to synagogue on the High Holy Days. But things kept getting worse . . . They thought maybe we could move to Luxembourg—the farm where our uncle lived. Thought we could start a new life there. But even that wasn't far enough." Daniel shrugged into his overcoat. "Germany came back for us and sent us to the Łódź ghetto in Poland. Detention, they called it. Without telling us what we were waiting for."

Rebeka couldn't let him tell the next part. She leaned forward, gripping her hands together. "Our older brother, Ari—he worked in the ghetto's administration office, and he overheard the officers discussing plans to ship us all off again. He begged us to run. As far as we could." She picked at a ragged nail. "And so we did."

"Ship you off? What, did they send your family to the work camps?" Liam asked.

A noise escaped her, a wild, frantic laugh. "Is that what they tell you?"

His brow furrowed, like he was grappling with a foreign tongue. "The *Times* says they're concentrating Jews and other political prisoners in labor camps. Like—" Liam ducked his head, cheeks darkening. "Well, like President Roosevelt's doing with Japanese Americans."

"Are they lying to you? Or are you just willfully ignorant?" Rebeka snarled. "They're killing us. As many as they can."

A muscle twitched along Liam's jawline. "I didn't—I mean, the papers say it's just—"

"It's a purge. Extermination. They've made monsters of us and won't stop until we're all dead." Daniel's fists curled at his sides. "So I won't stop either. Not until I've killed every last Nazi I can."

"You're sure?" Liam sank deeper into the hay. He didn't sound disbelieving, only—tired. Rebeka felt it, too. The endless capacity for human cruelty, weighing and weighing on her until she couldn't move.

"We saw it. When we stowed away on a passenger train out of Poland. We passed their camp at Chełmno, and you could smell it, the bodies burning. You could see the smoke." Her voice shattered. "And the other passengers—they were laughing about the smell. They all knew what it was, and it was just some big joke to them."

She watched the American, her mouth set in a firm line. Waiting for some kind of reaction, though she wasn't sure what she hoped he would do. She didn't know what she wanted—to rage and scream and tear the world apart? Most days it seemed like a good enough plan. Good enough to keep them alive for one more meal, good enough for her to believe what Daniel was doing was right.

Sometimes she just wanted to sleep. Burrow into the cold, damp earth and pretend it was her grave, the death she'd cheated. Sometimes she imagined the train came for her and she could sleep, sleep at long last.

But there had to be something on the other side of this nightmare—she had to believe it. It was the only way she could go on.

"We'll kill them," Liam said. "We'll kill every damn Nazi that gets in our way."

Daniel was leaning toward him, something unfamiliar in his features. It took Rebeka a few moments to recognize it as hope.

"You cannot promise that," Rebeka said.

Liam unfolded as he turned to Daniel. His seriousness was far quieter and cooler than her brother's, but the same fire burned under his skin. She didn't miss the way Daniel looked back at him then, either—and for a moment, she dared to hope Daniel might believe in *after*, too.

"If you'll help me get into Siegen, there isn't a German alive who can stop me." Liam's voice was threaded with steel. "Not the entire German army combined."

Daniel leaned closer toward him. "The shadow place," he said.

Rebeka cocked her head, confused. For the briefest moment, she blinked and saw the crumbling tower again. Kreutzer and his burning, hateful face. The darkness always waiting in the back of her mind.

"Did you ever feel like there was something more out there?" Liam asked. "Another world, just around the corner from our own?"

His words knocked the breath out of her, but she shook her head. "I can't say that I have."

"Well, it's real. I found it. A universe that exists just beside ours, and all it takes is the right frequency to bridge the gap." His eyes were wild now—the eyes of a true believer. "And it's full of this energy—a powerful energy. If we pull it into our world, we can do wondrous things with it. It's—it's easier if I show you." Liam glanced toward Rebeka, as if asking her permission.

What else could she do? Daniel had already made up his mind. She nodded for him to go on.

Liam stood, clenching fists, and drew a deep breath. For a long minute, nothing happened, and Rebeka fidgeted, wondering what stupid game this boy and her brother had cooked up.

But then the air shifted—tingling, needling at the headache that lurked behind her eyes. The starlight flared around her, gilding the hay and rumpled sacks of grain. The sheep bleated again, wary. The night seemed to gather around Liam, wreathing him, until only the whites of his eyes gleamed out of the inky black.

"I can reach into that world, draw on its power, and store it up, and then I can command it—give it form."

Liam opened his palm, and darkness unraveled like a ball of yarn from his hand, like he was a magician serving up a dangerous trick. Whispers surrounded her with gale force; a sickly violet light splashed over them all.

Rebeka's heart thumped, painfully sharp. It made no sense, what she was seeing—but neither did her visions. Why should this boy who twisted shadows to his will be any less real?

The hunger in her shifted. Sharpened.

"I saw him use it," Daniel said, his words rounded with wonder. "It shredded an entire cadre of SS officers like they were nothing. Rebeka, just imagine."

Just imagine.

Her brother wanted a way to kill with ever more cruelty and power, and this pretty idiot had appeared out of nowhere, offering him a terrible gift. And as the whispers slithered around her, she knew—the way she'd known in Berlin, the way she'd known in Łódź—it would be the death of them both.

But she'd have been lying if she said she didn't want it, too. As the whispers grew, she leaned into them and let her armor slide away. Why fight it? She didn't just want to kill Nazis—Kreutzer, Gerstein,

Himmler, and more—she wanted to make them suffer. She wanted revenge, even if not with the same blind fervor that Daniel did. Yes, the whispers reminded her—she wanted to see this through.

And she wanted to see Daniel smile. She wanted him to believe there was more for them than this. If this gave him hope, if this let him find an end to his dark road—

The shadows dissipated. In the creases of Liam's palms, she glimpsed a smear of blood she was sure hadn't been there before. A promise of greater power—or a curse to damn them all.

"All right." Rebeka swallowed. "I'm in."

CHAPTER FOUR
PHILLIP

Phillip Jones had never considered himself impulsive, exactly, but at times he could be both very dumb and very brave. Not that this insight into his character did him much good as he was barreling to the earth at ninety meters a second. *Don't pull the cord until you absolutely have to,* the pilot had said, after he cut the engine and dipped them into a slow, silent glide through the ink of night. *Don't wanna give Fritz a chance to aim.*

Small comfort as the dark forest reached up to claim him.

Several things happened so quickly he couldn't even be sure of the order: the snick of his chute unfolding, the jab of branches, the jerk as he pulled the cord, the instant between *very, very fast* and *not at all.* He bounced, snared high above the ground, and hit the release. Tumbled into dead leaves and loamy earth. *Get away from the 'chute,* his adrenaline managed to remind him. *Gotta be far away when it's found.* So he staggered forward in the darkness for a few hours until his brain caught up with his body and, instantly, he was asleep.

It started after the disastrous Connolly Surveying, Inc., Christmas party. The engineering school's colored lab was chilly from more than just the weather as Phillip stumbled toward his seat without lifting his gaze from his shoes. He felt his classmates' glares strafe across him like suppressing fire as he pulled out his chair with a screech. Then Darius sat down across from him, and Phillip's stomach wrenched so hard he expected to see his breakfast again.

"Don't." Darius reached for the soldering iron Phillip was holding and yanked it from his grasp. "Don't you even dare."

"Darius, it's not my fault." Phillip swallowed. "I didn't know. I was just trying to help, I swear—"

"Then you're a damn fool, Jones. Listen." Darius looked from Phillip to their professor. "We've got finals in just one week, and I'm sure as hell not failing this class, especially not now. I'll turn our final project in alone if I have to."

"But, Darius—please. You're my best friend."

"*Was*." He scoffed. "You really wanna take this away from me, too?"

"Please." Phillip hated the wheedling in his tone—the tone of a rich boy who rarely heard the word *no*. "I thought Mr. Connolly just wanted to help your team do your job better. Honest, I did. I wouldn't have designed it if I'd known." His mind raced, grasping desperately for something to hold on to. "I'll have my own funds when we graduate. I can hire you outright. We don't need his stupid firm, I can come up with my own designs—"

"The last thing I need is 'help' from the likes of you," Darius spat.

"Gentlemen," their professor said. "This is Lieutenant Colonel Jones with the United States Army. He'd like to speak with you all for a minute."

Lieutenant Colonel Aloysius Jones walked into the lab, hat mangled from being squeezed in his hands, and surveyed them with a face as long as the Arkansas River. The keening oscilloscopes and snapping soldering irons went deathly quiet. But all eyes whipped back to Phillip as the whispers stirred up again.

"Family of yours, Phillip?"

"Here comes another Jones to ruin our day . . ."

Phillip's eyes locked on Aloysius's—or Uncle Al, as he knew him. A decorated Harlem Hellfighter from the Great War. Three years ago he'd stormed off to the hills of Spain, rifle at the ready. And just three days ago, Emperor Hirohito had bombed Hawai'i. It was no coincidence that the army had sent him today.

"I understand you boys are very skilled in the ways of digital computing. Radio waves. Electronic communications." Like most men in Oklahoma, he drew out the first *e* in *electronic*—a slingshot ready to snap. "I'm looking for a volunteer to help his country. To make some history."

Darius was already rolling his eyes, but Phillip sat up straighter, something hardening in his spine. All his life he wanted to do more, be more than the relative wealth he'd been born into. His parents had made their mark on Greenwood with money, jobs, connections, but Phillip knew those weren't his skills. He'd tried to use his talent for science and design. But so far, the only history he'd made was nothing he wanted to claim, thanks to Connolly.

Maybe, though, the fault hadn't been in Phillip's skills at all— maybe he could use them for something good, something he wouldn't be ashamed of.

"What's the matter, sir?" another student, Patrick, called from the front of the lab. "All the white boys upstairs already turn you down?"

"Didn't ask them," Jones answered, surveying the lab. "I know your class has better grades anyhow."

Everyone mumbled their assent; no lie there. Darius raised his hand until Jones nodded to him. "What's in it for us?"

"Full tuition and GI benefits," Jones replied. "Pay commensurate with your level of expertise. And the warm satisfaction of knowing you're beating back the forces of tyranny and hate."

That earned him a few snorts. Tyranny was this classroom, the basement graciously segregated so they wouldn't "distract" the rest of the university. Hate was the smoke that had smothered Greenwood not two decades before when the white men stormed it, the blood, the firebombs and broken glass. Whether it was Hawai'i or Poland or Paris or London, those wars weren't theirs. Their hands were full with the hard work of building and rebuilding at home. Phillip's father had said as much over breakfast that morning, turning the pages of the *Tulsa World* with a sigh as the cook brought them freshly scrambled eggs.

"I know what you're thinking," Lieutenant Jones continued. "This isn't our fight."

The classroom went quiet.

"But I know another truth, and it's that sooner or later, these fights find you. Fascism is the enemy of all Black aspirations, and Germany's brand of fascism is one we can ill afford on our shores. If we can't smother it in its cradle, then I don't want to think what kind of monster it'll become by the time it reaches home."

Phillip had been gripping his pencil so hard his knuckles blanched.

The enemy was already here. Maybe not true Nazis like Uncle Al was talking about, but men all too happy to take advantage of him, to smile and praise his work from their mouths while their hands used it to harm. And he hadn't even known. He hadn't known.

All his life, his folks had tried to teach him that their way was the only way. Money had been their instrument of choice—and it had done its good. But Phillip just wasn't wired that way. He only knew how to act—to create. And right now, he needed to create something big. Something that put more good into the world than bad.

Now Phillip felt the pencil snap in his hands. "I'll go."

Darius whipped around in his chair, glaring. "Are you out of your damn mind? This joker's just going to send you to your death."

"Thought you didn't care what happened to me."

"What would Mr. Connolly have to say?" Darius laughed cruelly. "Don't think he's ready to give up the golden goose just yet."

Phillip's body tingled, the full realization of what he'd just signed up for rushing through him—some highly secretive mission for the US Army, one sure to call on his engineering skills. Was that why he was doing this? To prove he wasn't who his classmates thought? That he wasn't so swaddled up in the success of his inventions that he was blind to the rest of the world, its problems, even if he'd made problems of his own?

"Phillip," Darius said. "Phillip, what in the *hell*? You need this least of any of us."

No. Darius of anyone should know how desperately he wanted to prove he could do good deeds—that he didn't just make things worse. He wanted to laugh. Electrical engineering he loved—he loved the binary nature of circuits and how easy it was to chart their course, no matter how complex the system. People, though? He was finding them way harder to handle. An electrical system couldn't lie about its function.

No, it was more than that. He wanted—needed—to do something good. He needed to know he could use his skills for more than what that stupid company decreed. His family's money had protected him from a lot, but he hadn't earned that comfort for himself yet. There had to be some reason he had this talent for inventing—a good reason, not a poisoned one. That need was alive under his skin, an itch he couldn't reach.

"You sure about this, son?" Uncle Al asked under his breath. "If you're worried about finals, or—"

"No." Phillip sucked in his breath and locked eyes with him. "I'm in."

Uncle Al set his jaw. "I'll never hear the end of this, you know. This kind of mission . . . It's what you might call a leap of faith."

"Then imagine how good it'll be when I pull it off."

He tried to smile, but it came off strained. Because it was why Uncle Al fought, wasn't it? Where Phillip's parents worked their magic with money and with words, Uncle Al and Phillip worked better with their hands. Phillip wanted to use his hands, his skills, for good. He wanted to *do* good.

"Well. I know better than to talk you out of something when your mind's set." Uncle Al shook his head, a hint of a smile on his lips. "Let's step outside."

"They're just sending you to die in some white boy's place," Darius whispered. "What's the matter with you?"

"This isn't our war," Patrick said.

Phillip stood, the room swimming around him. Was he being sent to a certain death? Maybe so.

But it was better than dying in a soft bed while the world burned outside his gates.

Phillip couldn't recall the specifics of Uncle Al's brief that morning, but it hardly mattered. Once he arrived at Camp Davis, he learned it was mostly bullshit, anyway. He was rushed through the most basic of basic training; he scored high enough to qualify for Officer Candidate School, but Al assured him there were more important things ahead. Al juggled phrases like "suicide mission" and "adverse conditions" and "of great strategic importance and tactical significance" as if they were ticking grenades. When the rest of Phillip's fellow trainees got shipped out, Phillip was put on a plane that landed nowhere he recognized, then driven to a concrete windowless bunker where he was trained on radio sets and cryptographic machines. They drilled him on Morse code until he dreamed in dits and dahs.

In the scant few hours between the end of the day's training and sleep, he kept his hands busy with transistors and wires, with diagrams and switches, but when the instructor peered over his shoulder to ask what he was making, Phillip shrugged it off and told himself, *Not yet.*

And so he trained, and trained. Time blurred together; the days became a series of electrical impulses: on, off, on, on, on.

On and on and on.

And then, after eight months of never eating or sleeping or shitting alone, of constant orders and drills and briefings and practice runs, he awoke in the utter silence of the woods with a single code name running through his head: Magpie.

It was the kind of quiet that drove other people mad. Three days of a silence so deep it made his ears ache. He stuck to the forest when he could, where at least there was the steady crunch of leaves underfoot, the occasional birdsong threading through the September damp and chill. At night, he risked traveling the roads. He hugged the forest's edge and dove into the underbrush the moment he heard the distant growl of diesel motors or the drone of Luftwaffe overhead. His head hurt from squinting into the distance, and he could've killed for a slice of lemon chiffon pie. Sometimes he'd catch himself muttering, saying his stream of thoughts out loud just to have something to say, something to hear. But he needed to keep listening to the silence. Any sound could spell his death.

Nazi Germany didn't look how he'd expected: no bombs, no columns of goose-stepping soldiers, no dictators screaming into scratchy mikes. It looked no different from the land his folks owned north of Tulsa, their wooded enclave by the lake. But just like in Tulsa, it took only one person to decide he didn't belong.

Phillip stopped every few miles to make sure the compartments hidden in the soles of his boots hadn't worked loose. He'd check his compass and the tissue-paper map he was supposed to eat if he got caught. He should be coming across the farmhouse any minute now. Any minute now, and then the hard part of his mission would truly begin.

He wove his way through the final stretch of trees. The early autumn sunset cast the same grim splash across the cloudy sky as it did in Tulsa, an unsettling similarity. But nightfall would be worse. As soon as the sun went down, the Nazis would come to life like the roaches they were, Uncle Al warned: moving troops and munitions, patrolling villages, sending their planes east to bomb the Russkies, or west to make sure France wasn't getting any bright ideas. He had to make it soon.

There—down the sloping hill. An empty field carved out of the trees, the empty husks of harvest season scattered across it. Phillip hastened his pace.

All at once, the forest went silent. He'd thought it was silent before, but this sudden quiet made him painfully aware how much it hadn't been. This was a suffocating silence, like someone sucking all the air from the room. He froze midstep and pressed his palm to the nearest tree trunk for balance, then carefully lowered his raised foot so it made little more than a whisper in the dead leaves. He glanced up—made sure he was positioned under the densest part of the tree's canopy. Waited for the drone of airplanes overhead.

Nothing came. No cars, no humans, nothing to disturb the abject silence that felt dense as lead.

Phillip breathed shallowly, getting dizzy as he waited. He gave the forest one more scan, but he needed to move on—

Then, a crack—like peanut brittle. Like his arm when he'd jumped from the playground swing.

Phillip flinched. Al said the thing about sniper bullets was that at first, you might not even feel the pain. It hadn't sounded like rifle fire, but then, he only had basic training for reference. Well, if it was, at least they were a bad shot—

The crack sounded again, chased by a staticky hiss.

Oh, Jesus. A few hundred yards up ahead, what looked like a lightning fork tore between the trees. But unlike lightning, it lingered, crackling, wavering in the air: a thin scar of bright energy. The scar stretched taller, until a thick soup of darkness spilled from its heart.

Phillip thanked the US Army for issuing him rubber-soled boots and stayed rooted to the spot.

The darkness kept pouring out, tendrils of black smoke stretching—like arms clawing out of a womb. The limbs reached down toward the ground. Scrabbling. Dead leaves raked between its talons. A third tendril swelled and unfurled like an elegant, headless neck. The thick scent of decay filled the air. The first two limbs buckled—jointed now—and bent to yank free a torso with a knobby spine.

Phillip didn't believe in devils or ghouls or angels or anything he couldn't draw with a circuitry schematic, test with his oscilloscope. But he acknowledged there were limits to the known world, that the universe was infinite, and the observed portion of it was very small. So whatever the thing was slithering out of the tear in the air before him—he was all right with leaving it unobserved. Unobserved, and at a very great distance.

Phillip sprinted—wide to the right, then ahead, zigzagging through the trees. His footfalls were punishingly loud, but he couldn't stop to check if the creature was following him. He could only charge on.

And finally he saw it, the whitewashed farmhouse at the far edge of the field, glowing like a beacon in the twilight.

Phillip leapt over the low garden fence and flung himself at the side door. He didn't have time for subtlety—making a sweep of the perimeter and checking the windows for Nazi guests. He pounded flat-palmed against the wooden door, and only the rasp of panicked breath in his throat kept him from screaming—but the door easily gave way.

Unlocked. No one was on the other side.

Phillip plunged inside and slammed the door shut, then leaned against it to catch his breath.

No footsteps, no one calling out to see what all the commotion was about. His pulse buzzed in his ears, but he heard no other sounds. No shuffling chairs or scraping plates or Nazi boots pacing the halls. The farmhouse was supposed to be occupied—Al had assured him of that. They would let him in and show him to the root cellar, and there he would wait until his contact from the Magpie's network arrived.

Phillip sniffed the air. It smelled faintly rotten, like someone had left food out.

The vestibule branched off toward a modest kitchen and break-fast nook. He stepped through the archway; sure enough, a half-eaten meal was scattered across the table. Toast with bite marks. A break-fast sausage, sliced and swirled through wilted sauerkraut. A few flies lurched up and scattered as he approached, but otherwise, the house was dead.

Phillip swallowed the fear balled up in his throat and continued toward the foyer. There, the front door stood open, frosty air drifting in. He checked his corners, then approached the door. Were those—claw marks along its edge?

In the front parlor, the last gasps of a fire sputtered and coughed in the fireplace. Phillip grabbed the iron poker to prod the embers—somehow, it seemed even colder in here than outside—then hefted the poker. The army had issued him a sidearm, but he liked the weight of the poker in his hand. It felt more immediate in the narrow farmhouse. Poker first, he continued his slow tour of the lower floor.

The root cellar door was wide open in the hall, and leading down into it, like teeth ringing a maw, were sharp, jagged streaks of blood.

His afternoon MRE lurched back up his throat, but he forced it down. He had to think logically about this. A problem set—he could puzzle this out. Whoever the assailant was, they hadn't left bloody tracks exiting the cellar. Maybe there was an exterior cellar hatch they'd left through. They'd have no reason to stick around unless they knew he was coming, but if they were expecting him, why not clean up the mess? Wouldn't they want everything to look in order?

Maybe—Phillip forced himself to believe in this hope—maybe the farmers had just gotten lucky and shot a massive buck wandering through the woods, and had dragged it downstairs to dress it properly. It might explain the marks on the door—antlers as they dragged it through. His father had shot a six-point buck at their lake house once, but got it halfway into the cabin before realizing there was still fight in it left.

The third possibility—the one Phillip didn't want to explore—wrapped its thorny vines around him and wouldn't let go. That thing he'd seen in the woods. The inky, sinewy creature, slithering out of thin air. Surely he'd hallucinated it. But the ripple of those dark muscles, the awful smell and sharp crackle of electricity . . . could he have imagined that, too? How could such a thing be real?

Phillip hefted the poker, letting its weight ground him, then slid his pistol from its holster with his free hand. Just in case. If nothing else, he might have surprise on his side: for Nazis, deer, or anything else.

He descended the root cellar stairs into darkness.

No sounds but the faint groan of wood beneath him—nothing but the same wilted-vegetable stink and a pungent layer of dust and mold. Once he reached the bottom, he stopped and waited for any movement, any noise. Nothing. He risked a tentative step forward, but his foot struck something solid. Dense. He pulled back and waved his hand above him until he caught the pull string for an overhead light.

The bulb clicked on and washed the cellar in dull gold.

Two bodies glistened before him: a man and a small girl. As far as he could tell, anyway. They were mostly gleaming, blood-slick heaps, large swaths of skin missing to expose muscled limbs and torsos and patches of hair, their unbound intestines spooling off to one side.

Phillip was too petrified to scream: he could only stare, clammy sweat soaking him through, words nothing but a jumble of noise in his head.

Who—

Why—

Deep within the cellar, tin cans clanked together as something moved.

Nope. No thank you. Phillip whirled back toward the cellar stairs, feet acting of their own accord. But as soon as he started up them, heavy footsteps sounded overhead.

Trapped.

Mutilated bodies in the basement and God only knew what upstairs. And something else rattling in the darkness. At least upstairs there was a way out. But as he moved up the steps, the air congealed around him, shadows wrapping around his limbs like steel wool, chattering and screaming from inside his skull.

DON'TGOdon't go do n't g o . . .

His windpipe sealed up; his muscles burst with agony as he tried to pull free. His legs were ripped out from under him, and the darkness dragged him down the stairs, chin banging against each step. He skidded into the pile of corpses and rolled onto his back as the darkness spread around him, swallowing up all but a faint glimmer of the overhead light. Above him, a figure loomed: the little white girl, her body still mangled, shadows oozing from her many wounds.

Phillip did the only sensible thing and screamed.

She lifted one arm, rotten darkness spilling out of her seams. Stretched her hand toward Phillip, as if to caress his face, sending an array of images crawling like spiders through his thoughts. A world on fire, a circular chamber, a featureless face looming over him, waiting, wanting, demanding answers he couldn't give.

Somehow he had the thought to raise his pistol, but his limbs were locked in place. Of all the goddamned things Al had trained him for . . . Absurdly, he wanted to laugh. The army'd never guess in a million years how he'd gotten himself killed.

More, the girl hissed—the words like teeth and claws digging in. *We need more.*

Just then a rifle shot pierced the veil of darkness, whizzing over his shoulder from behind him, and a hole bloomed in the girl's face. She rasped with a scream, but it was like a deflating balloon, all rushing air as the shadows gushed out. In a gale of whispers and shrieking, the darkness collapsed on itself, leaving only the mangled body behind— just as before.

Phillip crumpled, the back of his head hitting the cellar stairs.

A young woman towered over him, her upside-down face snarling as she clutched her smoking rifle.

"You're late," she said.

CHAPTER FIVE

SIMONE

The American shoved off of the cellar stairs and whirled on her with a pistol in one hand and a fire poker in the other. "Who the hell are you?"

Simone slammed the barrel of her rifle against his poker in a riposte. Both rifle and poker clattered to the stairs. His eyes widened as he gripped his sidearm, and his thumb fumbled for the cocking mechanism. But she was already lunging at him, pinning his pistol arm to his side as she backed him against the cellar wall.

"Okay, okay." He held his free hand up. "You win. Let me go."

Using her forearm to hold him against the wall, she dug around in her hunting parka's pockets with her free hand until she found what was left of her pack of Gauloises and jammed one between her teeth.

"What," Simone growled, "is the code?"

He stared back at her with glassy, deep brown eyes. "Are you fuck-ing *kidding* me? Did you *see* that thing—"

"The code," she said again, fishing out her lighter.

"I—I thought you might prefer orchids!" he shouted. "Now get off of me and help me stop these—"

Simone scowled. She was kind of hoping he'd give her an excuse to use her rifle again. "They're dead." She let go of him and glanced toward the skinless bodies on the packed earth floor. "Or something like it. I killed two more on my way here." The lighter sparked under her fingertips. "Thought they were Nazi swine, but they didn't die the same."

"Then what *are* they?"

Simone shrugged, letting the smoke scrape out the tension from all the corners of her soul. How should she know? She was here to kill monsters. Didn't make much difference to her what form they took.

Her contact was still breathing shallowly, sweat clinging to his smooth forehead as he stared at the bodies—or whatever they were. Now that Simone allowed herself to look closely, she saw they were fairly horrific. Nothing like the stories of Nazi atrocities smuggled in from the far corners of Poland and Lithuania, but the visible organs were certainly unpleasant. And that shadow that oozed out of it, like coal smoke . . .

"Ph-Phillip." He offered her a shaking hand. He was trying to smile, the poor kid. He had a sweet face, with a sturdy jaw and thick eyelashes, better suited for the movies than the war zone. He was bound to be a colossal headache for her. "Phillip Jones. United States Army."

Simone stared down at his hand. "You told Georges-Yves you could help us."

"I have no idea what the army told your—uh—Georges-Yves." Phillip lowered his hand, then ducked to pick up his sidearm and fire poker. "I just know I was supposed to meet you." He glanced at her sideways. "Whoever you are."

Simone exhaled smoke instead of offering her name. Her fingers squeezed tight around the cigarette until they stopped trembling. "You have the equipment?"

He gestured, inexplicably, toward his boots. This was already taking too long, and night was falling thick. "They've got hidden compartments," he said. "The shoes."

"Okay." She wrinkled her nose; the cigarette was already nearly gone. "Are you ready?"

Phillip stared at her for a long moment before looking back toward the skinned bodies. "Shouldn't we, uh . . ."

Simone clenched her teeth as she followed his gaze. He wanted to bury them—as if they would care how they were treated now. She could just hear her mother chiding her about respect for the dead, as if the fascists had shown them all a single ounce of respect in two long years. "They knew the dangers when they agreed to help our network."

"They knew the Nazis were a risk. This . . . This was something else," Phillip said.

She frowned at him, but she didn't have time for this. Something sparked inside her—an unwelcome image, one she quickly tried to snuff out. A hand pulling away from hers. Snowy cheeks raked red with tears. A whispered apology that was no apology at all.

None of them had asked to face the Nazis. But the ones who chose to ignore the threat, the ones lucky enough to run—those she could never forgive. Those who cared enough to try, to even survive in this hellscape, for as long as they could—she could respect that grudgingly, she supposed.

"If there's something you feel you must do, do it quick." Simone sucked down the last of the cigarette and flicked away the ash. "Night is closing in, and we have a long way to go."

Phillip plucked the cigarette from her fingers before she could snuff it. He made a vague gesture over the bodies, uttered something under his breath, and then grabbed a canister of gasoline from the basement's corner.

"Won't take long at all."

It had been two years since the tanks rolled into Paris, since the bastards goose-stepped down the Champs-Élysées and Marshal Pétain threw himself at their feet in surrender. For the people of Goutte d'Or, though, the change hadn't been so momentous at first. They already knew how it felt to live with too many eyes following you on the streets and peering into your business. It was why the Khalefs no longer went to salaat-al-jumu'ah, where half the mosque's congregants were likely undercover gendarmes; only her mother still prayed the salah. It was how her rat of a brother could be laid off from the factory one day, then bring home cuts of meat and sport a new suit the next, all for the modest price of spying on their neighbors.

"This is only temporary. It will be all right," her mother chirped, shoveling potatoes and roasted goat into her mouth like she might never eat again. Her eyes were haunted with every cruelty they'd endured on Paris's unfeeling streets. "We've survived far worse."

But Simone had always wanted more than just to survive.

Several months earlier, April painted Paris with a thick smear of humidity, and nighttime was no better. Simone's skin was clammy with sweat that wouldn't dry, and Evangeline fanned herself relentlessly, her gaze somewhere far away. It was Thursday, their night together, when Evangeline could be sure her father would be trapped at work for hours on end, kissing the occupiers' too-shiny boots.

Yet Evangeline seemed unsettled. They'd dipped into Le Monocle nightclub, but she'd dragged them right back out again minutes later, claiming the smoke was giving her a headache (as she lit up her own Gauloises). The quays along the Seine were nearly empty; it was only them and the muggy air pressing in until they heard the motor rumbling down the cobblestones. Only the occupiers were allowed to drive now, leaving the rest of them to the Métro and bicycles and walkways. When you saw a car coming toward you, you knew it meant nothing good.

Simone yanked them into a dark alley without thinking, backing Evangeline against the wall. Whatever oddness had settled within Evangeline that night started to fade, and she tilted her face up, eyes sparkling in the starlight, eager as ever for a stolen kiss. Simone kissed her rose lips, her soft cheek, the point where Evangeline's jaw met her ear. Breathed in her scent of lilac and gin as chiffon shifted and crinkled under Simone's grip, her callused hand curling around a soft, pale thigh. She kissed Evangeline's neck and sank against her, constant terror weighing her down.

Three years they'd been like this, passion claimed on rooftops and in alleys and smoky corners of Paris's lesbian nightclubs. In the catacombs and in the many unused rooms of Evangeline's palatial home.

They'd never been barreling toward something, only seizing up each day as it came, clinging to each other when they could, but all too often, they could not. Not with a father like Evangeline's and an informer like Simone's brother. Not with the Nazis flooding the streets.

Evangeline tensed in Simone's arms.

"What's the matter?" Simone asked, then *tsk*ed as Evangeline started to protest. "What's *really* the matter?"

Evangeline smiled sadly and fiddled with her cigarette until Simone took it from her fingers and dragged a long inhale for herself. "You know Violette . . . the race car driver."

Simone wrinkled her forehead. "Violette Morris?" Violette was something of a celebrity in Le Monocle, tits lopped off, always dressed in a tuxedo with a pretty girl on each arm.

"I heard something at work, something I . . ." Evangeline slumped back against the stone wall. "Never mind. It's paranoid nonsense."

Simone folded her arms. She didn't wear tuxedos like some of the nightclub's guests, nor dresses; she preferred a breezy tunic and wool trousers with suspenders. In her line of work, carpentry and masonry, it didn't raise suspicion to dress like that. And in Evangeline's decorous world of diplomats and sycophants, her ethereal chignon of blond hair and floaty chiffon dresses suited her just fine.

"If you heard it at work," Simone said, "then it's not paranoid nonsense."

Evangeline snorted and reclaimed her cigarette. "Someone said she's a Gestapo informant. She sells out women like . . ." Evangeline didn't finish the thought, just huffed out a ribbon of smoke. "Said she reports to Göring himself."

Simone glowered. "Why? Why would she do that?"

"Protection, of course."

"That coward. And you were afraid for her to see you."

Evangeline stared at the ground. "Does that make me a coward, too?"

Simone bit back her instinctive response. They both knew what it would be, anyway.

Evangeline cupped Simone's cheek with her free hand. Her fingers were always as soft as rose petals, nothing like the hard calluses that crusted Simone's. Simone tried to look mollified, but the truth hung too heavy between them, thick as the April stink off the Seine as winter's secrets thawed. Simone would never have patience for surrender, appeasement, acceptance. Evangeline's gilded cage had been built with nothing but.

"They're getting more aggressive. I think they mean to punish us for de Gaulle."

"Because he has the good sense to fight back?" Simone asked. So many in Paris had accepted—been relieved, even—when Marshal Pétain delivered the armistice to the Nazi forces. France would allow themselves to be occupied, in return for a farcical modicum of self-governance. Curfews, deportations, all their liberties stripped off one by one in a great tease, like a burlesque show in Montmartre. And Evangeline's father was one of Pétain's accomplices. More and more each day, Evangeline was, too.

From the safety of London, Charles de Gaulle had put out the call on the radio: the Free French would not be stopped. In pockets and alleys and basements, informal plans were hatched and sewn together into a larger piecework quilt of resistance. Even in Simone's neighborhood, the whispers grew: here was a way to fight back. Not only against the Nazis. But against the French traitors who treated them like invaders when France was the one who had claimed Algeria for its own.

It was a call that grew ever harder to ignore, especially when Simone's carpentry jobs dried up. She was always at her most dangerous with nothing to occupy her hands. She needed work—a purpose. Craved it. Smuggling messages across Paris, learning how to clean a rifle—such tasks occupied her when nothing else could.

"Simone . . ." Evangeline bit her lower lip, eyes wide and searching. "I know you want to fight back." It had been an all-too-frequent argument between them of late. "But I'm telling you, it isn't safe. Informers are everywhere."

Simone narrowed her eyes. "You think I can't be smart about it? It isn't as though I'm going to strut down the boulevard with the Cross of Lorraine pinned to my chest—"

"You don't have to declare yourself a de Gaulle supporter to be punished." Evangeline's hands squeezed at Simone's hip. "Every time a resister kills a Nazi, they round up fifty French—a hundred—"

"That is *why* we have to stop them. Before they kill us all." She cut her eyes sharply toward Evangeline. "If they kill enough of us, they might even make their way to you."

Evangeline's hands fell away from her. "That isn't fair."

Simone's heart thudded. The truth was right there, on her lips— that she'd already joined the fight. She hadn't yet told Evangeline about Georges-Yves and Ahmed and Sanaz, their secret shooting practice in the woods, the network of messages they'd tapped into. She hadn't even meant to fall in with them, not really. Only Georges-Yves had found her wasting her days at the corner souk, hands fluttering over lumps of wood with a carving knife. He saw that restless energy and knew it needed a target.

You look like a hammer in want of a nail, he'd said, taking the seat opposite her as he blew steam off his cup of mint tea.

She'd ignored him at first. Men were always talking at her. The reasons they might be worth listening to were few.

Your brother, he'd continued. *He's a dangerous sort. Do you want to be like him?*

Simone stopped, the knife's blade pressed against the pad of her thumb. The extra ration cards. Promises of a new apartment bigger than the closet she and her brother and mother shared. Assertions that now that Germany had liberated Algeria, they could be free back home. Was it worth the screams in the middle of the night, the Gestapo storming up the stairs? The nervous smile that stretched across their mother's face as she pretended not to hear? It made the meat her brother brought home taste rancid. She'd rather have worked herself raw in a factory than go on that way.

I am nothing like him.

His smile glittered like broken glass. *Would you like a chance to prove it?*

It began as petty thievery, lifting supplies out of the back of military trucks and picking the jacket pockets of soldiers visiting Paris's many brothels. Simone's fingers had been made for that, slipping folded scraps of paper free. But as Georges-Yves's network grew, so did their opportunities. The missions that they'd planned, bigger and bigger, allying with the Partisans, with the Free French, with unknown entities who only existed in dits and dahs over the radio. And now Georges-Yves had offered her the biggest one yet, one arranged by the American government, no less, although Simone hadn't given him an answer.

In the three years they'd known each other, it was the first secret Simone had ever kept from Evangeline.

"You can't join them, Simone." Evangeline grazed fingertips against her face. "It's too dangerous. Their eyes are everywhere, and I couldn't bear it if anything . . ."

Simone blinked. "But you would stop it. You'd find a way to protect me. Wouldn't you?"

Wasn't that the point of working with those monsters? To temper what they did. Evangeline had spoken that way once. But maybe it was only a lie she'd told herself.

"I don't have that kind of power. No one does. The best I can do is—is watch them. Understand the way they work. Anything more is too great a risk, it would do more harm than good."

Evangeline turned a winsome smile on her, those green eyes glittering like the sea. Appeasement. Simone no longer felt guilty for not telling her the truth. She was her father's daughter above all else: a diplomat. A collaborator. A conniver and a schemer, selling out Paris and her own heart to keep a soft pillow beneath her head. Simone had worked herself into knots trying to justify all that Evangeline did or didn't do, but she could no longer ignore it.

"Things will get better," Evangeline said softly. She kissed the corner of Simone's mouth, but Simone didn't respond. "If we can endure it for a little longer . . . wait them out . . ."

Simone stepped out of her grasp. "Oh, yes. It's been a terrible hardship for you."

Evangeline sucked in her breath; it never took long for her offense to turn into cold anger. She narrowed her eyes. "You haven't a clue."

"You still live in that golden prison of a mansion, do you not? You eat three meals a day?"

"Don't, Simone."

"And all those days in the government offices, helping your father manage the bigger prison that is occupied France now."

"Better me than the Nazis—"

"What about those dinners at Place Vendôme? Has he found a sweet little Unterführer for you to wed?"

Evangeline lunged forward. "I would never—"

Distant shouts in German silenced them both. They shrank back into the shadows, and Evangeline reached for her hand, but Simone yanked it away. A car engine rumbled, and light swept over the mouth of the alley as a Hotchkiss drove past. Gestapo on the hunt, perhaps.

Simone had spent all her life as a stranger in someone else's land— Paris, the carpenters' ateliers, Evangeline's glittering diplomat world, with parquet wooden floors and lectures at the Sorbonne and waiting on the occupiers with a smile. It could never be Simone's world. She was done being an unwelcome guest, shrinking into the corner as if she were prey. She needed a purpose. She needed to hunt.

"Perhaps you're right. It *is* better if we aren't seen together," Simone said. "Perhaps we shouldn't see each other at all."

Evangeline reeled back. Tears marred her cheeks as she reached for Simone's arm. "Please, wait. You haven't given me a chance to explain—"

But there was nothing left to say.

"I would hate to soil your reputation." Simone brushed the stone dust from her hands. "You have such important work to do, after all. Watching idly while they tear us limb from limb."

"Simone," Evangeline hissed. "It is the safest way—"

But Simone was already walking toward the quays. Shouldn't she feel lighter, a burden lifted? Now Evangeline couldn't betray her to the Gestapo, endanger Georges-Yves and all the rest. Now she wouldn't taste appeasement on those too-soft lips. Like the appeasers themselves—Simone had been trying for so long to ignore what was right in front of her, and only now could she see past it.

But all she felt was the humid air, the hollow where her heart should be. Her hands itched without warm flesh beneath them.

Simone knew, then, how the next few months would unfold. She could lie unsleeping, hands itching, in the bed she shared with her mother. Curse herself for her temper, her refusal to succumb to the easy, passive path.

Or put herself to use. Any way she could.

They scavenged the farmhouse for supplies, then Phillip set fire to the basement on their way out. It would take at least five, maybe ten minutes for the blaze to spread to the rest of the house, which should give them enough of a head start. Enough that the fire would be a distraction rather than a homing beacon.

As long as they kept moving.

"What makes you so sure there aren't more of those things out here?" Phillip asked, after they'd been trudging in silence for half an hour. No signs of other humans yet, but soon they'd cross the main road west of Siegen.

"Nothing. But it doesn't matter." She scanned the roadway, but it was motionless. "We need to make it to Siegen tonight."

The town of Siegen had the misfortune of being one of the military operations compounds for the western troops, handling administrative matters and logistics for forces heading into occupied Belgium and France. Once the American helped them establish their secure and covert communications channel, Georges-Yves had explained, their network's contacts in Siegen should be able to flood the airwaves with fresh intelligence for the Resistance.

"You know," Phillip said, "you still haven't told me your name."

Simone motioned him across the road, catching a faint whiff of smoke. From the farmhouse, or something else? She closed her hand around her rifle strap where it crossed her chest. "Names aren't important."

"I'm supposed to be able to trust you." He shuffled forward so they were walking side by side. "Kind of hard to trust you if you can't even tell me your name."

He had a point, which only irritated her more. "Fine. Simone Khalef." She dug around for another cigarette. "Do you smoke?"

He shook his head. "Never saw the point."

"It helps file off the edges. But it can draw attention." She smirked as she lit up. "Not as much as talking does."

"Message received, geez."

They continued in silence, the dark forest pressing in around them. No stars tonight, only thick clouds that drank up what little light the villages offered and glowed dully overhead. The scout perimeter for Siegen shouldn't be for another three kilometers or so, but it never hurt to be ready.

"Watch the trees," Simone said under her breath. "If you see glints, red lights flickering, it may be snipers. They're my favorite."

"Your favorite?" he asked dubiously.

"To kill. Are you a good shot?"

"Ha. According to the US Army, I'm . . . adequate." He didn't sound too troubled by it. "You?"

"One of the best. That's why they sent me for you."

"You're from Paris, right?" Phillip asked. "They told me that was . . . well, kinda the base of operations for your network, I guess."

"Algerian." Simone narrowed her eyes. The safest option was silence, but she'd developed a sense for approaching patrols, and it felt good to speak after the oppressive stillness of her hike. But it was dangerous to let people in, to give them a set of keys. They could find all the weaknesses in your structure, all the failure points to exploit. Only Evangeline had ever seen Simone's before, but it had been enough to leave Simone with a gaping wound.

Evangeline. She shook off a pang and pressed on. *Stuck-up, spoiled, selfish, sheltered* . . . Simone ran through her well-worn list of reasons not to miss her, but her nerves were too wound up to put the usual force behind it.

"Have you killed one of them yet?" Simone asked.

Phillip was quiet for a moment. "No."

"Are you ready?"

His voice was thick when he answered. "Kinda thought that was your job." He turned toward her. "Does it get easier? Once you do it?"

"I never found it hard."

He laughed at that, at least.

"There is a funny thing about the way people think of the Nazis," Simone said. "Some like to pretend they are not people, but something other. A *real* Nazi has no emotions and is only interested in hatred and death, you know the line."

"Huh. Yeah." Phillip stared straight ahead. "Makes it easy for people to think they couldn't be one."

"Précisément. The danger in that is that when you meet one—when they talk and smile and fuss about little stupid things, go about their stupid lives—you believe that they cannot be the real Nazis. The *real* ones must be somewhere else. And that"—Simone exhaled—"is a mistake."

"So what's the *right* way to think about them?"

"You must see that they are people. That they are, in fact, like you and me. You can use this knowledge poorly—if you use it to scrape some semblance of forgiveness out of the dregs of your heart. If you assume that they must only do what they are doing out of helplessness, or obedience, or acting on bad information."

"Uh-huh," Phillip said, unconvinced.

"Or." Simone punctuated the air with the cigarette. "You can take that knowledge and use it to remind yourself that these are only people you are fighting. Fallible. Stupid. Cruel. They have made their choices. Like you, they are probably set in their ways. And also like you . . ."

Simone pushed the flat of her palm to her chest. "They are soft and fragile, and one bullet is usually enough."

Phillip's smile gleamed in the moonlight. He wasn't tall or short, a little soft around the edges, but there was a structure to his smile that put her more at ease. They may have sent her an amateur, but he could be a quick study.

"You're kind of scary, you know that?"

Simone couldn't help but smile. "I hope so."

She checked her compass and map. "We'll see the valley of Siegen soon." She pinched out the butt of her Gauloise. "Stay quiet. There may be scouts."

As she said it, though, she became all too aware of the stillness that had settled over the forest. When was the last time they'd heard something other than the crunch of their boots in dead leaves? She trudged ahead of Phillip in search of the ridgeline and strained to hear anything between the trees. Thankfully, he didn't ask questions, just pulled the rifle he'd taken from the farmhouse out of its loop on his pack.

Something shuddered deep in the earth then, a pulse like drums. For a moment, she thought it was the sound of her own heart in her ears, but no—it was all around them. Where the earth had been soft just moments before, it now sifted like ash under her feet. The trees had tightened, desiccated—as if some wave of sickness were coursing through them at record speed.

A tug in Simone's chest made her vision blur, and for a moment, ancient ruins loomed before her, then melted away again. It reeled her forward—she wanted to stand in the ruins, run her hands against the cool stones.

Idiot girl. A mirage, a trick of the starlight. She had to steady herself against a tree trunk to catch her breath. The forest was still the forest.

"Did you feel that?" Phillip whispered. He was panting alongside her, his features no longer clear.

Simone nodded, not caring whether he could see her or not. Then, with a tap to his wrist, she took off running toward the ridgeline, the stink of smoke heavy in her nose.

Below them, the town of Siegen and the military base stretched out, picturesque white stone and streaming river.

And a thick cloud of black smoke billowed over the blazing fire at the military base.

CHAPTER SIX

The Eisenberg siblings took it pretty well, all things considered. A world washed in darkness and fire and blood, the ruins, a shattered and unknowable past. The creatures who loped through it, each dangerous in different ways. Professor Einstein's theory called it a dimension, but that wasn't enough. It was the shadow of another world, a universe that lived beside theirs like the pages of a closed book. Given their similar geography, he suspected the worlds shared a common link, a common seed, but like dinosaurs and chickens, they'd somehow grown apart.

It was enough to send most folks screaming, or at least calling the warden at Bellevue. Daniel understood because he'd seen it; he saw its potential as a weapon for ending wars. Rebeka, though, seemed more resigned to their fate. She donned that long-suffering look Liam knew too well from their neighbors back in Hell's Kitchen: worn out and incapable of being shocked, betrayed so many times she just expected it.

He wanted desperately not to disappoint her—not to disappoint either of them. He wasn't crazy. He wasn't dumb. He'd always been the overachiever, the insufferable one, the youngest kid in class practically crawling out of his seat to answer the professor's questions. He never knew when to give up—he was always wanting. More knowledge, more power. He was going to get into Siegen whether they helped him or not.

But it'd sure be easier with their help.

Liam hadn't stumbled into the dark arts like in some Bela Lugosi movie: with a secret wish in his black heart; with candles, incantations, blood. That story came later. In the beginning, there was only the flame of his anger casting strange shadows on the walls. In the beginning, there was nothing but his own yearning and a sheet of numbers that wouldn't add up.

It began when he was sixteen, when, yet again, he hadn't been enough to stop all the evil in the world. He'd just started his second year at Princeton, and only visited his mother on weekends, like it proved he was all grown up and could take care of himself. (He wasn't, but he loved to pretend.) But when the call came from her neighbor that Tuesday night, he raced for the last train back to New York, feeling the whole way as if his lungs were full of glass.

As he raced down West Fifty-first Street, the shards twisted deeper, rooting around with agonizing ferocity. Something was wrong, something was wrong. His insides were already shredded when he raced up the stairwell to the brownstone attic they shared with two spinsters. The door to his ma's room was open. The other boarders and the police formed a wall in the narrow entryway, too thick for him to push through, but he could smell the blood.

She didn't come out of surgery until Thursday—morning, maybe, though he'd lost all sense of time and space, dimensions folding and tearing and unfolding all around him. The whole world was at once too bright and also nothing but shadows; the hospital was full of thin shapes that scurried away when he looked at them head-on. He could only smell bleach and the blood staining his hands. *The doctor will be with you soon,* and maybe it had been soon, but it felt like another century.

Once the doctor arrived, Liam wished he hadn't.

Five blows to the cranium and spinal column with a tire iron. Sustained damage to cerebral cortex, jaw, malar bone. We had to extract the right eyeball.

Might never fully recover.

Her speech is—

The doctor's words were only whispers, a taunting wind that blew and blew. He'd failed again. He'd thought they were safe at last, that he could leave her alone while he went to school, that they didn't have to worry anymore, but he'd been so wrong.

He sat on the edge of the twin mattress that smelled like witch hazel. Stared at his mother, her good eye. She stared through him.

What started it this time? he wanted to ask, he wanted to scream. But he already knew the answer: his father needed no reason at all. Just a belly full of whiskey after a night drinking with his red-armbanded friends.

They'd thought his father was dead, for a while. He'd been quiet, absent long enough. Liam had daydreamed about an accident at the docks, a cable snapping free and a crate crushing him beneath it. Maybe he'd been trampled at one of the German-American Bund rallies. Liam had stopped scanning the papers and obituaries, stopped snooping through his mother's mail. He'd been so sure Kieran Doyle had slipped back into whatever dark and gruesome crevice he called home.

Why he found them didn't matter—whether he'd come looking for money, a home-cooked meal, wifely duties fulfilled. To gloat over some new family he'd forged, maybe, or chastise her over their sissy of a son. To spout more of his hateful venom, the kind that used to poison every meal they ate together: that the Germans had some good ideas, the jobs of hard workers like himself needed protection, his family came over the *right* way and America had no room for more. He'd found them again, and because Liam had let his guard down, because he'd dared to believe he was in control, it was ripped away from him once more.

You'll need someone to care for her. A grown-up, the doctor stressed, looking him over in his ill-fitting suit. So he made the arrangements, reaching for his slender wallet with numb fingers. Moved them both to a rented room in Princeton, just a few blocks from campus. Divvied up his food stipend, added a few hours to his library shifts. The numbers still wouldn't add up.

He missed a week of classes curled up on the chairs of the hospital waiting room and steering his mother into their new life, even more hidden than the one before. He lived at the library then as he tried to catch up, building formulas and hypotheses into a wall between him and the world. Anything not to go back to that rented room, that stare.

Quantum mechanics, atomic weights, neutron signaling, dimensional shift. Dark matter flowing away, that mysterious negative sign in the universe's weight, throwing off everything he tried to compute. Dark matter seeping into the cracks and corners all around him, sticky as tar. Energy was neither created nor destroyed. It had to go somewhere.

And if it entered their universe, then surely it could be used.

He turned in his missed schoolwork and then some as he poked and poked at his formulas' holes. Turned seventeen. Hired a day nurse. Picked up a shift at the maintenance facility on campus, hauling heavy things around, throwing them down. Soon his shoulders pushed at the seams of the suit jackets that used to swallow him whole. And all the while, he worked numbers at the library from his position at the circulation desk.

The world beyond the library windows was black, a sea of ink, as night pressed in. After midnight no one bothered him. The stacks were his. In there, his theories made more sense than his reality, and he never wanted to leave.

He was standing by the coffee kettle one night, staring down at his half-empty mug and trying to remember whether he'd been emptying it or refilling it, when the other boy approached. Liam flinched—he'd thought everyone else had gone home. Thick eyebrows on pale skin and a healthy sheaf of black bangs, begging to be swept back—Liam momentarily forgot the mug in his hand. Had he seen this boy before? Surely he'd remember a face like that. The troubled crease between his brows, the dark glint in his eyes like a warning, the stylish glasses, the dimple on his chin.

The boy smiled—Liam's pulse galloped, not just from the caffeine—and pointed to the mug.

"Excuse me," he drawled, his accent something Bohemian and smoky that Liam wanted to breathe in. "I think you are using my mug."

Liam swore. Threw back the rest of the coffee. "Sorry. Damn things all run together. Here, let me wash it for you—"

"It's all right. Hey." The boy's hand closed around Liam's on the mug handle, silencing the never-ending stream of words Liam used like a reflex. Thick fingers, muscular, but smooth. Liam imagined them wrapped around his wrist. Cupping his neck. "You look like you need the caffeine more than I do."

Liam made a noise that was supposed to be dismissive. It wasn't.

"I'm Pitr. Medieval department." He gently coaxed the mug from Liam's hand. "I've been trying to finish this paper for . . . three days now? But I think you've been here even longer."

"Theoretical physics," Liam muttered, then, remembering himself, "Liam."

"Liam." Pitr's mouth did something to the vowels that scraped Liam's nerves raw like a blade shucking kernels of corn. His grin widened, revealing pearly teeth, full lips. A vein pulsed at the side of Pitr's neck, beckoning. "Maybe we both could use a break."

Liam wasn't stupid—you didn't get into Princeton at fifteen by being stupid—and he understood, in theory, how this was supposed to work. (Liam understood many things in theory.) He knew about the men who took the streetcars over to Brooklyn. Who went strolling in the park or the basement bar of the Savoy-Plaza.

But Liam miscalculated social cues on the best of days, and in the buzzing empty space of sleep deprivation, of his anger and desperation, he knew he might be misjudging. There were all kinds of computational errors that only revealed themselves by putting theory into practice, and—oh, had he theorized about this.

He was willing to take the risk.

Pitr tasted like coffee—everything tasted like coffee—as he locked the bathroom door and shoved Liam up against it. Liam's tongue melted against his like a sugar cube. This, *this* was what Liam had been missing, the error in his computation: how glorious it felt to be kissed, to have that sturdy hand untuck his shirt hem, graze over the bared skin of his abdomen, flatten against his sternum as if to still his stammering heart. An impossible task, given the way Pitr nipped at his lower lip, slotted a knee between Liam's, pressed against his thigh. Liam bit at that pulsing vein on Pitr's neck and lapped at his salty skin.

Liam did *not*, in fact, know what he was doing in practice. Fortunately, Pitr was an eager teacher, taking charge with a dark look and a stubborn smirk. With Pitr's help, Liam learned what his theories, his hypotheses had been all too inadequate to describe.

Over the next few weeks, it became a game between them: one would borrow the other's coffee mug, smirking as he walked past to join his classmates for a study group or to retreat to the carrels. Minutes later, they'd find each other in the bathroom, fumbling with the lock, with each other's clothes.

There were unspoken rules, too. Pitr would never acknowledge him when he was with his friends, would never so much as meet Liam's eyes. The one time Liam tried to approach him, Pitr's glare was so swift, so angry, it haunted Liam for weeks—weeks in which Pitr completely disappeared. Liam had messed up. He hadn't followed the rules that kept them safe, the ones Pitr already knew, and Liam had become a risk to them both.

But just as abruptly, Pitr returned to the library, Liam's mug in hand, as if nothing had ever happened. If Pitr could pretend, then so could he.

Because it was only a distraction, Liam told himself at first. It was better than his formulas that wouldn't add up, than what waited for him in the rented room. But then: a hunger. A yearning. He didn't want to have to hide. He wanted more than the scraps of Pitr's life offered up between gasps for air in the bathroom, the mirror over the sink thickly fogged. He wanted—needed—more.

If he voiced it, though, he feared losing Pitr completely. Damning them both.

Finally, toward the semester's close, long after most sensible students had gone home, they ended up studying side by side in the dark corners of the special collections. Pitr brushed his fingers against Liam's, and a secret frisson ran through him, crisper and more overwhelming than anything they'd already shared. He scooted his chair closer and watched Pitr as he scrawled out his thesis notes.

"Explain it to me," Liam said, though he would've listened to Pitr recite the tax code. Anything to linger in his orbit a little longer, forget the world where he hauled boxes and changed the dressing on his mother's face, his slender illusion of control ripped away. The world where he stopped existing inside Pitr's.

Pitr laughed, though there was warmth in it. "I'm not sure you'll understand it. You *are* two years younger than me, after all."

Liam pouted—not exactly helping his case—and hooked his ankle around Pitr's. Dragged him close. "Don't make me tease it out of you."

A heavy beat. Liam was sure he'd misstepped. That the rules inside the bathroom fell apart when exposed to the open air, as if they'd been written on one of Pitr's fragile tomes. For a moment, Pitr's expression turned hard, and Liam was overwhelmed with shame. There'd always been such darkness lurking in there, coals waiting to be lit.

But then Pitr chuckled to himself and ran a finger along Liam's forearm, Liam's pulse leaping in reply. "As fun as that might be . . ." He shoved away from Liam's chair and gathered a handful of notes. "I'm looking at a common thread between scattered writings throughout the medieval era. Medici Italy, Ethiopia, Bohemia . . . Mystics all over claiming to be following the guidance of some man named Tomasi Sicarelli to unlock another world."

"Mystics, huh?" Liam reached for a slender folio on top of Pitr's stack of books. *The Mysticism of John Dee.* "You mean frauds who make up angelic alphabets and burn poor ladies at the stake?"

"They weren't *all* frauds." Pitr snatched the book back. "Some of them genuinely believed in what they were doing. Not so different from your Newton or Einstein, really," he added, with a poke to Liam's ribs.

Liam rolled his eyes, but leaned closer. "Go on."

"Well, some of them call it the 'wrinkle'—a folded part of the world trapped out of sight. Others think it's a form of purgatory, a place where lost things go. But whatever the case, they all describe it as a world alongside ours that doesn't fit so neatly into any one religion's construct. Some even claim to have traveled there with Sicarelli and communicated with beings who lived there, who granted them access to a powerful energy source." Pitr shrugged, looking suddenly chastened. "I thought it was interesting, that's all."

Liam caught his mouth sliding open, the way it always did when he was running figures in his head. "A universe alongside our own."

Pitr blinked a few times. "I suppose. Is that—something that exists? Have you heard of it?"

"In theory." Liam snatched two sheets of Pitr's notes and held them facing each other, about an inch apart. "Imagine these are two universes. Maybe similar, maybe not. There are infinite universes, but these can be any two."

Pitr stared at the papers, that familiar hunger burning in his gaze. But this time it wasn't Liam Pitr craved. It was that thing Pitr loved far more: knowledge. Mastery. An academic accomplishment that would put the other medievalists to shame. Maybe, if Liam could be the one to give him a solution, Pitr might love him, too.

"They still follow the same scientific laws. Energy cannot be created or destroyed. And yet we see it happening all the same. Mass and energy slipping away where everything says it should exist. Then surging forward from someplace new."

"So you think it's moving between the two universes?"

Liam nodded. "If two universes are close enough, then yes."

"A wrinkle," Pitr said. "Purgatorio."

Liam set the papers down, one on top of the other, then folded their edges so they stuck together. He tugged one sheet up, and it lifted the other by the joined corner.

"If we can link them," Liam said, "then we can observe the other universe. Control the energy's flow. Harness it as a fuel source, even."

"I don't suppose you have any idea how to create such a link," Pitr said.

Liam dropped the paper and they fluttered apart. "It's all just a theory."

But Pitr started digging through his stack of books. "Maybe not."

"So every time you pull this—dark matter—from the adjacent universe, you are stealing it from there?" Rebeka had asked, eyebrows raised.

Liam had just demonstrated it for her: the frequency that let him reach through the veil, bridging the gap. He'd pulled the shadows into himself and turned them into strange shapes that twisted and writhed around the barn.

"I prefer to think of it as borrowing."

"I'm sure you do." Rebeka had wrapped her arms around herself and shrank into the corner of the barn. Daniel, though, had that glint in his eyes—the one that so perfectly mirrored what Liam felt inside. Potential. Something waiting to be cracked open like an egg. A hunger that couldn't be sated by this world alone.

If Liam could harness all of it, he'd never be too weak again. Maybe Daniel was thinking the same thing.

"And what you want from Siegen . . ." Rebeka prompted.

"A manuscript by Tomasi Sicarelli." Liam's voice went hollow. "It's supposed to describe how he stabilized a bridge between two worlds for a brief period in the 1400s. If I can stabilize it again, then I can harness an unlimited amount of energy, and not just what I can draw into myself."

"How do you mean?"

Liam's fingers twitched. "When I reach into the other universe, I can only harness a bucket's worth by myself. It's finite. My body can't hold any more." Certainly not without letting those dark whispers devour him alive, though he wasn't about to tell them that part. "But stabilizing the bridge—it would be opening the floodgates."

Rebeka scoffed, but Daniel had paused, no longer using his Nazi dagger to dig dirt from under his nails. His mouth was soft, open, but his gaze stayed sharp. Liam liked that stare—the way it pinned him in place like a captured moth. He wasn't sure which carried a greater promise of violence—that stare or those slender fingers curled around the dagger—but both sent a shiver down his spine.

"So you came all this way—in the middle of a *war*—for a stupid book?" Rebeka's tone dripped with doubt.

"I can end the war with it. Use it to topple the Third Reich."

He hadn't said it out loud before. He shrank back, realizing how naive he sounded, how stupid. Pitr had regularly called him a kid when he felt like being cruel, but it was true, he'd always been the hopeless idealist, the dreamer, the youngest person in the room. He blustered his way through everything with nothing but his wits and an unquenchable lust for more, more.

"This isn't your war." Daniel's voice was twisted tight, like a rag being wrung out. "What does it matter to you?"

Shame prickled like drying sweat on his skin. He remembered too well the panic he'd felt as he tore apart his room, the library, the laboratory in a desperate hunt for his life's work, ripped away from him. "I have my reasons."

His mother's face, her concave skull, her mottled eye socket, her crooked mouth: if he'd had the power then, he could have stopped it.

The men rallying at Madison Square Garden, his father one of them, screaming and screaming, their red and white and black banners spreading like the Spanish influenza through Manhattan, the whole country. He could make them pay.

Jozef Kreutzer, stealing *his* research, *his* accomplishments, so he could push Germany toward victory.

With access to the dark energy, Liam could hold them back. Stop every awful thing that lay in wait for him. Maybe erase them, if he chose. He'd never again suffer the helplessness he felt that night in Hell's Kitchen when he found his mother painted with blood. The frustration, the choking futility as Pitr slipped from his grasp.

Most of all, he tried not to remember his life before the shadows—life without that canter in his pulse, that fire stoking his thoughts. He needed it. He needed it with an urgency words couldn't explain. But he couldn't tell them. He should never admit to *that*.

"Kreutzer has *my* research. If he's using something I did to aid the Nazi war machine, then I have to stop him. I *won't* let this be my fault, too."

"Let someone else stop it," Rebeka said. "You're only one man—"

"There is no one else," Liam said, something animal in his tone. "And I'm sick of not doing everything I can. I know what it's like to wait and hope bad things won't come for you. I've gotta go to them first."

Both Rebeka and Daniel had stepped back from him. He was standing—when had he stood?

Oh. The shadows. They spilled around him, flowing from his palms, swirling at his feet. Blood welled under his fingernails from his clenched fists as he hummed the resonant frequency.

Liam sank down into the hay and closed his eyes, then forced himself to stop humming so the rift would close. In a rush of whispers, the shadows flowed back into him and curled up to wait.

"It's the best chance we have," Daniel said softly to his sister. His face was gentle now, pleading. He was asking for her help, or at least her permission.

Rebeka glanced sideways at Liam, then managed a stiff nod. "All right."

Daniel's shoulders dropped, relaxing. He wasn't smiling, exactly, but it was close enough that Liam wondered what he'd have to do to earn a full smile.

"So." Daniel pushed up his sleeves. "How do we start?"

Once their plan was set and they'd stolen a few hours of sleep, Daniel led him into the woods while they let Rebeka rest. Those slim fingers circled Liam's wrist as he guided him through the dark, but it was so quiet Liam thought he could follow him just by the sound of his breaths. Not that he minded being led.

Liam barely saw the truck, tucked beneath an escarpment just high enough to block most of its bulk, until they were right upon it. Daniel released him, and Liam pressed his hands to the cool metal in awe. The white stenciled Reich symbol on the door—an eagle clutching a swastika inside a laurel wreath—almost glowed in the dark.

"Do I even want to know how you got this?" Liam asked.

Daniel raised one eyebrow. "I am sure you can guess."

"You're a scary man," Liam said, meaning it as a compliment.

Daniel leaned one shoulder against the driver's side door. "I do my best."

Starlight traced the side of his face, much closer to Liam's own than he realized. Unlike in the shadow world, they were in Daniel's territory now. Liam tried to follow his lead and propped his head against the door, too.

"What did you leave behind?" Daniel asked, eyes glittering in the darkness. "What are you running from?"

Liam grimaced. "I'm that obvious, huh?"

"I know you are after this power." Daniel's fingertips ghosted against Liam's chest, and his heart leapt in response. "But it's not something you only run toward."

Liam curled his fingers against his sternum, though Daniel's hand was long gone. "There was . . . an accident. A couple of them, really. My mother, and then—"

Liam paused. He'd used up all his recklessness. But Daniel deserved to know. He pressed his hand against the driver's door and tasted the words on the tip of his tongue:

"And then the—the person I thought I loved."

Daniel exhaled. "Oh." His face scrunched up. "Did she . . . leave you?"

The taste turned salty, like blood. "I lost . . . *him*."

Too long of a silence, a hole dug too shallow, dirt filling it in as fast as he shoveled it out. He'd miscalculated. An ache was forming between his eyes, exhaustion and humiliation. And he'd just gotten Daniel on his side—

Daniel's fingertips came between their faces against the truck door, and he pressed his palm right beside Liam's. Liam imagined a faint current jumping between them. "Then I'm sorry for your loss."

Liam let out his breath in a rush.

They stayed there for a moment, the tension unwinding in Liam's chest as Daniel studied him with fresh eyes. Behind Daniel, a faint blush of violet was creeping up the eastern sky. With a nod, Daniel pushed off of the truck, then swung up into the cab. "It's probably better if you drive, in case we're stopped on the road. You look like one of them."

Liam nodded, mouth too thick to say more. His body was tingling. One threat had passed. But there were plenty still ahead.

Daniel dug around the steering column and tinkered with the electrical wiring. "It'll all be over the minute you open your mouth, but you can buy me some time."

"What're you gonna do, jump out and slit their throats?" Liam asked. A flush climbed Daniel's neck, and Liam couldn't help it—he laughed. "That really is your solution to everything, isn't it?"

Daniel grinned, and it lit up Liam's insides—there was one smile earned. "It's worked well so far."

After a few hesitant chugs, the engine sputtered to life. Liam raised one eyebrow, impressed. "Are you a mechanic or something?"

"Violist." Daniel swung back out of the cab, long fingers lingering on the door handle. "Let's get you a uniform."

By dawn, they woke Rebeka and loaded the supplies. She hid in the truck's bed while Daniel and Liam took the cab. The drive was deceptively easy, despite the black carrion shadows cast by the Luftwaffe planes constantly roaring overhead. Liam kept up a nervous stream of conversation as they went: the principles of energy and matter, mostly, because they were what he knew best and because Daniel asked. After a ten-minute lecture on Pauli's exclusion principle—two bodies cannot occupy the same quantum state at once—he stopped himself abruptly, a rush of heat taking over his face.

"Why did you stop? You care about your work," Daniel murmured, watching him through half-lidded eyes.

"I forget sometimes that no one else gives a fuck."

"They should, though." Daniel's fingers pressed a chord against his own thigh and quivered it in a vibrato. "It's how I feel about music. I don't even need to play the leading line. Violas never do." His fingers danced up and down, and Liam wished, briefly, they were dancing on his skin instead. "It is enough to give the melody its scaffold."

"You don't want to be the star sometimes?"

Daniel paused, smashed his fingers into a fist. "That makes it harder to hide."

Liam swallowed his gut response: *It'd be a shame to hide you.* Clumsy at best. And untrue. If the world were safe for Daniel, they wouldn't be here. Daniel wouldn't be shrinking, shrinking down from the windows, tucking knives inside his boot as he whispered what sounded like a vengeful prayer. Liam stayed silent the rest of the way and only stole furtive glances at the dark-eyed, rangy boy beside him.

They reached the outskirts of Siegen sometime around noon, the clusters of wood and whitewashed cottages huddled under a smoky sky that threatened rain. Just beneath the road sign welcoming him to Siegen, a rusted sign warned, JEWS ENTER AT THEIR OWN RISK. He glanced over at Daniel, but he'd fallen asleep, head lolling against Liam's shoulder.

"Daniel," Liam murmured. He tried to match the German cadence Daniel had used when he introduced himself, and savored the way it rolled on his tongue. "Daniel. We're almost there."

Daniel jerked up, sucking down air like he'd been drowning. He'd half pulled his knife from his belt before he took in his surroundings. "Ach, I'm so sorry. I haven't slept like that in . . ." He shook his head, collecting himself, then slid open the panel to the cargo hold. "I'll wake Rebeka and get in position."

Liam watched him climb through the panel for a second, then tightened his grip on the thin steering wheel, fingers wrapping all the way around. As his nails dug into his palms, he opened himself once more to the dark and dismal place. He'd been pulling from it every few hours, drawing out what he could, but now it was time for the final charge. The shadows suffused him, frothing and pulsing, before he tapered off his draw on them and closed the rift again.

His biggest challenge yet. He laughed to himself, body bristling with electric anticipation. He was ready. Holding the shadows inside for so long—it was both exhilarating and terrifying. Comforting and restrictive, like a heavy winter blanket. It both dulled and sharpened his senses like the buzz of a first drink. He craved this. He *needed* this. And the book—the book could give him more.

He adjusted his officer's cap, sat up as straight as he could—trying to look anything more than his eighteen years of age—and cranked the driver's side window down.

"Your name?" the guard asked.

Liam smiled, toothy, shadows deep and thick as oil around him. No other guards in the gatehouse. Abruptly, the shadows flowed over the windowsill and slipped into the guard's ears, his nose, snaring him before he could react.

"Sturmbannführer Junker."

Liam, the shadows whispered. Faint as spider's silk, but there all the same. Liam tightened his grip on the steering wheel and ignored them. There was nothing to fear. He was in control.

Pure black eyes stared back at Liam as the guard waved him through.

CHAPTER SEVEN
DANIEL

Daniel shouldn't have wedged behind the crates with Rebeka. The cramped space was too much—all he could imagine were the walls squeezing in, his lungs full of lead while his body was on fire. He was back on the train to Łódź, pinned in by sixty or seventy other bodies. His viola case had been ripped from his hands by the sheer mass of humans as the SS soldiers herded them aboard, leaving him with nothing but the clothes he wore. Rebeka had clung to his sleeve, and he'd clung to Ari's; their mother shed silent tears somewhere nearby, too far away to touch.

But who had Ari clung to when the next trains came? Had their mother held him all the way to Chełmno? Had they smelled it, the same thing he and Rebeka smelled when they stowed away on the passenger train—the stink of exhaust and burning flesh? Daniel smelled it again now, smelled it clinging to him, all over his skin and hair, as if he'd been buried alive with all those corpses. Like he would have been, if he and Rebeka hadn't run.

Rebeka took his hand and squeezed.

Daniel squeezed back as the truck stopped, channeling every last bit of his terror through their linked hands. It had to go somewhere. Any minute now, the guards would be poking around the wheel wells. He should be hearing the dogs' snouts snuffling on the other side of the canvas covering. But there was only stillness. No movement. The dull patter of Liam's German, too warm and chewy to fool anyone.

Daniel reached for the knife he'd taken from an SS officer's corpse. *Meine Ehre heißt Treue*, the blade read. *My honor is loyalty.* He liked the idea of the Nazis' own motto, declaring their unwavering conviction, being the last thing they saw before he slit their throats. A reminder that for fascism, there was only one cure.

The truck eased back into gear and moved forward.

Rebeka and Daniel exhaled as one, and he let go of the dagger's handle. "Looks like your American might know what he's doing after all," she said.

"He isn't *my* American." But Daniel couldn't keep a flush of pride from his tone.

"You like him, though."

Daniel glanced at her sideways. They'd never discussed it before, the way he always made excuses when her unmarried friends invited him to dinner. Rebeka was too observant, though, for her own good. She always seemed to know things without being told.

"He's very . . . determined."

Her eyes twinkled. "Like you."

Determined, and a little frightening. Being around Liam and his chaotic energy felt like standing outside in a thunderstorm. He was obsessive, relentless, clever—and yet beneath it beat a fragile heart that truly wanted to do some good. It pained Daniel how much he could relate to that, how much he wanted to see Liam pull off his crazy scheme. And what he'd said that morning—his confession offered like a secret handshake . . .

But it didn't matter. There could be nothing waiting for Daniel on the other side of vengeance. Siegen was just one step closer to the end: to finding Kreutzer, Gerstein, Himmler, and the rest. His purpose would be served.

The panel to the front cab cracked open. "Get ready," Liam said.

They shimmied out from behind the crates and gathered up their equipment. When they'd stolen this truck a few weeks ago, they'd been dismayed to find most of the food inside was potted meat of uncertain but vaguely porcine origin, which seemed cruel enough the Nazis must have done it on purpose. The crates of dehydrated milk helped, but after two weeks, Daniel would have gladly starved rather than force another draft of powdery dairy-water down his throat. He jammed the lid back on the crate where they'd stashed oats from the sheep barn and inventoried his gear.

Sidearm: three bullets in the chamber and a handful more in his pocket. Overcoat. Slender wooden box, the only real possession Rebeka had grabbed from their room in Łódź as they fled. He felt foolish—their parents had hidden it in their jewelry box, after all, rather than nailing to their doorway—but keeping their great-grandparents' mezuzah near his heart let him pretend their family was alive and protected still.

Rebeka pulled her knit cap low over her brow and gave him a nod. God, that girl was ready for any of his stupid schemes. After this, he'd have to get her further west, toward safety. He couldn't let her tag along with him toward the end.

Shadows slid over the weak light that had softened the truck's canvas top, and they crawled to a stop. It was just like any other errand he'd run back in Berlin, he told himself. Gather everything he needed and get out without making eye contact. Only instead of picking up bow rosin and matzo meal, there were men he needed to kill.

He checked the bullet chamber on his P38 and took a deep breath.

The door to the cab slammed shut, and Liam's footsteps circled the truck. There was a low exchange in German, then a single soft tap against the side of the bed: Liam's signal. Only one guard, then. A smile spread across Daniel's face.

"Yes, if you must, it's right in here," Liam was saying. His German accent was slightly better, thanks to Daniel's coaching, but it wouldn't get them far. "Step inside—"

The truck bed shuddered as the guard climbed in.

He was just on the other side of the crates. Daniel could hear him breathing, a slight, huffy sound, like the damp autumn air wasn't agreeing with him. It always pleased Daniel to remember the Nazis were humans—not that they were deserving of empathy, but that they breathed, they got sick, they too could be weak or dumb. They had soft tissue and organs that rarely tolerated bullets and blades.

Daniel stepped out behind the guard as soon as he passed the stack of crates and wrapped his free arm around the man's mouth. Before the thought to scream could even form in the guard's brain, Daniel's knife punctured his throat.

A quick slash was too good for him. He dug deeper and twisted the handle. Only total tracheal collapse would do.

Hot blood poured over Daniel's fist as he held the knife in deep. He wondered who this guard was. How long ago he'd decided that blaming Germany's Jews was the easiest answer to his woes. How many of his own neighbors he'd sold out. How much he'd longed for the structure and control of the Third Reich to relieve his need for thought. He wondered about who might miss him, a mother or a girlfriend. How many children he had who would no longer hear his hateful rants.

Killing him was like snipping a thread on its loom. It might have already been woven in, but at least it wouldn't taint the weaves to come.

Daniel breathed in. Rode through the guard's hapless efforts to thrash. Waited for him to go still. Breathed out. The guard's body was so heavy, slumped against him. Daniel took a step back and slowly lowered him to the bed of the truck. He took in the sad little eyes, the diagonal scar across the man's mouth. The useless fingers twitching at his side.

A few more pitiful gurgles, then the guard's eyes turned dull. Daniel pulled the knife free and wiped it and his hands on the corpse's coat.

Liam let out a low whistle. Shaking, Daniel stood up to face him. His expression was an even mixture of terror and awe, and Daniel felt that warmth again in his gut.

"Ready when you are," Daniel said.

Rebeka stepped over the corpse with her hand held over her nose and mouth. Her expression was harder to read, which Daniel hated. He knew she didn't regret what he did—how could she? How could anyone with an ounce of good in them? But her patience with their journey was growing thin. She didn't understand—each one he killed was only a drop in the sea of blood they were owed.

They moved to a corner of the concrete bay, shielded by rows of supply trucks. "The archives are in the old performance hall," Rebeka said, after scanning the shipping manifests. She studied a facilities map taped to the wall. "One thing these bastards are good at is meticulous recordkeeping."

Liam was standing with his jaw clenched and his fists tight, his stare somewhere far away. Deep shadows pulled at his features, more than they should have in the garage bay's lighting. It was the way he looked when he gathered energy, tapping into that shadow world with the trees that breathed, the ruins that echoed, the behemoth that fed on fear. Liam had called him scary before—but if so, they were two of a kind.

Liam inhaled deeply and opened his eyes, then smiled at Daniel. Tapped his elbow lightly. "Whaddaya say we thin out the SS's ranks a little more?"

Daniel sheathed his dagger and followed him to the door with a flutter in his heart.

They'd agreed to keep up their ruse for as long as they could—no sense pulling the entire compound down on their heads just yet. The moment someone challenged them, though, they were ready. Rebeka's pistol was wrapped in the jacket she carried over one arm, barrel pointed forward, while Daniel kept his shooting arm loose, ready to snatch up his P38. Only Liam appeared completely unarmed, but Daniel knew better.

The main compound at Siegen was a stucco and wood Bavarian

relic, badly outfitted with electric lighting that didn't so much illuminate as suggest. With their uniforms and bowed heads, they didn't attract a second glance in the dim and moldy corridor as they strode with purpose toward the archives. Wehrmacht and SS personnel crowded the halls, but there were also numerous civil servants—secretaries and accountants and maintenance workers and more.

It was the civilians whose presence tightened like a fist around Daniel's throat. They weren't career thugs like the soldiers; they were nobodies, just like the Eisenbergs' neighbors back in Berlin. That bored-looking blond woman clutching a stack of folders could have been the shopkeeper he bought sheet music from, the one who complained to his face about Jews as if they were a parasitic vine coiled around Germany before hastily assuring him that he wasn't like *them*. That boy, barely Rebeka's age, pushing a cart of coffee and sandwiches— he'd been fed a steady, meaty diet of disdain, of an unswerving conviction of the German people's greatness—and that if Germany were anything less, then it could only be the doing of the Bolsheviks, the Poles, the Jews. *If their pay cannot stretch far enough*, his mother once said, *they'll gladly blame anyone but the man who doles it out.*

Daniel blinked, trying to clear the red-soaked rage from his sight. He would kill every last Nazi responsible for his family's death. But he knew the Nazis alone were not to blame.

"Left," Rebeka said under her breath, when they reached a junction in the corridor.

Liam nodded and turned.

"Stop." A guard stepped toward them as they started down the new branch. "These rooms are forbidden to unauthorized personnel."

"Ja, ja." Liam patted at his uniform's pockets as if searching for credentials. "Give me one minute . . ."

The first guard was twenty, tops, while the second had the sagging shoulders of a man in his forties trying to cling to a former glory he'd never truly possessed. Maybe they chose this, maybe they didn't. Either way, they bore some responsibility: either way, they would pay.

"Ach. Here it is. In my pocket." Liam smiled and slowly withdrew his hand from his breast pocket as he hummed a strange melody.

Daniel slid his sidearm free, but it turned out there was no need.

The shadows erupted from the floor like lava and wrapped around each guard in an instant. Any screams they might have made were instantly shoved back down their throats as viscous darkness poured into their mouths, their nostrils, their eyes. They dangled, suspended by the bloody vines, and twisted back and forth as Liam curled his fingers. Then he slammed his palms together—and they folded away into nothingness.

The hallway stood empty before them.

"Wh-where did they go?" Rebeka asked.

"Through the veil." Liam's hands trembled as he dropped them to his sides, wisps of shadow still trailing from his fingertips. "Let the—the creatures over there deal with them."

Daniel recalled the faceless behemoth stalking through the underbrush and savored his sudden flush of cruel delight.

Liam cocked his head toward Daniel. "Now, as for the archives door—"

"Just a moment." Daniel slipped his makeshift lock-picking tools from his pocket and made quick work of the doors. They were finely carved, the wood trim swirling with flowers and the remnants of paint. Such a needlessly elegant building for such appalling purpose. Rebeka scanned the corridor while he worked, but Daniel sensed Liam's gaze on his fingers and felt a blush creep up the back of his neck.

The doors swung open.

The chamber had once been a music hall. The floor gently sloped and was studded with bolts where rows of chairs had been ripped up; a stage was shrouded at the far end. Now the hall was crammed with hastily constructed shelving and stacks and stacks of reinforced file boxes. Weak sunlight wafted in from the courtyard windows that lined one wall, but otherwise everything was dingy gray, redolent with decades of must.

"Well." Daniel swallowed. "Where do we start?"

"I'm after the confiscated property and inventory records. If you're looking for officer names and postings . . ." Liam met his gaze, some kind of judgment behind that stare. Not disapproving of his quest, exactly, but sad for it—sad that it had to happen, sad for where he feared it might lead. With a scowl, Daniel looked away. He'd had enough of that from Rebeka. Forgiveness was not a virtue. Vengeance was the least he deserved. What happened after—that was not Liam's concern.

"Inventory records are here," Rebeka called from the far-left row. She gave Daniel a similar look to match Liam's.

"Then I'll take the right." Daniel turned away from them.

"I'm looking for *Porta ad Tenebras*. Tomasi Sicarelli. The cover is pressed leather, looks like swirling lines feeding into an archway," Liam told Rebeka, but Daniel shut them out. He found a row of Wehrmacht and SS reports, and with a taste like gravel in his mouth, he forced himself to dig through them.

Boxes and boxes of invoices and receipts. Accounting records, troop authorization orders, payments, rations records, requisitions forms.

Carefully tabulated accounting and procedure for confiscating the property of deceased Jews.

He tried to move on. This wasn't what he was searching for. But then he came across the Einsatzgruppen reports—the SS's death squads—and he couldn't bring himself to look away. Men crowing over the results of their pogroms—blood and bone and brain flying in a hail of bullets, of shouts, of fire and shattered glass and hate—boiled down to nothing but numbers, sometimes in the thousands on a single ledger line.

Three thousand dead at a fort in Kaunas.

Thirty-seven hundred in Vilnius.

Eighteen hundred as reprisal for a German officer's death inside a Jewish ghetto.

A slow calculation of death and devastation, all the meat stripped from it, personalities flattened like tin, names erased, bones bleached to nothing but tally marks. He couldn't take in the volume of it, the enormity of its blandness, how completely and utterly banal—how exhausting—it all was. How drearily they'd had to codify murder and genocide as if it were just another thing to requisition, like filing folders and typewriter ink. So repetitious it required blank templates, boxes to be checked, forms to be filed in triplicate. So pervasive it filled this entire music hall—so blatant it cared nothing about leaving behind such a massive, meticulous record of its crimes.

Die Endlösung der Judenfrage, one document read. A report on the final solution to the Jewish problem. Slowly, methodically, he read through them all, unable to do anything but bear witness. Someone had to see these horrors for what they were—

And then he reached a contract—an agreement for the Chełmno camp to sell human hair to a candy cloth factory, at fifty Pfennigs a pound.

Cement was hardening in Daniel's blood. That's what did it—the weight of human hair. That's what turned him into stone.

Ari's loose curls, his mother's long, wavy locks, their father's thick hair—shaved from their corpses and sold by the bag so Germans could use it to decorate their hats. All while SS soldiers bickered about who got the gold fillings and shoes and wedding bands.

It wasn't a record of crimes. It was merely law now, from the repeal of Jewish citizenship to the Nuremberg Laws to the ghettos to the death camps. It was enough to crush Daniel where he stood. How quickly the Nazis had smothered down their humanity, how willingly a whole nation had turned human beings into things. A problem to be solved. An entire culture to be erased. How straightforward they had made it, how many checklists they had designed, so easy anyone could replicate their system, anyone willing to forget that they were people, that they were *alive*—

"I think I have something," Rebeka called to Liam, from the other side of the stacks.

But Daniel moved on to the next box.

A report on the testing of Prussian cyanic gas on Russian prisoners of war, dated August 1941. Stapled to it—approval to advance to trials in the detention camps. Far more efficient than the exhaust-fed vans method employed at Chełmno, the approval concurred. Permission granted to begin construction on such facilities in Auschwitz and Bełżec for administration of Zyklon-B gas.

Human beings, gassed to death. For daring to be alive. And so many of them to be killed that the Nazis had to worry about processing the sheer *volume* of them, about efficiency.

With eyes burning, Daniel ran through the names on his list again. If the Nazis could have checklists for their brutality, then so could he. Every SS officer responsible—every one that he would kill. Gerstein, the camp capo who sat back, boots on the desk, congratulating himself on a well-run system as the people sent to Chełmno were slaughtered en masse. Kreutzer, the man who stole people from Łódź for his experiments. And should Daniel survive long enough, then he could work his way toward the names at the top of every transcript: the very leaders of the Reich.

Daniel barely felt his knees hit the floor before the bile was burning at the back of his throat, his tongue, his teeth. He only knew what he and Rebeka had heard in snatches of rumors and the smell of Chełmno, but that had already been too much. Had his parents died screaming, clutching each other as gas filled their lungs? Had Ari been amongst the ones who hauled the dead to mass graves before he too was killed? Maybe at least he'd gotten to squeeze their mother's cold hand one last time as he lowered her into a yawning, hungry ditch—

Pale yellow spilled onto the wood, chunks of powdered milk in it. It only took one good heave to empty his stomach, but his body kept working, trying to wring the agony out of him. It didn't know any better—didn't know that what needed to be purged from his system was the entire world, that there was nowhere he could be safe from the poisonous potential of every human being alive. The Nazis in particular, to be sure; yet who were they but people who had been given too many assurances? Who'd never been challenged or had their voices silenced when they themselves were discussed?

He dragged himself back to his feet, clinging to the cheap plywood. Gerstein, Kreutzer, Himmler—where were they now? His hands raked over boxes, but he was uncoordinated, drunk with rage. Where were they now?

Approvals, so many approvals. For transfers, for requisitions. For experiments—so many experiments, some of them marked with Kreutzer's name.

Gerstein. Kreutzer. Himmler. He'd etched their names into his heart with acid. Their poison would not spread.

"No—this doesn't make sense," Liam was saying, a few aisles away. "The book should be here. Why would they transfer it to Wewelsburg?"

"Wewelsburg," Rebeka echoed, a frown in her voice. "But that's the headquarters of the SS."

Daniel clutched at the cheap wooden shelving to pull himself up. The SS headquarters—Himmler at the least would be there, and possibly the others, too. Plenty of guilty SS officers, in any case. He didn't give a shit about Liam's book, or Liam, or Rebeka, or anything else. All that mattered was killing his way through these men—

"Who's there?" a voice called in German. "Where are the guards?"

Someone had entered the music hall.

Daniel tore his knife free and stalked toward the door on unsteady legs, staying hidden behind the shelving. Nothing mattered but feeling another rush of blood over his hands, turning cold. Tremolo strings built under him, the churn of a Rachmaninoff or Mahler symphony threatening to boil over into chaos. Liam could continue his magical hunt, Rebeka could pretend the war would end and they'd go home someday, but for Daniel, there was nothing left but this: his rage and the Germans' soft flesh, the fear in the whites of their eyes as they saw their deaths reflected in his blade.

It was sweeter than the cascading opening of *Scheherazade*, darker and more devastating than the torrential sawing of Mussorgsky's *Bald Mountain*. He'd honed his fingers on études, but they had only been training for his true purpose: this.

He lunged from the stacks, knife raised.

The clerk ducked out of the way of his initial thrust, screaming as he stumbled. He was still screaming when Daniel fell on top of him, while the knife plunged crudely into his chest. Again and again. It took so much effort to stab a man to death, and Daniel had spent all his energy in the stacks. Nothing was left but wounded-animal instinct and fury. He'd lost his lunch, lost everything but this, his final act of contrition, his only way to atone for the fact that he and Rebeka survived where so many had not—

A hand fell on his shoulder, wrenching him back. "Daniel," Liam was saying. "Daniel. He's dead. Daniel—"

He stumbled off of the clerk's body and sprawled onto his back, hot tears mingling with the blood that peppered his face. It was everywhere. It dripped into his eyes and burned; it salted his lips and tongue. He wondered, with bleak, hopeless humor, whether maybe his body would appreciate it more than the powdered milk.

"They're coming." Liam gripped his forearm, bracing him. He stood strong above Daniel, gorgeous even in his fear, that little wrinkle between his eyebrows, his hair like dusty gold. It was almost a shame that there could be no after for Daniel—not even for this strange, magical boy.

"They're coming," Liam said again.

Daniel scrubbed the blood from his eyes and tried to find his feet as he shifted his weight toward Liam, letting himself be pulled up.

"How many?" Daniel asked. He didn't know why. It would be far too many for the three of them—even with Liam's abilities.

But Liam had no chance to answer. The door burst open, revealing a wall of rifle barrels aimed at them.

Then the world tore itself in two with a scream.

CHAPTER EIGHT
REBEKA

Everything was falling apart around her.

The music hall split open with a horrifying shriek, thinning the air. She was thrown backward, away from the doors where Daniel and Liam faced down a host of guards, and as she fell, she blinked and saw another place: a stone tower wreathed in shadow, breathing as if it drew energy into itself. It was burned into the back of her eyelids so no matter where she looked, it waited for her, shadows swirling around it.

This must be it: the vision she'd been trying to protect Daniel from. The grim conclusion to his quest. She'd failed them both—and the rest of their family, too.

The lightning faded, but the screams continued as Liam hummed a note that rattled her soul.

Daniel—was it Daniel screaming? She staggered to her feet, only to find the music hall flattened around her as if a tornado had landed on them. Shelves twisted and snapped, sheets of paper swirling past her—inventories and ledger papers and grim swastika letterheads. The guards who'd filled the doorway moments before now sprawled across the floor. Some cried out, their limbs bent at unnatural angles. Others were all too still. Scattered rifle stocks were shredded and spiraled like peeled potato skins. And in the epicenter of the torrent stood Liam, arms raised high as he commanded a spinning column of thick black smoke.

No, it was darker even than smoke. It was like burning pitch, and smelled just as foul. Inside the whirlwind, she heard—voices. Howls. Teeth snapping, ravenous.

The shadows whispered to her, achingly familiar: *Yes.*

"We have to go." Rebeka charged forward and seized her brother's hand, then reached for the American, too. "More will be coming."

"No—I need a moment—longer—" yelled Liam.

Boxes of paperwork were ripped off of the shelves, caught up in the vortex. Rebeka ducked low to avoid a piece of plywood as it whizzed past. "Your book isn't here! Let's go!"

"One more minute—"

But the sound of gunfire swallowed up whatever Liam was about to say. A fresh group of guards had arrived. Liam fell backward, struck in the shoulder, and dragged Rebeka and Daniel down with him. The vortex shifted in response as his concentration broke. Lightning crackled across its surface as the darkness stretched and yawned—a hungering void.

And then something taloned, something sinuous, slithered out of the black.

Rebeka staggered to her feet, hand closing protectively around Daniel's to pull him up with her. The shadows unfurled into a vaguely animal shape—limbs stretching, skin slick and viscous. But there were gaping sockets where there should have been eyes, a red fire smoldering deep within them. It crouched on all fours, but even so, it was eye level with Rebeka. It stared through her, and she felt—*felt*, like a shard of glass—the thing's slow smile.

Liiiiiii-ammmmmm, the thing purred, its voice hanging in the air like putrid mist. The thing crept forward on limbs with too many joints, its claws cracking deep into the slate floor. *We've been looking for youuuuuuu.*

Liam's breath hitched beside her as he stood, but she didn't dare take her eyes off the creature. She took another step back, pushing her brother and Liam behind her. The monster's head swiveled from side to side; more beasts gathered behind it. Some had snouts like wolves; others, tails that swished like hungry panthers. But their laughter, their insidious grins, their fiery eyes and dark intent were nothing of this world. The closest one pressed in toward Rebeka, and its snout scraped the length of her body with one long, mournful sniff.

Rebeka stared into its eyes, and the creature cocked its head at her. There was something beautiful, something graceful in its movement. Rebeka found herself leaning forward, desperate to reach out—

Then there were more screams in German as the beasts turned on the guards.

Bullets whizzed through the air, pocking the plaster of the music hall. They couldn't aim at the monsters through the smoke. The creature in front of Rebeka whirled around with a snarl and sprinted toward the gunfire, laughing as if it were all some game.

Rebeka slung her arms around the boys and steered them away.

The vortex had burst out the windows along the courtyard side of the music hall. They raced through the shelving, glass crunching underfoot, then tumbled over a windowsill. Another bullet zipped past as they fell, embedding itself in the plaster walls. Dry, dead bushes snapped beneath her and raked through her hair and across her face as she fought her way back to her feet, the pain vivid in the bitter twilight cold.

Liam wrenched himself up beside her with haunted eyes. Blood flowed from his shoulder where he'd been shot, but there was no time for babying if they meant to make it out alive.

"This way," Rebeka hissed, and charged toward a covered walkway that ran the length of the courtyard. If she was remembering the map correctly, they could circle back around to the truck bay. But she couldn't blink away the glow of the creature's eyes, seeing through her.

Behind them, screams continued as jaws snapped and unearthly howls rang out.

"Did you *mean* to summon those—whatever they are?" Rebeka asked.

Liam flinched as they steered down the walkway. "Um," he said. "No—not exactly."

"What are they?" Daniel asked. He was shaking—whether from the monsters or something else, she couldn't tell. It wasn't like him to fall apart, even if he did have half the German army on his ass.

"Well." Liam ducked into an alcove that led to an interior door, and Rebeka and Daniel pressed in beside him. "The thing about that other world is, it's not exactly . . . empty. And I think Sicarelli's meddling a few hundred years ago kinda . . . pissed them off."

Rebeka stifled a bitter laugh. This was getting better by the second.

"Whatever he did to mess up their ecosystem, it's left them a little . . ." Liam peered around the corner. "Let's just say they're drawn to the scent of human fear. Anger, suffering, blood."

"Like the smell of those Nazi bastards that you just shredded apart?"

Liam swallowed. "Yeah, pretty sure that was like ringing a dinner bell."

"And do you have any way to control them?"

"Sometimes. But—not as many as that."

As if she could have hoped for anything more. "Why can't you just close the rift?"

"I *did*," Liam cried. "But if I draw too much energy from the other side, it—it weakens the barrier. Takes longer for it to seal back up. That's when it's easier for the creatures to slip through. And when you hate humans as much as they do—"

Rebeka held up one finger for silence and pressed her ear to the heavy wooden door. A faint alarm bleated on the other side, tinny and mechanical. There wasn't much hope their soldiers' disguises would hold, not with her brother staggering around shell-shocked and Liam's wounded shoulder. Well, maybe Liam's monsters could serve as a useful distraction—at least up until they all got eaten. She closed her eyes, offered up a quick prayer, then threw her shoulder into the door.

Aside from the insistent alarm, the hallway was oddly, unsettlingly still. Like the other corridors in the compound, the electric lighting was too weak for the massive Bavarian monstrosity crumbling around them, but she saw none of the clerks or guards or secretaries or maintenance people, all those hateful little cogs in the Reichsmaschine. More importantly, she didn't hear any of those awful whispers—none of the wailing wind and creeping shadows that had poured from the vortex.

She supposed it was too much to wish the next world over had been full of sunshine. "Let's go before anything else comes out of the darkness."

Rebeka led them down the hallway, in what she hoped was the direction of the garage bay. To their left—back in the direction of the archives—some sort of massive gearwork system churned and scraped.

Liam limped onward determinedly, teeth gritted, one hand clamped around his wounded shoulder, but her brother was lagging behind. A tiny, hateful part of Rebeka wanted to leave him. She'd done nothing but save him for the past several months, and he'd repaid her by dragging her into *this*. Instead, she slipped her hand into his and tried not to mind the sticky, drying Nazi blood on his fingers.

"Come on," she said softly. "Let's live to fight another day."

Daniel nodded, but his jaw was tight. He wouldn't meet her eyes.

As they passed beneath the corridor lights—specifically, as Liam passed beneath them—each bulb flickered and went dead. She glanced questioningly at Liam, but he kept hurrying them along. Darkness pursued them down the corridor, and Rebeka envisioned grasping claws, coiling vines. Then the first bulb shattered—then the next, and the next after that. She jumped, her nerves scraped raw.

"What the hell?" Daniel muttered. But there was no time to stop and consider it. If they turned left at the next corridor, they should nearly be to the garage—

A fierce wind tore down the corridor then, rushing down the path they'd taken and whipping past them with an inhuman screech. "In here!" Liam shouted, and threw himself into the deep recess of a doorway. Rebeka and Daniel dove in beside him.

The wind shivered, lowed, then howled once more. In the center of the corridor, a lightbulb shattered, and the burst socket crackled with a surge of electricity. Ice flooded her veins as her vision split in two: the image of the corridor before her, and then the sight of *herself*, running, fleeing.

That was certainly a new development—but not one she had time to consider. She'd never been able to watch herself this way, or watch as if from two eyes—but whatever it meant, it couldn't matter right now.

"We have to go this way!" she shrieked over the clatter, and yanked them down a side hall. The second vision dissipated as if it had lost its quarry—she didn't dare look behind her. This building hunched all around them, unknowable, a labyrinth of horrors yet to unfold.

The wind flickered, a sad little whimper like a wounded animal, then stopped.

Silence.

"Well?" Rebeka asked, after a heavy moment. No hum of electricity, no distant shouts or footfalls. The nothingness was overwhelming. Suffocating. It constricted her with fear, wringing her nerves dry.

"Well, what?" Liam asked through gritted teeth. He still clutched at his wounded shoulder, and sweat glistened on his flushed face.

"Is it safe now?" She leaned out and risked a glance down the hallway. The twilight glow of the courtyard just barely penetrated the thick shadows that had engulfed the hall. Her eyes were starting to adjust, but only dull forms gave any hint of the corridor ahead.

"You tell me," Liam said, eyebrows drawn down. "You're the one who seemed so sure we'd be safe down here."

"I . . ." Rebeka couldn't answer that—not now, not without explaining so much more than she could put into words. "Let's just go."

Together, they stepped out, slowly continuing in the direction they'd been headed, but walking backward, facing the way they'd come. They didn't want to encounter any more awful surpri—

"Halt! Stop right there—"

A guard skidded around the corridor, sliding on some unknown slickness on the stone floors. His trembling hands betrayed him as he lifted his rifle, clutching a wobbly flashlight in his supporting hand. Rebeka raised her arm, gun in hand, while Daniel froze, glowering, and Liam took a threatening step forward.

An electric crackle echoed down the hallway the guard had come from. The guard gasped; the beam of his flashlight sliced back toward the hall as he turned to look behind him.

"Who's there?" the guard shouted. Rebeka took a step back; whatever he'd heard had snagged his attention. If it would hold him a moment longer—

Two black tendrils of smoke darted across the beam of light and coiled around the guard's legs.

The guard's screams were like silk ripping apart, shrill and anguished, as the darkness dragged him off. He fell face-first onto the tiles and scrabbled for purchase, but found none. All they saw was one last horrified expression gleaming in the dropped flashlight's beam before the guard disappeared the way he'd come.

Rebeka and Daniel both stared at Liam. "Did—did you—"

"I wish." He shuffled forward, taking a wide path around the corridor's mouth. "C'mon."

Before she could shout at him to wait, Liam went staggering, swaying, toward the junction ahead. Rebeka laced her fingers through Daniel's and chased after him, shielding her face with her free hand as another lightbulb exploded above them.

They reached the end of the corridor and turned left. Total darkness welcomed them, and still that soupy silence. She strained her ears for anything—a slithering noise, a hiss and rattle like something ready to strike. Her heart felt lodged somewhere inside her jaw. For a moment, she felt the rush and beat of powerful wings, like when she used to race across the banks of the Tiergarten pond, sending flocks of geese scattering. Then it was gone, as quickly as it had come, as smoky and intangible as all her other foretellings.

"Take my hand." It was Liam, somewhere on the other side of the corridor.

She started to protest that she was nowhere near him until she felt Daniel shift beside her to close his hand around the American's.

Three across, they hurried down the hallway, silence so humid it stifled their own footsteps, their own ragged breaths. Rebeka kept waiting for the grasping tendrils at her ankles and wrists, but it was no vision, only fear, raw and seeping. Narrowed eyes watching from the darkness. A hunger so sharp it shredded her apart. And those horrible arms, those living beasts of shadow and seething spilling out of a tear in the world—

Another screech of metal flooded the hall from the direction of the archives, and then, one by one, the overhead lights popped on, ticking toward them like a military march.

Liammmmmm, the wind whispered.

"Fucking hell," Daniel muttered.

"Hurry." Liam tugged them forward. "We're almost there." But in his free hand, Rebeka saw the darkness gathering inside his palm.

They all but ran down the rest of the hall until, at long last, they reached the garage bay. Smoke filled their nostrils as they ducked into its confines. The sky beyond the bay doors was red-tinged like a sunset aflame. Strange—it had almost been night a moment ago. Their truck was so close—Daniel's hand slipped from Rebeka's as she rushed toward it, ready to fling herself into the cab—

But then a guard rounded the corner, looming over her, his chin squashed down and his eyes bloodshot and cold.

Rebeka opened her mouth to scream. The guard opened his mouth, too—the mouth with the diagonal scar across it.

The mouth of the man Daniel had killed in the back of the truck.

Black smoke poured from the guard's lips, his nostrils, from the gaping wound of his throat, and a scream built up in that smoke. Rebeka wasn't waiting to find out what would happen next. She did the only thing she could think to do, and punched him square in the jaw.

A tuft of darkness gushed out of his face, like flour from a holey sack.

"What the hell—" Daniel started behind her, but then a surge of electricity raced up the dead guard-thing's limbs and crackled as his body was enveloped in static darkness that collapsed in on itself.

Liam stood behind her with an outstretched hand. "They're eating them from the inside."

"Excuse me?" Rebeka screeched.

"I told you—they like the taste of human fear." Liam twisted his hands, exertion flushing his face deep scarlet. "Quick, we've gotta bolt before it lets the others know where we are—"

Footsteps scraped and dragged behind him from the far side of the garage: more of them coming.

Liam, they called out, the name edged with laughter. *You're far too late. The book can't help you now—*

Rebeka shuffled back as the shapes came into view. Closer now.

"Go!" Liam screamed.

"But what about the truck—"

"JUST GO!" Liam shouted. "NOW!"

It was Daniel's turn to take Rebeka by the hand and pull her toward the bay doors. She was too stunned to protest.

They fled the garage for the main road out of the compound. No telltale winks of sniper scopes in the towers that dotted the fence line. In the distance, a scream was cut short and replaced with an electrical crack. Rebeka and Daniel kept running.

Eventually, Rebeka's feet slowed as they approached the guard post at the entrance. Daniel slowed with her, then tossed an anxious glance over his shoulder. Liam was running toward them with his face wrenched wide.

"Don't stop!" he shouted. "There's more of them coming—"

A horrific cacophony shredded his words as, behind him, twisted, blackened versions of the Nazis they'd passed in the compound corridors began to stream from the garage.

Liam . . .

"But the guards—" Rebeka started.

"They're all dead, or good as. RUN!"

That was all she needed. She charged on, Daniel close behind.

They passed the guard post and found it deserted. A slimy hunk of meat was collapsed on the side of the dirt road, raw, skinned fingers still clutching a rifle. Rebeka slowed just long enough to rip the rifle from what was left of the flayed guard's hands. *Don't think, don't think, just run.* She hugged the blood-slick rifle to her chest as she raced toward the other side of the fence and the trees beyond it, Daniel and Liam behind her—and behind them—behind them—

Rifle fire pierced the air with a fierce whistle and then a thud. Rebeka screamed for her brother reflexively, terror like acid eating through her chest. "DANIEL!" She spun around, but he was still behind her.

Another bullet sang out, and another of the horrible Nazi-creature hybrids fell—

"Keep running!" Daniel called.

Rebeka did. But too late, she turned to see just what she was running toward. She had just enough time to register the boy's face—wide-eyed, white teeth, and a mouth rounded in a shout—as she plowed into him head-on.

CHAPTER NINE

PHILLIP

The town of Siegen was wedged into the forested valley like a tick. Steep slate rooftops crowded around battered copper spires, but the military administration building, that whitewashed hulking monstrosity, was the easiest to spot: it was the one currently on fire. Thick, woolly black smoke blotted out the twilight as Phillip and Simone edged along the ridge. Just down the slope from them, the compound's perimeter was fenced in with razor wire. But the shadows prowling the fence's edge were not guards.

"Not again," Simone said.

Phillip unclipped his sidearm and crouched against a nearby tree. "The army really should've mentioned these things in training."

"Up ahead!" Simone called.

Phillip twisted in the direction Simone was aiming, toward their ten o'clock. He'd have to teach her to use clock-face directions later. A shadow figure had dropped down from a tree branch and was crawling toward them on all fours. No—all sixes.

M u U c h too late . . .

That goddamned voice again, the one that was both inside his skull and all around them, blaring like a pipe organ. Simone fired, striking it along its lengthy neck. The monster twisted toward them with a sharp hiss, but didn't slow its crawl.

"You sure that's how to kill them?" Phillip asked.

Simone ejected the spent bullet casing from her rifle and cocked the next. "It worked before!"

Phillip dropped his rucksack and quickly fished out gauze and the vial of camphor from the first aid kit. After snatching up a stick from nearby, he wound a strip of gauze around one end, then smeared camphor on it. Simone fired two more shots, but the creature was still advancing. Phillip struck a match and held it to the camphor-soaked end of the stick.

The hissing cycled up into a shriek.

"Not a fan of fire?" He waved the makeshift torch forward, warding the beastie off. It leaned back from him, reflected flame glistening in its dead eyes, but kept all its limbs firmly planted in the underbrush.

WILL not stop—

"We'll see about that."

The monster watched him for a moment more, then turned and leapt at Simone.

She screamed, rifle firing, but it was too close for her to get a good shot. Phillip pitched the torch at the monster's feet as its front claws slashed at Simone's chest.

"GET BACK!" he screamed at her, not that she needed the encouragement. She twisted in the monster's grasp and dove down, sliding easily out of her oversize hunting parka. The sea of dead, crackling leaves at the monster's feet sparked and hissed as Simone scrambled backward.

THEY MUST PAY—

The monster bared its needle teeth at him—then howled as the flames crackled along its body.

It didn't burn like he thought it would, like meat charring through. Instead its muscles turned stringy, dangling as it tried to scramble out of the rush of fire. A molten, limp arm flopped forward, claws swiping for Phillip, but then dropped to the ground and disintegrated into a tuft of acrid smoke.

"Congratulations," Simone muttered. "You're going to burn the whole forest down."

"A thank-you might be nice." Demons and mangled bodies and whispers and blood. Maybe, just maybe, he *was* in over his head after all. With a shiver, he slung his pack onto his back and skirted around the growing blaze, eager to get the hell on with their mission. He'd come here to help, but so far, it felt like all he'd done was fight to survive; the feeling settled, splinter-like, under his skin. This wasn't the way it was supposed to go. "Which way to the rendezvous point?"

They skidded forward, along the slope that edged dangerously close to the Nazi compound; it was either burning forests full of demons or burning buildings full of Nazis.

Then they heard the shouting from down the slope. *"Keep running!"* someone shouted. In English.

Simone's teeth were rattling, but she managed to slot fresh bullets into her rifle with shaking hands.

"Wait." Phillip yanked her by the sleeve. "That was an American."

"He must be who set the compound on fire." She glowered at Phillip. "I can see the resemblance."

Phillip bit his tongue and crept closer toward the trees, then ducked behind a thick trunk. Three figures sprinted across the narrow yard and the road that ran the length of the ridge down below. Behind them, more creatures lurched on unsteady legs, skin sliding and sloshing around.

"Oh, God. It's more of those mangled ones."

"At least I can shoot those."

The humans drew closer—two boys and a girl, all of them splattered with blood. Phillip ducked back behind the tree trunk as Simone took her first shots. "Try not to shoot the actual humans!" Phillip shouted.

"Why not? They look like Nazis to me—"

As Phillip peeked back out from around the tree trunk, the girl plowed into him, sending them both flying and crashing into dead leaves. "What in the hell—"

"Sorry!" She tried to extricate herself from him as she spoke in German—thankfully one of the handful of words the army made him learn. "Sorry—"

Her dark hair was wispy with loose waves, cut short around her ears. She wore a grimy dress that might have been blue once. He settled her off of him carefully; she weighed less than their mountain dog back home. Deep pouches under her eyes and a tightness in her face spoke of exhaustion, starvation. She wasn't one of the monsters. Same as them, she was prey.

"Who are you?" he asked. "Uh—Sprechen Sie Englisch?"

She blinked at him with wide, dark eyes—not anger, not fear. But Simone's rifle fired again before she could answer, and they both whipped around. Phillip crouched, defensive, but the girl looked ready to bolt like a startled deer.

"Don't shoot!" The American-sounding boy had reached the forest edge. He was dressed like a Nazi, but if he was one, his American accent was shockingly good. Phillip looked between the girl and him, then reached for his sidearm, but it had gotten lost somewhere in the leaves when the girl plowed into him. "Please don't shoot! We aren't with them—"

Simone kept her rifle trained on the guy as he came closer, pausing just long enough to fire over his shoulder at one more demon-human corpsey thing. There was another boy with him, dressed in a guard's uniform—at least, as far as Phillip could tell. It was covered in *quite* a lot of blood.

"Aren't with who?" Phillip asked, answering in English. "The Nazis? Or those . . . things?"

"Neither!" The blond white boy, the American-sounding one, stepped closer, though he kept his good hand raised. His right shoulder was crusted with drying blood. "Look, we can explain . . ."

But his explanation was swallowed up in a vicious growl as another monster dropped out of the trees. Its limbs seemed to sprout out of the mouth of a man's severed head; human arms and legs dotted some of the many appendages as they scraped through the dead leaves. The head swiveled toward Phillip and fixed its bloody eyes on him.

"Jesus Christ." Phillip took a step backward, but he was afraid to move too quickly. Was that how they hunted? Movement? Maybe he was thinking of lions. Dinosaurs. Carefully, he took another step back as the creature let out a rattling hiss.

Bang. Bang. Simone let loose a barrage into the creature's torso, shredding the head it had grown from. But all that did was prompt the creature to *unfold*, new dimensional horrors of body parts, blood vessels, throbbing organs crawling out of the skin it was shedding as it angled itself at Simone.

Blood will be repaid . . . Li-ammmmmm.

"You can only shoot them if they're using human bodies." The blond American stepped forward, stretching something between his hands like a shadowy Jacob's ladder. "These ones are a little sturdier."

"And how the hell do *you* know?" Phillip screeched.

With a grunt, the American snapped his palms together, and sparks of violet shot from his hands. The monster squealed, an ear-splitting noise, and stretched tall as though it were being hoisted into the air. Its flailing limbs skittered dangerously close to Phillip's face, revealing razor-like edges on the insides of its joints. Then the monster snapped free of whatever was holding it—and pounced right at Phillip.

"Motherfucker—"

The razor flashed right in front of his face—

And with another scream, the creature shrank back, curling in on itself before it *vanished*, like someone had slammed shut an invisible door.

For a moment, they were all silent. Phillip didn't know where to look. Up in the trees for more monsters? Across the field for more Nazis? The American staggered forward, clutching his bleeding shoulder.

"You gotta . . . send them back through the barrier," he said.

Then he dropped to his knees.

Simone tossed a sharp look toward Phillip as she leveled her rifle at the boy. She was asking his opinion, he realized, once the shock wore off. As to whether they could trust him. Well, there was a first time for everything.

"You a Nazi?" Phillip asked, shuffling toward him.

The boy grimaced as he shook his head. "American. Same as you, I'm guessing."

"What's the capital of Idaho?"

"How the fuck should I know? I'm from New York!"

Well, that much checked out. "Name the Andrews Sisters."

"Patty, Maxene, and . . . Shit, I don't remember. Maxene's the cute one anyway."

"The blonde?" Phillip challenged.

"No way. The dark-haired one."

Phillip couldn't argue with that. He jerked his chin at Simone, and grudgingly, she lowered her rifle.

The girl who'd plowed into Phillip was sitting in the dead leaves, arms wrapped tight around her chest. God, she was so thin, frail as a bird. The ferocity in her glare, though, was enough to warn off someone three times her size. She narrowed her eyes at him, and he realized he was staring.

"Don't suppose you know the capital of Idaho?" Phillip asked her.

She huffed and turned to Simone. "Are there more of them coming?" Her English accent sounded sturdy and husky, though her voice was worn out, like a threadbare towel.

"Not that I can see." Simone's thumb flicked the cocking

mechanism of her rifle, louder than was strictly necessary. "But if you don't start explaining yourselves . . . What those things are, and how you were able to get rid of them—"

"Liam. Liam Doyle." The blond boy moved to extend his right hand to Phillip, then thought better of it, wincing and readjusting his grip on his shoulder. "I can explain, but you've gotta give us something, too. We need help. We need . . ."

"Free French. Libération-Nord," Phillip said, to an annoyed groan from Simone. "Well, she is. I can't really go into details as to what I'm doing here, or why, but—I'm with her."

The dark-haired boy shuffled over to the girl who'd plowed into Phillip, and they murmured in German. Finally she lifted her head. "Rebeka. And my brother is Daniel." Her glassy brown eyes met Simone's, challenging.

"Listen," Liam said, "if you've got a safe house we can go to, or—somewhere secure—"

"If you've set a military compound on fire, nowhere will be safe for you," Simone said, her tone flat.

Liam gritted his teeth. "There's gotta be something we can trade you. Tell me what you want to know."

But Simone just laughed at him. "There is nothing I need to know that badly."

"You sure about that? Your Libération might," Liam countered.

This was getting them nowhere, and meanwhile Siegen burned, sure to draw more Nazis like rats to garbage. These people clearly needed help, and Phillip wasn't about to leave someone out in the cold. What was the point of any of this if he did?

"We *could* use their help," he said to Simone. "It'll make my job go faster. Give us some cover. And if they know how to deal with those *things*—"

"You are not in charge here. You—you *Americans* are not in charge." Simone's lip curled back. "Where were you when the tanks stormed into Paris, when Pétain rolled over and let those monsters scratch his belly—"

"Hey. We're here now, aren't we? We're doing what we can," Phillip said.

Simone swallowed and turned away from him, forcing down whatever rage she'd been about to unleash. In the little time he'd spent with her, Phillip had learned she was nothing if not a master of burying things: emotions, bodies. It made his own heart ache.

"Come on," Phillip said. "We're all on the same side. This is why we're here, isn't it? If we can't help three people who need it, how the hell are we supposed to help millions more?"

Simone worked her jaw from side to side. "Fine. You can follow us to our safe house at the next town and explain yourselves there. If you haven't burned it down, too."

Liam smiled, a bared-teeth grin. "Perfect. We'll regroup there. Figure out our next steps," he said to the German siblings.

"Answers first." Simone jabbed a finger eastward. "After that, I don't care what you do."

Rebeka glanced toward Phillip as they started their hike. The defiant glint had left her expression now that Simone had backed down, but she kept the look of someone far too used to staying behind her walls. "Sorry for running into you," she said in English.

"I think you had bigger problems at the time." He looked her over, the ragged dress and holey stockings. She carried herself as though she were used to being stronger, broader; he could see it in the proud jut of her chin, the determined tilt of her eyes. It made Phillip wonder what she was like before. Who she might become still.

"As long as those monsters burn," she said, jerking her head toward the military compound, "I'll be just fine."

He had to agree—the demons and Nazis alike.

Darius had laughed at him once, back when he explained the digital computer he'd been designing. *Still trying so hard to prove you're more than your inheritance, huh?* He always cut too close to the bone. Maybe he had been striving for acceptance, for something that would always be out of reach. In the end, it did so much worse than that—devastation he couldn't begin to undo.

Maybe that was why he wanted so desperately to help this weird bunch that burned down a Nazi base. The same reason he'd fled from Tulsa and jumped out of a goddamned plane. Because he wanted to prove his usefulness, his ability to do the right thing. But once again, he couldn't shake the feeling it was all about to blow up in his face.

Their destination was Hallenberg, a few towns east of Siegen. They'd planned to meet up with a Siegen shopkeeper in the Magpie network after nightfall, but instead of the stifling silence of curfew, Siegen was practically shimmering with activity as military vehicles and Gestapo trucks raced toward the administrative compound. The safest thing was to head to their next stop in Hallenberg, and they were all ready to put the smoldering wreckage as far behind them as they could. Phillip was itching to actually get to work on their mission. But he was here to help people, right? And these disasters sure seemed like they needed help. Anyone who'd pulled down the Nazis' ire was okay in his book.

"You will leave first thing in the morning," Simone told the newcomers. "Every last Gestapo thug will be hunting for you, and we don't need that kind of heat."

"And why not?" Rebeka asked. "What are you doing that's so important?"

"Nothing that concerns you—" Simone started.

"No one who saw our faces is still alive."

It was the first time Phillip had heard Daniel, the German boy, speak up. He was even taller than his sister, rivaling Simone for height, but where Simone had the sturdy muscles of someone who worked with their whole body, Daniel looked like yarn cast onto a wire frame. And Phillip didn't need his first aid training to tell that the blood on Daniel's clothes and face, drying purplish in the starlight, was not his own.

They marched for eight kilometers, ten. Liam and Daniel spoke in hushed tones, ignoring Simone's glowers, but Rebeka only stared into the darkness when Phillip tried to catch her eye. Small talk made him feel wound up like a transistor coil, all nervous potential and too much surface space. He was used to bumbling through champagne chatter at his parents' parties. She deserved better than that.

"You weren't afraid of the monsters," she said softly. Her accent made it hard to tell whether she thought that was a good thing.

"Then I guess I'm a good actor."

Her smile twitched upward. "You've been here long?"

"I, uh . . . I'm probably not supposed to say."

She nodded to herself. "And they only sent the two of you. Seems rather dangerous. You agreed to this?"

"It'll be worth it if we can pull it off." His breath lodged in his throat, caught on warring instincts as he scrounged for something more to say. None of the social rules he'd constructed for himself applied here. He didn't have a schematic for any of this.

"And if you can't?" she asked.

His shoulders dropped. "Then it was worth trying."

Her eyebrows rose with something like respect.

Phillip caught himself whistling "Boogie Woogie Bugle Boy" as they continued on. But it was at once too quiet and too loud in the vast emptiness of the forests around them. The sharp crunch of leaves trampled beneath five pairs of feet. The question of what in the hell they'd all gotten themselves into.

Finally Hallenberg emerged, a smaller hamlet curled up next to the forest alongside a dismal creek. Half-timbered Bavarian buildings clustered around a picturesque central square complete with a fountain, currently dry. Few lights sketched the shapes of curtained windows; the streetlights were dark husks against the starry sky. Probably just a precautionary measure against potential air raids. But there was an optimal volume of activity they needed to disguise themselves, and this fell on the side of too sparse.

"We head for the church," Simone said. "Act like you're supposed to be here."

The "church" turned out to be Himmel Kino, an old sanctuary converted into a movie theater, the marquee out front dark where it jutted from a plain whitewash-and-slate façade. They huddled beneath the entry, but the carved wooden doors had been locked. No showings tonight, Phillip supposed. With one hand on her rifle, Simone made five quick little knocks.

Nothing happened.

Dogs barked in the distance, the frantic, anxious noise of a pack eager to attack, then died down. Pigeons cooed down at them from where they'd nested in the eaves of the marquee. The air smelled smoky and stale, like fireplaces stoked to life for the first time after their summer rest.

Finally, there was a slow, dragging sound on the other side of the wooden door, then the clatter of chains being unwrapped. Liam shifted his weight impatiently at Phillip's side. Phillip couldn't blame him, with a wound like that. He was in for a rough night trying to patch himself up.

Was it the shadows under the marquee, or was Liam's face now edged in black? It looked like black veins shooting from his eyes. Phillip looked closer, eyebrows drawn down, but the illusion shattered. He must have imagined it.

At long last, the door cracked open, and a pale woman's face appeared through the seam. "Curfew. Showing's canceled for tonight," she said in German, and started to shut the door once more.

"Wait." Simone blocked the door open with her shoulder and continued in French. "J'ai besoin d'emprunter un parapluie."

Uncle Al had drilled Phillip on these phrases, but his accent was so bad he barely recognized them in Simone's flawless French. Something about borrowing an umbrella. He burrowed down into his coat.

The woman exhaled, like she was just as tired of this game as they were. "Rouge ou noir?"

"Je préfère vraiment le bleu."

The woman yanked open the door. She was broad, with a jaw made for chewing rocks and, as the full view of her revealed, was missing her left arm below the elbow. A neat knot in her olive coveralls concealed the truncated limb. She ushered them inside, eyes narrowing at each successive person who limped through her door.

"Sorry," Simone said, switching to English. "We picked up a few strays."

"I did not know the circus was in town," the woman muttered, though her accent seemed to feed the words through a cheese grater.

"We found them fleeing Siegen, or what's left of it." Simone gave Phillip a pointed look. "We're supposed to help everyone on our side, or so I've been reminded."

Phillip ignored her. "Is there a doctor or someone we could summon? He's been shot."

"Not by me," Simone added. "Yet."

The woman shook her head. "We're on curfew tonight because of an 'incident' at Siegen. That's what the loudspeaker trucks said, anyway."

Phillip steeled himself. "Guess I'll have to do it, then."

"You'll want to hole up in the projection room. It's a mess, but the sort of mess with good hiding places. There's a false panel behind the cabinets. Oh, but the projection equipment—be careful with it. You'll see I've added an extra switch to the side. Under no circumstances should you touch it, ja? Only in emergencies."

The woman introduced herself as Helene as she limped her way through the foyer of the church, under Gothic ribbed ceilings painted with strange, brightly hued images. Phillip was too used to Tulsa's clean lines, sharp Art Deco, forceful façades. This church, for all the drab white and slate of its exterior, was an untidy mess of primary colors creeping out of black and white. He kind of loved it.

"There's the staircase. The projection room's in the old choir balcony. If you need something to eat, the kitchen's in the rectory." Helene swung her right hand toward a doorway and twisting staircase beyond. "I'm supposed to host an officer matinee of *The Great Love* tomorrow, so I suggest you make yourselves scarce by then."

"And the radios?" Simone asked anxiously.

"We'll deal with them in the morning." With that, she waved them off and vanished into the rectory.

As soon as Helene was gone, Simone gripped Liam by the injured shoulder, thumb digging into his wound. "You promised answers. Now talk."

Liam groaned loudly in response.

"Jesus Christ, Simone!" Phillip rushed forward to pry her off. "At least let me patch him up first. Would probably help if we weren't leaving a blood trail to our hiding spot."

Liam managed a strained smile. "Do you know what you're doing?"

"They taught me how to do a field dress in basic." Phillip winced. "Aaaaand I probably shouldn't have said that."

"Fine. But then we need answers," Simone said.

They shuffled up the staircase in single file toward the projection room. Rebeka caught Phillip's gaze as they entered the messy converted balcony. "Thank you," she said quietly. "For helping us."

Phillip's stomach fluttered. "Someone had to, right?"

He settled Liam down against the wall, then started to work his arm free from the shredded sleeve of his jacket. "I'd figured you were army," Liam said. "Pretty sure I'm the only American moron who *isn't* out here on Uncle Sam's orders."

Phillip tore open the gauze pack and dabbed a vial of peroxide onto the wad of bandages. "You think *you're* a moron? I volunteered."

Liam relaxed with a grin. "Why'd you go and do a thing like that?"

Phillip flinched. Now it was his own nerve that was exposed. "Felt like the right thing to do, I guess." A pat, easy answer. He was used to the weight of his decision: the delicious look on his father's face when he announced he was leaving; the remorse he'd felt every time he built a new circuit diagram for Mr. Connolly, wondering how it might be misused next. But he wasn't ready to let these strangers in like that.

"Right," Liam said, but he didn't sound convinced.

Phillip pressed the gauze to the wound and scrubbed. It had to sting worse than an Oklahoma summer, poor bastard. The blood had started to dry, thick and tacky, on his collarbone, but Phillip could feel the hard nob of the bullet beneath it. Extracting it was a little out of his repertoire, but they had no choice. Maybe it'd be like threading a loose circuit back into place (though he doubted any patient would be much comforted by that analogy).

"You a Dodgers man?" Phillip asked, once he'd let up the pressure on the wound. He needed Liam nice and distracted while he worked the tweezers.

Liam shook his head. "Damn Yankees. Used to go to Dodgers games, though, with my . . ." Only the slightest pause, but Phillip felt it in the way Liam's muscles tensed. "My pops—*oof.*"

Phillip eased the bullet loose in a spurt of fresh blood and felt his own stomach flip. Liam hissed through his teeth and squeezed fists around his jacket, then slowly slumped back.

Phillip discarded the bullet, then cleaned the wound up once more. "It's LaVerne, by the way," he said, while Liam straightened up and tested his shoulder. "The third Andrews sister." A trust offering.

Liam smiled. "I guess I'm more a fan of Bing Crosby." He moved his arm in a slow circle, still wincing, but he was looking less waxy now, at least. "Not bad. You a medic?"

Phillip wet his lips, hesitant. "Engineer."

"Really!" Liam sat back with a grin. "Theoretical physics. Princeton."

Phillip let out a low whistle. "You study with Einstein? I usually don't give you theoretical boys much credence, but I gotta say, his theory of relativity . . ."

"How about you? Let me guess . . . Mechanical engineering?"

"Electrical," Phillip said. "Digital computing, radio waves, circuitry, I design it all." Or he did, anyway. Dimly, he wondered if he'd ever have the guts to design something new again.

"Frequency generation? I'll have to pick your brain about something I've been working on later. I'd love to see—"

"Enough." Simone pulled up a chair from the projectionist's desk and sat across from Liam, her rifle resting in her lap. "You said you had answers."

Liam exchanged a glance with Phillip, like he was asking for help. But Phillip knew better than to go against Simone's will. Slowly, Liam nodded, clammy sweat gathering on his brow.

"I do. But they aren't gonna be answers you like."

CHAPTER TEN
SIMONE

Simone was not what she would call a patient person. Nor a particularly credulous one. And while Liam, the idiot American who'd attached himself to them like a nettle, was doing his best to explain, she only grew more impatient and fed up.

"And these demons are crawling out of *another world*?" Simone asked. She'd seen the demons for herself, and yet. It was far easier to believe that he was as deranged as he appeared than that he was capable of summoning *creatures* out of the ether.

Liam slumped against the wall with a tired smile. "They despise our world because of what Sicarelli did to them, so they're determined to destroy every human they encounter. They're especially attracted to the energy signature of fear and pain."

"Is there any *other* way to feel when confronted with a demon?" Phillip asked.

Liam tipped his head, conceding the point. "But it's not just the creatures. It's the energy that suffuses their world. I can harness and channel it in interesting and painful ways."

"Dark energy," Phillip said, with an eagerness that made Simone roll her eyes. "That unaccounted-for mass weighing down the universe. You're saying it comes from the same place as those . . . those *things*?"

Liam's whole face lit up. "Yeah! I can show you the formulas. The energy passes between universes—there may be other dimensions, but our world seems to have the closest link to—"

"I wonder how it affects Kepler's gravitational equation—"

"I wondered that too. I can pinpoint the years when Sicarelli's bridge was open. It's all observable in interstellar background radiation—"

"Enough, both of you!"

Simone glared at Phillip. He at least should know better. He had a mission, same as her. Phillip hung his head, chastened, but was still grinning with giddiness over a new scientific puzzle to solve.

"So there are the monsters—those come from the other side. As does this energy you use. But what about when it seems to possess people?" Simone asked. "Like those guards that were chasing you."

"That's what can happen when the energy works its way inside someone, corrupting them from the inside out. People who are already angry, hateful—the darkness has an easier time attaching to them because they're primed for its corruption."

"Like the Nazis," Rebeka said.

Liam nodded, eyes narrowed. "Like the Nazis. As the energy suffuses them, they become stronger. Even more dangerous than they already were."

Simone pinched her nose, trying to fight back the tidal pull of her own anger. "And you want to meddle with these forces, why, again?"

"Because of what that power can do. You've seen what I can do by myself, wielding it. Now imagine that on a massive scale. How it could help the Allies turn the tide of the war."

"Or make the Germans even more powerful," Simone said.

Liam's head slumped. "Which is why I need to get Sicarelli's book away from them. The book—it's the key to drawing on an unlimited amount of that energy instead of the slow drip I can manage on my own. He supposedly stabilized a bridge between the two universes for a brief time, which means we can do it again."

Fine. She'd seen the results of this shadow world clearly enough, if not the world itself. The darkness that wore human skin, the shadows that slithered and screamed, and plenty of other kinds of monsters besides. There was no use denying it was real. But just because this boy *could* do these things didn't mean she wanted him on their side.

"The monsters. They were hunting you." Simone rubbed at her temples. "They were calling *your* name. Why?"

Liam went quiet at that. Of course. He drummed the fingers of his uninjured hand against his knee, a bundle of nervous energy. "Our universes . . . have a history," he said carefully. "They resented Sicarelli for meddling in their world. I'm sure they feel the same about me."

"So by being here with us . . ." Simone cast her gaze around the balcony turned projection room. "You've put a target on our backs."

He shrank back against the wall. "It's possible, yeah." At least he had the good sense to act embarrassed. "There . . . there was an accident, once. Someone I cared about . . . I think the monsters recognize me."

Rebeka made a strange sound at that, but Simone ignored her, glaring at Liam. Whatever help this idiot sorcerer boy could offer the

Resistance, whatever minuscule advantage, it couldn't be worth all this hassle. "I think it's time for you all to leave."

Daniel lunged forward. She'd forgotten he was there—the bloodied boy lurking in the corner, so quiet he might as well have been a cobweb. Now, though, he moved in front of her, fists raised, something like a snarl or a growl lodged between his teeth. He had the feral look of someone out of options. "We don't have anywhere else to go."

Simone reared back. "Get. Out. Of my. Face."

Her hands tingled with unspent energy. She was hoping for a fight. Let him try to swing at her. She stared him down, his tattered guard uniform and the freckles of blood across his face. She'd rather punch a Nazi, but she'd take what she could get.

To her disappointment, his shoulders fell. "One night," he mumbled. "You promised us one safe night."

She bared her teeth at him. "That's before I knew you were bringing monsters with you."

It was, however, the four of them against Simone. She saw that plainly now. Phillip, poor Phillip, wanted so badly to do the right thing, and the two siblings looked so worn through it was a wonder they were still standing. She couldn't imagine why they were following Liam, but if they'd survived in these woods this long, they were a damned sight more stubborn than she'd given them credit for.

Rebeka squared toward her, fists tight at her sides. "I didn't think you were out here because you were easily scared."

"Scared? No," said Simone. "Practical, yes. If it does not help my mission, then I have no use for it. Or you."

"You want something useful?" Liam asked. "You saw the power

that universe holds. It can shred through the Third Reich's forces when it's properly harnessed. Those 'monsters' are why we were able to face an entire outpost of Nazis and walk out alive."

"Barely," Simone said.

"In this war?" Rebeka huffed. "Barely is enough."

Simone fumed, but said nothing. The girl had a point. *If* they could contain those creatures, *if* they could harness that dark energy, it would be a great boon for Georges-Yves's network. Possibly as significant as what she and Phillip were doing.

Wait, was she actually considering it? This mission was going to be the death of her.

"I just need to stabilize the hole between the universes. Make it more reliable. I've sustained smaller tears in the past, but they all had this . . . unfortunate side effect. The two worlds bleeding together in uncontrollable ways."

"Unfortunate side effect?" Simone laughed. "We were kilometers away from Siegen, and still we saw these . . . these *rifts*. Monsters crawling through the forests. If they can manage to get through small tears, I'd hate to see what a larger hole might bring."

"I can fix it, I swear—"

"And if the monsters are after you, how is it safe for you to call on them at all? If that energy can corrupt the Germans, how long before it corrupts you too?"

"I can still control it, in small doses." Liam's voice took on a fervent edge. His skin had a grayish cast like wet clay, with bruised crescents lurking under his eyes. "Once I can stabilize a rift, I'll be fully in charge."

"M-maybe we can figure out how to do this without the book."

Phillip worried his fingers together like he was tapping out a code. "There's gotta be a way to stabilize it on our own."

"Could be." Liam dragged his gaze back toward the group. "Harmonic frequencies open the rifts. I can open a small one on my own, but for a bigger source of energy, I'd need a way to lock that opening in place."

Phillip gave him a crooked grin. "Well, you're speakin' my language."

Simone threw her hands up with a groan. "Just what you two needed—a peer group."

"You need something that can cycle the frequencies enough that they stabilize themselves," Phillip said. "So you don't have to do it for them."

"Yes. Exactly!" Liam exhaled a deep, satisfied sigh. "Someone gets it."

"Well, I don't know what some old manuscript's gonna tell you, but I've got something that might help." Phillip reached down for his boots and began to ease open the heel of one shoe.

"What are you *doing*?" Simone cried. "That is for our *mission*—"

"Our mission is stopping the Third Reich, isn't it?" Phillip plucked out a coiled, multipronged device. "I've been tinkering with this—it's like a frequency jammer, but with a more sophisticated routing pattern, multimodal scattering . . . The goal is to fold signals on top of themselves so the Nazis don't even realize, until it's too late, that the signals aren't syncing up. It's not part of our *official* mission, but—"

"Our official mission is none of their business," Simone said.

"You're setting up secure two-way radio comms, aren't you?" Liam asked. "Kinda obvious now that I think about it."

Simone's headache blossomed so quickly she was sure she'd popped a blood vessel. "Don't you dare breathe a word—"

Rebeka glowered at her. "We're on your side. Whether you want us to be or not. So try acting like it."

Simone surveyed the room. Liam, his eyes cold and dangerous, even with his shoulder bandaged and his skin pale as wax. Daniel and Rebeka, solemn and stormy, a unified front. And Phillip and his stupid device, ready to take on the whole damned German army like it was just some experiment. A pity. She was starting to tolerate him.

"There is one problem, though," Daniel said. "Sicarelli's manuscript was moved to Wewelsburg for a reason. What if the Nazis know what it does?"

The room went silent for a moment as everyone turned to Liam. "Dr. Kreutzer," he said, and the German siblings tensed. "He knows. He must know."

"He was conducting experiments on people in Łódź," Rebeka explained, looking at Phillip. "It's exactly the sort of thing he would want."

"So you would still need to get this book, regardless. To keep it from him," Simone said.

Liam sighed. "If it isn't already too late."

"I'll go." Daniel stood. "I can get it. Destroy it, if I have to. You know I can."

A look passed between Liam and Daniel that sent a phantom chill over Simone's skin: familiar and painful, the press of an old bruise.

"Please don't," Liam whispered.

"If you're going, then I am too," Rebeka said.

"No," said Daniel. "Stay with the partisan girl. Go back to Paris with them when they're done—"

"Y'know," Phillip said, "Wewelsburg's on our list of resistance pockets to outfit." He arched one eyebrow at Simone. "We can all go. Cause I don't know about you, but this thing he can do?" He gestured toward Liam. "I don't want the Nazis to have it, too."

She was outnumbered. There was no shaking sense into any of them. And just as she'd begun this mission, she'd end it: only the warm wood and cold metal of her rifle to pin her to this world.

"Fine," she said to Phillip. "Go play around in your shadow world all you like. Stay there, for all I care. But you ever feel like getting back to the task at hand—the one you were *sent* here to do—" Simone backed toward the door of the projection room, nearly tripping over film canisters. "Then you let me know."

The first time they'd fought about resisting was Lyon.

Simone had never been to Lyon—she'd never been more than a few dozen kilometers outside of Paris, aside from a brief visit to a dying grandmother in Algiers now lost to the blur of childhood memories— but she wished she had been. Lyon was unafraid. Lyon killed Nazi occupiers in train stations, on the street, at outdoor cafés like they were pigeons just begging to be kicked. When the Nazis demanded Lyon cough up its resisters, Lyon refused, no matter how many the Nazis insisted on killing in their stead.

That was the kind of stubbornness Simone admired. The fool-hardy, granite-carved stubbornness that yielded to nothing, despite all good sense to the contrary. The stubbornness of the stump in the field, the one that remained even after the offending tree had been cut down. It was that stubbornness that got Simone her first apprenticeship, and that got her stuck with the most detested woodworking gig in all of Paris. It was that stubbornness that drew in Evangeline, and that same stubbornness that sent her away.

Simone had to be hard, she had to be cold, because without that, she had nothing else. And if she died for it, well, at least she would die holding her convictions close. At least they would have to be pried from her hands, stiff, snapping away bone.

Georges-Yves saw some of this when he recruited her and gave her the tasks others were too afraid or unskilled to carry out. Her final test was at the Hôtel Ritz on the Place Vendôme, the glamorous maison where all the clever monsters like Hermann Göring lounged. When they weren't at sparkling soirées, or torture sessions at the Gestapo headquarters on Avenue Foch, anyway. Georges-Yves had access to the hotel's rooms, cabinets, corridors. He knew of gaps in the walls; he'd measured all the empty space the hotel's architects left behind. In true partisan fashion, he would turn that proletarian excess into his means of resistance.

After Simone installed a listening nook tucked beneath the wardrobe for Göring's many capes, she was brought deeper into the network: vetted, verified. Simone carried her secret in her back pocket, a bit of sandpaper to smooth out every irritation. The sight of SS strutting down the boulevard only reminded her of the secrets Georges-Yves's people snatched from Göring every night. It made bearable the rumble in her belly while she waited in ration lines. Even Evangeline's snide remarks had lost their sting, for Simone knew at least one of them was doing what they ought. It was intoxicating . . . and all she wanted was to do more.

Georges-Yves, as it turned out, had been counting on just that.

She was no longer content with little errands, collecting bundles of papers "left behind" at a bookstore or on a Métro seat. She wanted to be like the people of Lyon, picking off the vermin in the streets. Making them afraid. Finally, he took her to the range in the countryside with Sanaz and Ahmed and a few others, starting her with a snubnose pistol but quickly moving up to the hunting rifle when he saw how good her aim was.

Shooting was easy. It was like carpentry in just the right ways: angles and trajectories, curved planes, a sharp, measuring eye. Simone wished she could say she only imagined Nazis on the receiving end, but she didn't. Evangeline's father, her own absent father, her brother and his informer friends, all the cowards and crusty worthless sycophants of the Vichy—they all lingered in her mind as she fixed the rifle barrel, let out her breath, and pulled the trigger tight.

The first time she killed a man—a roadside convoy ambush on its way to Verdun—she didn't feel much of anything at all. The soldiers' angry shouts that she silenced. The wreckage of the German truck heaving and crumpling as it burned. It was only afterward that she felt the same satisfaction as completing a lengthy carpentry project. For a moment, however fleeting, it felt good and right for her hands to be still, accomplishment allowing her to rest.

But really, all she wanted was to do it again.

When she wasn't aiding Georges-Yves, her hands became restless as ever. She shredded papers between her fingers over stilted coffee with Evangeline. Itched for cigarettes constantly. She tried to listen, tried to persuade Evangeline in her own bumbling, brute-force way of the value of resistance. But everything inside her was too much. Evangeline's conviction, not enough.

The assassins of Lyon were heroes, she would say, as loud as she could without letting anyone else hear. *They died for it, but they got the work done.*

But Evangeline would only look at her coolly as she took another sip of coffee. *If they were really such damned heroes, they wouldn't have gotten everyone else killed, too.*

ILSE

Ilse Weber's morning had begun like any other. She unpinned the stiff skirt she'd worn yesterday from the clothesline and wriggled it over her hips, then uncapped her eyeliner pencil to draw thin lines up the backs of her calves. There was a war on—no silk or nylon to be wasted on such luxuries as stockings—but it was important to look the part. She had a terribly important role to play, after all.

She tucked her wheat-blond hair up into a stern chignon, then dabbed two circles of rouge on her cheeks. Lipstick was too great an indulgence, and drew the wrong kind of attention, she'd learned. She needed to look presentable to keep her position, but more or less invisible otherwise. It would come in handy when she needed it most.

Fully composed, she grabbed her identification badge, the one stamped with the swastika and laurel wreath, and called goodbye to her mother as she slipped out the front door.

It was only a short walk to work, but the early autumn air carried the scent of something dangerous in it, something smoky. Not the smell of burning leaves—too early—or the sharp, too-sweet stench wafting off of Niederhagen KZ. Something darker lurked in that scent, blowing in from the west like bad luck. It sent an uneasy trill down Ilse's back and quickened her step.

Ilse reached the entrance and flashed her identification at each successive tier of guards. Crossed the drawbridge, newly repaired, its stone masonry scrubbed raw. Entered the castle with its freshly exposed face, like a healthy spa peel in Switzerland. Gathered her over-starched lab coat and gloves from her locker and pulled them on. Then clicked her way toward Dr. Kreutzer's laboratory with a secret smile.

Ilse was always smiling in secret, because Ilse, unlike the earnest, sour-faced Nazis around her, was a spy.

She didn't like to dwell on it—didn't want it to seem like she was bragging—but Ilse had infiltrated the very highest echelons of the Schutzstaffel's administration at Wewelsburg. She assisted Kreutzer with his research and coordinated information across countless other departments, keeping the cogs of the SS turning properly.

For now, for now.

What the SS didn't see beyond Ilse's cool façade was the catalog she was building inside her head, the one she knew would someday aid the resisters in tearing it all down, stone by stone. Knowing this role she was soon to play—as soon as she figured out how—made each banal horror a little more bearable, made each cruelty she assisted in a little less cruel. Someday, she would do the right thing and turn over everything she knew. Someday, her trap would be sprung.

Once she knew what trap to set, that was. But that could all come later.

"Ilse, darling. You're just in time." Herr Kreutzer was waiting for her at the entrance to the laboratories. "We have a new arrival to assess."

Ilse's stomach curdled, knowing the sort of deliveries the Herr Doktor usually took, but she offered a polite nod.

"If it proves to be what I think it is, then we must move forward quickly. Come, let's find out."

Kreutzer pressed a hand to the small of her back, lower than was really necessary, to guide her toward an examination room. But Ilse kept her smile firmly in place. She'd grown up dreaming of a life on the silver screen, her face three stories tall as she played the Valkyrie, the mistress, the schemer, the star. Unfortunately, the war had rather limited the roles available to her. If the good National Socialist secretary was what she had to play to undermine the Third Reich, if that was what it took to stop all this tasteless, maudlin nationalism, this useless, isolationist paranoia, well, she was open to performing in a select intimate venue to further the resisters' cause.

This is not the way things are meant to be, her mother's friends whispered over the years, as their country shifted around them, becoming more and more garish like the German Expressionist set pieces of the film *The Cabinet of Dr. Caligari*. They kept saying it, that it was abnormal, but if that were so, then why did they all seem to inhabit the asylum while the abnormal ones, the Caligaris, ruled over them? It was all too normal, the true essence of Völkisch to be tyrannical, hateful, warring. Ilse accepted her abnormality. She would use it to her advantage.

For though she'd never known a different life, she couldn't help but feel nauseated by it. The pang deep in her chest when her neighbors and friends threw rocks at the Jews as they were taken away. The embarrassment that forced her to avert her eyes when someone picked a fight with an elderly yellow-starred woman on the streetcar. The shame down in her marrow every time the news broadcasts crowed over another swath of London destroyed, another nation trampled over.

Yes. This was the way to win the war—not with outright disobedience, violence, and discord. Ilse would win the war by standing up straight, doing her job, but knowing, deep down, the righteousness of her purpose. In her heart, she knew she didn't mean it when she went along with the Nazis' plans. She was good. She could be goodness in the dark.

"The masks, Ilse." Kreutzer held out a hand expectantly as they reached his laboratory's outer chamber. Ilse handed one over before strapping hers on, as well. Too often, the masks meant they would be conducting autopsies. But Kreutzer's research was so strange, so wide-ranging, it was useless for her to make any guesses.

They entered the room, where a metal crate rested on the examining table, roughly six feet in length. Ilse steeled her stomach as Kreutzer unfastened the crate.

"Oh," she said, sucking in her breath as she took in the corpse. It was almost completely black, as if burnt, but rather than being charred and ashy, it was . . . *slimy*. The closer she looked, the more certain she became that the thing in the crate had never been a person at all. Not just because of its eerie, burgundy-black skin, but also its overabundance of joints. Too many knees and elbows. Too many talons jutting from the backs of heels and palms.

If Ilse hadn't known Dr. Kreutzer, if she had not been working with him for over a year now, she might have grown ill at the sight. She might have screamed or fainted. But she was the sane one, the secret mole within Caligari's asylum. She was the only one who could expose Kreutzer, and in time, make things right.

"Fascinating," Kreutzer murmured, his smile scalpel-sharp. "Yes. Though I admit I am envious I was not the one to manage it first."

"Manage what, Herr Doktor?"

"To open a rift stable enough to permit these creatures to slip through." He snapped his gloves into place. "Decades of research, but the best I have managed is a trickle of energy. So many wasted trials . . ."

She'd seen only glimpses of the doctor's trials—people ushered into operating theaters, then reemerging with a hollow look in their eyes and ink in their veins. If they emerged alive at all.

Ilse had tried to read the doctor's papers about this shadow world, the Schattenland, but they put her to sleep every time. Prattling on and on about energy, blood offerings, some Italian idiot who spoke with angels or devils or whatever nonsense. It wasn't becoming for a man of science like Dr. Kreutzer. But he had been so methodical in his experiments thus far. Perhaps it was all leading somewhere after all—and she would be the one to witness it, to report it to the Resistance. A magnificent prize.

"We will need to work quickly. Once I have mastered the process, we must use the book very soon, to ensure we are in control. Not whoever is responsible for . . . for this."

"D-do we have everything that is required?" Ilse asked. With shaking fingers, she fumbled her gloves on, and hoped he did not see.

"Near enough to it." Kreutzer held out his hand for a scalpel, which Ilse hurried to provide. "Summon Herr Černik, then. It is time."

"But what *is* it?" Ilse asked before she could stop herself. She flinched as he made the first incision—the wet, squelching noise thick all around her.

Kreutzer's eyes crinkled through the lenses of his mask.

"It is as he promised." He peeled back flesh to expose deeply corded sinew. "The key to the Third Reich's conquest."

CHAPTER ELEVEN

LIAM

After Phillip gave him some sleeping pills, Liam lost track of what were dreams and what was reality. The film strips turned into black vines that slithered across the floor and coiled around his limbs. Daniel's soft lips shushed him as he changed the dressing on Liam's shoulder with nimble musician's fingers. Pitr's mouth wrenched open in a silent scream, hand stretched forward as blackness surrounded him.

Maybe it was neither dream nor waking. Maybe the behemoth in the shadow world had finally caught him, and was mirroring all his fears and failings as it waited for him to break. Maybe the faceless figures in the chamber room had caught him at last, and it was time for him to be judged.

"Daniel," he whispered once, or thought he did, reaching out to that dour face. "Please don't go."

Daniel gave him no answer. Maybe it was just the sleeping pills talking, sleep grasping for him again with bloody arms and too many memories. Maybe Daniel wasn't there at all.

Liam's mind tumbled downward, the past tugging him back.

After he and Pitr had embarked on their research, the end of the semester came all too soon, and Pitr went back to Czechoslovakia for the summer while Liam continued their work. They parted on uncertain terms at the end of spring. Pitr promised he'd keep researching while he was in "the old country," as he put it, with a heavy roll of his eyes. He was going to show Liam's diagrams to other researchers he'd been corresponding with while Liam tinkered around with frequencies, wavelengths in his lab.

Unspoken but heavy between them was the question of what *they* were. Liam yearned to belong to Pitr, for Pitr to belong to him. But Pitr still held him at arm's length, a secret for the library's darkened corners. He understood why. He just wished Pitr wanted more, too.

Liam's third year at Princeton was going to be the hardest yet. He was on track to finish his bachelor's degree by the next spring, just short of his eighteenth birthday, but among his studies, his mother, his many jobs, and his new project with Pitr (and Pitr himself), he barely had a moment to breathe. He brought dinner home for his mother and kept their room tidy so the landlady wouldn't complain, but it was too much penance for his lapsed Catholic sensibilities to bear. His mother would stare at him from her good eye, her face, her silence, her everything a screaming indictment of his failure. He hadn't been able to stop his father. He hadn't been able to protect her. As far as Liam was concerned, he might as well have wielded the tire iron itself.

There had to be a way to keep it from ever happening again.

But the summer semester drew to a close with no significant breakthrough, no answers, no nothing—and he could no longer ignore the world on fire around him. America was not yet in the war, but they'd heard the sirens blaring. They'd seen the ships of refugees hovering at their shore, only to be turned away—*America is full*, New York's English and Irish and Dutch families claimed.

It was all so useless, and there was nothing Liam could do to change it. Men like his father, with their red armbands and translated copies of *Mein Kampf*, were everywhere, angrier than ever about immigrants, Communists, heathens. Liam joined a student protest when Lindbergh and his America First goons came to campus, and shouted against the xenophobic monsters until his voice burned out, but it was as useless as sending a signal from inside a Faraday cage. No one cared. Nothing would change.

There had to be a way.

Liam tried to temper his excitement over his and Pitr's research, eager to have something to show when Pitr returned, but all through his summer classes, he found himself shoving formulas around like building blocks in want of a cornerstone. What was the key to opening up those neighboring realms? Based on energy observations, he was sure frequencies were involved—he needed to find the right vibration, the gap in waves. Professor Einstein spoke of bending space to cross distances and time, but that said nothing about worlds that existed parallel to their own. If they were two pages of a book pressed together, then there had to be some seam, some sentence that ran across them both.

Then fall came, and when the term started up again, Liam spied Pitr across campus a few times, but always with his friends, his sharp gaze scraping over Liam like he wasn't there—except for that once, that tantalizing day, when it was apologetic, hungry, wistful. That one time was enough to keep Liam's hope alive, a flickering ember hidden away.

He kept working nights at the library through the fall. Afternoons. Early mornings, too. He knew where Pitr lived, but if he showed up uninvited, he would never be forgiven. He knew too well the sting of Pitr's disapproval, a deliberate absence that pierced him through.

Finally, a shadow fell across the circulation desk, and Liam looked up from his lab notes to find Pitr watching him with a curiosity, a sorrow, that lodged Liam's heart high in his throat.

"We're having a small gathering tonight." Pitr gave him a scrap of paper with the address for the house he rented with two other history students. "You should come by."

"I—I'm working tonight," Liam stammered, but Pitr was already gone.

Bitter November wind rushed down the street as Liam made his way there straight from his late shift, the sounds of other campus parties fading into the distance. The porch light was out; the curtains pulled shut. Liam knocked, and the door eased open onto a poorly lit foyer. As he stepped inside, sounds wafted over him; somewhere, a radio played *The Adventures of the Thin Man*, complete with dire organ chords.

Pitr shuffled out into the corridor clutching a mostly empty bottle of potato vodka. "There you are." He was backlit, his features ghoulish, but they softened as he reached out and trailed his fingers against Liam's cheek. "Most people have already gone home."

His accent had gotten thicker during his time back in Europe. Liam wondered what it had been like there, if the specter of war hovered over everything, or if like everything else in Pitr's life, it was easily brushed aside and ignored.

"Sorry," Liam murmured, leaning into Pitr's touch. This was what he'd craved all along—this closeness between them, unafraid and full and bright. "I had to work—"

"Come."

It was an order, not a request. Liam's heart flipped over, and he took Pitr's hand. He'd follow Pitr anywhere.

They passed the living room, where a bow-tied boy snored on the couch, drink in hand. The upstairs was completely dark, but Pitr knew his way around, steering Liam into his bedroom. Heavy shadows loomed around them: a dresser, a bookcase, a four-poster bed that crowded out everything else. Only a distant streetlight offered any hint of the shapes around them.

"I—I think I found something," Liam started, oddly nervous. He had to say something powerful, something that would hold Pitr's exacting attention. "A frequency that might relate to the other world." He was elated to be back in Pitr's presence, brought to his home, no less. But as Pitr latched the door shut behind them, panic clawed at Liam—what if he was no longer enough?

"Shh." Pitr set the bottle down on his dresser and brought his massive paws to the buttons at Liam's collar. "Not now."

"But I thought you—"

Pitr quieted him with a kiss, stringent with alcohol and weighing heavy against Liam's mouth. Liam froze for a moment. He shouldn't give in to him, not yet. Not after the months that had passed with no word from him, not so much as a hint that Pitr remembered he existed. But he didn't last long. Pitr was here, Pitr wanted him still, had missed him, even, in his own way. It felt so good, so soothing to be wanted that Liam no longer cared that he was a secret to be hidden away.

But there was something new, mechanical in Pitr's movements, the reflexive way he kissed Liam, the possessive way he pulled him into bed. It was like a thin sheet of ice lay between them that Liam was desperately trying to break through, while Pitr sat impassive on the other side. Maybe it had always been this way, and Liam had just forgotten. Maybe he'd never been anything more to Pitr than he was right now: lean, tormented, precocious, and completely out of his depth.

It was worth it. Liam melted for him all over again, and the world beyond the cramped room crumbled into dust.

Afterward, Liam tried curling around him, kissing his shoulder and the thick cords of his neck, but Pitr didn't respond. Liam opened his mouth, breath hitching. What could he say? What would keep Pitr here with him, make him want the same something more that Liam craved? All he could think to blurt out were confessions of love, but he feared that would only drive Pitr further away.

When he looked again, Pitr was asleep.

Liam slipped out of bed, heart pounding. His eyes had adjusted to the darkness, and little details of the cramped room jumped out at him as he fumbled for his clothes. A box of Slovakian candy, empty wrappers piled beside it. Books on medieval hygiene and illuminated manuscripts. A stack of moth-eaten sweaters that stank of must from months in storage. A leather notebook jammed with loose scraps of paper, its cover bent and cracked in half, underneath a jar of pomade.

Liam glanced back to make sure Pitr was still asleep, then he eased the notebook free.

The first page looked like a bibliography scrawled in shorthand. Lots of words Liam didn't recognize, cloaked in the háčeks and čárkas of Hungarian, Polish, Czech. A few Latin words slipped out, though, amidst those sharp knives: just enough for Liam to follow.

Then came the sketches. Stone monoliths and buildings that matched no style Liam had ever seen before. A poorly drawn figure: Was it supposed to be a man? Its face was too long, its eyes lost inside deep vertical folds of skin. Liam's fingers skidded over the sharp pen marks that had rendered it, and an uneasy shudder rippled through him.

A folded note was wedged into the next page, warped from moisture and heavy use. Liam unfolded it to find it written in German. The letterhead was for a Dr. Jozef Kreutzer. Liam's frown deepened: the return address was a military posting in Łódź, inside occupied Poland.

At the time, Liam's German was perfunctory at best, so he could only skim the surface. Something about a book, *Porta ad Tenebras*, that had been confiscated by the German army but that Kreutzer was trying to track down. The key to wrenching open the gates. *It details Sicarelli's meeting with the beings on the other side, my research tells me. How he built the first bridge.* It might prove valuable later, Kreutzer said—but first their basic theories had to be confirmed. *My experiments continue apace, but we need more. Has your colleague found the frequency yet?*

Liam kept leafing through the notebook, a new urgency thrumming in his veins. The pages were wrinkled from being gripped with sweaty hands; Pitr's cursive was nearly indecipherable. Even the few passages in English were a challenge, and the deeper he went, the more the writing unraveled, panicked and swift. Strange creatures appeared in the margins, skeletal dogs with too many joints in their limbs and people with seams in their skin.

But then one page, the last, carried a single equation in English, splotched with ink and heavily underlined:

Two requirements for opening:

RESONANCE

BLOOD

Liam looked up, an unnamed fear gripping him. Just what had Pitr done?

And then he froze: There was a dark figure behind him in the mirror. Standing. Looming. Heavy bruises of exhaustion beneath his eyes. In the mirror, their gazes locked.

"Come back to bed," Pitr said. His voice was so low Liam felt it more than heard it; it traced a finger down his arm and held his heart in its grasp. Liam sensed something feral and unrestrained beneath the tone.

Resonance. Blood. The resonance part, Liam understood—it fit his own theories neatly enough. The right wavelength could create a gap in space itself, teasing open their universe like dough stretching until it tore in the middle. But blood—

Pitr reached for Liam's wrist. "Now."

Liam's foolish, petulant heart, the one that drove him to fight back against grade school bullies, that urged him to throw himself between his parents when his father was on a rampage—his foolish heart wanted to protest. He'd do anything to prove to Pitr he was old enough, clever enough, brave enough. That he was deserving. That he was worthy—of Pitr and whatever Pitr sought.

But the Liam who'd watched his father win anyway, who'd glimpsed the suffering men like him wrought, who had to handle the aftermath of a world he couldn't control and a heart he couldn't keep from breaking—that Liam deserved more.

"Don't be reckless," Liam said. "We don't know what we're dealing with. I can't lose you—"

Pitr curled his fingers around Liam's shoulder, digging in, sending a thrill down Liam's spine he both hated and loved. If he could see this through with Pitr—if he could keep from losing him—then someday, he could have what he deserved.

"You won't lose me," Pitr murmured. He turned Liam to face him, tightened fingers in Liam's hair. His kiss was metallic. Salty, like an oath sealed in blood. Liam felt something inside him shatter, but he didn't dare examine it. He wanted, too much, to believe.

Liam slipped from sleep and memory into darkness, a cold alkaline scent thick in his nostrils. He tried to reach out with his right hand for the glass of water he kept on the nightstand in his rented room. But this wasn't Princeton, and his right arm refused to obey. Pain spiraled out of his shoulder to remind him of everything that had happened yesterday, and Princeton felt further away than ever.

He did a little mental math. He'd had to sell his ma's golden medallion of Saint Patrick to afford airline tickets, but he'd been able to leave the home nurse with more than enough funds to last three months. Class would have been in session for two weeks now; they'd surely noticed he was missing, but his graduate advisor was probably too swamped to worry about him just yet. Still, this was taking far longer than he'd planned. And now the book had been moved to Wewelsburg—

Footsteps weighed on the stairs outside the projection loft. Liam wrestled himself into a seated position, propping up against a rough stone wall. There were no windows in here, but he felt well rested enough. It had to be midmorning at least. They hadn't kicked him out just yet.

The door opened, and Daniel turned on the lights. He carried a mug that smelled of weak coffee and a buttered pumpernickel roll. Liam's stomach growled as Daniel crouched down, and pink brushed over Daniel's cheeks. Almost a smile. Liam relaxed at that.

"You're looking better," Daniel said, offering him the plate and mug. His eyes were brighter today, but stormy as ever. He smelled wonderful—warm and damp, freshly soaped. Liam felt embarrassed by his sweaty state.

Liam took a long swallow of coffee, not caring that it was weak. "This helps. Thanks."

Daniel's gaze roved over him, taking him in. Immediately Liam had a flash of memory—something he might have babbled in the throes of pain—and it was his turn to blush.

"Listen . . ." Liam bit his lower lip as he fished around for the right words. "If I, uh—if I said anything that, that—embarrassed you, or—"

"You didn't. Embarrass me, I mean." Daniel's throat bobbed. "You did say a lot of things. Most of them unrepeatable."

"Oh, well. That'll happen when you get shot." *Don't leave us,* he seemed to recall telling Daniel, panic clawing at his throat at the thought of him throwing himself into a fight he couldn't possibly win. He took another gulp, then tipped his head back against the stone, looking at Daniel askance. "I meant them, though."

Daniel was still crouched before him, empty hands folded between his knees. He lifted one now, slowly, reaching toward Liam's face. Liam sucked in his breath, too afraid to move, not wanting to break whatever spell was between them. A quick flick of Daniel's long fingers, and he brushed a sheaf of Liam's hair to one side.

"That's good to know."

Liam wondered what Daniel would do if he reached up and took his hand, laced his fingers through his own. He didn't want to startle him away, this wolf in the forest who'd sized him up and crept closer, wanting, maybe, to be tamed. But maybe Liam was the one who should be scared. Daniel's intensity was molten, searing. Liam didn't fear it, precisely, but he knew it enough to grant it a healthy distance.

He kept his good hand wrapped tightly around the coffee mug.

"Do you think you'll be well enough to leave for Wewelsburg tonight?" Daniel asked.

Liam let out his breath. "That's the idea. We'll need a way in, though. And if—"

He stopped himself short. He wasn't yet ready to confess what he feared finding there. Not even to Daniel. It was his mess to clean up.

Daniel cocked his head, waiting for him to continue.

Liam swallowed the last of the coffee. Daniel deserved to know at least some of it. "I'm worried about Kreutzer. He knows about the book and the shadow world's powers, and he's got my older research. But I don't know how much else he's figured out."

"Ah." Daniel sat before him, close enough Liam could smell the coffee on his breath. "You think he may be able to use the book before we do."

Liam leaned forward. He was feeling more like himself now—the hunt, the promise of control a signal fire on the horizon. A chance to take all the badness he'd unleashed and use it for good. "There's still time. If we can get the book before Kreutzer makes sense of it, we'll be unstoppable. The entire Third Reich—demolished."

"I'm ready," Daniel said.

Liam set down the coffee mug and rested his hand on his knee, fingertips trailing onto Daniel's as well. "Whatever you thought Siegen was gonna be like, Wewelsburg Castle will be much worse."

"I know."

"It's Schutzstaffel HQ now. Heinrich Himmler himself holds court there—with all the other SS chiefs."

Daniel's knee twitched beneath Liam's fingertips. "That's why we're going, isn't it?"

Liam wanted—desperately—not to do this alone. And he wanted more time with Daniel than the past few days had offered, this tempestuous boy who always seemed to be at war with the music in his heart. But this was no picnic in the woods. And he knew Daniel's brand of chaos—the kind with no regard for his own life.

"Tonight begins the day of atonement. Erev Yom Kippur," Daniel said. "I promised Rebeka we'd eat together beforehand. We'll be ready to leave after that."

"Sundown, then." Liam nodded.

"What was your life like before?" Daniel asked suddenly. "What was it like back home for you? Was it really so bad that coming here seemed a better choice?"

Liam slumped backward with a tired smile. "Before? I pretty much lived at Princeton. The library and the physics lab. Always working."

Daniel arched an eyebrow at him. "You don't say."

"I, uh . . . I have a hard time letting go of things. I get something in my head, and I have to burn it out of me. I'm either all fire or cold ash—don't know how to be any other way."

"Yes, I can see that." Daniel smiled, hiding it behind his knee.

Another smile earned. Liam wanted to store them all up, wrap them carefully and tuck them somewhere safe. He wondered what Daniel might be like in a world where he could smile all the time, where he could walk down Fifth Avenue in clean clothes and laugh at something stupid Liam had said, smile because they'd stopped to pet a dog, frown over nothing worse than missing the IRT train headed downtown and so they had to linger on the station platform, nudging each other and sharing secret grins. He wanted Daniel's mouth to hurt from smiling and his sides to ache from laughter. He wanted his heart so full he had nowhere else to put it all except to funnel it through his viola's strings.

But it was no use imagining Daniel in New York with him, when Daniel couldn't see past the tip of his own knife.

"I wish I weren't this way," Liam confessed. "But I get these ideas in my head, and I want them so badly. I—I don't know how to *want* things less."

"But if you weren't so determined, then you wouldn't be here."

They held each other's gaze for a minute. Liam's mouth was too dry, too unwilling to cooperate; he drank the rest of his coffee to cover it up.

"You'd—you'd love New York," he finally managed, the words

tripping over themselves with sudden urgency. "It's like its own symphony. There's always a new melody to pick out."

Daniel's smile fell. "Berlin used to feel that way, too."

Liam allowed himself to imagine a world where he could be powerful enough to save this boy. Tear apart the Third Reich—not just because he had to, but because it was what Daniel, his family, deserved. He could almost believe it—that he could claim the book and the power he'd sought for so long.

He could taste it, the juicy steak after months of broth. The smile he thought would never cross his mother's face again. The power of two worlds in his veins, thumping, burning, searing—not Kreutzer's, not the Nazis', but his alone. He had uncovered this. He had tamed this. And he'd control how it could be used—not by Nazis, but by those who'd fight them off.

Liam regarded Daniel's face, this fighter's face, this boy who survived against the odds. They both deserved this.

"Well. We do this right, maybe we can find a way home."

"Maybe," Daniel said, but neither of them believed he meant it.

The shower was downright sinful, stripping off the top layer of Liam's skin, all of the grime and anger and failure that coated him like a film. Phillip and Simone had slunk off on their hush-hush mission elsewhere in town, while Daniel and Rebeka broke bread in the bell tower above and Helene went about her daily chores. Liam had offered to help her, but after a short quiz in German, she deemed him too much of a risk in case her customers got nosy.

So Liam helped himself to the selection in the film vault as he waited for nightfall to head out once more.

He tried *The Great Love* Helene had mentioned the night before, but his stomach was churning after only a few minutes in. A Nazi officer wooing a cabaret singer, and yet somehow it wasn't a horror show. He spooled the film back up and tossed it back in the heap.

Next up he found a stack of tins for an old silent film, *The Cabinet of Dr. Caligari*—two different editions, oddly, the older-looking one buried at the bottom of the stack. Both told the story of a world gone increasingly mad. A man was investigating the murderer Caligari and his sleepwalking, unwitting accomplice, only to find that Caligari is the director of an insane asylum and not one of its residents, like he should've been. A perfect parable for their time, Liam thought bitterly; that power was not to be trusted, not to be taken as an absolute.

Yet the newer edition nestled that story inside two bookended scenes. This version, unsurprisingly, bore the approval stamp of Goebbels's propaganda wing. The two framing scenes were brief, but revealed that in truth, the man investigating the murders was the madman, and Caligari the harmless asylum director trying to cure him of his delusions. Trust in the system. Any evidence the system is broken is only your own mind deceiving you.

Liam barely resisted the urge to rip the film right off its reel.

Wood planks groaned above and around him as people moved along the bell tower stairs. Instinctively, his hand moved toward the false panel where he'd hidden his satchel and P38, but he thought better of it. It was Daniel and Rebeka finishing their meal. He'd get confirmation first that the coast was clear. Then they could be on their way.

No sooner had he taken his hand away from the panel than the door to the projection room swung open. A yelp lodged in Liam's throat, bitten back just in time. In the doorway stood an SS officer, his cheekbones sharp, his cheeks hollowed out like shallow graves. A sour expression pinched his lips that could equally have been a sneer or a smirk. He nearly had to duck to step inside the projection room.

"Pardon the intrusion, good sir," he said in silky-smooth German. "We heard a vicious rumor some villagers were harboring unpatriotic fugitives. I'm sure you won't mind if we have a look around."

CHAPTER TWELVE

SIMONE

That morning, Simone woke in the church's sanctuary to their hostess, Helene, towering over her with her one hand propped on a generous hip. "Unless you want to watch *Die Große Liebe* with a few dozen SS officers at the matinee," Helene said, "I suggest you make yourself scarce."

Simone pushed off of the velvet-cushioned pew. Her pocketknife and a hunk of spare wood lay further down the bench, where she'd been whittling a bird figurine the previous night to lull herself into restless sleep. She worked her feet back into her boots. "Depends. What's it about?"

"The importance of waging war and marrying good Aryan girls. I assume. I try not to listen too closely." Helene stepped back to let her out of the pew. "There's pumpernickel and ham in the kitchens. Plumbing seems to be working for now if you'd like a shower. You should visit Karl and Guillerme soon to help them with your business—I'll show you the safe way there."

Simone moved past her, in the direction of the kitchens. "Thank you." She would never understand Europeans and their obsession with pork. "Have there been any updates out of Siegen?"

"Nothing yet." Helene planted herself beside the kitchen counter. She looked sturdy and unbreakable; Simone was glad to have someone like her on their side. "The only forces we get beyond our local Gestapo are those passing through on their way to Siegen, or the Occupied Zone. If it was as bad as you say, though . . ."

Simone winced as she tore off a chunk of dark bread. "We'll try to be gone quickly."

Helene made a huffing sound. "You are French?"

Simone swallowed the stale bread she'd been chewing. "Algerian. Though my brother and I have been in France for longer than we were in Algiers." She shrugged. "It doesn't feel like home, but then, maybe neither would Algiers." She thought, with a curious nostalgic itch, of the way their family, their faith had felt like a metronome keeping the tempo of their lives. As it fell away, as the invaders swarmed in, time itself seemed to have fallen apart.

"My parents were Belgian, but I grew up here," Helene said. "Married a German boy."

Simone tried to arrange her face into something like sympathy. "Did he . . ."

"Die? No. That would be too good for him." Helene spat into the sink. "He drives a tank for the Wehrmacht. Poland or somewhere. I get special benefits as a soldier's wife—*Kinder, Küche, Kirche*, children, hearth, church, all that rot. That's how I'm able to do all this."

"But why do you do it?" Simone asked.

Helene wrenched up the shoulder of her handless arm to rub her nose. "I voted against the Nazi party. Screamed and yelled and fought and marched against every law they passed. Until it became illegal to fight back. And legal to do all the horrible things they've done." She let out a shaky breath. "So I decided that if whatever I did was illegal anyway, then I might as well do it in the biggest, most illegal way I could."

Simone couldn't help but smile at that. "France and Belgium thank you."

"And you?" Helene asked, eyeing her. Simone didn't miss the way her gaze sliced her open.

Simone swallowed the last bite of pumpernickel. "I show my thanks in other ways."

After a long shower and a short stint checking the converted church's tower for vantage points, Simone went to fetch Phillip, who was watching while Liam poked around the film vaults.

"Well?" Liam asked. "Will you go with us to Wewelsburg?"

Simone glanced at Phillip, who was giving her a dubious look. "We can contact the Resistance cell there, and I'm not opposed to doing anything that sabotages the Third Reich." She narrowed her eyes. "But after that, we part ways."

"After that, we won't need to."

Simone didn't trust him as far as she could spit, never mind with a solid oak door and a whirring projector between them. But the sooner they dragged him off to Wewelsburg for his stupid manuscript, the sooner she could be rid of him.

Running, always running, Evangeline's voice teased inside her head. *Always from and never toward.*

As if Evangeline was one to talk. At least Simone had the courage, the stubbornness to do anything at all.

Helene showed them to the catacomb tunnels that stretched beneath the village's square, a forgotten relic of an era before radiator heat and snowplows. They thanked her for her help, and she grunted, nodded a curt farewell.

"And you're sure they have everything we'll need?" Phillip asked Simone for the hundredth time as they followed the tunnel that linked to the furniture maker's atelier.

"Everything your friends dropped for them last month," Simone replied. "But the rest is up to you."

They rapped on the trapdoor overhead, and an old man appeared behind it, staring down at them with bushy brows drawn. He helped Phillip first, then Simone, climb up into the hidden room.

"Nice design," Phillip said in English, surveying their radio setup. "Did you build this yourself?"

"Some time ago. Thought it might be useful." The man limped toward the cabinetry that housed a wide array of radio equipment. At one end, a man who looked like a younger copy of him was intently transcribing a Morse code message. "Turns out I was right."

"Only receiving messages so far, right?" Phillip asked, and the man nodded. "We'll get you set up here in no time."

"I'm Karl," the older man offered. "My son, Guillerme, he's the operator."

Guillerme finished notating his transcription and pulled off his headset to greet them properly. He gazed up at Simone with wary, shell-shocked eyes. Her gut twisted at that look. She was always feeling sorry for herself for what she'd been through; sometimes it was easy to forget how many others were relying on her.

"You're sure it'll be safe?" Guillerme asked. "I understand they have high-frequency direction finders. The trucks go through our village sometimes, looking for anyone who might be broadcasting."

Phillip fiddled with the latch on his tool kit. "Once I get these scramblers configured, the broadcast signal will look like it's just passing through from somewhere further down the line. Their huff-duffs won't be able to tell you're the source. And we'll bounce some extra noise off the ionosphere to keep 'em busy."

Guillerme eased, offering a tentative smile. "It would be a godsend. The information we're collecting . . . It's useful, but by the time we're able to pass it to agents, get it across the channel or into the Free Zone, it's too outdated. We want to be able to answer the Magpie's inquiries as soon as we can. He seems to get better results now that he's in our network."

"Who is this Magpie?" Simone asked. "Georges-Yves mentioned him as well. Said he's putting out a lot of radio traffic, leaking troop movements and so on."

He shrugged. "Someone in the Occupied Zone, I can only assume. But it's safer not to know." Guillerme lowered his gaze. "I've been able to defer service thus far, but if I'm ever dragged to war . . . I don't want to know all our secrets."

Simone flinched. He and Karl and Helene—they were Germans, banding together to do the best they could, given the circumstances.

But was it enough for them to fight back this way? What would they do when the Wehrmacht came and forced them to fight? At least they had each other, she supposed. Simone glanced at Phillip, and finally admitted to herself she was glad not to be here alone.

Phillip pulled a small electronic box out of his case and started teasing the braids of wiring from its slots. "This'll handle encryption for you. It's coded to roll over to a new scheme every few days, matching the schedule for our operators in Dover. Designed it myself with a few tweaks," he added, lips tugging toward a smile. Simone cocked her head to one side, watching him. "And then this—you can input your message, then it'll store the contents and parse them out over a longer period of time. Up to a day, if you need. As long as there's no interference on the line, we'll have no trouble picking it up. That way the goon squad can see your shining, happy face going about your business in town at the same time the broadcast is transmitting."

"That's amazing," Guillerme said. "They're starting to keep track of our comings and goings, you know."

As Phillip set up the equipment, Simone's gaze wandered toward a stack of books on the back table, spines cracked open, the exposed pages heavily marked in pencil. One in particular caught her eye— Rilke's only novel, written while he was in Paris.

The copy was in German, but Simone could practically conjure up the French translation out of nothingness, the words like a stylish perfume. Silk sheets, spring breeze teasing at soft curtains, Evangeline's lips moving over the haunting phrases like a prayer. *Those are the noises. But here, there's something more terrible: the silence.*

"Why do you have this?" Simone hissed. She'd caught herself

reaching for it, but had drawn back at the last moment, as if it might burn her.

"We use it as a codebook." Guillerme left Phillip to his work and joined her at the side table. His fingers traced a set of underlined words. "Different phrases to decrypt messages in the network. Something the Magpie set up."

Her fingers traced over one of the underlined passages for encoding. *One has to do something about fear once one has it.* Evangeline had hugged the book to her chest after reading that line, and Simone swallowed, recalling how tiny she'd looked—how tiny they'd both felt. They'd been the shape of loneliness and loss, of a simple truth that should have torn them apart so long ago. But Simone had wanted to believe. She wanted to believe they could someday overcome it.

She should have known, like a split in otherwise beautiful wood: no amount of sanding could smooth that fracture away.

"Do you . . ." Her voice came out all dried and cracked. She swallowed and tried again. "Do you have any of the Magpie's messages?"

"I keep his transmissions over here." Guillerme rolled his chair toward a stack of torn-off notebook papers weighted down under a coffee mug. "In case we come across any of the things he's requested."

Simone scanned through the unscrambled notes. Most of it was garbage to her—the message date and time, the sender's identification code, and the numbers signifying the length of the message to follow. Her eyes skidded over these clusters toward the meat of each message.

Request guest list for upcoming Wewelsburg conference 15 09 42.

Request update on munitions distribution to OZ.

Request last known location for Haupsturmführer Kreutzer.

And then, from just that morning: *Request details of Siegen attack.*

"The information he sends out—it has a lot to do with the Vichy government's distribution of munitions, food. I imagine someone in the network is able to use that to steal supplies." Guillerme smiled. "Whoever he is, he's pretty helpful. But it's always the helpful ones who get caught first." His smile faded. "He's only been active for a few months. Let's hope he knows what he's doing."

"The Vichy government?" Simone started, then stopped herself. Evangeline.

Stop imagining things. The Magpie could be anyone. Simone bit down on the inside of her cheek without any Gauloises to huff. "Are you going to answer this request about Siegen?"

"I thought I might, as soon as your friend is finished with his work. Why do you ask?" Guillerme twirled his pencil between his fingers as he said it. Too casually. Simone couldn't blame him for getting suspicious. She was being too naked in her hope. Her absurd, desperate belief that somehow Evangeline was not the callous coward Simone had branded her after all.

She dropped the stack of decoded transmissions and took a step back. "N-never mind. It isn't important." A fist of ice closed around her heart. "Not anymore."

Even if—*if*—somehow Evangeline had seen the truth of what Simone fought for every day. Even if she had devoted herself to fighting her way out of her cage rather than nestling up inside it, so comfortable while the world burned around her. What did it matter if she carried a vial of poison with her to every meal with their occupiers if she never found the courage to use it? What did it change for Simone?

Not a damned thing.

Something passed across Guillerme's face—a wrinkle in his brow, a frown, but gone just as quick. "If there was something you want me to put in the transmission," he started, "I'd be happy to—"

An electric buzz interrupted him. Karl, his father, bounded to his feet as he and Guillerme looked hard at one another. "Excuse me," Karl said in English, his face suddenly slack and pale. "I—I think I have a customer in the store."

Karl limped toward the far end of the room and shoved aside a panel that let out into what looked like a furniture studio. A tiny pang beneath Simone's ribs reminded her how much she missed her own work. Her fingers itched to reach out and grab a lathe, a sander. But curiosity and fear won out. As he fitted the panel back into place from the other side, she and Guillerme both crept closer to listen in.

"Keep working," Guillerme told Phillip in English, smile stretched taut across his face. "No need to worry." But the look he shot Simone was pure panic. Her heart squeezed. She wondered if he was aiding them for similar reasons to Helene's. A blessing that so many people were willing to risk everything to do what was right, she thought—and a curse that it was still nowhere near enough.

"I'm almost done." Phillip bound two wires together, then started packing bundles of cords back into place inside the machine. "Do we need to—"

Simone held up one finger as she tried to catch the tail end of Karl's conversation, but they were too far away. It was safer for her not to hear, but she needed some way to unfurl the tension so tight in her gut. She needed a cigarette. She needed to shoot another Nazi.

At last Karl limped back into the room, face white as paper. "They're looking for the people responsible for what happened at Siegen." He looked from Simone to Phillip. "I think you'd better go."

CHAPTER THIRTEEN

DANIEL

Yom Kippur was meant to be a day of forgiveness and atonement, but Daniel wasn't in a forgiving mood. He and Rebeka scavenged their pre-fasting meal in near silence: a sad bounty of canned broth, stale bread, and pickled vegetables from Helene's root cellar. Even as they shrank from their other traditions under the Gestapo's watchful eye, their Yom Kippur meals back in Berlin had been extravagant, multi-course affairs with egg soufflés and rich, fluffy bread loaves. At their uncle's farm in Luxembourg, they'd spend the day prepping the bread, speaking euphorically of how they would break their fast when Yom Kippur ended.

But even thinking of such a meal right now made his stomach churn. His stomach was shrunken, unsettled ever since their escape from Łódź another lifetime ago. Tonight was just another night with too little food in his belly and too much anger in his blood.

They took their scraps to the bell tower and spread out a pilled woolen blanket that smelled like a stable. He pulled the battered wooden mezuzah from his coat pocket and set it between them: an offering.

"We praise You, Adonai our God, Sovereign of the universe, who brings forth bread from the earth." The words in stilted Hebrew hung awkwardly between them, familiar and yet out of place. Rebeka unwrapped the stale bread slices with trembling hands. Daniel looked at the shafts of milky sunlight sliding between the rafters, the worn stone walls, the painted iron carillon dangling over them: anywhere but at her.

She chewed for a few minutes, then forced herself to swallow and faced him to continue the tradition. "Daniel?" she whispered. "May I ask your forgiveness? For . . . for anything I've done to hurt you this past year."

Daniel managed a dry laugh at that. "I'm not sure you're who needs to be forgiven."

She picked at her nails, breath drawn as if there was something she wanted to say, but no way to say it. Finally, she relaxed and shook her head. "I'm truly sorry I've tried to stand in your way. I know you want . . ."

Rebeka trailed off, and at last he found the strength to look at her. She was only a sliver of the girl she'd once been: no longer the tall, strong young woman he admired, but whittled down and folded up, like perhaps she could fold herself away into nothingness.

"I know you want revenge. And I don't blame you for that. I want it too." Tears rimmed her lower lashes. "But I've lost everyone else. I can't lose you as well."

He laced his hand in her slim fingers. Perhaps she was still that pillar—that rock that refused to be worn down. How much did she endure to stay so strong for him? He'd assumed it was their suffering that had robbed the life from her eyes, but maybe it was the way she always acted as though she had to be strong enough to carry them both.

Well, there was nothing he could do to change it. The only other option—not getting revenge—was no option at all.

"I'm the oldest now. I have to do this." His grip tightened. "For both of us."

"You don't have to give your life because our family lost theirs."

"Yes. I do." Daniel squeezed his eyes shut. Why couldn't she understand? "You don't have to go with me. It's not too late. Maybe the partisan girl and her contacts can get you some false papers, you can take a train west out of Wewelsburg—"

"*Stop trying to make me abandon you.*"

The fierceness in her voice threw him. Tears shook free from her lashes as she stared him down, trembling. His strong, resourceful Rebeka, the one who always had spare winter gloves in her bag when he inevitably forgot his own; the one who had listened to him practice études endlessly, noting just forcefully enough when his rhythm went astray; the one who had stayed up late into the night each month, long after their parents had fallen asleep over their desks, until she could make the shop's numbers balance out.

In that moment, he would have done or said anything to take away her hurt. He'd have lain down his knives and his pistol. He'd have pulled himself apart to keep her warm. She was his sister—she was all he had left. And always she'd been there for him, never questioning, never judging him, forever cheering on whoever he was or chose to be. She let him feel normal, she let him feel real.

But this was the only possible path for him. Why couldn't she love that part of him, too?

"Fine. I forgive you," Daniel said. He was done arguing about this.

She swallowed again and unscrewed the lid on the jar of broth.

His turn to ask forgiveness. Daniel shoved his knees up under his chin and stared at the floor. "Will you forgive me anything I might have said or done this year that hurt you?"

"I forgive you for dragging us across Poland and Germany," she said slowly. "I couldn't have asked for a better companion for it."

He flinched at that. Ari would have been better: Ari, the lion of their family, would have never gotten her into this mess. Their parents would have been better—Mama, who always saw the sunrise through the dead of night, and Papa, who never, ever let any of them want.

"I forgive you for entangling me in your countless schemes, because it felt so good to be doing something with my brother. Remembering how we could be when there weren't guards herding us around, people judging our every move."

Daniel let his shoulders drop.

She managed a soft smile. "And I forgive you for thinking it's perfectly reasonable to summon *demons from another world*. Though we both know it's really because you can't resist Herr Doyle and his damned dimples."

His face burned. "I never said—"

"You didn't have to." Rebeka brushed a hand against his shin. "I know you."

Daniel blushed, thinking of Liam's babbling after the morphine kicked in the night before. Mostly a bunch of astronomical jargon that only Phillip understood; but at one point he'd stopped in the middle of it to stare straight at Daniel. *You have beautiful hands*, Liam told him. *Promise you'll play viola for me someday.*

"You seem to know a lot of things," Daniel muttered.

He hadn't meant it as an accusation, but she reeled back as if she'd been struck.

"Rebeka?" Daniel reached out for her hand. "What is it?"

Sunlight danced across her face, making it look, for the briefest moment, flush and full once more. Then a cloud passed over the sun—she was nothing but shadows and hollow bones again.

"There's—" She caught her breath. "There's one more thing I must ask forgiveness for. A big one. But it's not fair of me to keep it to myself any longer. Not when I could lose you without a moment's notice."

He furrowed his brow. "Of course. Anything."

"No—you don't understand." She bit her lower lip. "I haven't been telling you the whole truth."

Rebeka clasped his hand with both of hers. He felt a sudden, sharp instinct to pull away, though he couldn't say why.

"I . . . I see things, Daniel. Visions, or glimpses of somewhere else, or . . ." She shook her head. "I don't know what to call them. It's like I'm watching other people through a foggy mirror. I learn things I shouldn't."

His brow wrinkled. "What are you talking about?"

"Usually it's—conversations, but sometimes worse." Her voice caught. "I know how mad it sounds. I never told anyone because of how mad it is. You wouldn't have believed me before. But now that we've seen this—this other world, these shadows, maybe it isn't so strange after all." She looked up at him, eyes gleaming. "You believe me, don't you?"

Daniel's hands trembled in hers. "I—I don't know. You're right.

It does sound mad. But I've seen a great many things that don't make sense recently." He tilted his head. "Why are you telling me this?"

"Because . . ." She took a deep breath. "I've seen the terrible things happening at Wewelsburg. You know what kind of man Dr. Kreutzer is. The things I've seen him planning . . . Please, Daniel. You can't go there." Her fingers dug against his. "You can't."

He felt a hot iron spike of anger. "You said you were all right with this. You said it was worth it, to destroy SS officers—"

"Well, I was wrong, all right? Kreutzer is doing terrible things— You can't open that bridge, Daniel—"

"How do you know that what you're seeing is real? Are you sure you aren't just imagining it?"

"I'm sure."

"But how?" he asked. "It doesn't make any sense."

She was silent a moment too long. "Because the visions never been wrong before."

A heavy shadow hung over his shoulder, a truth he didn't want to face. If he turned, if he looked at it, he could never be the same. "Rebeka . . ."

A tear slid down her cheek.

"Ari never sent you a warning, did he?"

The words came from somewhere outside of him, marching toward the answer he already knew. He felt the thick mud of the ghetto streets beneath his feet. He smelled the cramped tenement buildings and heard the hungry cries of other children through cracker-thin walls. He saw Rebeka running for him through the alleys, fist clenched around her book bag, her eyes wide with bottomless fear.

He would have given anything, in that moment, for her not to answer. He wished he didn't have to know. But he did, and it was like stepping onto the train all over again: that certainty, that doom.

Rebeka dropped his hand. "I *saw* them planning it. My vision—it was like I was in the room with them, watching from behind a mirror. Kreutzer and the camp officers, they were discussing how to persuade us all onto the transports, what was waiting for us at Chełmno . . . I panicked. I knew we had to leave right away."

There it was, the poison in his lungs, the cold dirt swallowing him up. She'd lied. She'd lied to him, but far worse—she'd left the rest behind.

Their parents. Ari. All their friends. They could have saved them—their path to escape had been so embarrassingly simple. Rebeka seemed to know just the route to take. The empty guard post, the hole in the fence, the unguarded alley in the judenrein city of Łódź beyond the ghetto fence. But she'd told him—she'd said—

"You were the first person I came across. I could see the empty guard post, but I didn't know how long we'd have that opening—if we'd tried to find them—"

"You killed them." His heart was scrabbling in his ribs like a trapped animal. "You could have saved them, but you left them to die!"

"No." Her tears had clawed angry streaks down her face. "I saved *you*."

What use was he? She could have saved Mama, with her laughter like wind chimes and her quick fingers on the piano and the rare holiday prayers that turned to melodies all on their own. Papa, whose butcher's hands never once turned harsh, never once turned to violence like Daniel's had now done; his eyes so soft and heart so full, he tried to rescue every sad stray animal that came across their path. And Ari— Ari, who was so in love with Tamar Adler on the next block, who talked of weddings and of beautiful little children he'd raise to someday be as strong and brave as his parents were.

She could have saved any of them. But she'd chosen him, with his short temper and brooding music and now his violent appetite—his helpless, flailing rage. She'd chosen the boy who used his hands so cruelly now instead of for the music he once loved.

Absurdly, a laugh bubbled up in his chest. Laughing at himself, his pitiful life, his traitorous sister. And now that he'd started, he couldn't *stop* laughing, at the cruelty of the whole world and all its gifts. She'd rescued him, but couldn't save the rest. So what use was his sister who saw things? Every outcome for them ended in pain.

"Daniel, please—"

He pulled away from her, and all at once, his laughter was gone. "You shouldn't have saved me."

Daniel stood, the world tilting around him. The jar of broth tipped over and spilled across the wood planks. He had to get out of here. Out of this church, this town full of hateful Germans, these woods that had swallowed him up with their shadows and whispers that promised if he could just kill the next Nazi, his debt would be paid. As if there could ever be *enough*. No, he had to get out of here, this life, this too-tight skin he'd been wearing. Rage had eaten up his insides like one of Liam's shadow beasts, and now there was nothing of him left.

He'd promised himself he would die avenging their family. But now—knowing she'd left them to die while he lived—

It changed nothing. Soon enough, he could join them. The sooner, the better.

"Please, Daniel." Rebeka tried to block his path toward the rickety stairwell. "Please, just listen to me—"

He ducked under her arm and continued down the stairs. "You're free now." Froth built up inside him, but he couldn't direct his rage at her. No, he had to conserve it. "Go live the life you deserve."

"Daniel, wait—"

The sound of several car engines below them drowned her out. They both froze, listening as the vehicles stopped at the front of the Kino. Car doors slammed. Boots ground against stone.

"You have to go," Daniel said.

She shook her head, tears still spilling, darkening the blouse of the too-large dress Helene had given her.

"Find Simone and Phillip. Stay with them. They'll keep you safe," he said.

"I'm not leaving without you."

"Yes. You are."

Then he bolted down the stairs two at a time.

CHAPTER FOURTEEN

REBEKA

The Nazis were crawling all over the Kino like roaches. Rebeka had scrambled up into the rafters with the carillon bells after Daniel stormed off, watching through the slatted tower windows, praying the soldiers weren't headed into the theater below.

They were.

Vainly, she tried to remember how long it had taken to climb up and down the tower's steps, how hidden the stairwell was from the main sanctuary, how quickly Daniel might have escaped, and where he could have gone.

Tunnels. Phillip had said something about tunnels underneath the town square. She touched a hand to her cheek, to the faint warmth that spread there as she remembered their conversation earlier that morning while everyone slept. She'd found him in the side chapel, hands folded before him like he might have been in prayer, but his gaze listless, wandering. With a nod from him, she sat down, and they were both too weary to let nervousness keep them from talking. A relief. Rebeka's mouth never seemed able to convey the too-big feelings in her heart and too-big thoughts in her brain, and Phillip, it seemed, was the same way.

Like her, he wanted to find the dawn in this endless night. He wanted to be a force for good. It was easy to believe in the dawn when they were surrounded by bright glass, unburnt candles, when their warm hands were so close. But it wouldn't help her now, not when the cruel darkness lurked just under her dangling feet. Not when she had no idea where Daniel had gone, if he was safe, if he was plotting, even now, to do something monumentally stupid and careless—

Footsteps thudded closer and closer as someone climbed the tower stairs. Rebeka pulled her legs up onto the rafter. She should be completely concealed from below. If the skirt of her dress would stay tucked under her thighs, the pockets flush against her torso—

The door flung open. Maybe two or three men, from the sound of it. Her heart pounded heavy as the bell's iron clapper; she was amazed they couldn't hear it ringing out halfway across the village. This wasn't like all the times she'd lain in wait while Daniel was off on one of his stupid missions, leaving her to wring her hands and sweat, or at worst, leaving her with a gun and ample warning time. All she had were the crumbs she'd scraped together for the meal and the old horse blanket they'd eaten on, which she'd stashed away in the tower cupboard before scrambling up here. And their family mezuzah in her pocket, a prayer tucked inside. It dug into her hipbone, bony where it had once been soft.

The men beneath her circled around the bell, but were oddly silent. It wasn't comforting. It figured that now, when she could use the visions most, none came. No, her curse was only good for ruining things. Like the fleeting, quivering chance she'd had to pull Daniel back from the brink.

Rebeka bit the inside of her cheek to stop the rush of tears. There was no going back. She'd made her choice—it hadn't even been a choice, just a matter of happenstance that Daniel had been the one she found just after the vision struck. Maybe if she'd saved Ari, they'd be at a café in London now, preparing for their Yom Kippur fast under the last of a summer sun, the Royal Air Force buzzing overhead on its way south. Maybe if she'd saved Papa, they could have lived off the land until the war ended one way or another. If she'd saved Mama, they could have melted into the anonymous cities of southern Europe, donned new lives, worn new faces.

Or they all could have died. And she'd have saved no one at all.

There was no changing it. There was no forgiveness. No atonement. Only this moment, right here, the rotted rafter pressing into her gut. Her breath a flood she was trying desperately to hold back. The wooden box in her pocket hot as an ember with everything she'd done, all the mistakes she could never correct.

Pain lanced through her head, between her eyes. She stopped just short of sucking in her breath, shocked at the suddenness of an impending vision. Her heartbeat nailed her in place while, below her, the soldiers shuffled around, poking into the various corners of the tower.

The soldiers—

Rebeka's vision warped and took flight, startled like a moth shaken from a curtain. She saw the bell tower from beneath her—looked up toward the rafter where she hid—

Both the soldiers looked up. And then she *was* the soldiers, seeing through their eyes. Hearing the dull drone of insect wings beating, thousands and thousands of them, as they caught sight of her body spread across the rafter, the skirts of her dress dangling down.

She slammed back into herself, with a suddenness that nearly knocked her over, and she jolted forward, gasping for air. It had been so much more intense than her previous visions—as though she weren't merely watching, but actually *there*, occupying that new space outside her own body. She twisted to the side. Had the soldiers really spotted her? If she needed to run, if she was caught—

Both soldiers stared right at her. But they weren't soldiers, not really. They were emptiness and shadow, their eyes and mouths hollow. Dark smoke wafted around them, seeping from their flesh.

Bile rose in her throat. They looked similar to the soldiers in Siegen who'd been consumed by shadow. But no, these men were in between that and normal men. Like the shadow had gotten its talons hooked in them, but they weren't fully gone yet. Like their transformation had just begun.

And they were looking at her. Motionless.

Expectant.

Her tongue was woolly and thick. With a flicker of vision, she saw: from the soldiers' eyes. From her own. From that dark and frightful place, far away, where all her visions led—the place of ink and shadows. When she experienced her visions, she'd always watched them as if from the other side of a dark mirror. A shadow world all her own.

Perhaps like Liam, she was bound to it, too; but unlike him, she'd never had a choice.

Rebeka stretched her fingers, cramped from her death grip on the wood beam. In her mind, she extended the soldiers' fingers. And below her, they eased their grip on their rifle butts.

Her heart leapt in her throat. Controlling the shadow and its movements—this, too, was new.

They stared at her, and she stared back. Pulse hastening, she imagined them pulling the rifle straps up and over their heads, then setting them down on the wooden tower floor. They did so, no resistance, no complaints, no urgency—just a straightforward, careful execution of her command. Glittering onyx eyes looked back up at her. Still waiting.

Still under her command.

With trembling arms, she pulled herself upright on the rafter. Her body felt miles and miles away from here, as if it belonged to someone else entirely. She felt the possibilities now, the boundless potential like a simmering river, its current just waiting to be directed.

Was this what Liam felt? Was this the energy he tugged at and knitted into his own? She didn't feel like an outsider twisting it around, subject to its corruption and hate. She *was* the current. She was that energy—

And in the distance, the current rippled. An undertow, pulling her another way. And just as quickly, the spell broke, as if the connection between Rebeka and the creatures had been snipped to a thread, only a single fiber still remaining. The calmness Rebeka felt receded, and in its place surged fear.

Rebeka tried to steady herself.

"Go." She waved her hands at the soldiers, scrabbling to recover that calmness, that *one*ness she'd felt moments before. "You never saw me. Get out—"

The undertow pulled harder now. Angry, churning. Someone else was trying to wrest control from her.

The soldiers' expressions changed. They narrowed their eyes—started reaching for the rafter. She couldn't sense one of them at all now, and her hold on the other was slipping, fraying, about to break.

No, she screamed, silent, and dove back into the darkness, like falling backward into deep waters.

The second soldier's vision snapped into hers. With monstrous arms, she made him snatch his rifle back up from where he'd dropped it. Aimed it at his companion, just as a hand wrapped around her ankle. Tugged at her.

Br–r–rap.

The bullets struck the first soldier in the back, and he dropped immediately to the tower floor. There was a rush of shadow, buzzing and roaring like a gale, then nothing but blood spreading across the planks.

Rebeka was shaking all over now. But she forced herself to look at the remaining soldier, the one holding the smoking gun.

Seeing through his eyes, she brought the gun's barrel under his chin.

She was ready for it, but still yelped as the bullet spray wrenched away his jaw, his brain, his hair, smearing it across the tower walls. She *felt* it, a dull pain, but there nonetheless.

Rebeka gritted her teeth. She would not empathize with these Nazi monsters. Whether they were under the influence of the dark energy or not, they deserved all of their pain and more. She only wished . . .

The corners of her eyes burned. She only wished she'd understood how to control them sooner. Whatever—however—*this* was.

She eased down from the rafter and stepped over the first soldier's body. She had to find Daniel, before the other soldiers—and there were surely others—found him first. And Phillip and Simone—even Liam, the only person who might have the slightest clue how this all worked. And if the Nazis were here, then Helene was in danger, too. All of her Resistance contacts.

Oh, God. Rebeka sank against the stone wall, throwing a hand out to catch herself just in time. What had they done? How many more innocents were going to die because they'd killed a few monsters in Siegen?

Rebeka's head was buzzing so hard she barely felt the tidal wave until it was all around her, black vines choking her, tangling around her limbs. A wall of hatred and fury, crushing her under its weight.

She fell forward, and fell, and fell. She crashed into what felt like mud, thick and slurping as she tried to scramble to her feet. The bell tower had disintegrated around her. Nothing surrounded her but black trees against a rusty night sky.

This is not yours.

A figure stepped out of the trees before her, darkness pouring off of him like sheets of rain. If he'd been human, it had been some time ago; his skin was marbled, veined with black. Rebeka stared up at him, hands fisting in the glop beneath her. When she reached out for the currents of energy, they quivered, caught between her and the figure.

You don't belong here. The figure stepped closer. Rebeka rocked back, mud thickening around her. His words swelled all around her like blood vessels ready to burst. *THIS IS NOT YOURS.*

Rebeka closed her eyes. She'd been here before: the dark woods that smelled of smoke and blood. It hadn't made sense then, how much it felt like home. It still didn't now. But now she also felt—what? An opening? An escape?

No. She felt at peace.

The shadows swirled around her, slicing through the air, and the figure staggered back, throwing a hand over his head. *Intruder,* the whispers chattered. *Intruder.* Yet she felt certain that only one of them didn't belong here. And it wasn't her.

WHO ARE YOU? the man howled. *HOW CAN YOU CONTROL THEM?* He was pushing back against her attack, but there was something ragged in his words, something that spiked into her veins.

No one. She was no one at all.

The shadows snapped into her then with that same sense of oneness she'd felt in the bell tower. She pulled out of the mud effortlessly. The trees parted around her, their pulsing breaths relaxing as she passed. Rot and metallic tang hung heavy in the air, but she no longer feared them. She breathed in; breathed out. She would survive. She always survived.

And then: another figure, blocking her path.

It pressed against her thoughts as she looked up, around. She'd found herself in the center of ruins, once built from massive slabs of granite that jutted at strange angles. The figure was giant, but it wasn't threatening her; it was only watching, peering around in her head, the same as the other shadows had done.

Well. She could hardly blame it. Friend or foe? Wasn't she making the same calculation now?

It swept a meaty arm before it, and the air shimmered and warped.

Rebeka staggered back as the ruins seemed to repair themselves around her, building into what she could only describe as a temple. Intricate designs had been painted over the granite, geometric shapes that might have been some kind of text. The creature swept its hand again, and more creatures flourished around her, standing in the circle of the chamber, and she got the distinct sense they were passing some sort of judgment.

The presence in her mind grew more insistent. Memories of her own life mixed in with images she didn't recognize. She saw herself watching from the window of her uncle's farmhouse as her crush, Joachim, worked in the garden next door; he'd been killed by Einsatzgruppen during the seizure of Luxembourg. She saw the creatures arranged in a circle once more, only they were recognizable now, their faces almost human, their expressions guarded, as an oddly dressed human man—breeches and livery—bargained before them. The man looked through Rebeka, and she tasted a name on her lips: Tomasi Sicarelli.

His bargaining concluded, he turned from the creatures with a cruel smile, and they collapsed, screaming and writhing, as their features were torn away.

Fire. The fire consuming their synagogue in Berlin. The fire and ravage of human hands tearing through the shadowed forest. The creatures aching as Sicarelli pillaged their world, the color and life gone from the lands, their muscles and faces shriveled.

Rebeka closed her eyes, shaking. This world . . . it had suffered, too.

Then the presence retreated from her mind. The creature drew itself up, cartilage snapping as it straightened high. Was she going to be punished for what had been done? For being another intruder and conqueror, like Sicarelli, like whoever this other man was?

But with a flicker of violet, that world disintegrated—the shadows lifted like veils parting wide.

And then it wasn't the ruins at all, but a narrow stone path. Buildings pressing in on either side. The buzzing was gone, the current was gone. She felt nothing now, heard and saw nothing except the dull twilight muffling the town of Hallenberg.

Rebeka gulped down stale autumn air. She wasn't in the bell tower anymore, but looking at the church head-on from the other side of the town square. Her mouth hung open as she tried to piece together what had happened the past few minutes. The soldiers, the shadow, the forest, the ruins—and threading it all together, her.

The shadows were inside her—and she had a home in them.

CHAPTER FIFTEEN
LIAM

They detained him in the projection room. Through the window onto the sanctuary, the images of *Die Große Liebe* flickered across the screen draped in front of the altar. The Nazi and his singer embracing. The Nazi heading off to drop bombs on London. The singer tearfully but patriotically being one with the Völkisch, surrounded by other sturdy Aryan women who kept the Nazi war machinery churning. The Nazi and the singer reuniting once more as the Third Reich celebrated victory.

"We just want a brief look around," the officer assured him. "We won't interfere with your work."

His work. They thought he was the projectionist, just a village boy earning a wage until he was old enough to join their ranks. Liam kept to one-word answers as the officer questioned him about comings and goings, about Helene's patriotism, about whether he'd ever been to Siegen. He did his best to look distracted, occasionally ignoring them completely to rack and queue up the next film reel the way Helene had showed him, then drop the completed reel onto the heap of tangled-up footage at his feet.

"It is good work you are doing here," the officer said. "Keeping morale high."

Liam had plenty of things to say to that, but only nodded in response. Better they thought him simple, unable to offer more than a few words in reply.

"It is easy to become complacent out here," the officer said, "away from Berlin. To allow unsavory elements to fester. To forget why we fight." He gestured toward the sanctuary and his soldiers below. "But it is this. The heartland, the good hardworking Germans like you and my men, that we are fighting for. Don't you agree?"

Liam hummed. He kept himself at the right frequency to hover on the edge of the shadow world, enough that he could draw on the energy in a trickle, but not a flood. He didn't dare press any deeper. The longer he held on to it, the deeper he drew from it, then the more likely he'd attract the monsters again.

They had *known* him, in Siegen. They'd been waiting for him to dip too deeply into their world, to become greedy and overeager. He'd opened a rift too wide, and they'd seen their chance.

They'd known him. Everything he'd done. And they would punish him for taking from their world.

Perhaps he deserved to be punished.

Another soldier entered the room, clicked his heels in salute, and reported in hushed tones. The officer bobbed his head, a smile crossing his slimy lips. "Excellent. Bring him to me."

Liam's pulse ratcheted up. He adjusted the film ratio with ice flooding his veins.

"Now, you were telling me, friend . . . that you had never been to

Siegen?" He spoke the words in English, clipped as neatly as his nails. "I'm afraid we both know that's not true."

Liam's nostrils flared. Something hung heavy in the air—the stench of the other world. Rot and blood and pain. He looked past the officer to the pair of guards who flanked him. Darkness clung to the corners of their eyes. They held themselves unnaturally, dangling as if from puppet strings, their joints sharp and raw.

They weren't shadow-consumed. Not completely. But the shadow had gotten its hooks in them and was eating them from the inside out. The warning trill in the back of Liam's mind was blaring now.

"My name is Jozef Kreutzer. But I believe you already knew that, yes?"

Liam's tongue was glued to the roof of his mouth. "I . . ."

"Liam Doyle." Kreutzer tucked his hands behind his back with a smirk. "Graduated from Princeton just short of your eighteenth birthday. Pursuing a master's in theoretical physics . . . A real shame about your mother, though. And they never did find your father to bring him to justice? So tragic."

A commotion in the doorway—more soldiers were joining them. Wrestling someone into the room. Liam swallowed down a cry. Daniel.

"I owe you some thanks, I believe, for your astounding work revealing the path to the shadow world. But your research was limited by a pitiful lack of imagination, Herr Doyle. You fling the shadows around like a child with paint. But I . . . I have the power to create a masterpiece."

Kreutzer approached one of the soldiers and caressed the man's cheek. Wisps of darkness followed his gloved fingertips as the man stared straight ahead, unblinking, his body rigid and strained.

"I can merge the shadows with man to create the perfect soldier. Perfectly obedient. Empowered with a raw, limitless energy that can devastate and destroy far beyond what any single soldier should be capable of. It took a great deal of trial and error to reach this point, but finally, I've perfected my technique." Kreutzer narrowed his eyes at Daniel. "Shall I give you a demonstration?"

Daniel met Liam's gaze with those dark, storm-cloud eyes of his, mouth opening. Liam squared his shoulders and dug his nails deeper into his palm, let the salty warmth build there, let the pain in his shoulder, his hand, his heart take root. Damn whatever waited on the other side—he had no choice. He faced Daniel and tried to convey meaning in a single look: *Do you trust me?*

Daniel tipped his head forward in a nod.

"Your methods of harnessing the energy are way too sloppy," continued Kreutzer. "You can barely keep control of yourself, much less the creatures you try to command."

Liam started to stand up, fists clenched. But Kreutzer rushed forward and shoved him back into the chair with a firm grip on his bad shoulder. Kreutzer's smirk deepened as he drove his thumb right into Liam's wound.

"Your shadows won't help you. They are no longer yours." His lips curled back as he bent forward, hissing right into Liam's ear. "They belong to the Third Reich now. And with them, we shall be victorious. Ruling this world—and the next."

Another soldier rushed into the room with the same dead eyes as the rest. "We've completed our search of the building, Herr Doktor. The proprietor is in custody now."

Kreutzer leaned away from him with a frown. "There were no others in the building? You are sure?"

"Only these two and the proprietor." The soldier spoke in a flat, rusty monotone. "But she will give us whatever information we need."

Kreutzer whirled back to Liam. "I know there were more than just you two at Siegen. Where are they? Who else knows how to access the shadow world?"

"Dunno." Liam shrugged, deliberately letting his bad shoulder drive into Kreutzer's thumb. The pain spiraled through him, sparking behind his eyes. He welcomed it, letting it feed the darkness in him. He'd kept the rift open for far too long already, but he needed just a minute more . . . "But I know something else you don't."

Kreutzer's smile didn't touch his beady eyes. "And what is that?"

Liam focused on Daniel, calculating the distance between them. He had mere moments to act. Would it be enough? It had to be. The soldiers had said it themselves—no one was left in the church but Nazis now. Dozens of them down in the pews, watching their false gospel of triumph and tyranny. A handful here in this room.

Liam smiled at Kreutzer, then dove forward, freeing himself from Kreutzer's grip and catching the switch on the projector with his free hand. The switch Helene explicitly told them not to touch.

An exposed wire sparked along the side of the projector and crackled, and the scent of ozone surrounded him.

Everything happened at once. Kreutzer jumping back, Liam leaping forward, the shadows unfurling around him like a cloak. The spark catching on the highly flammable film strips and their silver nitrate base. Helene certainly knew what she was doing, Liam had to give her that. She'd known this moment might come. Only he suspected she'd been prepared to burn herself down with the Nazis, if that was what it took.

The rush of flame whooshed around them as it leapt from reel to reel, the whole mess of film tangled all over the projection floor. And then the shadow closed around him and Daniel in a tight embrace.

Kreutzer's face wrenched into a scream as he dissolved into a blur of fire and shadow when their world faded from view.

Liam and Daniel crashed into a muddy swamp inside the shadow realm. Only a dull outline of the church was visible around them, the soldiers screaming as the fire spread hungrily, eagerly from reel to reel.

A moment later, Kreutzer emerged beside them, wreathed in flame.

"You think you are the only one with tricks?" he growled.

The flames sputtered and congealed on Liam's skin, rolling away from his face and down his arms until he held them in a single ball of fire in his palm. Kreutzer glowed, furious, as he concentrated to keep the flames contained.

Liam pulled himself up out of the mud. The shadows were all around, waiting for him to command. But as he pulled at them—

Nothing happened.

Kreutzer smirked at Liam. "This world is ours now. Enjoy it while you can." He flung the flames at Liam's feet.

"Stay back!" Daniel cried, catching hold of Liam's ankle. Kreutzer was already vanishing, slithering off into the darkness beyond the fire wall he'd left behind. Liam strained forward, raw fury powering him. He couldn't lose Kreutzer now. Kreutzer had the book, he was using the shadows to further his own horrific purpose—

But he'd escaped. Liam dropped back into the mud with a groan. Once again, he'd been too late.

Daniel pushed to his feet in the slurping mud and helped Liam stand. "We'll find him. He must be headed back to Wewelsburg. We can stop him there."

Liam nodded, too exhausted to argue. It was the best they could hope for now.

As they trudged out of the mud and into the darkened forest, the ghostly image of the church continued to burn through the shimmering veil of the opened rift. Fires with silver nitrate burned brutally hot and fast, with such a fervor they could even burn underwater. Had it been anyone else, Liam might have felt some sliver of remorse for just how painfully the soldiers inside were dying right now. He and Daniel were safer on this side.

"Thank you." Daniel took a step closer toward him. Liam's heart was racing, but the shadowed woods were oddly quiet and calm compared to the chaos back in their world. As Daniel came nearer, his pulse ratcheted higher. "For saving me. For . . . everything you've done. You didn't have to do any of it, and I—"

"Of course I did," Liam said. In the darkness, Daniel's eyes were no longer stormy: they glittered, fathomless like stars. "It's the least you deserve."

Daniel's lips parted as they held each other's gaze. Had Liam only imagined it earlier, when he felt Daniel's fingers running through his hair? When Liam admitted who he was—who he *really* was, not the boy on whatever dossier Dr. Kreutzer had been fed. The darkness inside Liam's heart, his desperate need for control, his brutal search for more and more power. And his fragile truths too: his vulnerabilities, the wounds inflicted on him by his father, by his schoolboy infatuation, by every step of his life. Liam had told and shown him all those things in just the few days they'd known each other, and still Daniel stood at his side.

Still Daniel looked at him like he was a mystery worth unraveling.

Still Daniel's breath quivered between them as Liam moved closer, bringing them nose to nose, heart to heart.

"Daniel," Liam exhaled. He was at once a churning sea and deathly calm. "I—"

Liam . . .

Liam jolted back as the whisper rattled through the trees.

"What was that?" Daniel asked. The trunks shifted around them, crowding in. Insects shrieked in the foliage. The mud gurgled beneath them, growing warmer and warmer.

"We have to get back to our world before the rift closes." Liam reached for Daniel's hand. "Now."

The outline of their world was growing fainter by the second. Liam steered them east, out of the muddy banks of the shadow world and the stream east of Hallenberg, into the thickened heart of the forest. The woods drew closer around them, the tree trunks like bars.

Oh, Liam. There's no point in running anymore. The words echoed all around them.

"I'm not running from you," Liam muttered under his breath. Not that either of them believed that.

We have the manuscript. We have the power. And soon, all the world will see.

They wove through dense, bristling vines. Up ahead, Liam spotted a patch of bushes with razor-sharp leaves tangled together, and jerked Daniel away from them just in time. A tendril of thorns stretched out for them, then snapped back, disappointed.

Will you help us usher in a new age of darkness?

The earth rumbled under their feet. To their right, tree branches split and shredded apart—a massive shadow loomed overhead. The behemoth was nearby, the behemoth that had descended on them the first time he brought Daniel through the gates. "Don't look," Liam hissed back to him.

Oh, yes, run! We already know how much they like Doyle blood.

Laughter rose all around them like sulfurous stink. Through the trees, red eyes drew closer. Unblinking. The tree branches rattled as darkness slithered and coiled around them, poised itself, readied for a strike.

Liam reached out to seize control of the creatures surrounding them. Left to their own devices, they'd gladly devour him or anyone else who crossed their paths, but if he could seize on their energy, he could manipulate them. But there were so many—and the figure was fighting back, trying to control them for himself.

Liam's grasp slipped, and the roars and hisses rose around him. Wings thrummed overhead as a shadow fell across them. The fear-eater's senses tickled at the back of his mind, trying to probe his thoughts for new horrors to feast on. If he looked at it, it wouldn't have to dig far at all.

He couldn't fight this. Their only option was to run—head back to their world—even if it was full of Nazis, fire, worse. But the silvery outlines of their world's shapes were almost gone. He could barely make out the ghostly wisps of soldiers, the military trucks, the fire. He had no choice. He had to trust that they were far enough away from the church. He had to trust—

Something swooped down from above with a brittle shriek. Talons sank into the collar of his shirt and wrenched him forward, his feet dragging through mud, until he was brought face-to-face with darkness, with eyes deep as hell, with teeth turned needly and long. *You* will *pay,* the figure seethed. The words were all around them, in his lungs and in his blood. *You will pay for everything you've done to me.*

"What *I've* done to you?" Liam cried. "How is this my doing—"

"Liam!" Daniel called, then stumbled forward, dagger drawn. Liam tried to twist toward him and opened his mouth to cry out, but the talons dug in deeper as a fist of mud reached up to clench around Daniel. His mouth rounded with fear, but only for a second; then he was the boy that Liam knew once more. Fierce. Fighting back, even as the mud squeezed around him.

"Let him go," Liam said. He pushed back, grasped for more and more darkness to control. But every time he thought he'd grabbed enough, it was ripped from him again.

The figure snarled, *This world obeys me. They are* mine *to command now.* Violet flames licked up the figure's palms and wrapped around his arm. *And when the darkness consumes you, I'll command you, too.*

"You can't have me just yet."

This time, Liam reached for the silvery threads of the rift that would take them back to their world and tugged. It seared into his mind, the blinding brightness of it, and the harder he pulled, the more the darkness unraveled around him. With a snarl, the taloned claws dropped him, and he scrambled back until he found Daniel pulling free of the mud and took his hand once more. His skin was burning, hot as the film reel fire back in the town, burning the shadow away as Liam tore open a pathway home.

Trees coalesced around them as the darkness faded. He pulled Daniel to him while the rift sealed up behind them: the darkness, the hatred held at bay.

For now.

They were back in their world on the eastern bank of the stream, stoic oak trees shedding orange leaves around them. To the west, they could hear screams amidst the crackling flames in Hallenberg's town square. Gunfire rang out, a single rifle crack: Simone? Or one of the soldiers?

"We have to get to Wewelsburg. Kreutzer's got the book—"

"What was that . . . thing talking about?" Daniel asked. "Doyle blood—paying for what you've done." Daniel's breath quivered; he took Liam's hands. "Liam. What was—who—"

Liam squeezed his hands back, then dropped them. He turned to keep moving, but Daniel stayed rooted to the spot. He'd seen it in the firm line of Daniel's mouth: he would have to give him the truth, all of it, if he wanted his help.

If he wanted . . .

Liam closed his eyes as he gulped down air. He'd never meant for any of this to happen. It was why he'd come here alone, why he'd been fighting so brutally for control: he was the only one who could set things right, because he was the only one who'd let them go so wrong. So massively, so painfully. This was his trial. His mistake to undo.

Liam's shoulders fell, and he opened his eyes once more. Only minutes ago, he'd almost kissed Daniel, but now Daniel was looking at him like one of the shadow world's monstrosities. Something dangerous, something not to be touched.

Daniel was more right than he knew.

"I . . . lost someone in the shadow world. Someone I loved."

Daniel lowered his gaze, resigned. "The boy you mentioned. Pitr."

Hearing Pitr's name—from Daniel's mouth, no less—made it all too real. There'd been a time when all Liam wanted was for it to be real, for the world to know what they were. How easy it had been, back then.

"I thought I knew what I was doing. All my theories and formulas. I'd even found the right frequency—" Liam leaned back against a tree trunk. A simple tree, shaded and quiet. In the twilit woods, even the fires of Hallenberg felt far enough away. "But the truth is, I wasn't strong enough to control it."

Daniel stepped forward. It was a trusting gesture, far kinder than Liam deserved. Yearning stitched tight in Liam's chest. He wished he could have met Daniel anywhere, anytime else—an easy, uncomplicated place, where demons and humans alike weren't circling them like wolves, all too ready to kill them over nothing more than who or what they were.

He wondered if such a place could ever exist.

"It was an accident, then?" Daniel lifted his gaze. "You can't blame yourself for that. That doesn't make it your fault." Then, hesitantly:

"This is why you want the book, isn't it? Because you want to bring him back. You want to save him, don't you?"

Liam stared at him for a long minute, and his fingers traced the ghost of Pitr's touch against his cheek. *Bring Pitr back*. Was that what he wanted? Could it have been, once?

But then he couldn't help it: he shook with a laugh.

"No. No, getting trapped there was the least he deserved." Liam's voice ran cold. "The only problem is that I didn't finish the job."

CHAPTER SIXTEEN

Sniper work was one part blood rush—calculations whirling through her head faster than she could examine them, sights lining up perfectly—and nine parts insufferable dullness. Not the dullness of having nothing to do, but of knowing she had something to do yet being unable to do it until some unknown time at which she would have to move too fast—but not now, not yet, not close enough that she could be ready, not far enough she could look away.

Simone hated and loved it. She hated the wait that was a constant itch between her shoulder blades and loved the moment that itch went away. She loved the bloom of red from a Nazi's skull, those flowers she so carefully planted blossoming over and over. She hated being kept from that joy.

And most of all, she hated sharing the waiting with someone else.

"We should check on them," Phillip said, for the thousandth time. "No one's gone in or out for a while now. If they found anyone, they'd be hauling them off already—"

"But they aren't, which means they are still in there." Simone twisted her neck from side to side, earning a satisfying *crack*. She was stomach-down on the roof of the furniture shop, rifle propped on the roof's lip, aimed toward the church. A handful of military trucks and a single officer's Mercedes were parked on the town square. "Do you want to walk into a Kino full of Nazis? I'm not so sure you could avoid notice as convincingly as Liam."

Phillip scowled at her, but they both knew she had a point. Not that she would fare much better. Sometimes she wanted to laugh with how mad this whole journey was, traveling hundreds of kilometers into the heart of Nazi Germany to find a boy who'd dropped out of the sky. And get them both safely back out again—not that Georges-Yves or the US Army had been too forthcoming about how they'd manage that. A frequency, a preassigned code. That was her only hope of ever escaping this nightmare land.

Part of her didn't care about escaping. Part of her wanted to cling to the feeling of the rifle firing in her hands, deafening her frantic thoughts and puncturing the pain she kept bottled inside of her. She hated Evangeline, hated her for her cowardice. She hated France and the narrowed stares other Parisians gave her, their muttering about immigrants, as if they weren't the ones who'd claimed Algeria for their own. But she loved Evangeline, too; her ambition barreled through nearly every *no* that stood in her way. Loved that it was almost too plausible to believe that maybe, despite everything, she just might really be aiding the Magpie.

She loved France and its colors and chaos and opportunity, woven loosely and brightly like a Berber rug. She missed her mother holding fast to the deen, reciting a du'a into silence, into nighttime, into the ear of a god who knew what lay before them and behind. She missed the feeling of wood melting under her fingertips, shrinking and shaping itself into whatever she dreamed.

And yet like a dream, it crumbled in the light of day. She could try to hold on to it, but she could never go back. Also like woodworking: a wrong cut could never be uncarved.

Simone checked the rifle sights once more. Her gun wasn't really made for long-distance work—the scope's magnification was minimal—but it was the best trade-off she had, not knowing from day to day whether she'd find herself perched in a tree or face-to-face with the enemy. A few men stood guard under the Kino's marquee, waiting with nervous energy. It didn't look like they were smoking, or on any sort of break, but they weren't directly acting on orders, either. They looked . . . listless. Wrong.

Simone tightened her grip and leaned forward.

"Wait." Phillip stopped his pacing. "The alley. There's someone down there."

Simone gritted her teeth. "Soldiers?"

"No. It's—" Phillip sucked in his breath. "Shit, I think it's Rebeka."

Simone forced her jaw to unclench. "What the devil is she doing down there? They could see her—"

"I don't know! I didn't even see her walk this way. Hey!" He hissed down toward the alley. "Up here!"

Simone ran her thumb back and forth over the rifle's stock. She wasn't about to take her eyes off the soldiers. Behind her, Rebeka's shoes thumped, wet, against the metal of the fire escape. Before her, two more soldiers exited the Kino. No—three—no. Simone's stomach dropped. The third person was being frog-marched between them, red-faced and stoic—

Helene.

Promise me, Helene had asked her, away from the others. *Promise me that if you must, you'll do what needs to be done.*

"What happened?" Phillip was asking Rebeka behind her. "You look spooked."

Simone pinched the bridge of her nose and tried to shut them out. The Nazis would do terrible, terrible things to Helene: dig for any truth they thought they could bleed and beat and scrape out of her before discarding her husk. She didn't deserve it. She'd only done the same as Simone—she'd fought. She was better than Simone, in truth. She actually cared for people, tried to save as many as she could, while all Simone wanted was—

Was what, exactly?

Simone had been so caught up in running away, in the pressure-valve release of each bullet she fired, that she couldn't see the cliff edge she was racing toward. She didn't dare wonder what would remain of her when there was no more pressure to unleash.

At least Helene had a purpose. She knew why she did what she did, all while knowing it might cost her everything. She deserved so much more.

She deserved to be spared.

Simone braced herself against the rifle. Caressed the firm barrel and the wooden stock, her intricate design only halfway carved into it. She settled into the rifle's sights, that funnel that stripped away all her fear and uncertainty and animal urge to escape.

Helene's hair had wormed loose from her tight braid and wisped around her head, halo-like. Her cheeks were flushed, but she held her chin high. Her broad face was solid and sturdy as granite. The Nazi on her left kept having to readjust his grip on her half arm, unable to manage a decent frog-march, and the tiniest smile tugged at the corner of Helene's mouth every time he did.

This would be how she'd want it. Not hours or days from now, after they'd stripped her down, beaten her, brutalized her. Not after she'd learned how much it took to wrest the secrets from her soul. She would want to die proud.

Simone took aim.

The crack was too loud in the autumn air; the rifle's butt jolted beneath her, petulant. Without a sniper's stand to brace against, the sight had slammed into Simone's eye, and a hot welt was already forming. *Dammit.* Behind her, Phillip and Rebeka had fallen into a shocked, perilous silence threatening to teeter over into screams. But Simone ignored them and brought the scope back up to her eye once her vision cleared.

They should already be running, but she had to be sure. For Helene's sake.

"What are you doing?" Phillip whispered, quietly but with searing urgency. "What in the hell—"

Helene's body had gone limp, sagging between the two guards who'd dragged her from the Kino. The guards were just now turning, bewildered, to stare at the red fountaining from her forehead. The blood framed her cheeks, her chin; between those crimson streams, it almost looked like she was smiling.

The guards looked up. Looked at each other. Sputtered something Simone was too far away to hear.

Then they dropped Helene and started to shout.

Simone curled her arms around the rifle and sat back. Her relief was so warm and all-encompassing, so sharp, that for a moment she felt tears gather in her eyes. They should all be so lucky, if they were caught. *To God we belong, and to God we return.* To hell with all the rest.

But there was no more time to waste. "We need to head back to the tunnels."

"You killed her," Rebeka sputtered. "All those Nazis in the street, and you killed the woman who helped us—"

"Do you have any idea what they would have done to her? To the rest of the Resistance members, once she gave them up?" Simone swallowed down a rush of bile in her throat. "Adab al-qital. The way of war. She asked me to do whatever it took, and so I did."

Sacrifices. So many sacrifices lining her path. Too often she felt like one of her idle carvings, shaving off strips of herself in a vain effort to whittle down into something that felt right. Her homeland, her family, her dignity, her love, her respect for human life. She was the artless hunk of wood that remained.

But she had done the right thing, whether the others could see it or not. Maybe in that, she'd reclaimed something.

Phillip's eyes were still wide with disbelief, but Rebeka lowered her head. "You're right."

"Yes, I know." She slung the rifle over her shoulder and hoisted up her pack. "But if we don't move soon, we're going to be next—"

The rush of fire was immediate. Simone turned back toward the church at the noise, just in time to see the windows burst out of the second floor. The projection room. The shouts already filling the town square ratcheted into shrieks, the frantic pounding of boots.

"Now," Simone managed, her tongue too thick in her mouth. "Let's go now."

Phillip and Rebeka were too stunned to protest.

They dropped down onto the workshop floor of the furniture atelier and made their way through the radio room. Guillerme was hunched over the transmitter, sending out a frantic message, but Karl rushed toward them. "What's happening out there?"

"Nothing good. You need to hide everything." Simone gestured to the stacks of decoded messages, the radio equipment, Phillip's freshly installed transmitter boxes. "Quickly. Somewhere they'll never find. Destroy anything you don't absolutely need to keep."

"But we were finally making progress—answering the information requests—"

Like the Magpie's. Cold iron gripped Simone's limbs. "Did—did you answer the request about Wewelsburg—"

Karl glanced toward his son, but Guillerme was wrapped up in his sea of dits and dahs. "Not yet. You said there was nothing to tell—"

"Change of plans."

She was going to regret this. Jeopardizing their mission on the whim of that idiot American boy and her own desperate hunch. "Tell the Magpie we're headed to Wewelsburg." She glanced at Phillip, who gave her an encouraging nod. "We'll report from there as soon as we get communications established safely."

Karl kicked open the hatch to the tunnel systems. "Then we'll barricade this room from both sides."

Simone started down the hatch. Phillip and Rebeka followed,

hands and feet slapping along the metal rungs. The tunnels had a fetid, stale smell to them from disuse.

"When we are safe," Simone muttered, "you'll tell me how you made it out of that flaming hell."

Rebeka stumbled behind her. "I will."

"What about your brother?" Phillip asked suddenly. "Where is he? Oh, God, was he still inside—"

"No." Rebeka's voice was steady enough that even Simone felt comforted by it. "He's safe. For now."

Simone noticed she didn't say the same for them.

Simone had learned a great many things about silence in her life. There was the silence of her and her brother huddled underneath their bed while their parents raged in Arabic just outside. The silence after their father left, went back to Algiers with scarcely a goodbye. Her mother's silence was always pointed, the silence of shame and grief and embarrassment for raising her children alone, letting their faith fade, packed up with all the things that marked them as outsiders in a chest in the corner of their room. The heavy silence of night in occupied Paris, the long wait for the sound of boots, the crash of kicked-in doors.

Silence could be beautiful too. Simone loved the way the night seemed to hold its breath when she joined Evangeline on the sloped slate roof of Château à Pont Allemagne. The wind stilled and the starlight bent a little closer when she took Evangeline's hand in hers, when she kissed whatever part of her she could reach: a creamy shoulder, a knobbed spine, a mess of hair just loosed from its bun. But Château à Pont Allemagne held many, far more wicked silences in its newly restored walls. Simone hated every one.

She'd grown accustomed to the invisibility cloaked around her when she worked at the château. It was a beautiful architectural monument, Baroque and overflowing with scrollwork, cherubs, marble, and paneled wood. Nymphs and satyrs lurked in the corners of rooms like eavesdroppers, and more than one passageway through the mansion's interior facilitated the easy, unseen movement of servants and paramours alike. It was a house designed for burying secrets, for speaking the unspeakable so it need never be spoken again.

That was certainly how Monsieur Gaturin used it. It was how he intended for Evangeline to use it, too. She and Simone buried a great many secrets in its walls, confessions that could never have survived in the open, but the château was a wonderland mirror that made even the impossible seem real. Now Simone wondered what further secrets those walls were hiding. If they saw Evangeline undergo the same transformation Simone had, from prisoner to aggressor. If the real Evangeline was hidden in the silence between the dits and dahs of the Magpie. If that Evangeline could ever be coaxed out.

But Château à Pont Allemagne held a strange grip on whoever entered those garish, swirling bronze gates. When you looked out its windows, all you saw were bright and careful gardens. You never saw the snakes.

CHAPTER SEVENTEEN

PHILLIP

After everything they'd seen, Phillip had about decided he liked the forest the least when it was quiet. The quiet was too heavy, too suspicious. The quiet was just a dam getting ready to break.

It took them a few hours of hiking before anyone seemed willing to speak. Simone's head was swiveling around madly, scanning the rapidly darkening trees for signs of anything that might be hunting them. Helene's death hung heavy as gunpowder around her. Maybe she thought nothing of it, but when Phillip looked at her, it was all he could see.

Rebeka was harder to read. Whatever ordeal had led her safely out of the church before it became a conflagration, it must have rattled her—hadn't it? There was a stubbornness to her calm, a determination in the way she trudged on through the densely overgrown forest floor. But there was pain, too. It made his heart ache to see it, the pain etched around this proud girl's mouth.

He'd seen too far much death in the past day, but it only hardened his resolve. A vivid, gruesome reminder of the world his parents and uncle had known, all the pain and suffering they tried so hard to armor themselves against. He'd never really known how it felt to be right in tragedy's grip, even if he saw that sorrow, close enough to touch. He wanted to stop it the way that only he could.

"Wait. Hold here," Simone hissed back at them.

Rebeka's hand caught his sleeve reflexively before she flinched and muttered an apology.

"What is it?" Phillip asked.

Simone started into the forest, hands at her waistband. "I need to piss."

Rebeka stifled a laugh. Phillip couldn't look at her, or he'd start laughing too. But then their eyes met, and it felt so good, so pure.

"Should we be looking for your brother?" he asked, still grinning.

"We know where he's headed. I doubt we'll be able to catch him before they reach Wewelsburg."

"And you're okay with this?" Phillip asked.

Her mouth flattened. "I have to be."

Phillip exhaled. "I'm sorry. You shouldn't have to be worrying about—well, any of this. Maybe you can head back to Paris with Simone, like he said—"

"No. I want him to . . ." She gazed into the darkness around them. "I want us to get through this. Together."

"Then we'll do our damnedest to make that happen."

Simone reemerged from the twilit trees and beckoned them over. "This way. I spotted something."

They followed her for a few hundred yards, then crouched down, the escarpment overhead deadening even the sound of the breeze. In the starlight, Phillip just barely saw the shine of Simone's and Rebeka's eyes, the latter staring straight ahead without seeing much that he could tell.

"There're lights up ahead," Simone said under her breath. "A cabin or farmhouse, maybe. But if there are lights, it probably isn't empty."

"Should we keep looking for one that is?" Phillip asked. "Or if they have a barn or shed that we could sneak into—"

"I'm not afraid of them." Simone and Phillip both turned toward Rebeka. Her English, already choppy, had turned to blunt little jabs. A challenge twisted on her lips.

"The Nazis or the monsters?" Phillip asked.

"Either one."

"Well, you should be." Simone's fingers played with the straps on her bag. She'd gotten a new hunting jacket from Helene, Phillip realized with a pang. It was much too broad for her, the shoulder seams falling somewhere around her biceps. He wondered if she could ever forget where it had come from.

"Maybe," Phillip drawled, "we could keep going, and look for another place—"

"No. We need to rest." Simone clicked her tongue. "Tomorrow we can regroup at Wewelsburg, catch up with your brother there. But I don't want to face these shadow things without the American's help."

"I . . . I don't think the shadows will be a problem now," Rebeka said, looking down at her hands.

Phillip's eyebrows crawled up his forehead. "Because Liam isn't with us?"

She shrank into her shoulders. "No. Because I am."

"You might need to explain that one," Phillip said.

Simone gripped her rifle strap. "If you're some kind of demon magnet now too—"

Rebeka shook her head and dropped down onto the ground, tucking her knees under her chin. She looked either very brave or very scared, and Phillip couldn't decide which. "It doesn't work that way."

"And you know this how?"

"I've seen with their eyes." A laugh wrung out of her; it sounded too much like a sob. "Apparently I've *been* doing that. For quite some time."

"Rebeka . . ." Phillip said. "You're tired. We've been through a lot—"

"Don't patronize me. I know how mad it sounds. But I shouldn't have feared it. I should have seen it sooner for what it was, before . . ." Her gaze fell, and she tucked herself together tighter. Disappearing. "They won't hurt me. We have an . . . affinity, I think. A bond."

"You *think*," Simone said, sour. "What in the *hell* do you mean?"

But Phillip's mind was fuguing on what she'd said before. *I should have seen it sooner for what it was.* Those words clanged around in him like a tolling bell, guilt bricking itself up around him. He'd come out here to smash it all down, prove he could help, too, in his own way. But was he really saving anyone, or was he only putting them in more danger?

Now he dropped to sit beside her, knees falling wide until he was cross-legged. Karl and Guillerme—had they avoided being found? Or had he only sealed their fate?

"Why are we all sitting down?" Simone asked. "I'm trying to make a plan—"

"We should take this cabin," Rebeka said. "If you don't want to travel at night, it's our best choice."

Simone issued a few short sputters, then looked to Phillip for support. Oh, no, he wasn't playing that game. He shrugged, head tilting toward the cabin as if to say, *Worth a look.*

With a growl, Simone stood back up and unslung her rifle. "Fine. I'll search it." She trudged forward two steps before whirling back and adding, *"Don't go anywhere."*

Once her footsteps retreated, Rebeka sagged forward and squeezed her eyes shut. A tear gleamed in one corner of her eye.

"Hey," Phillip whispered. "Are you all right?"

She gathered her dress's hem into a fist. "I wish I'd understood sooner."

"How do you mean?"

"I see—things. Places other than where I'm standing. I didn't realize it before, but it's like I'm watching them *from* the shadow world. And the shadows themselves, they . . ." She shook her head. "I don't know how it's possible."

"Well, it's another universe, right?" Phillip's mind was whirring on frequencies, circuitry. Liam's explanation had made so much sense, just the kind of diagram he needed to understand the world. Hell. It made more sense than anything else he'd seen out here. "If it's that close to our world, then some people might have a—a sensitivity to it. A frequency, maybe. They can probably sense the weakness in the barriers and maybe even glimpse through those barriers without realizing it."

"So there is nothing mystical about it. Just science." She didn't sound too thrilled.

Phillip winced. "Doesn't that make it better?"

"It's not better or worse. But . . . I don't want to have this—this *connection* to a world like that."

"An evil world?" he asked.

She pressed her lips together. "A place of darkness. I want there to be more than just the darkness."

He leaned forward, intending to tuck back a brown lock of hair that had drifted into her face. He wasn't even thinking as he did it; it felt natural, instinctive. He stopped himself just before touching the lock, and their eyes met.

"Sorry," he said, at the same time she told him, "Don't be sorry."

He laughed softly and secured the hair behind her ear. Her skin was so cold, but then, he supposed, so were his hands.

"There's more than just the darkness," he told her. There was more to the world than the paths that had been laid out for them. The opportunities lost. The wounds they'd inflicted. He had to believe it because the alternative would crush him alive. "There has to be."

"I want to find it," she said.

Phillip opened his mouth to answer, but Simone returned then, towering over them.

"I don't know how, but it's completely empty. No sign anyone has been there for days."

Phillip scrambled to his feet, the thought of a safe haven too much to resist. "You're sure?"

"Sure as I can be." She shrugged. "They still have electricity, but we don't touch any lights, don't turn anything on or off. We leave it exactly as it is. And we take turns guarding." She fixed her stare on Phillip. "You're first."

Despite Simone's proclamations, they did use the stove just long enough to heat up canned broth and toss in some cubes of vegetable bouillon, which was unfortunately all the flavor they could find. They sat around the cabin's tiny breakfast table as they slurped down their sad little soups. The cabin looked like someone's hunting lodge, and a modest layer of dust blanketed the bedsheets and tables. If the owners were around, they hadn't come here in some time.

After another sweep of the woods, Simone beckoned them both onto the porch and held her hunting rifle out in both hands. "Now. I think it's time you both learned how the hell to use these things."

Phillip huffed. "I got decent enough marksmanship scores—"

"Sure." Rebeka reached for the rifle. "I'm too clumsy with the P38."

"Do you know how to check that it's loaded? Without blowing your face off?" Simone gestured toward the chamber. "How you slot the bullet, prime the firing mechanism . . ."

Rebeka pantomimed taking the steps. Her breathing seemed to slow as she went through the motions, and some of the tension left her face. Phillip raised one eyebrow at Simone. He'd thought she was just like him—far more at ease with diagrams than people. But even if she didn't intend to, she knew just the thing to put Rebeka more at ease.

Probably helped that it involved killing Germans.

Simone stretched out, long-limbed, on the cabin's porch steps. "Now bring it to your shoulder. The thing is, you'll always know the kick of the butt is coming. You have to be ready for it, but not so braced that it makes you rigid. Think of it like . . . the next step in a dance. If you step too soon, it'll mess up the step that came before."

Rebeka smiled faintly at that. "It's been a long time since I've danced."

Phillip's mouth—the goddamned traitor—was already opening to offer before he clamped it shut. She'd told him what sent her and her brother into the woods—the halting, panicked escape from Poland she'd recounted the night before. She certainly didn't need him fawning all over her while she wrestled with everything else.

"Line up your shot, but don't forget the rules of physics, all right? Gravity, wind, the rise and fall of your own breath. Wait for a space. A silence. See the arc of the bullet, how it will move. And then—boom."

Boom. Phillip shivered involuntarily. But the woods were a wall of darkness staring back at them, a lazy trickle of birdsong giving comfort that nothing worse lurked in the trees.

Yet.

Rebeka moved through the steps of firing a few times more until her focus drifted. She returned the rifle to Simone and slumped back on her palms, looking for all the world like she was relaxing.

What did he say to someone like her? Phillip's talents lay in his knowledge, his ability to build and transform. But that wasn't some universal adapter that could be plugged effortlessly into any conversation. Small talk, the weather, the markets, the symphony—his parents' idle chatter bored him at best, and out here, it seemed impossibly wrong.

Yet the silence felt easy. When Rebeka looked over her shoulder at him, he smiled, and she smiled back. Easy. Maybe words were overrated for her, too.

"So. The demons." Simone tore at her nail cuticles. "Why aren't you worried about them?"

Rebeka nestled into the woolen blanket she'd brought from inside.

"I can't speak for all of them. But I think I have an understanding with some."

"What about Liam?" Phillip asked.

"Some of them want him dead. They made that *very* clear." Her gaze hardened in a way that sent a chill through Phillip.

"And why is that?" Simone asked.

"He's the same as all the others who've used their world before." She shrugged. "Just wants their power for himself."

Phillip braced himself. "What about your brother?"

For a long moment, she was silent, gathering up her words. There was a way her lower lip twisted when she was being careful, this pensiveness that had weight to it.

"He will do what he always intended to do," she said finally.

Phillip had one more pressing question. He fiddled one hand into his pocket and rubbed his fingers over a radio crystal nestled there. Just one tiny geode offered enough energy to power an emergency field radio. It seemed more like alchemy than science. And yet, expanding out from the small crystal, from radio waves, he had arrived at something world-changing. Secrets sent around the globe.

"Liam said frequencies were a part of opening the path between the two worlds, right?" Phillip asked.

"Something like that." Simone cut suspicious eyes toward him. "I didn't understand half of what he said."

Rebeka nodded into her arms. "A combination of finding the right frequency, and using . . . pain . . . as bait. To draw the dark energy out."

"Right. You need the bait to open it, pull them into our world." Phillip let go of the crystal. "But maybe not to close it again."

Simone scoffed, but Rebeka chewed at her lower lip, lost in thought. Phillip caught himself staring—at the bow of her mouth, the long cast of her eyes as she retreated back inside her head.

"If it is about frequency . . . then that might explain why it 'chose' you, too. By which I mean—it didn't choose you at all." Phillip nudged her foot with his own. "Everyone gives off their own little bit of radiation. You just happened to get the lucky number."

"What, you think I'm tuned to the same frequency as the shadows? Like a radio set?" Rebeka asked.

Her gaze had lifted. Despite the dark circles under her eyes, she looked lighter—brighter, somehow. Like there'd been some light inside her switched off for too long, and he was only seeing it glow now for the first time. God, he wanted to do anything it took to keep it burning bright.

But then it came crashing back down.

"You're kind to think that," she said, too carefully. "But I know better."

"Rebeka . . ." He shook his head. "Whatever you're feeling about this connection you have—I promise you, it's not your fault."

"You have no idea." She grimaced. "You don't even know me."

The words stung when they landed because he knew she was right. They hovered in an uneasy silence, so unlike the comfortable one they'd shared before. This new silence was too much, a hunger he couldn't sate. And as much as he *wanted* to know her, more than that, he wanted to help. No. He *needed* to.

And suddenly, he felt that tingle under his skin, like when he saw past the mess of a schematic or circuit diagram to the system it could create. He felt like just the right switch being slotted into place. He might not be able to build bonds like his parents did, or tear through enemy lines like Uncle Al. But he could solve a problem.

"What if—what if I could close it?" Phillip asked. "Maybe even keep you from sensing it anymore." The question felt too fragile, like a tissue-paper flower he'd made his mother once at school. She'd frowned at it, clucked her tongue. *Don't ever settle for something so false*, she'd told him then. But now he would pin his hopes on something flimsy if he had to. He'd pin his hopes on whatever he possibly could.

"You really think you can do that?" Rebeka asked.

"I'd like to try."

Rebeka looked at him thoughtfully, then nodded once, careful. "But only after I find my brother."

Phillip knew how it felt to bear a gift that looked more like a curse. To be celebrated for something that made you feel sick inside. It was why he'd let himself be thrown from an airplane into a war-ravaged forest, wasn't it? To desperately prove that maybe his talents didn't have to be used for harm. But everywhere he looked, while others saw the shining light his gift cast, he only saw the gruesome, chilly shadows it left behind.

Simone stood then, and retreated to another room of the cabin to rest. But Rebeka was still looking at him, with more uncertainty now than before.

"Why are you really here?" she asked, and when he opened his mouth—"The truth. Not because of the army. Why are *you*."

Phillip tangled his hands together to keep them from fluttering around. "I'm afraid it's not so heroic as you may think."

"Tell me about it" was all she said.

He liked that. *Tell me about it.* No empty platitudes, no absolution that wasn't hers to give. It gave him the confidence he needed.

"Well, I've had it pretty easy all my life. As easy as a Greenwood family can have it, I guess. But I was never going to be a businessman like my parents. I was never that good with people, connections."

She smiled softly. "Not everyone can be."

"Yeah, but I respect them for it, you know? They were always the first to pitch in when our neighbors needed help, when someone's business got hurt. I don't want to take it for granted, everything I have. I want to help out, too. I went to college to earn my own place, to make something of my own from all the little designs I was always fussing with, but it just didn't feel like enough."

"Your radio encryption systems? I wouldn't call those little."

He blushed, strangely proud. Like maybe he wasn't so pitiful for looking at her like she was the sunlight that trickled through the trees, dappling the world with flecks of gold, that little spot of brightness in all the cold shadows.

"Well. It didn't work out so great."

Rebeka's smile faded.

"Last year, I ended up working an internship at Connolly Surveying—an oil company in Tulsa. A bunch of us from the engineering college did. Kind of came as a shock that this white man wanted us to work for him and that he'd actually pay us fairly.

"But he was polite, and encouraging, worked right alongside us to build out mathematical models for picking drilling sites or improving extraction techniques. When he asked me to build a digital computer to help the mathematicians run their projections, I was all too happy to help."

With the soldering iron running, Phillip almost couldn't hear the laughter and tinkling glasses from the rest of Connolly Surveying's offices at the top of the Philtower. His parents had all but ordered him to attend his employer's Christmas party, much to his dread. It wasn't that he hated being around people, though that was hardly his favorite thing, either. It was the added layer of tension, like a chewy cake fondant, draped over all his interactions with them, and in a company owned by a white man, the layer may as well have been concrete. He felt like some kind of jack-in-the-box everyone kept cranking, waiting to see what he'd spring up with next.

Not even Darius, his best friend, was soothing his nerves this time. When Mr. Connolly dragged him out for a toast to his newest engineering success, Phillip had found Darius and several of the other mathematicians conspicuously absent. The other interns from the engineering school only glared at him until he lowered his gaze.

He hated that Mr. Connolly was making such a big to-do about him anyway, like his freshman project was somehow world-changing. He'd designed a new tabulation machine: a massive system of levers and pulleys and vacuum tubes and rotating gear sets that could take in a complex set of data—like, say, the geological and survey data on a given piece of land—and output an array of mathematical projections for what an oil well drilled there might yield. What once took Darius and the other interns almost a day to calculate could now be computed in under an hour, thanks to Phillip's creation. Mr. Connolly called it a marvel, said it was bound to revolutionize their work.

Not Phillip. He couldn't shake the feeling that he'd finally earned his place in the larger world, but in doing so, he'd left something just as valuable behind—something he could never get back.

At least he had an excuse now to hide away in his lab in the office's corner. There was always some gear set for him to tweak, a circuitry board for him to refine. Phillip liked the feel of the soldering iron in his hands and the burning, snapping ozone smell it left behind. He liked the way a circuit always did exactly what it was supposed to do. People were too unpredictable. Imposing. He never knew what inputs to give them. The only safe thing for Phillip to do was not engage.

"There you are, Jones." Mr. Connolly's voice punctured the crackle of the soldering iron. "You're missing out on quite the party."

Phillip switched the iron off and shoved his goggles on top of his head. Marty Connolly stood in the doorway of the lab, clutching a tumbler of scotch like he might have to use it as a bludgeon.

Phillip shrugged. "Felt like making some adjustments."

"Always working, aren't you? I like that. It shows good character." Something in his words set Phillip's teeth on edge, but he couldn't quite name it.

Mr. Connolly moved toward the dark leather armchair next to Phillip's desk and settled into it. Phillip's chair, usually. But Mr. Connolly inhabited it like his personal throne. He took a slow sip of scotch as he watched Phillip, and carefully, Phillip turned his attention back to the wiring in front of him: a replacement part intended to upgrade the data storage on his electrical computer from twelve-digit integers to twenty-four. Mr. Connolly hadn't come here for no reason—that much was clear. But if he wasn't going to make his purpose known, Phillip wasn't going to make it for him.

"It isn't very comfortable, is it?" Mr. Connolly asked.

Phillip looked up at his boss shifting in the armchair, leather creaking in protest beneath him.

"Pah. All this money, and I can't get you a proper chair." He stood and continued, "C'mon, Jones, I think it'd mean a lot to the folks if you'd mingle with them. Just because you can invent something that does the job of five mathematicians . . ."

"It's not like I invented the concept," Phillip said, scalp prickling. He knew what Mr. Connolly meant, though. He was worried about the rest of the office seeing Phillip as "uppity." He didn't know which bothered him more—that they might think it or that Mr. Connolly cared if they did. "Besides, I, uh . . . I noticed none of the mathematicians were here."

"Wasn't that your idea?" Mr. Connolly asked. "I mean, machinery like that . . . It'll eat some electricity, sure, but at least you don't have to pay it a salary."

Phillip tried to breathe in, but his ribs felt encased in ice. "I'm not sure what you mean, sir."

"You saved us a lot of money, Jones. No matter how much all those fancy tubes and wires cost, it's still cheaper than paying the five of those boys."

The ice spread into his lungs, his blood. "Well—it still takes men to run it. People, I mean," Phillip added quickly. "People have to run it."

"Oh, sure. But not *five* of them. That'd defeat the whole point, right?" Connolly took another sip of scotch and licked his slimy lips.

"Mr. Connolly?" Phillip squeezed the bundle of wires so hard they crimped. "What did you do, sir?"

"Your friends from the college didn't appreciate that I've got to make hard choices." He narrowed his eyes. "But they don't know how to turn a profit like we do. You and I."

Phillip swallowed, but nothing washed away the taste like acid that was filling his mouth. "But the internship—"

"Was always on my terms." His teeth flashed with a vicious smile. "I'm so glad you understand, Jones. I think you're going to go far."

Rebeka's hand covered his. For all her boniness, she felt . . . sturdy. Like an anchor keeping him from getting carried out to sea.

"Did you trust Mr. Connolly not to fire your friends?" she asked.

"I should've known he would. But it—it never even crossed my mind. I was so busy trying to prove myself, that I could make my own way, give something back, and not just rely on my parents' name . . ."

Rebeka's fingers curled tighter. "You made the machine for the right reason. But you didn't think of the consequences."

"Sure. Everyone *thinks* they're doing things for the right reason. Even Mr. Connolly." Phillip pulled his hand from hers.

Rebeka didn't say anything more for a long moment, which he supposed was only fair. The whole world was on fire, eternally smoldering with the flames of good intentions. People who thought they were doing the right thing. No one, he supposed, ever did a thing because they believed they were in the wrong. They just accepted any bad they caused as the cost of something greater.

He didn't want her pity. Not when she'd suffered so much, from so many injustices carried out by people who believed wholly in what they did. Was there any good to be done in this world? Or was it always only a choice between bad and worse?

"Now you can do better," Rebeka said, a quaver in her voice. "You care enough to want to help. That alone means something. It was enough to drive Germans like Helene and your radio operators to do bigger acts."

A lot of good it had done Helene. "I wanted to prove I could make a difference out here. But what if I only keep making things worse?" He shifted forward in the darkness, his hand itching where she'd touched it. "All these technological advances, these modern marvels of science, and all we seem able to do with them is make everyone's lives miserable. Bigger bombs, deadlier wars. And even though I think I'm helping the right side of this hell . . . am I really helping at all?"

The corners of her eyes shone too bright in the starlight as she lifted her chin. Proud, determined. "You already have."

Phillip's voice stuck in his throat. "Rebeka . . ."

His instinct was to deny it. Put himself down and everything he'd done. But he'd made a difference—the tiniest of a ripple, and she was right. They'd rescued her from almost certain death at Siegen. The village they just left could send back word to the Resistance—warn them of what was coming. And if they could answer that informant's request for information out of Wewelsburg . . .

"I let a terrible thing happen to my family, even as I saved Daniel," Rebeka said. "I knew what was happening. But there wasn't time to save them all."

"But you did save him. And yourself."

Rebeka shrank back. Disbelieving, maybe. But he'd only spoken the truth. Even if she couldn't see it.

"I did," she said at last. "And what you did . . . What you created . . ." She shivered in the cold air. "Maybe there's still some good it can do, too."

He bit back a sour laugh. "We'll see about that."

"Quiet," Simone whispered. They hadn't even heard her stir.

She padded toward them through the cabin on bare feet and crouched down. Something had shifted in the darkness outside; Phillip could feel it. He could no longer hear the roar of insects.

He shot a look toward Rebeka, the question unspoken in his eyes—*Shadows?*—but she shook her head once, quickly.

Simone's hands squeaked in the darkness as they curved around her rifle barrel. Phillip reached down, too, for his sidearm, before remembering he'd left it in its holster halfway across the room.

In the stillness of the cabin, the door handle twisted with a click.

CHAPTER EIGHTEEN

LIAM

Liam was leaning against the shiny beetle shell of the officer's Mercedes-Benz when the man emerged from the beer hall. The officer paused midstagger, tipping precariously toward the left, before catching himself and assuming something like an outraged expression. With the slack elasticity of intoxication, his features turned downright grotesque.

"Guten Abend, mein Herr," Liam said, his voice too chipper and too sharp. "So glad you could join us."

"Do I know you?" The officer curled his fingers through the ring of keys in his palm, so that the jagged bits of metal jutted from between his fingers.

"Not yet, my friend. But we'll know you very soon."

The officer suddenly remembered his P38 and reached for it in what he probably believed was a subtle fashion. Poor Fritz. His hand never even connected with the grip. Daniel emerged from the alleyway behind him and easily ripped it out of its holster before the bastard had time to react.

Daniel then jammed the pistol's nose into the officer's ribs as his other arm locked around his throat, blade in hand. "How about you show us a good time?"

He maneuvered the officer into the Mercedes-Benz's back seat while Liam climbed into the front. The motor started up with an effortless purr, nothing like the chug of his landlady's truck when he drove her to the grocery store.

Liam ran his hands along the smooth steering wheel, bracing himself. This wasn't going to be easy without touching the shadow realm. Its absence throbbed through him like a toothache he kept worrying with his tongue. Maybe he could just dip in for a moment, grab a fistful of shadow before it could sink its claws into him or alert Pitr that he'd returned—

No. That was the darkness talking. He'd overused it already—that he was thinking these thoughts was proof enough of that. He could do this without the shadow. All he needed was that fierce spitfire boy grinning at him through the rearview mirror. Liam returned Daniel's grin, chest swelling with pride.

"Where are you taking me?" the officer asked. "What is it you want?"

Liam smiled. "We're asking the questions here, Klaus."

"My name is not—"

"I really don't care."

Liam steered them down the narrow streets of the village. They'd stumbled on the ski resort when it emerged from the thick of night like a Bavarian oasis of wood and plaster. There wasn't enough snow to warrant a tourist infestation yet, but the taverns and inns were open for a smattering of visitors.

When they'd spotted the officer's pristine Benz parked out front, they knew they had quite a catch waiting for them inside. When they entered the beer hall and found he was only an Untersturmführer, certainly not important enough to be loaned such a magnificent piece of machinery for a night out, they knew their luck had just ramped up. Now to press it a little bit further.

"Where'd you get the car, Klaus?" Liam asked, as casually as he might ask about the daily special.

Klaus huffed indignantly, but shrank back when Daniel pushed in closer with the edge of his knife. "I am an officer of the German army, and as such, I am afforded—"

"Oh, no. Nuh-uh. Not with those measly little squares on your lapel, you aren't. Bet that line works all right with the Fräuleins, though, huh, Klaus?"

Klaus glowered at him. "All right, so I borrowed it. What do you care? You aren't German."

"I wouldn't get too clever, Klaus. Who we are isn't your concern."

Liam turned off the main road and onto an access trail, deeply rutted and rattling with muddied-out tracks. The nose of the car tipped upward as they climbed, their teeth chattering all the way. The darkened ribs of trees closed around them as the village began to fade below.

"Where are you stationed? Wewelsburg?" Daniel asked.

"All right. You sound German." Klaus whirled toward Daniel. "But you *look* like a filthy—AUUGHHH!"

Liam tried and failed to stop himself from laughing. He didn't need to look back to know Daniel had embedded the knife in Klaus, carefully missing his vital organs for now. "Sweetheart, you were supposed to wait until *after* we got his uniform off."

"Couldn't help myself." Daniel flashed him an embarrassed grin in the rearview, lighting Liam up from the inside. "My *filthy* parents were butchers, so I'm fairly certain that right now, the blade is beneath your left lung," he told Klaus. "But if you make any sudden moves, it'll take nothing for me to puncture it. That'll be considerably more painful than what you're currently feeling."

"You fucking bastards—"

"Answer the question, *Klaus*," Daniel hissed.

"Yes! I'm stationed in Wewelsburg! Why are you only asking me things you already know?"

"Just want to make sure we're on the same page."

Liam clenched his jaw against a particularly sharp jolt in the road. The trees were parting to reveal the star-smeared sky above them. As they crested the ridge, he turned toward the left and scanned the ridgeline for the chairlift.

There it was, hunkering down in the darkness like a primitive beast. Daniel was right—maybe they didn't need the shadows to have some fun.

"Now," Daniel said, "for our real questions."

Liam brought the Mercedes to a stop and opened the back door. As Daniel climbed out, silver starlight limned his face; it sent a flutter through Liam's heart. Daniel negotiated Klaus out of the back seat while keeping the knife firmly planted inside of him, like meat on a spit.

Liam yanked the covering off the chairlift, sending pollen and dead leaves flying. It took some digging around with only the stars to guide him, but finally he found the pull chain for the prime mover's engine. A couple sharp yanks, and the diesel rig woke up from its long summer slumber with a dry cough.

"Not much gas in the tank," Liam called. "Better think quick, Klaus."

"What? What is it you want to know?"

"What Dr. Kreutzer's doing at Wewelsburg."

Klaus allowed himself to be jerked forward by Daniel, closer to the chugging engine. The chairlift began its slow processional, bobbing high over the hillside. It was a pretty sad slope, as ski villages went; even upstate New York offered better courses than this. But it would serve their purposes just fine.

"What do you *think* he's doing at Wewelsburg? It's the SS head-quarters." Klaus glowered at Liam as he pulled a length of rope from his pocket and lashed Klaus's hands together in front of him. "Reichsführer Himmler is stationed there, and the head of the Einsatzgruppen—there's quite a lot of paperwork—"

"I think you know that's not what we mean." Liam yanked him forward by the rope, and Daniel reluctantly pulled the knife out with a thick slurp of blood and a pathetic whine from Klaus. "Kreutzer is experimenting with things better left alone. Dark things. Isn't he?"

Klaus's whole body went rigid; he gained the shifty-eyed bravado of subterfuge unique to drunkards. It was like a dog playing dumb when its owner tried to pry a mystery object from its jaws.

"I—I wouldn't know anything about that," Klaus said, his voice growing more labored. "As you said yourself, I'm only a lowly Untersturmführer—"

"Oh, don't be so humble." Liam tossed the second length of rope to Daniel, who headed over to the chairlift engine and pulled the lever to switch it into manual mode. The engine whined, eager to get back to work. Daniel climbed up and looped the rope over the cable, then tied Klaus to that loop. Once they were in the air, he'd dangle a good five feet below their chair.

"After you," Daniel said with a dramatic sweep.

Liam beamed at him, then settled into the pollen-flecked chair like it was the finest chariot. Daniel joined him, then tugged loose the rope he'd wrapped around the braking system. They set off careening down the mountainside.

"Are you crazy? The minute I'm out of these ropes, you fairies are—YAUGH!"

Klaus was abruptly yanked off his feet as they descended. He dangled only a few feet up, for now. But the terrain was changing soon.

"These *fairies* get to decide whether you live or die, Klaus. So think very carefully about what you want to say next." Liam pressed his knife's blade against the rope that suspended Klaus below them. "Kreutzer's project. What's he doing to his soldiers?"

"Okay, okay, I only know a little bit—there's this man helping him, this awful man, he looks like Death, all darkness and hatred—"

Even though he'd known it was coming, it still struck Liam like a kidney punch. "Pitr Černik." He closed his eyes and saw that dark face looming behind him in the mirror. Heard the awful screams.

"Yes, that's him. They're manipulating—energy, I think they called it, imbuing soldiers with it. They were asking for volunteers—"

"Imbuing?" Liam asked. "Imbuing, how?"

"I don't know! I didn't sign up! Sounded like suicide to me." The chair swayed as Klaus twisted against his bonds. "That's all I know, I swear!"

"You said it sounded like suicide." At a nod from Liam, Daniel swiped his blade against the edge of the rope; just enough to slacken the tension as Klaus dropped further. They were nearly over the river ravine now. "How do you know that?"

"My friend, he . . . he signed up for it. Said it was better pay, and it's supposed to—do something, he said. They promised it would help him achieve his true Übermensch potential. But I didn't see him for a week, didn't know if he'd gotten deployed, or—" Klaus yelped as the rope frayed further. "Then I saw him again, in the bowels of the castle. But he wasn't . . . *himself*. His movements were all wrong, his eyes were off, there was this horrible stench of decay to him—and his skin, God. It was like he'd been taxidermied, like there was something underneath that wasn't *him* anymore . . ."

Liam set his jaw in a hard line. Kreutzer still hadn't perfected his technique, but he was getting close. If he stabilized the bridge, there was no telling how many more soldiers he could transform at a time, or how many of the shadowy monsters he could chain to his control. And if he'd rescued Pitr from the shadow world and was using him too . . .

They reached the ravine.

Daniel stood up to hit the emergency brake, and the chairlift shuddered to a halt. Klaus twisted and turned, yelling out in fear as he dangled and swung over the cleave in the earth, the jagged rocks far below that lined a rushing stream. Liam's mouth was dry, but he forced himself to go on, despite the false bravado now apparent in his tone.

"Long way down, Klaus. Time to tell us the rest about your friend."

"He—he grabbed my arm, looked at me with those awful, dead eyes, and then he—he wheezed something. I'm not sure what he said. But then there were aides upon him, wrangling him back into one of those basement laboratories. They said he had pneumonia, some bullshit like that. But I know what I saw."

"Good job, Klaus. You're almost there," Daniel called. "Now, about Wewelsburg. How do we get in undetected?"

"*You* don't." Klaus laughed, bitterly. "You must have an identification badge. There're multiple checkpoints. It's locked up tighter than a Jungfrau's thighs."

Liam rolled his eyes. "There must be *some* way in."

"There is." Daniel sawed at the rope once more, and it stretched further. "And he's going to tell us."

"Scheiße, okay, you maniacs!" Klaus kicked his feet helplessly, fraying the rope further. "But you have to let me go after this. Swear it."

Daniel and Liam exchanged glances. "Fine. You've got a deal," Liam said, though Daniel tensed with displeasure beside him.

"Your best bet is through the garage. It's how I got the Oberführer's Benz out."

"Is it unguarded?" Daniel asked.

Klaus grimaced. "No, but the guards are bored, easily bribed. I offered to bring back some pretty Edelweißes for them if they let me out for the night."

Liam blinked. "You bribed them with flowers?"

"He means girls," Daniel muttered. "Pure-blooded German girls."

Liam glared down at the guard. "Aren't you a charmer, Klaus. Now, what about watch schedules?"

"Men are posted along the battlements at all hours. Only a complete idiot would try to infiltrate it."

"This castle has battlements?" Liam asked Daniel.

"The papers say that Himmler likes to fancy it his new Camelot," Daniel explained. "And all his SS commanders are the knights of the Round Table. It's vile."

"Is it?" Klaus asked. "His lieutenants already wield a power mightier than Merlin's. Once they make more of those soldiers like my friend . . . They'll be unstoppable. A thundering wave of destruction."

"I'll bet we can stop them just fine," Liam said, but with a certainty he didn't feel. With Pitr helping them, lying in wait to strike the moment Liam dipped into the shadow realm . . .

"Then come and find me if you do. Perhaps we shall have a drink and a laugh, ja, meine Freunde?"

Daniel flicked out his blade once more and held it to the rope. "I'd rather not."

Klaus screeched as the rope pulled taut, the fibers splitting one by one under Daniel's knife. "You bastard! You promised me—"

"And your friends in charge of Łódź promised we'd be safe," Daniel said.

Darkness lurked in his gaze, gleaming like volcano glass in the night. Liam's breath caught at the sight—at the fury radiating off of him, the barely controlled rage that guided his every movement. He was a thunderstorm shaped like a man, and Liam wanted the storm to break over him. Drown everything else.

"I have nothing to do with the camps—I simply do my part—I promise I—"

"Perhaps you should ask my parents, my brother, how much your promises are worth."

Daniel gripped the rope in one hand and sawed the remaining threads through.

The cut rope slipped easily from his hold. Their chair rocked forward, then pitched back, bobbing furiously on the stopped cable. Klaus's scream twisted around them as he fell, torquing at Liam's nerves, and then stopped abruptly in a wet slurp several dozen meters below.

Liam looked toward Daniel, but he was staring straight ahead, into the looming trees, the moonless night.

"Should we check . . . ?" Liam asked, after a long minute that stretched out like eternity. It felt like the moment between the frequency waves, when the universe itself began to fray, worlds and worlds caught in a held breath as they waited to see what new realities would spin forth.

"No." Daniel's throat bobbed as he swallowed. It was pale, exposed. Liam felt the urge to press his fingers to it, feel Daniel's frantic pulse. "If he's not dead yet, he will be soon enough."

They were both silent a moment longer, then without a word, Daniel reached for the override switch and the chairlift lurched back to life.

After they got back to the top of the lift, they drove to a ski chalet around the backside of the hill, the small cluster of wooden huts like gravestones in the silent night. None of the cabins were lit; the heavy stillness of an early fall night tucked around them like wet wool. They worked together quietly, side by side, to scavenge food and bedding, then decided to risk lighting a small fire in the fireplace as the night turned sharp and cool.

"You want something to eat?" Liam asked, holding out the can he'd turned up. He frowned at the illustration of jellied eels on the label. "Well, maybe not *this* specifically, but—"

Daniel smiled softly at him. "I've got some potatoes from Helene's we can boil. I'm ready to break my fast, anyhow."

"Never thought I'd go wild for boiled potatoes, but you've got me there," Liam said.

They found a pot in the kitchen and made their way back to the living room to cook. "So, according to Klaus back there, sounds like the garage is our best way in. Like Siegen." Liam chattered, anxious, as he gathered bedding and pillows while Daniel busied himself at the fireplace, heating a coffee kettle. "We can find Kreutzer's office, nab the book, and get the hell out."

"But Kreutzer knows your face. Pitr too."

"I have ways around that," Liam said.

"I thought it was too dangerous for you to use the shadows now. Won't they alert Pitr, or something?"

He hesitated. Pitr's voice, echoing in the woods. "This is too important not to take the risk."

Daniel headed toward him with a mug of coffee. The smile on his face, both shy and hopeful, set a fire in Liam's gut.

"You're a goddamn angel," Liam said, as he took a sip.

Daniel closed his hand around Liam's on the mug's handle, then let his lithe fingers trace down Liam's wrist, along the divot of his elbow.

Liam held his breath, afraid to startle him away. Daniel's fingers fluttered hesitantly at Liam's side before dropping.

"Kreutzer doesn't know my face," Daniel said. "At least, not as well."

The coffee turned cold in Liam's mouth. "No. Hell no. We do this together. It's safer this way."

"You're right." Daniel worried his lower lip with his teeth. "I just . . . I don't want you to get hurt."

"And I don't want *you* to get hurt. So I guess we're even."

Liam tipped Daniel's chin up with his fingertips. He wanted to burn everything about Daniel into his mind—the flinty dart of his eyes, the plushness of his lower lip, the dark curl that lingered over his brow no matter how many times he shoved it back. No matter what became of Liam, he wanted to remember this, and how giddy it made him feel.

"Daniel . . ." Liam murmured, throat tight. *Please don't be afraid for me,* he wanted to say. *I can still control this darkness. My days of being powerless are gone.* But he wasn't willing to tell Daniel any more lies.

They sank down to the couch, and Liam tossed back the rest of the coffee. Daniel's hand found his once more, its weight a comfort, something solid he could hold tight. Daniel shifted, drew in a breath to speak.

"I need to see this through." In his lilting accent, it sounded so grave, so official.

Liam turned to face him. "Daniel," he murmured. His fingers slid into Daniel's hair, cupped the shell of his ear. How had everything felt like a struggle with Pitr, and with Daniel, it came so naturally? "Daniel, I want—"

Daniel captured his hand and dragged it to his mouth. Chapped lips brushed along the ridgeline of his knuckles. The faintest nudge of a tongue along the seams between his fingers. Something in Liam's chest caved: an avalanche he had no chance of holding off.

Time worked differently in these cursed woods. He'd spent months and months with Pitr, but never shed the feeling he was taking a stressful exam; three days with Daniel, and already they'd built a lifetime of trust and familiarity. Liam already wanted another lifetime of it more.

Daniel's mouth rounded on the tip of Liam's finger, and Liam whimpered.

"Shit." Liam forced himself to sit up straight. "Wait. I'm sorry. I need to tell you something. Before we . . ." Liam cleared his throat, very much hating his conscience. "I feel like you deserve to know what we're facing . . . and why."

Daniel's grip loosened on his hand. "Pitr, you mean."

Liam nodded slowly. He squeezed Daniel's hand once, trailed his index finger down the center of Daniel's lips, then forced himself to pull his hand back.

"He and you . . . you were . . . lovers."

If only that had been true. The words had danced on Liam's lips plenty of times, but he'd been too scared to voice them. His earlier admission to Daniel had been the closest he'd ever come to saying it out loud. "Something like it, anyway."

Slowly, Daniel unwound at Liam's side. Liam turned to stare at him. He'd never imagined he could fall for someone again, not after Pitr's casual cruelty that later turned to viciousness. Liam couldn't put his heart out there on a string for someone to use like a leash. He needed to maintain control—not just of the shadows, but of himself.

In Daniel's eyes, he found softness. Not judgment. "Whatever you have to say, it doesn't change who you are right now. I see you."

"Jesus Christ, I wish I could bottle you up and drink you for liquid courage." Liam shook with a frantic laugh. Daniel's whole face went red, and Liam couldn't stop himself—he kissed that infuriating curl. The thrill it sent down his own arm, straight to his heart, would have to be enough to give him strength.

"Let me start from the beginning."

Liam explained about his father and the rages that threatened to shred their apartment, rages that Liam was too small and weak to stop. How the first time he grabbed his father's fist on its path to his mother's face, and the beating that followed, should have warned him off. But Liam had never been any good at taking a hint.

Even after Liam's mother had kicked his father out, it didn't help. Liam would never be able to save her.

He told Daniel about how the last two years passed like a knee pressing into his back. All the doctor's appointments he could barely afford, and the three jobs he juggled just to manage that. The late, late nights deep in the stacks to keep on top of his classwork and hang on to his scholarships. The mocking jeers of his supposed peers, who regarded him like a sideshow attraction: the little boy who thought he was a man. His voice cracked well into his second semester at Princeton; he wasn't gangly, or short, but he never seemed to fill out his suits properly all the same. He spoke of his papers that mysteriously went missing, the books he needed that always seemed to be checked out, and the thousand little taunts and slights that added up until they were a morass, threatening to pull him under.

Why shouldn't he have seen Pitr as a life preserver tossed out to a drowning man? Secrecy was just the price he paid to have one good thing, one moment of solace in this world.

But after that night in Pitr's room, the world grew darker, more hateful, more afraid—and Pitr with it. Liam had craved control—true control—for as long as he could remember. He craved it so much that he couldn't see how badly Pitr wanted it, too, until it was too late.

Pitr thought the realm they sought demanded sacrifice. Not himself, of course—Pitr was too vain for that—but he theorized, correctly as it turned out, that the frequencies Liam's oscillators generated weren't enough. The shadows required blood. They demanded pain. A rift between the universes exacted a heavy toll, and Pitr was clearly ready to pay it, whereas Liam was not.

Into winter and the cold comfort of the new year, Pitr haunted Liam like a specter, desperate to persuade him it was worth the cost. "We can forge an opening to the shadow world," Pitr said one night, catching him in the bathroom where they'd first embraced. "All we need is a sacrifice."

"No. I won't do it."

"But, Liam." Pitr paused. "Not everyone deserves to live."

Still, his voice was a low rumble that brought Liam's nerve endings to life. And because he knew Liam too well, because Liam had given him everything while Pitr had parceled out only the slimmest glimpses of himself, he knew just the toehold to seize in Liam's thoughts.

"Some people aren't deserving of life, Liam. Do you think your father is?"

Liam swallowed back a growl. His father was not up for discussion. "Why? Why do you want this so badly?"

Pitr laughed. It was his same laugh as always, but only now did Liam hear how cruel it had always been, how superior he thought himself. "Because it's there. I have the knowledge, the power to take it. The power Sicarelli tried to claim before the creatures on the other side beat him back for his weakness. I am not weak. And I will not be beaten."

Footsteps in the hallway. They both dove into separate bathroom stalls as someone else entered.

Liam's mind whirred over Pitr's words as the intruder went into the third stall. No—he couldn't do it. He wanted to access the shadow realm and the control it offered because he wanted to *stop* people from being hurt, not because he wanted to hurt them. Even monsters like his father, who was toiling away at the docks under a new name, last he'd heard; his German-American Bund pals had bailed him out after a scant few months in Riker's. Liam had done everything needed to keep his mother safe. He kept the curtains pulled tight around their new life in New Jersey. As much as he hated the man, not even Kieran Doyle deserved to pay the price Pitr was suggesting.

So Liam tried to tell himself.

The toilet in the third stall flushed; the intruder moved toward the sink and turned the faucet on.

"*Think about it,*" Pitr whispered from the next stall.

Liam flew out of the bathroom and didn't look back.

He'd thought the matter was settled, and for a few months, at least, it was. As he carefully avoided Pitr, the spring of 1942 broke over Princeton like a storm, flooding the campus with pollen, grim news from the African and European fronts, and panic as finals approached. Army recruiters set up camp outside every lecture hall, touting the fast track to officer candidate school a college boy was guaranteed—and wasn't that better than waiting for the draft? Liam considered it, but he was set to graduate with his bachelor's and start his master's work immediately after. He wanted that, he was certain, yet he couldn't muster the requisite enthusiasm or relief his classmates seemed to feel. Pitr's unsettling presence throughout the winter had now become a heavy absence, a black hole.

Liam spent his nights in the laboratory when he couldn't pick up extra hours at the library. He tinkered endlessly with his stupid oscillators, those two curved metal columns that came up to his chest to generate the harmonic frequencies he sought. They should be working, if his calculations were correct. He was sure he'd unearthed the correct frequency. He'd mathematically proved the other universe's existence, living and breathing beside him like a stranger standing too close at the bus station. But no matter how hard he tried, he couldn't bridge that gap. Couldn't find a way to cross over. And he was growing increasingly worried about exactly what might happen if Pitr gained access first.

Liam had just plugged in the oscillators and had begun to power them up for another futile attempt when he became aware of someone watching him from the door.

"Is that it?" Pitr asked, and Liam nearly jumped out of his skin.

"Christ. What're you doing here?" Liam's grease pencil slipped out from behind his ear. "I don't have anything to say to you."

Pitr stepped into the lab. As frightful as he'd looked that night in his room last winter, he looked even worse now. His hair hung in filthy clumps; sleeplessness was smeared under his eyes like oil stains. Liam could smell the musk of exhaustion and coffee on him from across the room. He looked like a balloon a week after the party ended, sagging and deflated.

"I've brought you something. A . . . a peace offering."

Liam took a step back, wishing he'd locked the door.

Pitr wheeled in a dolly, wheezing with the effort. A wooden crate rested on it, hastily hammered shut. It still smelled of fresh-cut pine, the cheap resiny kind used at questionable warehouses.

The ones by the Brooklyn docks.

"No." Liam stepped backward until he pressed up against one of the oscillators, their dual posts nearly as tall as he was. Cold sweat trickled down his spine. "Pitr, no—"

But Pitr had produced a snub-nosed pistol from within his coat. "The machine, Liam. Turn it on." He bared grimy teeth in a desecration of a smile. "You know the frequency."

Had Pitr been keeping tabs on Liam all spring long?

Liam clenched his jaw to keep his teeth from chattering. This was a nightmare, brought on by stress and exhaustion. Any minute now he'd wake up in his rented room, alarm screeching, ready to start another early morning at the bakery before rushing to his first exam—

Pitr aimed the pistol at Liam's feet. *"Now."*

Heart thudding in his ears, Liam fired up the oscillator.

For a few seconds, nothing but a dull hum filled the dank basement air. Then the space between the two oscillator posts stretched apart, like taffy being pulled. Moments became separated by the rotating thud of the ultradense sound waves. Liam felt his body stretching and contracting with each oscillation, atoms realigning, his thoughts syncing with that grim metronome. Between the two oscillator posts, the air shimmered and warped. This was as close as he'd gotten without attempting the blood offering Pitr had mentioned before, this fogged-glass glimpse at the other world: no real hint of what lay on the other side.

Pitr's face contorted with a hideous grin that made Liam's stomach flip over. How had he ever had feelings for this monster? He was seeing Pitr for the first time now, all his scholarly airs and sly confidence flensed away. All that was left were the cruel sinews of his ambition, an ego that couldn't be satisfied.

"Yes." Pitr's smile was oil-slick. "I knew you'd figure out how to reach it eventually."

Liam took a step back, hand fumbling behind him for his tools, but Pitr wasn't as distracted as he looked. The gun's barrel followed his every move.

"Don't get clever. It doesn't suit you."

Liam held his empty hands in front of him. There had to be some way he could get the gun out of Pitr's hands—but every time he latched on to the beginnings of an idea, the oscillators rolled over again with an agonizing thump, chasing all the thoughts from his head.

Pitr yanked the dolly closer to the line of air between the oscillators and kicked at the flimsy pine boards. "Now for our sacrifice."

Even knowing what was coming, Liam's head swam, revulsion and terror and hatred hitting his bloodstream all at once like poison. And just a little, despite himself, the sweet hint of anticipation.

Pitr ripped the torn boards away to reveal the crate's contents. Kieran Doyle was curled up inside, densely bound with rope, attempting to shout through a tight gag. The stench of alcohol and sweat hung around him in a thick miasma; Liam could barely see his face between the filthy chunks of strawberry-blond hair. But it was him. The monster in Liam's nightmares. The tyrant who almost turned their room in Hell's Kitchen into a slaughterhouse. The hateful coward who'd robbed the light from his mother's eyes.

And here he was—just a sad, pitiful lump, dirty and destitute, bound and gagged in a basement. Suddenly, all Liam wanted to do was laugh—at this sad, miserable fuck and at himself, for letting the man rule his thoughts and *life* for so long.

He wasn't worth the shit stains their landlady's dog left on the carpet.

"A worthy sacrifice, don't you think?" Pitr asked, snapping Liam's attention back. "No one to miss him. A perfect vessel of sickness and uselessness and rage. We'll transmute him into pure misery and pain to open the gates."

Could Liam do it? Kill him. His own father. Exact vengeance for his mother, for the twenty years of terror this man had wrought on her. The question wasn't whether he deserved it—because Liam knew he did. What Liam didn't know was whether it was worth whatever gruesome taint the act would leave on his soul. Whatever further darkness it might invite in.

But Pitr knew him too well.

"Come on, Liam Doyle. Take back your name." Pitr smiled. "Take control."

He'd always known just what strings to pull.

Liam shuffled forward until only the thin pane of throbbing air separated him from his father. Kieran's eyes were rolling wildly, but when they settled on Liam, his whole demeanor shifted. Hatred burned deep in those glassy eyes. From behind the gag Pitr had tied around his mouth, he tried to spit out a few epithets, and Liam was glad not to have to hear them.

"Kill him. Free yourself." Pitr extended a knife toward Liam through the thick haze of shimmering air. Its handle was ornate; its blade curved. "Take control."

Liam's breath caught in his throat. *Control.*

His fingers spread wide, ready to grasp that knife. Was it wrong to kill monsters? No. Far from it. Nazis, tyrants, abusers—every last one deserved nothing but pain. His father among them. He deserved a muddy ditch and his own vomit clogging his throat, or a bullet in the base of his skull from any number of the cut-rate mobsters he owed.

But for Liam to do it? Now, like this? This wasn't control. Not like Pitr claimed.

Forever binding himself to Pitr and his father with this act was no freedom at all.

"No."

Liam dropped his hand. His father snorted, twitched.

With a snarl, Pitr raised his pistol toward Liam's chest, his grip shaking. Liam felt his muscles tense, as if that would do him any good. But then Pitr shrugged and lowered the gun.

"Suit yourself."

The first shot shattered Kieran's kneecap. His scream filled the air, rolling with the rise and fall of the machine's oscillations. The second shot tore open one of his palms. Blood gushed onto the laboratory floor until it ran and met that wall of warped air, and then it flowed up along the surface of the air—weightless—swirling in the space between the oscillators.

"Look." Pitr had to shout to be heard over Kieran's grunting and the machines. "It's working."

As the blood tinted the ribbon of air red, it began to shift. That stretched space—that was the only way Liam could describe it—began to hint at something beyond the strange shimmer. It looked like a membrane pulling thin, hinting at something on the other side. A landscape—shapes like trees, like leaves, too dark and muddled—

"I told you. All we needed was some pain."

Pitr reached down with his knife then and began sawing at Kieran's ear, each creak of splitting cartilage loud as gunfire. Something chattered within the darkness between the oscillators, and Liam imagined a thousand hungry, gnashing teeth.

And then the gnashing was inside him—it was thrumming in his veins. His heart beat faster and his breath quickened as he absorbed his father's screams, his pain. Liam felt heavier, like his bones had turned to lead. An energy raced inside him, cracking and pulsing with a heartbeat all its own.

The dark energy he knew existed, on paper and pencil scratch, was here. He felt it. He welcomed it. And the more Liam focused on it, the more he felt, with certainty, that he was pulling it *into* himself.

It sighed and shivered inside him—as though with relief. Like coming home.

Pitr must have sensed it, too, because he stopped the torture to look up at Liam with a glare. "What are you doing—No!"

Pitr lunged forward, crossing directly in front of the space between two worlds. He reached for Liam, but the gap pulled at him, its force magnetic. It sucked away Kieran's blood from Pitr's hand—feasted on his screams—

Then Pitr's eyes turned black and the shadows deepened across his face. He was harnessing the power too.

"Yes. It's mine." A chorus of voices undercut Pitr's as he spoke, skittering like spiders. "Mine. I gave it the sacrifice—*I* deserve the power—"

The darkness throbbed in Liam's mind, whispering all the ways he could use it to make Pitr pay. Liam drew his hands apart and imagined the energy stretching out between his palms, tugging it back from Pitr's grasp.

"No! It's mine!" Pitr shouted.

He whirled to his captive and slammed the dagger into Kieran's chest. Liam's father groaned. It shredded at Liam's eardrums. But it fueled him, too. All the torment this pitiful man had wrought on him and his mother. All of Pitr's manipulations, all of the lies and heartbreak and subterfuge and denial. Liam drank it all up, even as he sensed Pitr doing the same. Binding that energy. Drawing it into himself.

But he couldn't hold on to it forever. He needed to unleash it.

Pitr's eyes widened. He sensed what Liam was about to do. They were playing tug-of-war with the very fabric of time-space, the dark energy trickling through the hole between two worlds. He staggered forward, even as his legs stretched, swirling deeper into the hole. "It's mine!"

But Liam found it was easy to command the energy that it was now inside him. As natural as walking, breathing. He'd been born for this. He knew how to take control. And the darkness promised him power far greater than Pitr could handle—the things it promised—

He thrust his hands together, compressing a mass of shadows into a ball. Relativity. Fusion. Explosion.

The shadows tore out of Liam as though he were casting a net. They spun around Pitr, coiling up his limbs. Pitr was screaming—even over the hungering oscillators, Liam could hear it—but as the shadows engulfed him, they stuffed the sound right back down his throat and slithered inside.

Pitr staggered into the undulating wall, the tear between the worlds. His hand still gripped Kieran by his bonds, though Kieran was slurping his last breaths through a punctured lung. Liam should feel something, he should feel relief or anger or regret—but all he felt was a dark smile bubbling out of him. Power coursing through him. Limitless.

The tear stretched wider. Inviting. After all, this was what the shadow world had been waiting for. A suitable offering. The perfect sacrifice.

But Liam had acted too fast. He'd expended all the energy at once. He dropped to his knees, the sudden weightlessness leaving him dizzy, nauseated. The other world had gotten what it came for—and now it was retreating, leaving Liam empty and cold.

"*You'll pay*," Pitr wheezed—

And then the portal closed up around him.

Too much, it had been too much all at once. The air where the portal had opened condensed, thickening. The oscillators screeched and snapped and pulled inward from their moorings, the gravity of the collapsing rift between worlds sucking them in. They crashed against each other, their whirring noise rolling frantically, then they fused together as the noise wound down, like a top losing its rotational momentum.

Liam sat back on his heels with a strangled cry. Pitr, his father, the blood, the gun, the dagger—it was all gone. And with it, the energy he'd harnessed from the other world.

But it had worked. Liam laughed, tears burning his eyes. Pitr had been right after all.

Oh, God. It was real. The shadow universe he'd only glimpsed in the space of his calculations, in the decimal-point error of his numbers. It was terrifyingly, undeniably real—just on the other side of reality, waiting for the right frequency.

And just like Pitr said, it was hungry for their pain.

CHAPTER NINETEEN

PHILLIP

The cabin's door creaked open on dry hinges. The whole room was a vacuum, Phillip's and Rebeka's and Simone's breaths collectively held, their muscles taut as stretched springs as they waited for whoever was on the other side. From the corner of his eyes Phillip spotted Simone, her arms perfectly still as she kept her rifle ready.

A man reached into the room and flicked on the light switch.

"Don't move," Simone growled in German. "Or I feed bits of your fascist brain to the wolves."

The complete bewilderment on the man's face morphed as he took in the scene before him. The Algerian woman training a rifle on him. The Black boy clutching a tool kit. The Jewish girl huddled under wool blankets. His lip curled up, and his eyes bulged into something like parody.

"What in the hell are you mongrels doing in my home?" he bellowed in German.

Simone pulled back the cocking mechanism with a resounding click—

A woman with her wheat-colored hair in perfect plaits beneath a knit cap. "Sigi, what's the matter?" she purred as she ushered two tiny, flawlessly adorned children into the cabin's doorway. The youngest of them, the boy, stumbled forward, heedless of his father's outstretched arm until he caught sight of Phillip and stared.

"Mama," the little girl said. "Monsters."

Simone's grip on the rifle slipped. *Dammit, Simone.* Now wasn't the time for her to discover some shred of sympathy for fellow humans. The kids weren't a threat, not yet, but if the woman ran to summon the Gestapo, or—or—

"Yes, they are monsters, Fritzi." The mother snatched her little boy by the straps of his lederhosen. Yes, Phillip realized with a groan, he was wearing honest-to-Kraut lederhosen over a ribbed sweater. "Go back to the car. Fetch Mama her—"

"No one's going anywhere," Simone said, and turned the rifle toward the little boy.

"Go, Fritz," the man Sigi—Sigmund, maybe—urged. "Don't listen to these *people.*"

"Papa—"

"Don't you do it," Simone said.

"*Go!*"

Fritzi took off running. Simone lined up her shot. Her finger pressed down on the trigger—

Then with a snarl of frustration, she stopped herself. "Khara," she swore under her breath.

Sigmund laughed, the sound harsh as gravel. "You're all the same. Vicious like animals, but weak-willed." He took a step into the room, even as his wife shot out her arm to stop him.

"I don't kill children. Unlike you," Simone replied.

"But you've lost your bluff now. Do you even have bullets? Let's see."

He reached for the barrel of the rifle to snatch it away, but Simone yanked it back. Swung it around to crack the side of his head. As he reeled from the blow, she brought it up to aim again, the woman screaming, until—

"Stop," little Fritz shouted. He'd reappeared in the doorway wielding a pistol, the weapon comically large in his shaking hands. With a smirk, his father took it from him and clapped him on the shoulder.

Phillip's left hand was still under the woolen blanket. He had half an idea forming. Carefully, he stretched his fingertips for the sole of his boot and started to slide open the panel.

"Well done," Sigmund cooed to his son. "Now. Help me tie them up."

The family moved into the room. Again the man snatched Simone's rifle by the barrel and this time managed to yank it out of her grip.

"Stand up," the woman barked.

Reluctantly, Simone and Rebeka got to their feet. Rebeka's shoulders were squared, but her hands trembled as she moved them behind her back. *Shit.* Phillip was almost done. He'd eased the components out of their hiding place—he just needed to fit them into the receiver—

"You too, Blackie. Stand up!"

Phillip palmed the components into his jacket sleeve and stood, clutching his pack. It was just inside the main pouch, it would take him five seconds—

"Mama," the little girl said again, stepping into the cabin to tug at her mother's wool trousers. "*Monsters.*"

"Yes, darling, I know. But we'll take care of them, the Gestapo will take them away—"

Though it was the last thing he wanted to do, Phillip turned his attention back to the open door with a heavy sickness in his gut.

Monsters. The little girl had no idea.

Red eyes blinked from the darkness beyond the cabin steps. Prowling, circling. He might not have noticed them if he didn't know what he was looking for. Phillip risked a hasty glance at Rebeka, whose hands were shaking.

Well. He swallowed. Maybe the monsters would offer a quicker death than the Gestapo.

The woman spun Rebeka around to fasten her hands behind her back, and Rebeka faced Phillip. She mouthed three syllables at him, twice, to be sure he caught it. Jaw tight, he dipped his chin slightly to confirm.

Frequency.

At Sigmund's feet, tendrils of shadow slithered into the cabin. Phillip forced himself not to look at them. The woman finished binding Rebeka's hands and turned toward Phillip.

"They'll have fun with you," she sneered, pulling out a fresh braid of rope.

"Not as much as we will," Phillip replied.

Her arrogant expression wrinkled for the briefest moment.

Then the screaming started.

Whump. Sigmund hit the floor face-first as the tendril of darkness yanked him backward. His daughter shrieked, banshee-like, but didn't take his hand as he grabbed at her. The woman turned away, eyes widening, and Phillip plunged his hand into his satchel.

Where was his goddamned jammer? As soon as the monsters were done with the Germans, he had to try—he'd have to hunt for the right counterfrequency to lock them out. But even as he thought through the plan in his mind, he saw all the points of failure, the unlikeliness of success—

Rebeka closed her eyes and rocked back and forth on her heels. If she was communing with the shadows again, he hoped it was working.

Crunch. Sigmund's shouts went abruptly silent with the gnash of bones and teeth, replaced by the screams of his family. Phillip forced himself to look: the first monster stood in the cabin's doorway now, grinning at them with a blood-slick smile. It sucked down Sigmund's headless body with a fierce slurp.

"Anytime now, Rebeka," Simone shouted, stepping backward from the monster. It turned flaring nostrils toward her, sniffed deeply . . .

Then swiveled its focus toward the German woman.

Something bumped up against Phillip's leg, and he looked down to find Sigmund's bitten-off head staring back up at him. Bile roiled in the back of his throat. But it was the reminder he needed to get to work—

"You devils have done this! With your—your wicked magic and your—"

The German woman had no time to finish before the monster raked her into one massive, multijointed claw and held her aloft. One talon punctured straight through her lungs, dissolving her words into a damp gurgle.

Finally Phillip found the jammer and tore it free of his pack. He snapped the crystal into place and rattled the box until the dimmest frequency came in. *Come on, you know how to do this.* He clicked through the frequencies, but his invention was designed for portability, not fine-tuning. Before him, the monster took its time feasting on the woman while its companions munched on the Reichsjugend.

There—he found one frequency that made a curious shimmer in the air. It was almost as if, for one second, the monsters were a chalk drawing on a blackboard that someone had smudged. But then they righted themselves and turned, snarling.

Oh, you felt that, didn't you? Phillip spun back to the frequency, and the same effect happened. But it wasn't enough. Liam had told him that the frequency opened the rifts, so countering that frequency should push it closed again. Right? If he was going to force them back into their realm, he'd need more power.

"You found it," Rebeka said, locking eyes with him.

Phillip winced. "I don't have enough juice. I need a bigger generator. I need—"

"A car?" Simone asked, peering out the cabin window.

Phillip's face fell. Yes, a V-6 engine ought to do the trick. But there were at least two monsters between him and that horsepower. "They're blocking it—"

"I can buy you time," Rebeka said.

"Please—don't—"

But she was already facing down the first monster, now finished with its feast. It crouched back on powerful legs, watching her with a cruel smile on its gore-smeared face. Rebeka extended one hand to it, and it took all of Phillip's willpower not to scream at her.

"Trust me," Rebeka said softly. She averted her gaze from the monster just long enough to meet his eyes. "Like I trust you."

And then Rebeka collapsed to the floor, her heap of a body shimmering—as if caught between both worlds.

Phillip froze. "Rebeka!" he shouted, despite the monsters—half a dozen of them now—despite everything. "Rebeka, please—"

The cabin rumbled like the beating of a thousand wings. The air around them turned dense and scraped at his arms.

Go, the monster roared, its voice multitonal, a frightful chorus. The word was coming from the other monsters' mouths now, too. *Go, Phillip. Hurry!*

Phillip gathered up his tools and raced for the cabin door.

CHAPTER TWENTY
REBEKA

Rebeka both was the monsters and wasn't them. She could move them like marionettes, but they bobbed and writhed on strings in ways she couldn't control. They were her eyes and nose and ears, but she was never fully in command of them as she straddled the two worlds, two times, two lives, and maybe more.

The man she'd encountered before in the shadow realm hadn't found her yet. Maybe he didn't know she was here. Maybe by staying halfway in her own world, she could evade him—but then again, he might be busy with something else.

She shuddered, not wanting to imagine what that something else might be.

In truth, the shadow realm was a lot less frightening this time. It wasn't a dead place; the plants writhed with their own breath, and the drone of insects and other nameless creatures spoke to a vastness she couldn't begin to comprehend. These ruins were where entire civilizations had once thrived, in the past the other being had shown her. The shadow energy sustained this dark place and gave it life with the same relentlessness as the sunlight in her own world. Apparently, that dark energy had been pulsing in her all along. And yet feeling it, accepting what it had given her . . . she felt brighter than ever.

She stumbled past another cluster of eerie ruins and thought of the faceless figure, the time it had shown her from before. Before humans had reached through the barrier and stolen some of the shadow for themselves. She remembered the figure approaching her, reaching inside her head as if passing judgment. Had it trusted her not to betray them like Sicarelli did? It must have known she was unlike that angry man who prowled the shadowlands now, conquering some of the more predatory monsters. The being had shown Rebeka for a reason. It trusted her to be better.

Just because she had an affinity for that shadow energy, drew it to herself unintentionally, magnetically, didn't make it hers. She hadn't asked for it, no more than the shadow energy had asked to be used. They were stuck together, along for the vengeful ride.

Look, Rebeka. Wasn't it what their mother was always telling her? (Had always *told* her, she corrected herself.) *Look at what's in front of your face. Stop trying to get ahead of yourself—you'll only trip over your own feet.*

It was true. As a little girl back when they'd attend synagogue on the High Holy Days, she was always squirming, waiting for the closing prayer, eager to rush out and feel the cool Berlin air on her face, the possibilities of the empty night ahead like a gulp from a crystal mountain stream. By the time they banned Jews from attending movie theaters and concert halls, she'd already charted a different life for herself. Business school in Switzerland, accounting classes, all the ways she would take over their butcher shop and turn it into a bustling enter-prise, maybe somewhere other than the hateful streets of Berlin, their shop becoming a good thing instead of a leash that kept snapping her parents back.

But her visions weren't enough to stop the night of smashed win-dows, of their neighbors being marched through the streets like cattle. Their flight to Luxembourg hadn't been part of her plans. While their uncle tended his crops and Ari rolled up his sleeves to enjoy their new life, she felt ready to burst out of the too-tight cocoon of her skin. Every day she tried to formulate a new plan, bringing her parents news of a ship bound for America or signs that London was push-ing back the Blitz, and wouldn't it be better if they found something more permanent, somewhere they could truly begin again? She was so tired of being derailed, her plans thrown out of gear, so that sometimes she couldn't even see what was staring back at her from the darkness, from that humming aura that crowded her sight and tunneled her into another world . . .

She stopped, and breathed, and looked, and felt.

Humid air, swampy and fetid with the endless cycle of vegetation flourishing and dying and rotting and feeding life anew. A rumble in the earth, the steady percussive beat of giant feet or hooves or claws in the distance. *Look, Rebeka. Look and see what's watching you.*

She forced her gaze to lift.

In the distance, flickering. A faceless thing, a behemoth hunched down like a massive mountain, calling her, begging her to look. But her stomach tightened every time she tried.

The darkness shifted. Swallowed her. Became infinity.

It was like a pond, still and heavy all around her, punctuated only by the occasional distant drip of water that rippled outward through her thoughts. Dimly, she was aware of the shadow realm, of her world, and all those layers of possibility between them. What was she looking at? Why had the shadows guided her here?

Look.

The faceless figure was beside her again, its countenance solemn and lowered. That pressure in her mind steered her forward, toward a broken circle of stones.

As she stepped into them, they lit up, like a spotlight piercing a dark stage. The air around them warped. She was seeing this land's past; she was seeing her world's present, and they were all entwined.

Look. If you take too much darkness, this is what you will become.

The sight shifted again until she was peering back into her world through a darkened scrim. But she was no longer in the cabin. The shadows had ushered her somewhere else. A pathway winding through lonely forests, shuttered houses. A castle's tower on the hill.

She moved across rain-slick cobbles toward the shaft of light until she reached a stone archway. Not rough and wild like the shadow realm— human hands had built it. The spotlight, she saw now, was streaming down into the room beyond the arch, filling the chamber within.

She rested her hand on the archway and stopped. There was something too ritualistic about this room's design. It was bell-shaped, rising up toward a round opening with an intricate carved design, a lattice, laid over it. Four sectors, four arms, bent and then bent and then—

Her throat felt swollen then, buzzing. A Hakenkreuz. When simplified, it became a swastika.

Menacing busts dotted the chamber's periphery, twelve in all. Faces in white marble that she only knew from grainy photographs in *Der Stürmer*. Stoic, as if they were Roman gods. No. Aryan ones. Arrayed around the central depression in the room as if awaiting a ceremony.

And in the center of the depression—a lectern. A book.

Look, Rebeka, the Faceless whispered. *Do not miss what is coming.* Another watery vision—a reminder of Sicarelli wrenching the life force away from the Faceless and its people. *What has already come for my kind.*

She reached the pool of light. A handwritten manuscript, bound in deteriorating leather, rested on the lectern, the light glinting off its gold-edged pages. The book's cover had been pressed with a symbol not unlike the Hakenkreuz, but this one had a dozen jagged arms, like rays of a sun, reaching out of a doorway. The Black Sun: some fabrication of Aryan lore teased out of half-remembered historiographies and misinterpreted wood carvings and ledgers that didn't get burned with witches. (Oh, how those Europeans did love a good witch hunt, a convenient bin for disposing all their woes.)

Dread bubbling in her stomach, Rebeka opened the manuscript cover.

Porta ad Tenebras.

Was this Wewelsburg Castle, then? It felt so different from war rooms and officers' banquet halls. As if the chamber had been prepared for this purpose. For ritual. For sacrifice.

The tower in her vision. It was leading her here—

She lifted her hands from the book, but they were already sticky with some thick substance.

"Isn't it beautiful?"

Rebeka nearly jumped out of her skin. She stepped back from the manuscript, and now she could clearly see: it was seeping shadows and blood, not unlike an infected wound. Opposite her in the darkness, a man stepped forward—the angry man who'd confronted her in the shadow realm last time. The one who'd commanded the demons, who wanted the shadow world for his own.

Dark eyes, loose dark curls—he looked a little like Daniel if she squinted, but there was something whittled and starved about him, like if he bared his teeth, there'd be nothing left of him but fangs. He wore round-lensed glasses perched halfway down his nose that made him look both old and young at the same time.

"Don't worry," he said. "You'll be right on time."

Movement from the manuscript caught Rebeka's eye. The blood had cleared from the open page, revealing an illustration. A black rectangle of ink, only now it was shifting—stretching wide. An arm took form, reaching up out of the page—grasping for her—

Rebeka stumbled backward. The arm connected to a complete figure—a man. But he was far from a normal-looking man. His skin was shrinking, pulling tight around his skull. Shadows wisped out of his nostrils and mouth as he laughed.

Please. This time it was the voice of the faceless ones. The civilization who'd lived in the shadowlands long ago, before Sicarelli desecrated their world. *Please. Our energy will corrupt your world as surely as yours corrupted ours. You cannot let this pass.*

Lightning crashed beyond the chamber, the hot white flash revealing the man was only a black void in the shape of a person. His smile was licked with flames.

"Don't be late," he said. "We need all the blood we can get."

But the vision was collapsing around her.

Rocks shook loose from the chamber walls. A bust of a senior Reich official tipped forward and smashed to the ground. The rubble fell straight through the man as if he were a ghost. In the distance, a pitch rose and fell, rose and fell on a frequency as it adjusted, dialed itself in.

"Wait—" Rebeka cried.

But it was too late. Phillip had done what she'd asked.

She awoke on the blood-strewn floor of the cabin.

"Rebeka!" Phillip rushed toward her. "Are you all right?"

She flung a hand out in front of her face, patting around until she could grip his shoulder. "Did you . . . What did . . ."

"I found it," Phillip said. "The frequency. I reversed the amplitude, sent the waves in a different direction, and it was just like—"

Simone clicked the safety on to her rifle, the sound riotously loud in the dead of night. "It was like they evaporated."

"It shut the rifts," Rebeka said.

That rectangle of blackness on the book's illustration, the hands grasping out. The gate between worlds.

The gate that Liam sought to fling open for good, with the aid of the book at Wewelsburg Castle. If these other men didn't open it first.

Rebeka looked into Phillip's eyes, so brimming with hope, with pride. Her fingers crept up to cup his cheek. Like her, he'd only ever meant to do what was best. Like her, he couldn't see the consequences

7

beyond his periphery—the men who lost their jobs; the family members she couldn't save for the one she did. It shouldn't have to be this way, this zero-sum game of fortune and failure. Light and shadow. They shouldn't have to trade darkness from their world with darkness from another. There had to be a force for good in this world, one that didn't carry with it an equally bad cost.

But it would mean staying firmly planted in their world. No more shadow. No more connection to the other world. No more control for Liam—or anyone.

"I saw the book. At Wewelsburg. The Nazis know what it can do. They are going to use it to open the bridge, and soon."

Phillip's eyes had lidded as he sank into her touch. Now they opened slowly. She felt his regret, too. She wanted nothing more than to savor this moment with him—to look and really see what was right in front of her.

But she knew what awaited them.

"My brother wants to get there first." Her next words sat heavy on her tongue. "But it will get him killed."

Simone had been rummaging through the German woman's discarded purse, but paused at that. "The book will kill your brother?"

"Yes—no. I'm not sure. The man who wields it. I've seen him in the shadow realm before. He's been hunting us."

Simone unearthed a packet of cigarettes. Her nose wrinkled as she read the label, but with a shrug, she fished one out and fetched her lighter from her bags. "And he will use its power for the Nazis, yes?"

Rebeka nodded. She didn't trust her voice any longer. "Liam thought he could use the book to stop them. But he was wrong. No one can. The shadows will corrupt us all if we keep the rifts open. We can't leave any sort of connection to the other world at all."

"So we must stop him instead of help him," Simone said with a heavy sigh.

"We can do it," Phillip said, though the words came out sluggish. "Cancel out the frequency. I'll need to make some adjustments, but—"

"Might as well leave now, then," Simone said. "I don't think we're getting any more sleep tonight as it is."

They packed up their things and left the bloodbath of the cabin behind. It was hard to see anything at all in the dead of night, but every time Rebeka closed her eyes, the behemoth was waiting: its surface ready to drink up all her fears. Its mountainous spine called to her, a siren singing her into the dark.

CHAPTER TWENTY-ONE

EVANGELINE

Stefan Neumann was a perfect gentleman, and he worked very hard to make sure everyone knew. Despite the shortages, Evangeline's desk was never devoid of fresh-cut flowers, though of course he didn't attach his name to their delivery. He arrived at Château á Pont Allemagne in a Mercedes polished until it gleamed like a wicked stepmother's enchanted mirror. He held the door for her always, black leather gloves freshly oiled beneath the sharp cuffs of his uniform. And when they arrived at Maxim's, he never used his rank to secure them the choicest table.

Not that anyone was going to deny anything to the Torturer of Troyes.

He waited until their lobster bisque had been brought out before he began that night's interrogation, a shift Evangeline noticed only because he paused after inhaling before he spoke. His hair gleamed a gentle chestnut under the gas lamps, parted on the side as she'd suggested instead of straight down the middle, and he looked at her with a gaze he must have believed was boyish. Charming. Men were always so pleased when women returned their smiles, not realizing those smiles were like the jabs of knives, forcing a hostage's response.

"I stopped by your office to bring you coffee this morning," he said. "We got a new shipment at the headquarters, and I wanted to share."

"What terrible timing!" Evangeline said, not missing a beat. "It must have been when I stepped out to fetch my sweater from home." She rubbed her arms and tried not to cringe at how dry and scaly they'd become without her usual regimen. "This weather's turned so suddenly, hasn't it?"

"A pity. You should tell someone where you've gone next time. I'd hate for you to miss something important."

Evangeline hovered over his phrasing longer than she should have. He couldn't possibly have hidden a double meaning in it. He couldn't possibly know what she did—the games she'd been playing since that awful April night. It was a casual remark, not the scalpel incision of a man trying to pry back her flesh. But even if it was . . .

She played it casual too, smiled prettily, and sipped her bisque.

"Well?" Stefan asked, pushing his emptied bowl away. "How was work, then? Once you were suitably warm."

She set down her spoon as well, her appetite quickly leaving her. "Oh, the usual. This province upset we haven't set aside enough rations for them, that politician running out of excuses to give the Americans."

"Such a precarious position you occupy," Stefan said. "You must still be friendly with our enemies, even as they snatch at lands that have willingly joined the Third Reich."

"Well, it's that damned de Gaulle, running his mouth on the radio." She batted her lashes. "Or so I've heard."

Stefan leaned over the table, and one hand fell on top of hers. He'd removed the buttery leather gloves, leaving only rough, caustic skin as it closed possessively over hers. His hands were always so dry. They had to be, she supposed. How many times a day did he have to scrub away blood? How many electrodes had he applied that morning to some poor Frenchman's balls? When he closed his eyes and hummed Wagner, was it to drown out the echoes of screams or to bolster them? She tried not to flinch.

"Please, my dear. Don't play foolish with me. Some men may appreciate it, but I am not one of them."

Evangeline's pulse rushed in her ears. He was exactly one of those men.

"You are a beauty, it is true. But it is not only for that that I admire you." His thumb scraped over her knuckles. "A Sorbonne woman, learning the art of diplomacy at her father's side for all her life. Such a rare intellect is unmatched behind a face like yours, hmm?"

It wasn't the Sorbonne, though, that had taught her what she knew. And it certainly hadn't been her father. She let a blush rise on her cheeks; Stefan didn't need to know the shape of the face that put it there. He didn't need to know about the girl who'd slapped her out of her stupor and compelled her to act. And he certainly didn't need to know *how* she acted—how once she'd started, she couldn't stop.

"I must confess. While I waited for you, coffee turning colder, I couldn't help but glance at some of the figures on your desk. It was the most curious thing, though—I could not seem to make them add up."

Something shattered in her chest, sharp as glass. "Are you sure you were reading them right?"

The waiter arrived with their next course, roasted leg of lamb, and Stefan reluctantly drew his hand back. Evangeline's stomach groaned at the mere smell. For all her father's scrabbling and bowing to the occupiers, they still never got meat at home. Not anymore.

"Well, perhaps I was not. Perhaps you can explain it to me, yes?" Stefan said. "I don't fully grasp your job with the Vichy."

Evangeline took a sip of champagne to buy herself a moment to think. She had a speech perfectly memorized for whenever a supervisor or colleague questioned her. She'd run through it a dozen times. But all that flew through her mind just then was a memory like a blade through her ribs: the look of betrayal on Simone's face, that moonlit face, those dark eyes so full of pain.

You were right, she wanted to scream at that girl. *I'm not cut out for this. I'll never escape this cage.*

She was trying. Dear God, she was trying. But it couldn't do anyone much good if she got herself killed.

"I must approve requisitions to the Reich's forces within the Occupied Zone." She smiled sweetly, the way a schoolteacher might while explaining simple arithmetic. "We have our inputs, we have our outputs. So I must allocate where it all goes."

"I understand that much." Stefan waved his fork, irritated, and a fleck of juicy lamb's blood splashed her dress. "I mean that they are asking for enough to feed our men and keep the electricity churning at the command posts, yet you are not requisitioning it for them."

"Well, that is the funny thing about occupations. A system that kept one country running cannot instantly be made to accommodate two."

The warning flashed in Stefan's expression, his genial mask gone in an instant. But she couldn't be cowed by him. If she backed down now, he'd know she was bluffing. It was better to keep up the indignant front, even if it meant a smack on the wrist, than retreat too easily and reveal it all for a sham.

"Well, I suppose you understand it better than I do," he said at last. "I just want to make sure nothing is being sent *awry*, is all."

Like entire warehouses full of rifles, dispersed to the Libération-Nord in the dead of night. Like half a shipment of grain bound for a German marshaling yard that wound up in the hungry village of Lyon. Like a careful inventory tracking how requisition requests moved across the Occupied Zone, the spikes indicating where German forces were building up and when, the sort of information that was so easily tapped out in Morse code and bounced off to London and even further.

It had been so easy. So easy to make the contacts she needed—so easy to misfile paperwork, lose correspondence, copy ledger pages. The hardest part had been convincing the Resistance network that she wasn't a plant. Spying was the easy part. Not getting caught was still a work in progress.

"If I could produce supplies out of thin air," Evangeline said calmly, "then I gladly would have done so by now."

"Funny you should mention that." Stefan spoke with his mouth full of meat bright as rubies. "There was a crate of Wehrmacht ammunition that turned up in a partisan bunker we raided yesterday."

"You see? It's hard enough trying to stretch our resources for our own forces without these idiot Resistance fighters picking off our transports." God, she hoped he couldn't hear her heart knocking against her ribs right now.

"Very few people are privy to those transport movements," Stefan said. "And you are one of them."

Evangeline bit back her first instinct—to deny it. Instead she rolled her eyes, like this was a fight they'd had many times. "You said yourself I'm too smart to play such a stupid game. Would I really let a Gestapo officer court me if I had something to hide?"

"Remind me," Stefan said, "how we met again, ma chèrie." He smiled, a scrap of flesh stuck around his left canine.

"You were in my office, questioning all our employees." *Looking for the person who'd given away troop positions for a secret convoy that the Brits promptly blew to bits.* "I was one of the last you called for questioning." *I'd gotten sloppy. Stupid. I'd been everything Simone thought I was, and worse. I couldn't even do the right thing properly.* "After you asked me about my daily routine, places I frequented, friends I kept, you asked me if I was seeing any fellows." *Easy enough to say no to* that.

His lips spread, slick with champagne, though she didn't dare believe the test was over. "I liked your demeanor. Your unwillingness to back down."

"I don't like having my work disrupted, that's all." Too late she thought to add, "And you *are* a rather fetching fellow, aren't you, mein Herr?"

God, her hubris. Thinking she could play a Gestapo interrogator for a fool. He'd offered her very little in the way of solid intelligence, anyhow—only the vaguest hints that she could send out, half of them likely to be traps. But men like him didn't know how to be denied.

"And you," he purred, "are a divine prize, indeed."

Her stomach curdled as she smiled at him. She'd strung him along this far. Meals, strolls through the Tuileries, nights at the opera watching that insufferable *Götterdämmerung*. But he was circling her closer and closer, and the closer he got, the more perilous everything became.

"It would be a dreadful shame if you got too clever for your own good."

Evangeline could practically feel Simone glowering at her when she answered, "I'm clever enough to know my place."

There was a commotion at the front of the restaurant then: Gestapo officers storming in from the rue Royale. The maître d' scrambled back, flattening himself against the Tiffany stained glass to keep out of their way. Numbly, distantly, Evangeline's thoughts blared with a warning: that it had all been an elaborate setup, a monthlong game, and now, *now* when she was finally about to get the information out of Wewelsburg that her network desperately needed, now that cells in Hallenberg and other command points were finally coming online, it was all going to crumble around her and crush her in the rubble. And yet she felt the oddest sense of peace, a buzzing sensation that permeated all of her limbs. Perhaps, if her remains were ever recovered, Simone might know that she'd been wrong. That Evangeline had tried to do right by her.

"Obersturmführer Neumann." The men stopped at their table, and the leader spoke: a lowly Scharführer by the look of his insignias. "You are required immediately."

It wasn't for her. Evangeline forced herself not to collapse with relief. They hadn't come for her.

But they must have captured someone else.

"A pity." Stefan wiped his mouth, tossed his napkin onto his half-full plate, and stood. "Perhaps you would like to accompany us, Mademoiselle Gaturin? You might find this enlightening. And afterward, we can have a drink and a laugh at La Coupole, ja?"

"Obersturmführer . . ." the soldier said, gaze darting toward Evangeline.

"Don't be silly. She's one of us. Isn't that right, Mademoiselle Gaturin?"

"Sieg heil," she said bitterly.

Stefan led her to the waiting Mercedes, and they rode through the heart of Paris, her Paris, to 84 avenue Foch. The Gestapo's counterintelligence headquarters. It was far too beautiful a building, steep Beaux Arts roofline, marble columns blossoming all over its façade, to be used for such an ugly purpose.

She kept her eyes to herself as they climbed to the fifth floor, though she couldn't help but note that the second floor housed an unusual amount of radio equipment. She'd long suspected too high a percentage of supposed Resistance chatter was coming from just such a source, but now, seeing it for herself, she felt ill all over again, wondering just who she'd been telling the wrong sort of secrets to.

How long would it take for her to break? Would she break even now as Stefan delivered this warning, this test?

"You can wait right here." Stefan ushered her into a cramped closet-size room where a metal grate offered a glimpse of the room beside them. She barely swallowed back her gasp at the sight of the man on the other side, bound to a chair, one eye swollen shut and ringed in blood.

Then Stefan entered the interrogation room and smiled at the man. "Possession of illegal radio electronic devices in addition to the crate of Wehrmacht ammunition we discovered on your property." He clucked his tongue. "You have been a busy man, Georges-Yves Sauvage. Let's find out what more you've been up to."

CHAPTER TWENTY-TWO
DANIEL

"You're always one to burn the ships," his mother once said. She was reading—always, her evenings filled with stacks and stacks of books in three different languages that disappeared at alarming rates—and this time, she was drumming her fingers against a copy of Homer's *Odyssey*.

Daniel frowned at her from behind the sheet music he was studying. "I don't know what you mean."

"You force yourself to move forward by taking away your escape route. Burning the ships you arrived in so you can't sail back to safety."

Daniel twiddled his pencil, uncomfortable with his mother's stare. Besides, she didn't have it quite right. He didn't sabotage things so he was forced to be brave. He just ruined whatever he touched.

The thing about playing viola was that not every great composer knew how to write for it. Sometimes you played Vivaldi, who teased beautiful harmonies out of every part, fitting them together like architecture, scaffolding. Bliss. Then other times you played Pachelbel. Wagner. Haydn, even. Those composers who didn't know what else to do with you, so they slapped you on an ostinato line, sawing back and forth like the metronome for other, more important roles.

In a sense, then, it was Pachelbel's fault that Daniel had time to stare off into space, to start memorizing the lines of the second violinist's face. Daniel was fourteen, and he was overflowing with yearning, fire in want of a wick.

Ernst—that was the second violinist's name in the youth chamber orchestra. Like the flamboyant late leader of the Sturmabteilung—the stormtroopers—Ernst Röhm, the other chamber orchestra members would darkly joke. In the windowless practice hall, Ernst was sunlight, never serious, never satisfied, wearing his superiority and glibness like a suit of armor. (Daniel didn't know, then, the difference between true light and a false, furiously stoked glow.)

He should have recognized the warnings. He should have done the calculations. The snarky utterings after their practice sessions as Ernst smoked and chatted with Liesl and Rudolf, the way they would cut their eyes toward Daniel and change their posture whenever he approached.

Sometimes Ernst was like all the rest, dropping hints that soon there'd be no place for Jews like Daniel in chamber orchestras or anywhere else. But not always. He could be funny—though usually when making fun of someone. He could be brilliant at the violin—but that, too, was often an effort to show up Liesl, to compete for her seat. Daniel didn't care. He was smitten, and Ernst paid him attention from time to time, not all of it bad. Daniel had so much to learn.

And so he burned the ships, not even realizing the torch that was in his hands.

It was after a performance at the Youth Activities Hall, the son of casual venue that people like Daniel weren't yet barred from. Their quartet had woven flawlessly together into the flow of Chopin, sweat dripping from their noses as they played, their breathing aligning into a single lung, in and out. Daniel had never felt closer to his quartet mates—never felt closer to a greater power. If they could play this well at the championship, the prize was surely theirs.

He was confident. It made him reckless and foolish.

At the beer hall afterward, he drank three beers, four; Liesl's cheeks burned bright red, and Ernst's voice carried with a resonance Daniel felt in his bones. He leaned into Ernst's words like they were a warm spring breeze. Liesl and Rudolf left to dance, and suddenly it was only Ernst and Daniel, facing each other, an unspoken vastness heavy and present between them.

"So," Ernst said. A smile played at his lips.

Daniel took a step toward him.

The corner was dark, shielded from everyone. Ernst's hand reached out, caught Daniel's elbow. When their eyes locked, Daniel saw—later he would swear he saw—Ernst had been waiting for this, too.

When they first kissed, it was with an exhalation of air. Then another. Ernst moaned—Daniel was certain of it. Leaned back, inviting Daniel closer.

But then Ernst was shoving him away and shouting and cursing, calling him every filthy name he'd ever heard, for Jews, for homosexuals, for soft boys with too much music in their hearts to wield a butcher's knife the way their fathers hoped. And of course Liesl and Rudolf manifested from out of nowhere at the commotion, they heard Ernst's furious shouts as he described Daniel's "attack," and in that moment, that look, that moan, Daniel lost everything. His love, his quartet, his songs.

In the end it didn't matter. They'd already taken his citizenship; next they forbade him from concert halls. The stormtroopers marched through the streets and shattered windows and dragged his neighbors away. The Eisenbergs abandoned their shop for Luxembourg. But because he hadn't been careful with his trust, because he hadn't fully grasped the world and all its dangers—he'd only made things worse.

It was his gift. More than music, more than murder. His gift was to destroy.

Liam was still holding his hand in the dark, cool silence of the chalet. He'd unraveled his story of Pitr's betrayal and the rift opening to accept its first sacrifice. It should have terrified Daniel; it should have warned him away from this angry, hungry boy. Instead it made him fall harder.

"You found out how to control it better, though. Afterward."

Liam hunched his shoulders. "I got better at opening rifts on my own—by digging my nails into my palm, mind you, not by any more sacrifices. I wasn't about to look for him, though. I'd seen how twisted the creatures on the other side were—some dark, horrible, hateful version of our world. Always figured that if Pitr survived, he'd end up that way."

"Hard to believe that's even possible," Daniel said grimly.

"They were . . . corrupted. Sicarelli stole their energy away, and it destroyed their civilizations. Left behind those hungry, ravenous monsters."

"And now Pitr has learned how to control them. He's working with Dr. Kreutzer to imbue soldiers with that energy. You're certain?"

Liam nodded slowly, his thumb making slow circles over the back of Daniel's hand.

"He was always obsessed with medieval mysticism, alchemy, all that nonsense. Convinced he was the greatest, that his breakthrough would make some kinda celebrity out of him. I'm sure he'd cozy up to all kinds of monsters to get the power he thinks he deserves—and that includes Kreutzer."

"You think Kreutzer helped him find a way out of the shadow realm?"

"He must've. Though someone like Pitr . . . he probably likes that world better than our own. There, he gets to play God." Liam shook his head. "There's no telling how much his time in the shadow realm has twisted him. And if Kreutzer's offering him the manuscript, a permanent way to link our two worlds . . ."

"You want the manuscript too, though."

Liam's thumb stopped. Shadows stretched along his face, and the air between them felt suddenly cold. "We need that energy. All of it. And if we're gonna have it, then someone has to be in control of the gate between the two worlds. Better me than him."

Daniel watched him for a moment. "Are you so certain it isn't the corruption driving you?"

Liam blinked. "I—no. I can resist it. I *have* been resisting it, I promise." He scratched at the stubble on his jaw. "And once the bridge is open—"

"But what if instead you were to close it for good?" Daniel asked.

"Seal the rifts, like you and Phillip talked about. So no one could access it. Not you, not them."

Liam was quiet a minute too long. "That isn't a choice for me."

Something unfolded inside of Daniel, like a tightly clenched fist finally forced to relax. He knew what it was to have no choice. He'd been working his way through the SS with every chance he got, but now they stood on the precipice of an incredible discovery. Kreutzer was sure to be there. Heinrich Himmler wouldn't want to miss such a momentous event. So many SS officers, ready and waiting . . .

His heart sank. It was a suicide mission, no matter what Liam thought. Especially if Pitr was there, ready to counter him. He couldn't send Liam to his death—he couldn't bear it.

This ambitious, mad, and maddening boy—he deserved to live. He didn't have to wallow in the darkness any longer, desperately seeking control. But for Daniel, the darkness was the only possible ending to his path. The wrong Eisenbergs had paid with their lives; he had to repay that debt. His debt, and no one else's.

"Don't you see?" Liam asked him. "I can harness the shadows and keep them out of the Nazis' grasp. I'm strong enough to do it. I can end the war." He looked hard at Daniel. "You'll be free."

There was no freedom for Daniel. But he smiled, the pain of it sharp. Liam didn't have to know what it would cost.

"Daniel," Liam breathed. He swallowed, the sound so loud Daniel felt it like a blow. Liam's lips were parted, and Daniel yearned to lean in . . .

"I'll fight for you, Daniel." His eyelashes fluttered as he glanced away. "I'll fight to keep you here. I know I'm obsessive, disastrous—"

Daniel laughed, throaty, and climbed onto Liam's lap. With a gasp,

Liam's arms fell open, inviting him closer. Daniel's knees bracketed Liam's hips as he settled onto his thighs.

"I'd rather fight along *with* you."

Liam started to laugh, but Daniel quieted him with his mouth. The sound dissolved into the cool darkness of the chalet until they were only two boys, kissing like it could hold off the dawn. Liam's lips were an embrace all their own; they were salt and sorrow and promises of something Daniel could never deserve. He kissed Liam tenderly, like he might fall apart if Daniel pushed too hard, but then Liam's hands came to his hips and held him firm. An anchor. A bond.

It didn't matter what darkness waited for him. He would have this, this moment of goodness and warmth, before farewell. He used to find release in music, then with a knife in his hand. Though the killing wasn't over yet, he could experience this, too: a gorgeous, soft, brilliant boy beneath him and a desperate rhythm in his heart.

Liam's lashes feathered across his cheek as he pulled back, looked up. "I want you," he whispered. "I want whatever you'll share with me. Your words. Your breath—"

Daniel slid his legs wider until their hips were flush and stifled a groan. Liam's body was burning, it was so sturdy beneath him, and it did horrible, wonderful things to him.

"I don't know what I'm doing," Daniel confessed. But he wanted Liam to absolve him. He wanted his forgiveness.

"Whatever you like," Liam breathed.

Daniel's fingertips skimmed Liam's chest, the buttons of his shirt. Their mouths drew them together again as Daniel worked the buttons open, kissing and gasping for air, kissing and pausing to look into

Liam's eyes, a question at each step. And each time, Liam nodded, biting at his swollen lower lip and stoking that fire fiercer in Daniel's gut.

Daniel kissed the pale skin of Liam's chest, his muscles, the fine golden hairs. God, he was beautiful, lean and powerful where Daniel, in less dire times, had been gentle and soft. He'd been embarrassed by his body then and by the feral thing he'd become, but as Liam stripped Daniel's shirt away, the sly grin on his face eased Daniel's fears.

"Just gorgeous," Liam murmured, then melted back as Daniel mouthed at his neck. Liam's back arched and he bucked forward with a groan as Daniel's hands teased lower, tugged and tugged until finally he worked Liam's belt free.

"Show me," Daniel gasped. "Show me everything."

"You're sure?" Liam's voice had twisted with yearning, but he held himself very still. Waiting.

"Yes." Daniel cupped Liam's face in his hands, thumbs grazing those strong cheekbones. "Completely."

Liam seized him by his hips and rocked forward, and—*oh.*

And slowly, fumbling, hands linked to steady each other, they found their way. They moved together, and Daniel quickly realized he'd had nothing to fear at all. Everything felt—right. Like he'd been wearing his shoes on the wrong feet until this moment, like before Liam, he'd never really known how to breathe. He'd fretted for nothing. It was the most natural thing in the world to love Liam Doyle, and the sensations Liam teased out of him, the things he whispered—

Daniel wanted more of this. He wanted it to never end.

Just for one night, he dared to believe in an after. Murmuring, kissing, caressing—Liam let him believe.

The fires would rage tomorrow. The dark depths of Wewelsburg Castle could wait. For tonight, at least, Daniel no longer felt the blade pressing into his back. He forgot, just for a moment, the sword dangling over his head. The world ablaze around them. He felt bliss, he felt this boy he was in love with beneath him, and the rest of the world fell away.

CHAPTER TWENTY-THREE

SIMONE

It was hard to remember now, but Simone had been thrilled she'd been offered the apprenticeship at the Pirripin brothers' atelier menuiserie off rue Tourneux. The French school system had no use for her once she became a teenager, and she'd worked hard to grasp a new purpose; long hours at the drafting table after vocational classes ended for the day, her hands stained from cyanotype paper and her pencil wearing a groove into the side of her finger, followed by work at the jigsaw and miter saw until sawdust filled her lungs. But she'd wanted it so badly. The vocational schools had taught her, had put her hands to use, when France itself would not. She ached to shape wood into something else altogether, leave her fingerprint in the slate-roofed palaces on the Champs-Élysées or in the mosques of her fragmented memories of Algiers.

She'd *wanted* something, like she feared she might never want something again.

But the atelier was nothing like what she'd expected. Jean-Pierre had no intention of giving his secrets away, and his brother,

Jean-Claude, no interest in advancing the career of an "invader," or so he said. She became little more than their errand runner, sorting lumber, haggling with vendors, organizing the desk drawers bursting with crumpled receipts that were the atelier's recordkeeping system.

So when they came to her with a new project—a project all her own, to manage unsupervised!—she was already looking for the catch.

She found it as soon as she reached the client's address.

"I want you to understand something, mademoiselle," Monsieur Gaturin drawled, steering Simone through room after room of saccharine opulence with an iron grip on her shoulder. "The bones, yes, the *bones* of Château à Pont Allemagne are flawless. I don't want you injecting your foreign . . . sensibilities . . . into this storied estate."

Simone could already spot several flaws in the "bones" of the monstrous mansion that, unaddressed, would lead to complete foundational collapse, but Monsieur Gaturin left her no opening to speak.

"I told those damned brothers this is to be a cosmetic repair only, to restore the carvings to their former glory and save us from this regrettable water damage. *You*, however, do not appear up to the task."

"I have completed all the requisite exams, monsieur." Simone's grip on her satchel tightened as she felt her old anger rising. Blistering the air around her. "But if you would rather let your home crumble around you—"

His nostrils flared like a cobra readying its strike. "Do you *dare* to speak back to me?"

"Papa. Are you tormenting the help again?"

Simone looked up to find the most stunning girl she'd ever seen standing in the peeling, crooked doorway. Not beautiful—not in the way of Château à Pont Allemagne, with its gold leaf and wooden parquet and elegant plaster—but *stunning*. Her aquiline nose stretched long on a long face and longer neck. Her arms floated, ethereal, at her sides, their pale creamy color framed by breezy teal sleeves. Her lips were brushed a pale rose that nevertheless looked riotous against her bone-white face. And the way her green eyes turned on Simone—

She was a Gorgon, Simone was sure of it. One look from those eyes and Simone felt made of stone.

"Do you see this?" Monsieur Gaturin cried, gesturing at Simone like he'd been delivered another man's suit. "They sent me a bloody Arab. A *girl*. Not even a woman, a *girl*, and they think somehow she can salvage the dining hall—"

"You're hardly in a position to judge someone's carpentry skills, Father." Simone slipped forward silently—she might as well have been floating. "And if you have such a strong dislike of Arabs, then maybe you should stop voting in favor of continued annexation."

"That's *quite* enough, Evangeline. This is not your concern." Evangeline—alhamdulillah, but the syllables even *tasted* good as Simone tested them on her tongue.

"The dining hall wouldn't need salvaging in the first place if your tasteless guests hadn't left the bathwater running while you occupied yourselves with—"

"Enough. And you dare to wonder why the Villiers' son fled from you the first chance he got."

"No, Papa. I don't wonder at all." Evangeline lifted her chin. "I only regret he didn't do it quicker."

Monsieur Gaturin's hand twitched at his side; Simone knew all too well the gesture of a man just barely restraining himself from delivering a blow. She leaned forward on the balls of her feet, ready to stop him forcibly if necessary. Damn whatever these rich people thought of her.

Evangeline paused in front of Simone and examined her in a way that felt both formal and gloriously, painfully intimate at once. "You are a carpenter with the Pirripin brothers? You can fix the damaged paneling and carvings?"

Simone nodded and matched her defiant gaze.

"Then you are quite welcome here." Evangeline turned on her delicate heel and, with a viper's strength, snatched her father's arm and steered him from the dining hall. "Don't you have better things to do, Papa? A meeting with the German ambassador or something?"

Simone wondered if Evangeline herself might not be better suited to that task.

With a smile, Evangeline turned back around, and Simone's heart stuttered at the sight of her.

"Please," Evangeline said softly. "Don't let me keep you from your work."

After sketching up her proposed alterations and presenting them to Evangeline for approval, Simone began her work at Château à Pont Allemagne. But it wasn't easy. She worked slowly, painstakingly, her desperation to do right by Evangeline stifling her progress, sending her elbow skidding every time she tried to carve the perfect cornice piece. She'd spend long hours at the Pirripin atelier, long after the brothers had left for the night, repairing the pieces she'd botched.

And Evangeline was always at the château—nearly always. She'd sip tea while studying for her entrance examination to the faculté des lettres, sometimes narrating her notes to herself. Or she would play piano—Saint-Saëns or Ravel or Chopin, her delicate fingers too small to hit the big chords, but what she lacked in technical prowess she more than made up for in emotional sway. More than once, Simone had to remind herself to breathe, her heart was so full inside her throat as Chopin's mournful journey pulled her along and laid her soul bare.

Once, Evangeline spread out a blanket next to Simone's drop cloth and unpacked a picnic. A veritable feast, even though she claimed it was nothing, really, just a little something she'd picked up on her way home. Cheese and bread and succulent roasted quail, which Evangeline assured her was every bit as good as the cured jambon she kept for herself.

Simone never said much during their afternoons together, but she didn't need to. She worked with her hands like she was untangling all the knots she didn't know had been present for so long inside her soul. Evangeline filled the vast, chilly mansion with her carefree chatter, and it warmed them both.

Simone sorted her own life out in her head while Evangeline talked, doling out bits of herself like delicate confections. Her fear of spiders, her disastrous experiment with ballet. Her desultory habit of picking the pockets of her father's dinner guests, lifting pocket watches, opera receipts, once even a letter from a mistress that would have caused quite an international incident if she'd revealed it. She drew—and drew well, judging by the charcoal sketches of herself that Simone found one afternoon, even though Evangeline laughed it off later.

But mostly Simone learned of Evangeline's dream of becoming a diplomat. Like her father. A civil servant of great esteem. And then, a prized wife to someone much like herself, and yet this mystery man was sure to take precedence, her work only a slim shadow of whatever glowing accolades he'd gain.

This last bit, Evangeline disclosed with her face partially hidden behind the knees she'd drawn up under her chin. But Evangeline wouldn't admit to being afraid. She wanted—needed—to be too strong for that.

Slowly, inevitably, Simone's work drew to a close. She'd been dreading it; she dreamed about her afternoons with Evangeline, who never complained when plaster dust drifted down on her head or when Simone's finger slipped and she cursed in Arabic. She found herself working slower just to postpone the inevitable.

Fortunately, Evangeline rescued her in this, too.

"It's too gorgeous a day to spend inside," she declared as Simone finished installing a new panel casing. "I simply must go for a walk. You'll join me, right?"

"Your father doesn't pay me to walk."

Evangeline leaned closer, conspiratorial. "My *father* is detained in a lengthy parliamentary debate on how we should respond to the annexation of Poland, and it's expected to last well into the evening. So he's in no position to judge how either one of us spends our time."

Simone's breath fluttered. She'd been taking care with how she dressed, but she was still a girl from the immigrant neighborhood of Goutte d'Or, after all, scraping and scratching and clawing for work. Evangeline had braided her white-gold hair and coiled it on top of her head; in the sunlight streaming through the room, it gleamed like a halo. Her delicately draped sundress further canonized her. And Simone, well—she wore trousers and a tunic and boys' leather shoes; wood shavings lurked in every crease of her clothes. Despite her best efforts, tufts of her fluffy hair had drifted free from the cap she'd pulled snug on her head. She had no business walking around Trocadéro—with Evangeline besides.

Evangeline gave her an assessing look, as if reading her mind. "Let's brush that dust off you. Maybe I could style your hair?"

Simone's breath rushed out of her. "I'd love that."

Evangeline winked and beckoned her into the closest powder room.

She twisted up the sides of Simone's hair, then joined them with the rest to sweep it into a carefree bun like showgirls wore. There wasn't much to be done about her clothing—she was too tall and broad-shouldered for anything of Evangeline's, not that she dared ask—but Evangeline wiped a smudge of grease from her nose and declared her perfect.

Perfect.

Simone clutched the word close to her chest, like it might fly away.

They stepped out onto the promenade, and Evangeline immediately slipped her arm through Simone's, smiling and staring straight ahead. Simone became painfully aware of her own gait, the way she bobbed and jerked, and tried to even out her paces so she wasn't yanking the smaller girl around. She couldn't think of anything clever or insightful to say, but the silence between them carried its own cool melody. Slowly, as they moved further from Château à Pont Allemagne, Evangeline began to relax and pointed out whatever shiny bits caught her attention: an old woman with an oversize hat, a pair of dogs wearing bow ties, a willow tree whose branches shimmered like a waterfall.

It was a beautiful Paris that Evangeline lived in, impossibly far from Simone's 18th arrondissement, and the more Simone took it in, the less comfortable she felt.

"So what is it you wish to do after your apprenticeship?" Evangeline asked as they neared the campus of the Dauphine. "Will you become an architect, or . . . ?"

The glass bubble in Simone's chest shattered, and the illusion broke. She was only pretending here. She had no business with Evangeline on her arm. She had no business on this clean, quiet street, pretending she belonged here, when every person she passed surely knew otherwise.

"I'm not going to university."

Evangeline blinked a few times, then cocked her head.

"You understand I'm Algerian, yes? My family, we—we live in Goutte d'Or. Surely you know that life can never be for me."

Evangeline bit her lower lip. "I'm sorry. I wasn't trying to—"

"It's—it's been very lovely, living in your world for a few months." Tears prickled at the corners of Simone's eyes. "But this isn't my world. It never will be."

Evangeline's throat bobbed. "I like my world better with you in it."

Simone's mouth inched open, but she had no words. She wasn't used to working with people. They didn't obey geometry and lathes and planes. "You hardly know me." Simone's temper, always simmering beneath the surface, was threatening to boil. "I'm a novelty to you, a funny glimpse beyond these landscaped boulevards—"

Evangeline dropped her arm out of Simone's and whirled to face her. "I know you are meticulous but impatient. You'll do any task a countless number of times to get it right, but you resent it, you resent that you can't shape things just the way you like. I know you swallow down insults and slights but they sit inside you like stones, refusing to dissolve. I can't imagine what kind of weight that must be inside you all day."

Simone crossed her arms over her chest, feeling very exposed. She should have known Monsieur Gaturin's daughter was more than just a pretty objet d'art. She was crafty, shrewd, calculating—and it made Simone love her all the more.

It also made her fear the day Evangeline might turn those weapons against her.

"I think you like your work, but you don't feel respected for it. And it frustrates you. It poisons the whole process. I'm sorry they treat you that way—you deserve better." Evangeline's fingers darted out to tap against her cheek. "I wish I could give you better."

Simone turned her head away from Evangeline's touch, even though she craved it. "I don't need your pity."

"I'm not offering it. I just wanted you to know you aren't some . . . passing amusement." Her smile was lopsided—not at all the polished smile she wore around her father. Simone wondered if she was glimpsing Evangeline's real smile for the first time.

"Look." Evangeline pointed down the street to an archway made of bone. "The catacombs are open."

Simone blinked a few times. Trying to follow Evangeline's thoughts wasn't so much chasing a train as winding through a labyrinth. She wanted to go back, back to the moment when Evangeline touched her face. Wanted to linger there a while longer and forget all the reasons she shouldn't.

"I like to get lost in the catacombs when I need to think. They're comforting." Evangeline held out her hand to Simone. "Want to see?"

Simone nodded and took her hand.

Evangeline led her into the caverns, dark and moist as a mouth. They passed various tour groups who'd no doubt come there to appreciate the same. Skulls leered all around them, but the hollow eye sockets felt welcoming, somehow. No judgment, no eyes to see the humiliating infatuation she was sure burned bright crimson on her cheeks. She'd been to the catacombs once when her father still lived with them; he acted like they were something gruesome to put the fear of God into misbehaving children, to warn them that they ought to respect their parents, for death, and judgment, was always lurking around the corner. That it lived in their bones, just beneath their own skin.

Whether that constant reminder of mortality was what Evangeline liked about them, though, Simone didn't know. She tried to see them through Evangeline's eyes now as they crept, soft as cats, down a winding central corridor. More than bones, Simone now saw architecture. Structure. More than impermanence, she saw eternity, the power of enduring in a shifting world.

And she saw this magnificent girl she was hopelessly in love with.

She saw a glimpse of something she never dared dream could be hers.

"I think they're beautiful," Evangeline said at last. Simone didn't know how far down they'd gone, but they'd lost all other sounds of living things; the tour groups they'd passed were many turns behind. "I wish I could put my bones here someday. It's a form of immortality, isn't it?"

"I'm sure you and your father will have gaudy monuments towering over Père Lachaise for all eternity."

Evangeline rolled her eyes, then slowed to a stop when they reached a metal gate blocking off one path. "What do you suppose is behind this?"

Simone pretended to think long and hard before answering, "Bones?"

Evangeline giggled and squeezed her hand. "You're hopeless. Come on. Help me with this lock."

"What?" Simone whisper-hissed, but Evangeline was already tugging at it.

"If they've locked it off, it must be because there's something good on the other side." In an instant, she produced a hairpin from her bun. "Watch. I used to practice this on Papa's desk drawers."

Simone bit back another disbelieving cry. All she could do was watch while Evangeline worked the pin in the gate's lock and toss anxious glances over her shoulder. Maybe for Evangeline this was all fun and games, but Simone knew the way the gendarmes and Goutte d'Or informants looked at her and her family—they'd never get the harmless chuckle a politician's angelic-faced daughter always would.

Evangeline must have sensed something of this in Simone's

silence, because once the lock popped, she glanced at Simone shyly—guiltily. "I'm sorry. You probably think I'm a dreadful brat."

She *could* be a dreadful brat, but that wasn't the point. "I envy the freedom you have, that's all."

Evangeline looked away, blinking rapidly as she eased the lock and chain loose from around the gate's bars. "I didn't choose to be who I am."

"Neither did I," Simone said, more tartly than she intended. There was that temper, boiling over again.

Evangeline sniffed—were those tears gathering at her lower lashes? Simone's stomach dropped out from under her. This wasn't at all how she'd wanted this excursion to go. Not that she had any illusions how it might go, only that she didn't want *this*—

The gate screeched open, and they stepped through.

"I know as fates go, mine could be far, far worse. But that doesn't mean I want it. I don't want to be his heir. Some pawn my father can shove into whatever marriage looks most convenient at the time. I want—"

"Hey! What are you doing—"

They both froze as a shout ricocheted across the bones.

Then, once more Evangeline seized her wrist, and they ran.

Finally, Simone had the advantage, thanks to her trousers and sturdy shoes. Evangeline's Oxfords kept sliding out from under her as she skidded across the winding path; a stray bone spur snagged her stockings with a horrible rip that cascaded down the fabric. The footsteps drew nearer. Evangeline pulled her down a side corridor, darting underneath a workers' oilcloth spread across an archway of femurs and skulls. They were plunged into darkness in the narrow gap. Evangeline clasped a hand over Simone's mouth as they faced each other in the alcove, and Simone could feel their hearts pounding together frantically as they tried not to breathe.

The footsteps drew closer. Closer. And then with a heavy grunt, went back the way they came.

They sagged down, Evangeline squeezing her forearms tight. Simone couldn't bear to let go. Evangeline's warmth was intoxicating, a strong perfume she couldn't stop breathing in. All she wanted was to drown and drown.

Finally, she drew a ragged breath. "What . . . What is it, then . . ." The boil threatened to overtake her. "What is it you really want?"

In the dim lighting, Evangeline almost glowed, her face drawing closer. She pushed a loose strand of Simone's hair back from her face, eyes luminous.

Simone didn't dare breathe. She couldn't startle whatever delicate thing lived between them. She wasn't ready to give it up. Not yet.

"I want you."

Evangeline cupped Simone's hand on her face and drank her in with her lips. Simone was so startled at first she almost pushed back, and Evangeline faltered—but Simone surged forward then, and more than made up for her misstep. Their arms were warring as they reached for each other, but their lips were in harmony, working together like they'd been made to do this all along. Evangeline tasted sweet and a little salty, creamy like the wedges of Brie she brought home. And the gentle sighs she breathed against Simone's cheeks were as soft as any of her gauzy dresses. Simone wanted to grip them, feel that fragile fabric in her hands. Her knee slid between Evangeline's thighs, and Evangeline tightened around it with a moan.

"I want you," Evangeline murmured when she gasped for breath. "I want you, I want you."

"You already have me," Simone said. She found the tender space beneath Evangeline's ear and kissed it. "Since the day we met. But—aren't you afraid?"

Evangeline leaned back from her, eyes wide and gleaming in the electric light that trickled around the corners of the oilcloth. The concern scrawled so plainly on her delicate features fractured Simone's heart.

"I'm always afraid." Evangeline's voice wavered like it might break. "But isn't it better than being afraid alone?"

Simone pushed away the memories and shoved through the thick oak branches that slapped her with wet leaves like tongues. Every step, she waited for the whistle and sting of death. But nothing came. Whoever was watching them either didn't realize they'd been spotted—unlikely—or was waiting for them to act first.

Rifle hoisted, she scanned the forest's edge across the road below them and waited for something to budge.

There—a flash of gold, then green and gray. Someone was crouching on a tree branch. The branches were stubbornly dense with brown and orange leaves, but Simone made out a slight figure doing their best to hide.

Simone locked the bullet in her rifle chamber, relishing the sharp crack it made that echoed across the ridge.

"Don't shoot!" The figure's arms rose. "We're on your side!"

Simone had heard that before. Thanks to the pose, she could approximate the location of the figure's chest, their head—

She stumbled backward, rifle slipping from her shoulder. She was going mad. That had to be it. For a moment, she saw a flash of gold and rosebud lips—for a moment, she saw Evangeline—

The figure dropped down from the trees with a crunch of dead branches. Of *course* it wasn't. Simone cursed herself. First the agent on the radio, now this. She was losing her edge, and it was going to get her killed.

The figure—the young woman who did, at least, have blond hair twisted up around her skull in braids—approached the side of the road.

"We don't mean you harm," she said in slow, deliberate German. "But you should know I have two more companions you haven't spotted."

Against her better judgment, Simone turned around. Sure enough, Phillip and Rebeka stood with their arms raised, a German man and woman pressing the muzzles of hunting rifles to their backs.

"Fine." Simone dropped her rifle. "What do you want with us?"

"We're supposed to meet Resistance contacts sent from Hallenberg," the man said.

Simone groaned and bent to pick up her rifle. When the first girl glowered at her, she slung it on her back and held her empty hands out. "You idiots. Suppose I weren't with the Resistance? Now you've just told me that there's a cell in Hallenberg and one in Wewelsburg, which is where I presume you're from."

The cocky smile faded from the man's face. "But you're—I mean, obviously you're not Nazis—"

"They said there would be only two of you." The blond girl made her way up the escarpment to join them. "The guard and the radio operator."

Rebeka bit her lower lip. "I don't want trouble. I can go—"

"Go where?" the man asked. "Don't you know what Wewelsburg is?"

"I know that we're supposed to be vetting you and your little social club of Germans who are playing at Resistance now that it's far too late," Simone said. She stood up straighter, scanning their faces. "You're doing an abysmal job of proving yourselves so far."

The man narrowed his eyes, but none of them mustered a clever retort to that.

The blond girl, the one Simone had first spotted in the trees, stepped into the midst of Simone, Phillip, and Rebeka in some strange sort of negotiation. "I'm Ilse. These are my colleagues, Mitzi and Jürgen." Mitzi and Jürgen stared back with tight jaws. "Please forgive our harshness. It's been very difficult for us to watch the world unraveling around us. Even in our little town."

"I can't imagine," Rebeka said in a tone that was pure venom.

"You misunderstand me. There's something terrible happening at Wewelsburg Castle," Ilse said. "Something that has to be stopped."

Simone and Rebeka exchanged a look. That horrible ceremony Rebeka had seen when she stepped into the shadows. Those bloody demons were going to follow them everywhere.

"We'll need to set up your radio system first so we can get word out about what's happening," Simone said. "But then, if you're willing . . ."

Simone felt a tug deep in her gut as Ilse's gaze landed on her. She stared back, challenging, and hoped Ilse didn't know it for the pitiful bluff it was. "I'm sure it's nothing we can't handle."

Ilse laughed like shattering glass. "We'll see about that."

CHAPTER TWENTY-FOUR
LIAM

Liam awoke to birdsong. Sunlight tickled his nose as he stretched along their makeshift pallet on the floor, savoring the raw, swollen feel of his mouth. "Daniel," he murmured, fingers stretching, grasping. "C'mere."

But his hand landed only on bunched-up blankets, already cold.

"Daniel?"

Dust motes swirled in the sunbeams as he stood. The air in the chalet was too stale—ash and sex and musty bedding. Too silent. Sudden panic jerked Liam upright like a puppet string.

"Daniel?" He whispered this time, pushing to his feet. "Daniel, where are you?"

The only answer was a dark crackle in the back of his mind.

Liam forced himself to take a slow, steadying breath. He hadn't so much as touched the shadow world since their escape from Nazis and then Pitr the previous evening. He didn't *need* the shadows to guide him, to bolster him. But they certainly made things easier. Thoughts of the darkness circled him like a hunter outside the cabin.

If Daniel was in danger, or if Pitr had found them—maybe he could just snatch a fistful of energy, only enough to protect them—

Liam opened his eyes with a gasp. His nails had torn into his palm, and blood welled there. Hands he'd touched Daniel with last night, had cradled his jaw and traced along his throat and his hips and more besides. *What if you closed the rifts for good?* Daniel had asked him—forever sealed off the pathway between the shadow world and theirs. The very thought curdled in his stomach, crushed his chest with a panicky weight.

He needed the power—*needed* it. His whole life had been pushing him toward this victory. He'd no longer be the helpless, powerless, too-young boy struggling to grow up, struggling to care for his mother, struggling to prove his worth. For himself, and for countless others suffering. The chance that Pitr and his Nazi friends could claim the shadow world for their own was just the risk he had to take.

He forced his palm flat to his side as he crept across the great room of the chalet and peered into the kitchen. No one. Nothing.

Nothing except a note on the counter.

I know you'll try to stop me, or demand to come with me, which is why I must go now. I can't let anyone else get hurt—and that means not letting the darkness eat you, too. Know, though, that you gave me one last reminder of what it is to feel joy—that for a moment, I could pretend there might have been another fate for me. For us.

I'm sorry. I wish I could have spent another lifetime learning you.

The cry wrenched out of him, dropping him to his knees. He was imploding—his sadness and fury collapsing into a single dense point. *Daniel. You idiot.* Darkness pounded in his head, crowded his vision. *It didn't have to be this way.*

He crumpled the note in his fist, leaving smears of blood on the paper. Unthinking, he drew on the darkness. The first trickle of shadow was like ice, but the more he pulled, the more it thawed.

A quick glance out the window showed the Mercedes was gone. But if he moved through the shadow world, he could go faster. He could catch up to Daniel. Maybe even beat Daniel there.

The shadow pounded in him, an executioner's drum. It demanded to be let in. It was a great carrion bird, hungry and eager to stretch its black wings in his heart. Tear through his skin. Consume him. Make him its vessel of rage.

The chalet shimmered around him as oily nighttime flooded it and the shadow world stretched before him, beasts circling, trees hungering, wind laughing with his name—

Shit.

Liam shoved it all away with a snarl and slid into a heap on the floor. "God damn it!" The rift wavered and closed back up. Blackness slithered out of him and scattered to the far corners of the cabin, evaporated, burrowed, fled. "God damn it."

Could he make himself close the rift for good? Daniel had asked him to. Daniel had seen what the shadow world was doing to him.

Liam raked his hands down the sides of his face. If he closed the rift now, then it would all have been for nothing. He'd be an empty shell, the hollow, precocious boy who'd pushed too hard and come up short, when all he wanted was to drink up the shadows until there was nothing of himself left—

No. The shadow was never going to grant him everything he needed. He blinked back tears. But the shadow could help him save Daniel still—take down the Nazis at Wewelsburg. If it didn't destroy him first.

A loud banging tore him from his thoughts. Someone was pounding on the door.

Liam was crumpled in the corner of the kitchen. Not exactly hidden from sight. He should stand up, find a hiding place. But his body didn't seem too interested in following through. It was futile—it would take so much effort; it would cost him so much more than he had to give right now, with his heart wrenched open and the shadows just out of his reach, a danger in themselves. The bloody paper wadded in his fist was taunting him as fiercely as the darkness had. Another thing he couldn't change.

"Werner? Are you here?" a voice called in German.

Liam said nothing. Did nothing. He'd been scooped out.

The polished boots stopped in front of him.

"You are not Werner." The man reached down and forced Liam's chin up. "So why did you have his car?"

The soldier's compatriots flooded through the chalet, circling him. It would be so easy to touch the shadow and shred these men. But Liam was drained now; he reached out for the frequency but everything unraveled at his touch. Even if he could access it, Pitr was waiting, just waiting, to snare him again. Liam did nothing as the soldiers bound his hands and steered him toward the waiting truck.

"Let me guess," Liam muttered as they shoved him onto the low bench. "You're taking me to Wewelsburg Castle."

The soldiers surrounded him on the bench as the truck lurched to life. "Oh, no. We have other plans for you."

CHAPTER TWENTY-FIVE

PHILLIP

The more Ilse, Mitzi, and Jürgen talked, the less comfortable Phillip felt.

They'd believed themselves fairly inured to the Third Reich's upheaval until Himmler chose their beloved castle for his Camelot. *We thought surely this fad of ignorance would pass,* they explained as they trudged through the woods. *After all, this isn't Germany, not really. Real Germans would never behave so cruelly.*

Ilse had secured a position in the castle's secretary pool, which gave her access to all kinds of information, and Jürgen worked in the garage, driving shipments to nearby towns. "Some days I like to fantasize about dropping the shipments off at the wrong location. Sowing a bit of chaos, you know?" He smirked as he explained it. "Let the Wehrmacht bastards go hungry for a few days."

"Then why haven't you?" Simone asked.

Jürgen frowned at her. "Well, it's too dangerous right now. They'd know exactly who'd done it."

"We're waiting for the right chance," Ilse said. "As soon as we can figure out a safe way to go about it, then we'll really make them pay."

Safety. As if there was a safe way to resist. If things were "safe," there was no *need* to fight back.

"What have you actually done that's useful, then?" Simone asked.

Phillip and Rebeka exchanged a look. They clearly both had more experience biting their tongues. Though at that realization, Phillip wondered, maybe for the first time, if it had ever done him any good. Certainly not with Mr. Connolly. He wondered what Darius would say if he were here instead.

"I keep records of unusual shipment requests. For instance, they recently brought in archival material from Siegen," Jürgen said. "And shortly afterward, the administrative building there burned down. Doesn't that seem suspicious to you?"

"Terribly," Rebeka muttered. Her terse expression hadn't budged, and Phillip couldn't blame her.

"It will be . . . difficult . . ." Mitzi studied them from the corner of her eye. "To hide you three. We'll do our best, though. I think you'll find Wewelsburg is a relatively safe haven in the shadow of the beast."

"I find that hard to believe," Simone said.

Ilse scowled. "We're not monsters. Just because a few hateful fools seized power against our wishes—"

"Have you had any other refugees come through?" Rebeka interrupted. "Two boys around our age, maybe?"

The Germans looked at one another, then shook their heads. "Should we have?" Jürgen asked.

Rebeka bit her lip. "No. It's nothing."

The Germans muttered amongst themselves, in the sly way of

teenagers talking about someone they dislike. Given his rudimentary language training and how quickly they were speaking, Phillip couldn't catch their words, but there was definitely something disconcerting in their tone. He darted his hand out to squeeze Rebeka's, fleetingly, and she let out a weary breath.

They reached the last hill, and the town of Wewelsburg spread open before them like the pages of a fairy tale. White stone buildings and slate streets, picturesque cottages and a babbling brook, and guarding it all, the elegant but imposing spires of Wewelsburg Castle. A shiver ran through Phillip at the sight of it. If Rebeka was right, the SS could be gathering inside right now to summon all kinds of dark and deadly monsters to unleash. But in the champagne wash of late-afternoon sun, it couldn't have looked more innocent.

They neared the quaint stone bridge that led into the walled town, but as soon as they started across the path, a strange and schmaltzy melody drifted out of the gates.

Die Fahne hoch, die Reihen fest geschlossen . . .

"Who's singing?" Phillip asked, dread like a cobweb brushing the back of his neck.

Their hosts stopped just short of the bridge. Ilse glanced at Jürgen, who jerked his head to one side. "We're going to take the tunnels," Jürgen announced.

"What's going on?" Phillip asked again, an edge now in his tone. The dread was sharper now—nails digging in.

Ilse fluttered her eyelashes as she made her way down the escarpment to the creek below the bridge, then led them toward a pair of ancient stone tunnels set into the town's bedrock. "Just some idiots having drunken fun. It's better to ignore them."

"Stormtroopers," Rebeka muttered. "Brownshirts. They like to patrol the streets, keep 'order' for the Reich."

Phillip stopped in his tracks. "I thought you said your village was safe?"

Ilse twisted back to face him. "There are plenty of reasonable people in our village. But there are also many bored and restless soldiers stationed in the castle, ja? So when they find a bit of fun to have, it's best to let them have it and stay out of their way."

"Great strategy. Ignore them, and they'll go away," Phillip said. "Seems to be working wonderfully so far."

Ilse stopped again, bristling. "You want me to go fight every single Nazi I see? I can help you more like this."

Further behind him, Phillip heard Simone checking the chamber on her rifle. Phillip clenched his jaw as he followed along. At least he was here—he and Rebeka and Simone could defend themselves. Maybe they couldn't fight every single Nazi, no, but they didn't have to turn and run from them, either.

He locked eyes with Simone, and she gave him a silent nod.

They reached the runoff tunnels, and Mitzi climbed in first, shrouded suddenly in total darkness. Ilse and Jürgen followed. Phillip helped Rebeka up, then Simone took up the rear, casting glances behind her all the while.

"So what exactly are these stormtroopers?" Phillip asked. "What do they want?"

"They used to round up any Jews or 'Jew-lovers' they could find, and parade them down the street for humiliation," Rebeka explained as they slowly crawled down the tunnels. "Make them wear humiliating signs. Or worse—much worse."

"Sounds like back home," Phillip said under his breath. When Rebeka stared at him quizzically, he shook his head. "All it takes is a few crocodile tears from a white lady for the Klan to attack our neighborhoods. Sometimes not even that."

"Is that not illegal in America?"

"Are you kidding? Half the time, it's the sheriff or the mayor under those hoods."

He shook off the tension that had settled onto his shoulders just thinking about it. Of everything he'd had to fear this past week, the unnerving sensation of white eyes watching his every move hadn't been among them. Back home, they waited, breaths held, for him to slip up while carrying out the simplest tasks of buying a cup of coffee or getting a drink of water from the correct fountain. Now he strung up illegal radio transmissions and shot demons, and no one was around to judge.

Maybe he should walk around with the solemn intent to kill every fascist he encountered more often.

"You said the stormtroopers *used* to do this," Simone said.

Rebeka laughed bitterly. "No need to now that they're making every city judenrein. I suppose the brownshirts will have to find new targets to torment soon once all the Jews are gone."

Ahead of them, Ilse started humming the same melody, until Mitzi shushed her. "What? It's catchy."

Finally they reached their destination. A rattle of heavy keys, a latch, and they entered a dank basement, wet and slimy like the tunnels.

"Here we are. Our little cellar social club." Ilse smiled wryly as she waved them inside. "It isn't much, but it's safe and it's ours."

"Technically it's my father's," Jürgen said with an air of disdain, "but he's been sent elsewhere for the war, so I'm in charge."

Phillip flinched as he realized which side of the war.

"This is . . . a beer hall?" Simone asked.

The cellar before them was a low-ceilinged tavern, complete with wooden benches and booths, electric wrought-iron chandeliers, and a wall of beer taps. Half-moon windows ringed the tops of the low walls, presumably offering a view onto the streets of the town, though they'd been covered with newspaper.

"It's the private party space. The beer hall is upstairs." Mitzi sauntered over to the wall of taps. "We only let people we like down here."

Phillip didn't miss the warning in her tone, in her sharp look. But he'd about had enough of tying himself in knots to fit in someone else's box. He met her gaze, calm and quiet, and she finally looked away.

"We meet here once a week to discuss our efforts for the Resistance," Ilse explained as Mitzi started filling steins of ale. "Though unfortunately there isn't much we've been able to do yet, since we cannot transmit safely."

"We've been listening, though," Mitzi said. "I monitor the radio waves from the keg room. That's how we found out you were coming."

"So what exactly *have* you accomplished for the Resistance?" Simone asked.

The pause grew thick enough to stuff a parka in winter as Ilse's mouth flapped open, closed. "Well, nothing, *yet*," she finally said. "But we've been gathering intelligence—like the Magpie's requests. I record the minutes of my commanding officers' meetings, their research projects."

"Then what are you waiting for?" Simone asked.

Ilse narrowed her eyes at her. "When it's safe for us to make contact with someone, we will."

"Oh, I see. You're waiting until you have nothing left to lose—"

Ilse sputtered. "That isn't—"

"Surely our intelligence can help." Mitzi shrugged her shoulders. "The soldiers like me well enough. They tell me things sometimes. They all want to sound more important than they really are when they're trying to get me into bed." She looked at her nails. "And our other friends, they all work in the castle, too. We hear things."

"We're doing what we can, don't you see? We hate the Third Reich—we know this isn't Germany, not really," Ilse insisted. "We'll do whatever it takes to get our country back."

"But this *is* Germany," Rebeka said. "Germans did this. Germans continue to do this."

Mitzi sighed. "Well, not *all* of us. This whole business with sending the Jews and Communists to camps and so on, that isn't right."

"But those are German laws. Germans agreed to do those things," Rebeka pressed.

"Well, *I'm* not doing it, and I think it's gauche, and I'm not even a Jew." Ilse folded her arms. "So there you have it."

"One of my best friends in grade school was a Jew," Jürgen piped up. "He was always so kind and honest and eager to talk to everyone. Not at all like . . . well, you know, like they say. Isolated. He didn't speak Hebrew. Hell, he probably spoke better German than me."

Mitzi brought a tray of ale toward them and gestured toward the booths in the alcoves. "Sit, sit, this is too dire a topic to discuss sober."

"So your friend didn't deserve this treatment . . . but the 'stand-offish' ones do? The ones whose German isn't perfect?" Rebeka asked. Phillip gently guided her into the booth, but her limbs were like steel, bending under considerable strain as she sat.

"That isn't what he meant," said Ilse. "Only that, you know, stereo-types aren't . . . Well, you get my point."

"Clear as mud." Phillip scooped up one of the steins.

"And it isn't just about the Jews, either," Ilse continued. "The Nazis are vile in other ways. Restricting what you can say, requiring patriotism . . . Maybe other, more backward countries are that way, but we're a cosmopolitan people. We should be better than this."

"Then why aren't you?" Simone asked.

Ilse huffed at her. "What do you think it is we're doing here? Why we're helping you? Goodness. You'd think you might be a little more grateful. We're on your side, you know. A thank-you might not be out of place—don't you realize the considerable risk we've put ourselves in by bringing you here?"

Outside the papered-up windows, the brownshirts drew nearer, boisterously singing the "Horst Wessel Lied." They must have been right next to the town square. Phillip and Simone exchanged an anx-ious look.

"I know what will help. Let me head to the kitchens! Jürgen, why don't you put on some music?" Mitzi asked.

"Um—if it's all the same—" Phillip started, but she'd already dis-appeared up the twisting staircase. A heavy door groaned open, letting in a burst of drinking music, then slammed shut. The door, apparently, was the only thing separating them from the drunken stormtroopers. Jürgen turned on the radio in the corner, and cranked it high to drown out the singing on the square and in the tavern above.

"So. What has it been like? Working with the Resistance?" Ilse leaned across the booth to stare at them wide-eyed.

"I'm not with the Resistance," Rebeka said. "My brother and I barely escaped from getting sent to the Chełmno death camp."

"*Death* camp?" Ilse echoed, then giggled. "Well, that's a little dramatic, don't you think?"

"No. They sent my family there to kill them." Rebeka glared at her, her voice trembling. "I've seen it."

"That seems like an exaggeration. I mean, we know they're moving people into concentration camps, detaining them and such, which, don't get me wrong, I happen to *strongly* disagree with, I think it's horribly inhumane. But there's simply no evidence that they're killing them. I mean, it doesn't even make sense. Don't you think, Jürgen?"

"If I were a heartless Nazi bastard, I'd use them for labor," Jürgen called from the radio set as he adjusted the dial.

"See?" Ilse said. "It just doesn't make sense."

Rebeka seethed while Phillip spoke.

"Where I'm from," he said, "we fought a whole damn war about that, too."

Ilse rolled her eyes. "Please. Everyone knows your civil war was about economics."

Phillip glared at her. "Yeah. The economics of losing your free labor source because they're *human beings*."

Rebeka gripped the edge of the table, her fingernails splintering into the wood. "I've seen the camps. I've smelled the fire from the burning bodies. The other Germans were *laughing* about it, because they knew exactly what was going on."

Ilse faltered at that, and paused for an overlong sip of her ale. "Well." She set her drink down. "If true, that is a very serious accusation indeed."

Phillip's head was starting to throb. "She just told you it's true."

"Mein Gott! No need to be so angry!" Ilse flattened herself back against the bench. "I was only trying to be certain we got the facts right."

"No, you were refusing to believe her. A survivor of your own goddamned Nazis and their goddamned German-as-hell laws."

Ilse narrowed her eyes. "For the last time, I'm on your side, all right? But if I'm going to help, then we have to make sure we get everything correct. We can't afford to exaggerate or act before the time is right—"

"I need some air."

Rebeka shoved her way out of the booth. A syrupy Bavarian waltz was playing on the radio now, punctuating her steps with croony marching lyrics, *Liebe* and *Lebensraum*. Phillip and Simone exchanged a glance.

"If it's all the same to you," Simone said, her English especially clipped, "we'd like to get on with our business with the radio sets and be on our way."

"Oh," Ilse said, setting her drink down carefully. She licked those red lips of hers, bright as a fresh wound. "Well, I'm afraid it can't be done just now."

"You said the radio's in the cask cellar," Phillip said. "That it's right over there."

"Yes, that's all true, but . . . We'll have to wait for Jürgen's dinner workers to leave first. They're in and out of the cellar all the time, you see, and if any of them were to spot you, it could cause . . . problems."

"So we have to wait." Phillip gripped his beer stein so hard he half hoped the handle might snap off. He was so tired of playing nice, of ignoring every stab. He hadn't come here to give a strained smile at the same callous people he could have smiled at back home.

"It won't be too much longer now. Just a few hours!"

"And I've got dinner," Mitzi announced, returning down the basement steps with a tray.

Despite himself, Phillip's mouth watered. The camping rations he'd scarfed down that morning, scavenged out of the bags of the dead German family in the cabin, had barely served as an appetizer. Mitzi's tray was loaded with stacks of grilled sausage links glistening with grease and creamy cutlets. The smell of roasted meat unleashed a mighty rumble in his gut.

Then he noticed the looks on Simone's and Rebeka's faces.

"I can't eat that," Simone said.

Rebeka stared. "Me neither."

"Oh, surely you can make an exception. You're half starved," Ilse said.

"That's my decision."

"But you can't do the Resistance much good if you're dead," Mitzi said, around a mouthful of sauerkraut.

Phillip glanced at Rebeka, the tension in her mouth and her

hollowed cheeks. Maybe he could convince her to have some of the bread rolls, or the sauerkraut—just something to get her strength up before they started the search for her brother—

Rebeka spun from the booth with a miserable cry. Phillip dropped the sausage link he'd been pulling toward his plate and rushed toward her, but she was fury and wounded pride, shoving him away. "Don't touch me," she wheezed, then slumped forward. "I'm sorry, I'm sorry, it isn't you, it isn't you."

But it was the whole world. It was people who blamed their troubles on those with even less power than them. It was the "believers" whose mouths prayed as their hands shoved away the suffering, the sick, the poor, the oppressed. It was the nonbelievers convinced that empathy was a weakness they needed to evolve past.

Rebeka clasped Phillip's hands in her own. "This is why we're here," she whispered feverishly. "This is why we're carrying on. Because I'll be damned if we put our fate in the hands of people who can drop our cause the moment it becomes too heavy for them to carry."

Phillip shook his head. "I'll never be clever enough, smart enough, innovative enough to prove my worth. I already tried, and I only made things worse."

"Your worth as a person isn't something you have to prove."

Phillip tipped forward, legs going weak beneath him. Such a simple idea, but one he'd never even considered. His whole life had been about proving himself. To his successful parents, to Mr. Connolly and the white world south of Archer Street, to himself. He was trying to make himself tall enough that no one could push him down. But maybe he was already enough. Or, could still be yet.

He tried to smile at her, but relief overwhelmed him, a wave that threatened to break on his face. "I still want to help," he managed.

Rebeka raised her hand and brushed her thumb along his lower lashes. He knew it came away damp, but didn't care. "Then let's wreck the Third Reich."

CHAPTER TWENTY-SIX

EVANGELINE

By the time they left 84 avenue Foch, the first rays of sun had already stained Paris's eastern flank. It all looked so wrong, given the night she'd had. Twilight Paris was seductive: glamorous and mature. But predawn Paris should look more innocent; its hands should not ache from being too long clenched in fists; its teeth should not throb from a tense jaw. Its eyes should not be dried out and swollen from exhaustion, terror, tears.

If Stefan saw anything wrong with the morning, though, he was careful not to show it. He was still onstage—for how could any of this not have been part of a careful performance, one he'd possibly been scripting since the day they met? If the act was wearing him out, if the hours of Georges-Yves's screams had taken any toll on him, he gave no hint. He whistled as he opened Evangeline's door for her, then slid in behind the chauffeur.

More than anything, she was shocked he was letting her leave Gestapo headquarters at all.

"I apologize for the long evening," he said, as the car nosed its way toward the Champs-Élysées. The Arc de Triomphe seemed like a cruel mockery as it loomed into view. "But given your position, I am sure you recognize how terribly important it was. That interrogation simply could not wait."

He folded his overcoat between them on the bench. Her gaze swept over it, the pockets, the lining, all the little creases and folds she'd carefully memorized. Her father once called her a thieving magpie, an insult she took to heart. Now, the Magpie's fingers twitched.

"I see the point," Evangeline answered carefully. "However, I'm not sure it has much to do with my office." Through the blear of exhaustion, she managed to chain together an alibi. "We only deal with requisitions, after all. Not counterintelligence."

"Ahh, but that is where you are wrong. Counterintelligence is the duty of *all* subjects of the Third Reich." Stefan folded his hands neatly over one knee as he leaned toward her. "Those requisitions your office manages—why, it is just that kind of critical intelligence that someone has been leaking across the airwaves that poor imbecile's network established."

The hours of fear and visceral horror as she watched Stefan conduct his interrogation had wrung her out, leaving a frayed, filthy dishrag of a girl behind. She scrabbled for purchase in some kind of lie, some kind of subterfuge, but only came up with broken nails.

"That's why you came to my office in the first place," she said slowly. "You were hunting a mole."

He smiled, far too pleased with himself. "That's right."

"But you caught them. Did you not? Three people left the office quite abruptly, shortly afterward." Which was true. At least one had been a reassignment, Evangeline knew, but Stefan didn't have to know she knew that. She'd changed her tactics, slowly, carefully, after his investigation had begun. Gradually enough that he might not notice the mole had been tipped off to his attentions. She was doing everything right. By God, she'd done everything so carefully that she feared she hadn't made any real difference at all.

But she'd done enough to send the Gestapo scrambling. She'd done enough for Simone to be building some sort of damned ridiculous campaign into the heart of the Third Reich. She'd done enough that Georges-Yves was going to pay for it with his life, and who knew how many more. She'd done enough to sign her own execution orders, if Stefan was steering this where she feared.

And still the Nazis held her city, the world, in their brutal grasp.

"I thought we'd caught them, but no," Stefan finally said, the tinge of remorse in his voice far too phony. "It would seem we have not. But it's no matter. I'm sure we will very soon."

They had reached the 16th arrondissement. He could not possibly be taking her home for real—could he? This was just another stage of the hunt, of whatever snare he was trying to draw around her. She'd been caught, and he was drawing it out for as long as he could, waiting for her nerves to fray and snap. She didn't need to be sitting in that same bloody chair where Georges-Yves had slumped for her interrogation to have already begun.

"It has been a long night, and I've been a terrible excuse of a gentleman by keeping you out so late." He patted her hand; she didn't bother to hide her instinct to recoil. "Take the day off. Get some rest. You work far too hard as it is."

"Some rest," she repeated. As if she could possibly sleep after that.

Yes. He wanted her scared, panicked, thrashing about to pull the snare tighter. He was letting her go so he could follow her back to her den. He had all the pieces of the network sorted out: now he wanted to see how she would assemble them.

"I'll do my best," she offered with a smile. And let herself into the mansion, his eyes burning a hole in her back the entire way.

CHAPTER TWENTY-SEVEN

SIMONE

One hour and far too much awkward silence later, they were finally allowed into the keg cellar that smelled of wet and yeast. Beside her, Phillip nearly choked at the pitiful receiver they'd been using to listen to Resistance communiqués. "I'm amazed you can even get a signal with this thing."

"It's verboten to buy anything more powerful," Jürgen said with a shrug. "And even if it weren't, it's a sure way to expose yourself as a spy."

"How did you learn the transmission codes? Where to listen?" Simone asked.

"My mother has friends in Paris who connected us. They promised we could do some good," Ilse said.

"Well?" Phillip turned toward Simone, lips pressed into a thin line. "Shall we get to work?"

She didn't know him well, but it was palpable, his reluctance. It was heavy in her, too. Neither of them trusted these bumbling fools, these pampered Germans who played at Resistance like it was a low-stakes dominos game. They only placed bets with spare change, and not their very lives. It made Simone sick to think how very many lives they'd be placing in these idiots' hands as fresh bargaining chips.

But then she thought of the Magpie, waiting expectantly on the other side of the vast fields of static. They were running out of time: to gather intelligence on Wewelsburg, to stop Rebeka's brother, and then, if they knew what was good for them, to flee this cursed forest for good.

"Let's do it," Simone said.

Phillip let out his breath. Trusting her. She hoped that trust wasn't misplaced.

"All right." Phillip rubbed his hands together. "First, I'm going to switch out your power source. This thing you've got is barely better than a crystal diode. Then we'll get you set up with the huff-duff foilers and a TX box—uh, a transmitter, that is. Then, if it looks like everything's functioning as it should, I'll leave you with this—" He held up the device he'd designed, the frequency folder. "This will cover all your encryption and decryption needs, and confuse even the most dedicated direction finders. You can get rid of all of this." He waved his hand at the stack of loose papers they'd been using to unscramble the Resistance ciphers. "Under one condition."

They all stared at him wide-eyed.

"At the *first* hint, and I mean the *very* first hint, that someone might stumble across it, you take your shoe and you smash that cipher box." He pantomimed crushing it with the heel of his boot. "Smash it as hard as you can."

After a fair bit of work and some creative rearrangement of the cellar's circuitry, they had a functioning transmission station. The German kids crowded around it like it was a new toy, arguing over whose information would get sent out first, but Simone spoke up anxiously.

"Actually, I need to transmit something."

The Germans looked at each other; Jürgen shrugged and headed back upstairs to entertain his patrons.

"We were supposed to report in to the Magpie once we reached Wewelsburg," Simone said in a low voice to Phillip. "I don't know if the network ever received our previous message, but . . ."

"But?" Phillip asked, one eyebrow raised. Simone didn't answer, her jaw tightening. Stupid, wishful thinking on her part. Could she really ask him to trust her once more?

With a sigh, Phillip stationed himself at the transmission station and switched on the encryption box. "All right, what should we send?"

Simone tugged at the sleeves of her hunting jacket, pulling them down over her hands. "Send it urgent to Magpie. Say that . . . that we've reached Wewelsburg and are ready to gather any shiny bits the Magpie requires. Standing by."

Phillip tapped out the message slowly, painstakingly, the dits and dahs taking an eternity. It dropped out into the ether, and across Europe, hidden in basements just like this one, men and women hunched over their radios turned down low and rushed to scribble down the message before it slipped out of their grasp. But none called back out. The receiver stayed quiet.

"Sorry." Simone shrank into her jacket, her stomach sinking. "I guess I just thought—"

MAGPIE. TX BEGINS.

Phillip scrambled to grab a pencil. Simone almost ripped it from his hand, then thought better, and wrapped her arms around herself as he rushed to transcribe the new message. She hovered at his shoulder like a bird ready to spook.

YOUR MAGPIE WELCOMES ALL SHINIES FOR HER NEST, the message continued. CAN PROVIDE LIMITED SUPPORT.

"Ilse! Ilse, where are you?"

Jürgen rushed back down the stairs, his face flushed. Simone gritted her teeth, willing Phillip to concentrate on the Morse code while the Germans gathered in excited, rushed tones.

ENTERING CAMELOT BUT SOME CHANNELS COMPROMISED, Simone answered. CAN YOU HELP US?

TIME LIMITED, Phillip transcribed as the response came in. CAN ARRANGE SAFE EXTRACTION AFTER TWO HOURS—

"You're needed at the Castle. Kreutzer's orders. The guards are waiting for you upstairs."

—BUT THIS NETWORK UNSAFE, the response finished. ADVISE ON NEXT STEPS, OVER.

The floor opened up beneath her, the sinkhole that was her heart threatening to swallow her alive. Could this Magpie really be her Evangeline? Her flighty, thieving, mischievous girl. She had been orchestrating countless tiny coups, not the ones that lived in her own head like Ilse's and Jürgen's did, but the thousand cuts that just might strike the right artery. The bitterness Simone had felt that swollen April night still burned inside her—it had grown pleasant to hold on to—but no, even that comfort was washed away in this new flood of relief.

"Yes," Simone pleaded. "Tell her we'll take the two hours."

Phillip watched Simone for a moment, and for once in her life, she was too happy to want to hide her happiness behind the shield of her scorn. He laughed once, quick, to himself, and began to type out their response.

"What's going on?" Ilse asked, crowding over Simone's shoulder.

Her shrill voice brought Simone back to earth. She turned toward the Germans, Jürgen and his rosy cheeks. Rebeka unfolded her arms from where she'd been lurking in the shadows and stepped closer, eyebrows drawn.

"Why do they need Ilse at the castle?" Rebeka asked.

"They captured a Jewish boy inside the castle compound. Apparently he'd made his way into Dr. Kreutzer's office. Was trying to assassinate him."

Rebeka sucked in her breath like she'd been punched in the gut. Simone felt the blow, too. She could only think of one Jewish boy stupid and angry enough to try just that.

"Kreutzer wants your assistance with the questioning," Jürgen said.

CHAPTER TWENTY-EIGHT

EVANGELINE

Were it not for Simone, none of it would have happened. She would have gone to work in the Vichy alliance; she would have bowed her head and avoided any attention the Nazis shot her way. Maybe she would have allowed Stefan to court her, maybe not, but it would not have been the same. She would have been nothing but a coward then, the coward Simone believed her to be—the coward she really was.

This wasn't bravery, even now, that compelled her to go on. It was its own cowardice, the fear of Simone actually being *right*.

For Simone always saw through her, saw her skeletal structure of privilege and comfort and wealth. She had worked hard to make her way to the Sorbonne, it was true; but plenty of people worked hard; plenty of people were at least as smart as she was. Only they didn't have the silver platter of the Gaturin name, the Gaturin money, the Gaturin comforts to serve up that hard work. Simone exposed her to the bone, revealed every last layer of who Evangeline really was. Evangeline hated it; she hated what she saw when at last she was able to look at herself through Simone's eyes.

And yet, despite it all, Simone had loved her. For a time.

God, what was she doing? Was she risking countless lives just to prove Simone wrong? To run from the person she knew she really was? She was doing the *right* thing, the bold and stupid thing, true, the most that could be done by anyone in her position. But it was so minuscule; it was so, so late. Even in this pathetic act of resistance, she'd now been caught.

Georges-Yves had given Stefan everything he knew. The Resistance node locations. The radio frequencies. The codes.

Simone was in the dark of the forest now, stumbling blindly, no idea that the only lifeline she had was now compromised.

Evangeline stared around the darkening mansion, around her bedroom of silk and gold and brocade. Stefan's men were almost certainly watching the house, waiting to see what her next move would be. He wanted her to rush straight to her radio set and try to warn the others in the network, implicating herself and them. He wanted to see her in action.

Well, Evangeline was well versed in the dangers of wanting too much.

She moved to the far corner of the upstairs sitting room and found the corner piece just beside the fireplace mantel. Simone's work was so flawless that she doubted even the finest Nazi spy hunter could ever detect the faint dip and groove in the molding that Evangeline was now prying loose.

Deep in the bones of Château à Pont Allemagne, something clicked.

Evangeline rushed back to her bedroom and wrenched open

the panel that had been unsealed. She pulled it all out—all of it. The cipher books, the transmissions she'd yet to make, the radio and Morse code communicator and signal booster and everything else, everything someone might possibly need to hang her for subversive acts against the occupying forces.

Evangeline's hand brushed against the frame of the large panel, and she stared into it, into the space where once they'd huddled together, legs dangling out, arms intertwined, lips like bruises as they kissed and mouths like sacrament as they did more. And then she closed it. Perhaps for the last time.

She assembled her radio kit. Recalibrated her ciphers. Scratched out a few rough drafts of the million billion thoughts dancing around her head: the apologies, the pleas, the promises to do something meaningful. And then she sat down before her radio set and waited.

Waited.

It wasn't too late. Not just yet. It wasn't too late to pack it all away or smash the radio to bits or burn the cipher books. She was only listening in, the silence deafening now that Georges-Yves was gone. No matter how many Gestapo agents Stefan had set around the château, none could catch her if all she did was listen in. It was only when she began to transmit that her fate was sealed.

She crawled toward her bedroom window. Peered around the thick damask curtains, careful not to let them shift. Stefan's men were surely listening for her to give herself away.

She dropped back down and gripped her face in her hands.

You will never understand what it's like to be hungry, Simone had said. *You will never know what it is to truly want. And without that need, then you will never have the courage to do what must be done. We fight because we have everything to gain. But you will never fight, because no matter how righteous your purpose, how just your cause—by fighting, you will only lose.*

But she'd lost Simone all the same. Now, with one act, she would lose her country, her whole world. She did not need to be executed alongside the Resistance for France to die around her. She did not have to throw herself in front of a tank to feel the ache, that nagging tug, that told her she could have prevented all of this. She could stay locked inside this beautiful home, its bones built long ago by starving peasants and its floors swept by threadbare immigrants and its wood refurbished by a young Algerian woman that people spat on and called names—she could stay locked inside its comforts forever, but it would not take away the knowledge of the suffering and torment and hatred that continued beyond the seeded-glass windows. If she didn't fight—there would be loss all the same.

She might as well do whatever she could.

The radio mumbled to life once more, beginning with the code name, long and short, as the operator identified themselves. Evangeline raised the volume just enough to hear it clearly.

CARPENTER.

Simone's code name.

She bit down hard on her finger to keep from sobbing. Her other hand closed around the thing she had slipped from the pocket of Stefan's coat, her fingers Magpie-quick. It was not too late. It was not too late to save her own life.

It was also not too late to save Simone's.

Her fingers flew over the transmitter as she parceled out her response, their back and forth, all the gaps between the letters filled with things they could not say. The static on the line was heavy; Evangeline could almost imagine Stefan breathing into it, excited, delighted that he had caught her in the act. The Magpie. The mole within the requisitions office that had chipped away at the Wehrmacht, bit by bit.

Can arrange safe extraction after two hours, Evangeline told her. Her heart was a fist in her throat. *No more.*

They signed off.

Downstairs, so far away in the cavernous mansion she barely should have been able to hear it, Evangeline heard the front door splinter in its frame.

CHAPTER TWENTY-NINE
LIAM

Clear the streets for the brown battalion, clear the streets for the storm battalion! Millions gaze upon the swastika, full of hope, for the day of freedom and plenty shall dawn!

The brownshirted thugs of the Sturmabteilun hadn't had a good public humiliation in a while, and it showed.

His captors parked the military transport truck on the outskirts of Wewelsburg, under autumn leaves that sparked gold and orange like embers as they frog-marched him across a stone bridge. They were joined by a handful of stormtroopers scarcely older than Liam, with lopsided haircuts and red lines on their throats from too-tight shirt collars. They hung a sign from his neck—FOREIGN AGENT—and sang the "Horst Wessel Lied" to commemorate a fellow fascist who'd been killed by Jewish agents, one of the boys claimed.

The Nazis were killing unfathomable numbers of Jewish people, but it figured the one dead German got his own song.

By the time they reached the town square, they'd attracted a meager crowd of off-duty soldiers and teenage boys too young and gawky to join the army just yet. Someone ran out with mugs of ale from a nearby tavern so they could drink and gossip while Wewelsburg's residents hurried past, trying not to make eye contact with him.

And Liam just let it happen. He felt the castle's shadow hanging over him like an executioner's blade. Maybe Daniel was in there now, murdering Dr. Kreutzer; maybe he'd been captured or killed himself. Maybe right this minute Pitr was tearing open a rift between the two worlds and stabilizing it with Sicarelli's book. Could Liam even stop him if he did reach out for the shadow once more? Could Liam stop himself from being consumed?

"Nothing to say for yourself, spy?" One of the boys, an acne-pocked kid practically swimming in his uniform, jabbed a finger into Liam's sternum. "It's a lot more fun if you fight back."

Liam hung his head. He was so tired—too tired, even, to keep himself upright against the post where he'd been tied. "What makes you so sure I'm a spy?"

"That terrible accent, for one." The SS officer who'd found him in the cabin smoothed out Daniel's note against his knee. "And your girl-friend's letter is in English."

Liam clamped his mouth shut.

"'I wish I could have spent a lifetime loving you,'" the officer read in a squeaky falsetto. "Where is she, anyway?"

"Far away from you," Liam growled.

The thugs burst into laughter and clanked ale mugs together. "Maybe we should go find her. Show her a real good time."

Liam bared his teeth. "You wouldn't stand a chance."

Daniel had encouraged him to close the rift for good. Deny himself and the Nazis both the shadow's power. What Liam hated most was how right Daniel was—how close he'd already come to succumbing to the darkness. What right did he have to criticize Daniel for doing the same?

Maybe it was their fate to always lose, to be beaten down, to see their dreams snatched away. Daniel could try to destroy the SS High Command, but it would likely kill him. If Liam pursued the shadow world once more, it would devour him, too. Either way, he lost. Either way, men like his father, like Pitr, like Heinrich Himmler and all these smug Nazi bastards would win. He and Daniel were only two boys standing against a tide of tyranny, a civilization built on hate.

Worse still, Liam hated that even as he felt like surrendering, the shadows called to him, his desire to tap into them again a living urge trying to break out of his skin. All but begging him to harness them one final time.

Another soldier came to join them then with a fresh round of beer. His grin, mossy and leering, lingered on Liam for too long. "Getting thirsty, spy?"

Liam didn't answer. It didn't stop the soldier from sloshing half his mug onto Liam. He sputtered as ale drenched the front of his shirt.

"What'd you do that for?" one of the brownshirts whined. "Such a waste of good beer."

"It was worth it for the look on his face." The guard drank from the rest of his mug and exhaled. "Ahh. Did you hear from the castle? They captured a Judenschwein trying to assassinate Dr. Kreutzer."

Liam's heart stuttered in his chest.

"Kreutzer? Ach, that man gives me the creeps. My brother

volunteered for his trials, and he just . . . hasn't been the same since."

"Your brother was an asshole. Besides, the doctor's project is supposed to make us even stronger, even better at fighting off enemies of the Reich . . ."

Liam clenched his fists tight, trying to drive off the insistent hum inside his skull. Whispers of power, promises of vengeance. Just one more time—what was one more time, if it meant he could save Daniel? Save the world? What was one more time feeling the power surge through him again, until he *was* power, until he could devour his enemies and destroy everything, like they'd destroyed him?

No—this was why Daniel hadn't wanted him to do it. This was why he couldn't let it in. Even if it would be so easy to give in, to defeat the Nazis—easier, even, than doing nothing at all—

Liam started humming. A single note, a sustained frequency. He found the dark tendrils swirling around his bound hands like an old friend.

Oh, Liam. There you are.

The voice echoed across the town square as the brownshirts went hazy. Darkness shimmered across the stones, bloodied trees and burned-out ruins overlying the whitewashed tavern and stone cottages as he opened the slightest rift. Eyes blinked at him from the blackness as something slithered past his feet.

Liiiii-aaaaaaam. I knew you couldn't stay away . . .

No—this was wrong. As soon as he felt the shadow, he felt its talons sinking into his flesh, shredding him. It flooded into the gaps between his thoughts, crowding out his senses.

Don't be shy, Liam. You are *powerful. You always were.*

"I don't want to be powerful," Liam managed through clenched teeth. "Not if it means being anything like you, Pitr."

Oh, but you are like me. And you still have a great purpose to serve. I need you, Liam. I need your command of the darkness. But if you won't do it for me . . .

The darkness warped again, revealing a stone chamber. A figure crouched in its center, gagged and bound. Daniel, his head bowed, his body slack.

A sacrifice.

The darkness burned away, leaving Liam back on the square, the brownshirts still arguing around him. They barely noticed the bitter laugh that rose from Liam's throat and the oily black that swirled in his palms.

"You win, Pitr." Teeth bared, Liam wrenched the ropes on his wrists apart like they were thread.

"Hey, wait!" one of the guards shouted.

"Which of you idiots untied him—"

Liam stood, and a swarm of screeching insects burst out of his palms. In an instant, they surrounded the brownshirts, swallowing up their screams in a torrential buzzing as they ripped away chunks of flesh. Liam was instinct and adrenaline now; if he stopped to think, if he stopped to worry about anything beyond this moment, he would fall apart. He was the shadow's tool.

But for just a little longer now, the shadow would be his.

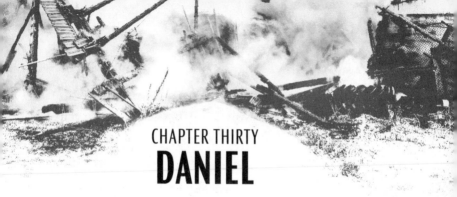

CHAPTER THIRTY
DANIEL

For one desperate, beautiful moment, Daniel almost thought he'd be able to pull it off.

After returning the Mercedes-Benz to the motor pool, he slipped unnoticed through the garage bay, the morning shift's soldiers still bleary-eyed and half asleep. He followed two men to the dining hall, and from there, found the directory for offices. Kreutzer's was in the basement, attached to the laboratory space, which should have been ideal: fewer witnesses, thicker walls. The yawning secretaries paid him no mind as he stalked past them in a freshly stolen uniform. The office door was unlocked.

And inside, the doctor was nowhere to be found.

Daniel cursed, then shut the door behind himself. It was the safest place for him to hide, for now. He hadn't done anything too rash just yet. He hadn't fired his gun, given away his purpose. Maybe the book was here, under the stacks of lab charts, bundled-up papers. He could take it back to Liam, forget his assassination plot, leave his vengeance for another day. Maybe he could even destroy the book. Keep it from everyone's hands. Run away with Liam and forget everything.

But he'd burned those ships.

Daniel stepped out of the office, his heart a heavy timpani line. Stravinsky's *Rite of Spring*. He was here for his own ritual, one last act to balance the scales of the Eisenbergs' deaths. The corridor was empty, but somewhere in this stone prison, Kreutzer waited. Maybe even Himmler himself. Any one of them would do.

The drumbeat heightened as he drew closer to the end of the wing—the laboratories the Unterführer had mentioned. Where Kreutzer wove his vile magic, where his victims gasped for air but breathed in only shadows as Kreutzer and Pitr infused them with energy from another world. A bass line underpinned his heartbeat now as he moved closer, rising and falling, over and over. One hand closed around the doorknob, the other around his knife. He wrenched it open, not knowing what horrors would await him on the other side—

Kreutzer looked up from the body spread before him. His white lab coat was thin and too starchy; it had been washed too many times, with too many blood stains leaving behind a faint yellow residue. And the body—it hurt Daniel's eyes when he tried to focus on it. Shadow and smoke and fast-twitch muscles, a pained shudder of breath—

"Ah. Herr Doyle's accomplice, aren't you?" Kreutzer asked. "A pity he didn't come himself."

Daniel lunged forward, knife raised. He aimed for the doctor's throat, mottled with puckered burn-scar scabs—

The body lurched up from the operating table: shadow and smoke and emptied-out stare. It socked Daniel square in the gut, dropping him to his knees, then shot out a foot to kick his knife away. Kreutzer snapped his fingers, and the soldier wrenched Daniel's arms behind his back with impossible speed.

Kreutzer stood before him, fresh burns glistening with puffy skin along one side of his face. It was almost enough to make Daniel smile, the memory of the Kino fire Liam had set. He crouched down low, the machine behind him humming with the alternating frequency to open the rift, and regarded Daniel with a smile scalpel-sharp.

"Don't worry. I think I have a use for you yet." He turned to the soldier. "Take him to the dungeons while Herr Černik and I prepare."

The soldier dragged him away, his failure weighing him down, heavy as shackles. His cell was tiny, closet-size; the door slammed shut with a finality that stung. He curled into the corner to wait. He could almost hear Rebeka scolding him for trying to be such a hero, such a fool. His traitor brain conjured up memories of the pale field of Liam's throat, his muscles tensing and relaxing as Daniel's fingertips charted them. Had he felt that passion still, when he found Daniel's note? Had he awoken with regret and felt only relief to know Daniel would trouble him no more? For Liam's sake, Daniel hoped so.

And yet deep down, he supposed he'd been hoping Liam would find a way to stop him.

No, hope was foolish and wasteful. Why should Daniel cling to hope in such a worthless world as this? Why should he fight to make it better? There was nothing to fix. At least the shadow world was more honest about what it was: darkness and blood and endless agony and rage. Humans were the real monsters who wore the skin of innocent creatures while underneath, they festered with hate.

After very little time, the door to his cell clanged open. Daniel glanced up, squinting into the harsh burst of light as Dr. Kreutzer stepped inside. But it was the boy who followed him into the cell who gave Daniel pause. He was shorter and a few years older than Daniel. Perhaps. The sallow, haunted expression in his eyes spoke of someone far older. His dark hair was swept to one side over bottle-lens glasses. And when he moved, he—

Daniel squinted. He didn't know how to describe it, except as an *echo*, shadow trailing behind the boy's limbs. An uneasy tide rose in Daniel's gut, his subconscious working out something his mind hadn't yet put into words.

Kreutzer wrinkled his nose at the stench of hard water and molding stone and human waste that permeated the cell. "You're certain this will work?"

The boy's smile was brutal, carved out of his face with a rusty knife. "He smells of Doyle's spells." He stepped forward, one hand raised, and instinctively, Daniel jerked his head away. Yet this only made him laugh with a wretched, metallic scrape.

Revulsion flushed over Daniel. "Pitr."

Pitr's eyes narrowed to hot points of fire as he gripped Daniel by the chin and forced Daniel's face upward to study him. His touch was clammy; his movements jerked awkwardly, like a marionette. And still he smiled and smiled.

"I am so much more than Pitr now."

Daniel tried to shrink back, but Pitr held firm.

"Did he love you?" Speaking low turned Pitr's voice scratchy, and it felt like claws raking over Daniel's skin. "Oh, I hope he did."

The doctor regarded Daniel like a beautifully marbled cut of meat, making Daniel's skin crawl. "You will pay for what you did to me." He turned his face into the grimy light, the burn scars from the fire at the movie house in Hallenberg shiny like sausage casing. "I look forward to it."

Pitr trailed a fingertip down Daniel's jaw until it rested against his collarbone where it jutted from his torn-open shirt. His touch felt like venom, burning Daniel alive from the inside.

The air around Pitr shimmered then—his touch faded away as if he was backing off. But he hadn't moved at all—he'd only *thinned*. Pitr sighed like he was scolding a child. "I will need to ready him first."

Kreutzer narrowed his eyes, then nodded. "I'll have my tools brought to the chamber."

"Yes," Pitr said. "That would be ideal."

Then Pitr became solid again. His grip was now a fist clutching Daniel by the throat. His mouth stretched into a rictus, rotted teeth sharp and grinding beneath glowing eyes.

"I want him to feel it. Each excruciating moment of your pain. I want you to cry for him. I will break him, and his power will be mine. Do you understand me?"

Daniel said nothing, despite the cold dread filling him. Bait. They wanted to use him as bait for Liam.

"I want him to come try to save you. Hear you begging for mercy. And I want him to watch as you die."

Daniel closed his eyes. "I died a long time ago." How many times had he dreamed of this moment, of telling these men exactly what he thought of them? And yet he had no words, no knife or pistol in his hand either. It had all been a waste. "You bastards killed me when you sent my family to Chełmno."

Pitr's grip loosened, and he slithered back.

"Come." Kreutzer seized Daniel by his bound hands. "Maybe we can make your death mean something more."

"Welcome to the Realm of the Dead."

The chamber they dragged him to was a cavernous, ritualistic space, gaudily appointed like some sort of medieval sanctuary, with curving stone walls and too many candles to count. A shaft of light illuminated a sole lectern in the center of the room. Daniel's head felt woozy; whatever they'd given him had imbued the whole space with a misty, hazy atmosphere that threw garish shadows onto the rough sandstone walls. Daniel knelt, hands bound behind him, while Pitr held a dagger under his chin. Thin rivulets of blood ran down his neck and arms, trickling with warmth.

And then there was the machine—the two machines—

Liam's oscillators. The curved metal posts emitted a noise that rolled over and over at a painfully low frequency, thousands of times stronger than any radio wave. It threatened to tear open Daniel's thoughts.

A girl appeared in the opening to the chamber, taking in the sight with wide rabbit eyes. "Herr Doktor . . . ?"

"Ilse, my dear, there you are. Better late than never."

The girl—Ilse—blinked, trying to regain her composure. Her gaze skittered toward Daniel's, but just as soon darted away. "J-ja, mein Herr. What is it you need?"

"This one"—Kreutzer jerked his head toward Daniel—"he's

showing remarkable resilience, isn't he? Come. Help me make use of him yet. Prepare the oscillators."

Pitr chuckled. The sound was almost inhuman, rumbling deep in Daniel's marrow.

"Perhaps it is . . . too cruel to use a prisoner for this, Herr Doktor." Ilse clutched her clipboard to her chest. "We have so many volunteers—"

"Nonsense." Kreutzer waved her off. "Now, help us prepare for the ritual."

Ilse clipped past him on high heels that echoed through the chamber. As she came alongside Daniel, she knelt down, studying him with a quizzical look. Daniel looked back at her with drooping eyelids.

But then she mouthed a single word: *Rebeka.*

Daniel sucked in his breath. "Here? No—"

Ilse's eyes flared wide as she pressed a finger to her lips, then stood once more and joined Kreutzer at the lectern in the chamber's center. He ran his fingers along the page open before him. The illustration showed a darkened doorway, thick shadows pouring out of it in spiraling waves. As Daniel tried to focus on the waterfall of darkness pouring off the lectern, he felt even more disoriented, nauseated.

Rebeka. Had she come after him? What about Liam and the others? He prayed that if any of them had sense left, they'd find one another, stay together, leave him to die and not risk their own lives as well—

"You shall be a sacrifice. To fuel the transformation of our troops and the unlocking of boundless energy for the Reich," Kreutzer crowed. All around them, the air had taken on a shimmering quality. "You remember the creature we examined from Siegen, Ilse?"

Ilse's smile was strained. "How could I forget?"

"We will command an army of them. Infuse our soldiers with their powers. An army of monsters to devour our foes."

"And a new world to conquer," Pitr added. His blade skipped across Daniel's arm, making a shallow nick.

Kreutzer waved his hand with annoyance. "But only if you hurry up."

"He's fighting it," Pitr growled, studying him. "He doesn't feel enough pain."

The machines gurgled with a new sound—the frequency had changed. Daniel felt a tremor in the air like the trill of the strings section, the low rumble of timpani. He knew the sensation. It was the same feeling of teetering on the brink that he'd felt all around Liam. When they were about to kiss. When he was about to tear the world in two—

A tremendous explosion ripped through the chamber. Not an artillery strike—something more, something primal. Something deep and vast and hungry.

Yes, *hungry*—that was the word Daniel thought as he was tossed into the air, the ground beneath him bucking wildly. Hungry like a deep, deep well that could never be filled. As Kreutzer and Pitr and Ilse went flying skyward with him, he imagined they felt the hunger's pull, too, and none of them were afraid.

Then they landed on the shattered Black Sun mosaic at the chamber's center. Daniel groaned, fingers stretching out along the tiles as he tried to wrench his arms around. The book skidded across the broken stone floor, pages rifling in the wind. Sulfur and smoke danced heavy on the air.

A figure stepped out of the smoke, soot smearing his face. Dark tendrils wisped from his blond hair, his outstretched fingertips, his glowing eyes. He strode across the tile, something dark and wondrous trailing behind him like a veil.

"Liam," Daniel breathed.

With a ripple of whispers, Liam stomped on Pitr's wrist and wrenched the dagger from his hand. "Hello, Pitr."

CHAPTER THIRTY-ONE
PHILLIP

"**We have to go in,**" Rebeka said. "He'll need us. We have to stop the ritual—"

Simone spat on the cobbles of the alley mouth where they were watching the castle. "If the Nazis caught him, your brother is already dead."

Phillip shrank back into the shadows as a pair of guards goose-stepped along the castle's entrance bridge. This was insane, this was all insane. They couldn't barge through the front door, and if Daniel had been caught sneaking in, the castle was sure to be on high alert. He wanted to help Rebeka, but as far as he could tell, the best thing they could do was send word to Simone's Resistance contacts—maybe they could even summon military assistance from RAF pilots off in Wherever-the-Fuck-by-the-Sea—and let them handle it.

Let them handle it. Not our fight. His father's words and Mr. Connolly's rang in his skull. Just like the German kids they met, who'd gladly endure a death by a thousand smaller cuts if it spared them a larger single discomfort. It was easy to ignore any problem as long as paying attention hurt worse.

Phillip looked at Rebeka, the tears clumped in her dark lashes, the hard set of her jaw.

This girl was going to be the death of him.

No. The determination she set in him was.

"Your brother has a death wish," Simone pointed out. Softer now. "We may already be too late."

"I have to fight for him." Rebeka tilted her head. "Just as you're fighting, I think, for the person on the radio."

Simone whirled on her, rifle clenched tight. "What the *fuck* do you know—"

"Hey! Both of you!" Phillip shouted. "None of this helps us get inside."

Or that was what he mostly said, before the blast of energy kicked him in the chest like a drunk mule, sending him sprawling deep into the alley. Lightning burned through the sky; when he blinked, he saw the afterimage of Wewelsburg's main tower split with a bolt that came from inside. He groaned, waiting for his vision to clear. Simone had landed somewhere to his right, and Rebeka landed on top of him.

"Oh," she said, facing him, her eyes round with shock. He imagined his own expression was something considerably dopier.

"You all right?" he whispered.

She smiled shyly, nodded, and tucked her hair back behind her ear. He raised his hands, overcome with the urge to tuck it back, too—

Then the shards of stone began to rain down on them.

"Merde! Right in my eye."

Simone sat up, and Rebeka did the same, scrambling off of Phillip, delicate as a hummingbird. He sat up too, and realized he wasn't only winded from Rebeka. His whole body ached.

"What . . . what was that?" Phillip asked.

Simone finished digging around in her eye and shook the rest of the dust from her hair. "I think *that* was our invitation inside."

He followed her gaze to the north tower of the castle. The bare stonework had shredded upward and split open like a trick cigar. Dark smoke spewed out of it—too dark for normal smoke. Too rank with an oily stench.

"The ritual chamber," Rebeka said, her voice quavering.

"Got a feeling Liam has something to do with that," Phillip said.

"What tipped you off?" Simone asked with a roll of her eyes. "The explosions?"

"Let's hope Daniel's with him." Rebeka was already standing, wriggling her foot back into a loosened shoe strap, body primed to bolt.

"Rebeka, wait." Phillip stood too. "If you're going to charge in there, at least tell us your plan."

"Okay. Liam wants to keep the portal open. But he can't control it all—not for good. Not without the shadow devouring him, too. And especially not with Kreutzer and that . . . man." Rebeka gripped his arm, pleading. "They need my help. Humans have ruined the shadow world enough. We can't keep stealing their energy, just as they can't keep drinking up ours. We'll corrupt each other until there's nothing left."

Simone and Phillip both turned toward her, assessing. "But . . . but you can control the energy," Simone said.

Rebeka shifted her weight, shoulders drawing up toward her ears.

"No. It's too much. There's so many, there's so much hatred—I'm—I'm afraid I can't hold on."

Phillip tapped her wrist with his fingertips. "But I've seen what you can do."

She rocked back on her heels and wrapped her arms around herself. "I don't want to be like those monsters. The angry ones, the vengeful ones." Her voice broke. "It doesn't matter who started it. We'll tear each other's worlds apart."

"You're not like them. My God, you're not. Is that what you're afraid of? That this connection somehow makes you . . . *like* them?"

"I don't want to be this evil, ravenous thing. I don't want to be able to control the shadows."

"Hey. Hey, listen to me." He placed his hands over her too-sharp shoulders, waited for her to give him a tentative nod. "You didn't choose to have this affinity. And it isn't because of something you did."

She squeezed her eyes shut, but didn't argue.

"It's a thing that happened, all right? It's not your fault. You didn't *do* this."

"But I could have used it. I could have used it to save our whole family. I didn't. I'm no better than one of those things, angry and starving."

"You saved Daniel," Phillip said. "And you can save him still. You understand it better now. You know what it can do, for better or worse." His voice hitched; he felt the force of Mr. Connolly's carefree dismissal of all the harm his invention had done. But he chose to do better. He had that choice. And so did she.

Rebeka blinked. When her lids opened, her eyes were filled with blackness; her body felt thinner in his grip, like he could close his palms around her shoulders and move right through her. Then she blinked again and was herself. No—that wasn't right. She'd always been herself. Darkness, grief, rage—why shouldn't she feel those things? Why shouldn't they all? What use was it to try to act so noble when fighting monsters who believed in no such thing?

"You can ignore the darkness. Pretend you don't feel it," Phillip said. "Or you can use it to stop people who'd use it for far worse."

Something tugged at Rebeka's lips: the dimmest hint of a smile. To him, it felt as warm, as real as spring.

"You're right. I didn't ask for any of this to happen." She stood up straighter. "But that doesn't mean I can't use it now."

Simone stepped toward them from the alley's mouth. "It's been almost an hour," she said. "One more hour until I have to hail Magpie."

"When we're done, we have to close the bridge to the other universe. For good." Rebeka swallowed, her slender throat bobbing. "This has to be the end of it. Otherwise it could destroy both our world and theirs."

Phillip's fingers moved involuntarily toward the pouch where he kept the frequency folder. It could help negate the pull of the other universe. With enough juice, he could help seal it for good. But they'd still need Liam and Rebeka to do it, too. "And you really think you can convince Liam of that?"

She drew a slow breath, twisting her fingers in the folds of her jacket. "We have to try."

An air raid siren groaned to life on the streets beneath them.

"Shit." Simone peered around the corner. "They're going to call for reinforcements. If our stupid American isn't careful, he's going to summon the entire Wehrmacht."

"The comms room. We've got to get there first. Jam their outgoing signals. Their equipment should give me the juice I need to help close the bridge, and then we can coordinate with Magpie." Phillip gestured toward one of the triangle sides of the castle, where thorny radio antennae sprouted from it like a cruel crown. Between that and the ring of transponder towers they'd passed on their way into town, it should be more than enough.

"Magpie," Simone echoed, glancing away. "I'm sure she's afraid, same as us. But it's better than being afraid alone."

Amid the screaming sirens and rancid smoke, Simone led the charge toward the chaos of Wewelsburg Castle.

CHAPTER THIRTY-TWO

LIAM

The shadow world was no longer just around the corner. At Wewelsburg Castle, the two worlds had collided and twisted together like crumpled metal in an auto accident, and it was impossible to tell where one ended and the other began. They bled into each other in a nightmare of whispers and shrieks and shadow and stone.

Pitr crawled to his feet, skin slipping over the knot of shadows beneath. He was more shadow than man now. Liam supposed a year lost in this horrible place would do that to anyone, especially someone who already nursed so much darkness in his heart. No wonder he and Kreutzer had found each other; if Pitr hadn't chosen Princeton, he probably would've gladly worked his way up the SS ranks alongside his research pal. Pitr's sunken chest puffed up with a gulp of air, and then he laughed. It sounded like the wails of the dying.

"Thank you for the added pain." Pitr's smile glinted like a knife's edge. "It's just what I needed to begin the stabilization ritual."

"Let Daniel go. You don't need him for this."

"Oh, but I do." Pitr snatched Daniel up by the bindings around his wrists. Strange winds swirled around them, echoes of sorrow stitched into the gusts. "He means something to you. So he is worth everything."

Daniel locked eyes with Liam then, those dark pools pulling at Liam's gut. *Dammit, Daniel.* Liam swallowed, throat bobbing. Why did Daniel care so little for his life, even now? Why hadn't Liam been able to convince him to stay alive?

"You shouldn't have come for me." Drying blood coated Daniel's upper lip, cracking as he spoke. "You deserve to live."

Liam bit his lip to stave off a rush of tears. "So do you."

Daniel's eyelids fluttered as he fought against blood loss. "You don't need this other world. You're strong enough without it."

How Liam wished that were true. He'd never been strong enough, and now he'd let his weakness ruin them all. He had to command the shadow one last time before it consumed him. If he could just be strong enough, he could keep it from the Nazis and whoever else sought to claim it. If he sacrificed—

The castle chamber shivered and quaked, straining to hold both worlds as they melded into one, sending him off balance. The shadow world and his world were aligning, folding together, and the ground where they stood was the hinge. The chamber's stone walls crumbled away in a torrent of wind, exposing only the shadow realm around them and a crude altar of ceremony and sacrifice.

Liam saw, then, what Pitr meant to do: bleed Daniel to draw out more of the monsters—monsters Pitr meant to command.

Liam's body felt ragged with the immense energy he'd gathered into himself. He'd unleashed plenty when he tore into the castle, but now, in this twilight plane between two worlds, he didn't need to draw the energy into himself any longer. It was already here, spilling around them, infecting his world more and more by the second as the universes bled together. He could command it all. He could do anything.

But so, potentially, could Pitr.

Liam closed his eyes and reached out. A hundred thousand heartbeats hammered in the distance as dark creatures circled the confluence, weighing their options. He heard their hungry whispers, their purposeless yearning to punish the world that stole from theirs, to feast on the taste they loved most. Pressing even further into the shadow, he caressed their thoughts each in turn, teasing them with the promise of countless Nazis to devour if they'd just fall under his control. He needed them on *his* side—not Pitr's.

They raised their heads and drew nearer. They were hungry—and they would obey whoever let them feed. Whoever gave them a whole new world to conquer.

Liam opened his thoughts to them, their energy, their wants, their ravenous cravings echoed through him. He saw glimpses of the worlds as they saw them: trickling anger and fear, sweet and cloying as perfume; the world was measured around them not in light and shadow and form, but in its raw potential for violence and decay.

He could give them that.

Here, this is yours. Feast. He saw what they saw; he steered them through the maze of the crumbling castle walls as it bled into the shadow world. A cluster of SS officers on that floor, foot soldiers gathering in the common rooms—let the monsters sate themselves.

Screams rang through the corridors of what was left of Wewelsburg Castle.

Liam saw them popping behind his eyes like mortar shells bursting: the monsters, *his* monsters, feeding. The Nazis' agony and pain sustained them. The fierce, relentless gnash of teeth and claws and a hunger that had no bottom, just like his power, his boundless power.

Someone wheezed with laughter behind him. Frowning, Liam turned, letting his focus slide away from his monsters and their glorious feast. Kreutzer was dislodging himself from beneath the rubble. Bright red blood glistened over the fine coating of stone that powdered his face and hair; it smeared across his chin the color of a ripe pomegranate. He swayed as he pulled himself up to one foot, then the other, and dusted his hands across his knees.

"You have some skill, Mr. Doyle, I will grant you that." He cracked his neck from side to side; his tongue darted out to flick against the blood beneath his lip. He stooped down and grabbed the battered *Porta ad Tenebras* manuscript. "But you lack that crucial ingredient that will see our Aryan warriors to glory. You lack *conviction*."

Liam took a step back as the doctor moved toward him. With a roll of his hand, he wrapped a strand of shadow energy around his wrist. It shivered in his touch, desperate to be used. Desperate to use Liam. "I wouldn't say that."

"You think I underestimate you, little runt? No." Darkness slithered across Kreutzer's eyes, purple and silver galaxies spinning in its wake. "I've seen it. I've seen through you. Through all of this . . ."

Kreutzer took a deep gulp of the fetid air around him. The castle *smelled* like the shadow world now, that spoiled-meat stink full of rot and dampness. Liam had always fought against its influence; for all he felt it corrupting him, he hadn't realized, before, quite how much he'd managed to stave off. It had eaten Pitr from the inside out. Latched on to that cruelness in him and let it metastasize. Pitr had already been a creature of the shadow world, its ruthless laws and rabid pursuit of selfishness and cruelty; he just hadn't yet found his home. And now that he had, it was no wonder the world had bent toward him far more confidently than it had ever yielded to Liam.

But the darkness was pulsing through him, and he couldn't keep control of it forever.

Pitr and Kreutzer struck as one.

It was a wave of force, black and sparking with electricity. Slamming Liam to the ground. Crackling across his skin. He only panicked for a moment, but it was enough to loosen his grip. One by one, the leashes of the monsters he was controlling slipped free.

Shit.

Above him, Daniel dangled, blood dripping down his forearms. He stared at Liam with an unfocused gaze. Too unfocused—he was losing too much blood.

The monsters' howls were at the chamber doors now.

"Enough, Dr. Kreutzer," a woman's voice said.

Liam blinked from his position on the floor, his vision still rattled, just in time to catch sight of the pretty blond secretary steadying herself on her heels. She'd produced a snub-nosed pistol and pointed it now, shakily, at Kreutzer and Pitr, back and forth.

"You've done enough. To Germany, to her people, to all of us. I can't stand for it. I won't stand for it any longer."

Kreutzer struggled to keep himself from breaking into a laugh.

"I—I will be strong against the tide of hate," she stammered. "We must—resist—"

The chamber door shattered in an explosion of wood splinters. The beasts were here.

They poured forth like a poisonous gas, filling the chamber. Joints creaking back the wrong way, skinless muscles bunching, wounds seeping and oozing. The pack leader crouched and sprang—and before she could summon a scream, they descended on her.

In seconds, she was nothing but shreds of flesh.

"Sweet, stupid Ilse." Kreutzer clucked his tongue. "Far too little, my dear. You're far too late."

The beasts circled Kreutzer, teeth snapping, but Pitr held them back with an upturned hand. An eyeless rust-colored snout snuffled at Liam's torso, his neck and throat.

Liam slowed his breathing and savored his own fear. He welcomed it. It would fuel him. Biting down on his tongue to add to his pain, he reached out to unleash the rest of his stored energy—

But there was nothing left.

"I told you you didn't want it enough," Pitr said. "You strive and strive. But you'll never be willing to do what it takes to seize true control."

A thousand eyeless faces pressed in, their razor teeth dripping with fresh blood.

Liam flinched as their hot, decaying breaths raked across his skin. Maybe Pitr was right. Maybe he couldn't seize complete control over the entire shadow realm.

But maybe he *could* do whatever it took to close the rift for good.

CHAPTER THIRTY-THREE

SIMONE

Wewelsburg Castle was a crypt, and it was quickly suffocating them.

"This way," Phillip called. The electric lights dotting the corridor flickered once to reveal a partially collapsed doorway, then fell dark again. "The antennae were up here."

"The electricity's barely working. How will we power a signal?" Simone's heart was beating furiously, a trapped bird trying to take flight. Evangeline was waiting, just out of reach, past the shadow-touched soldiers and monsters and whispers. Evangeline had promised to find them a way out—she could summon the full force of her Resistance network—if they could just hold out—

Another flicker of electricity, enough to remind Simone of the concrete walls squeezing in around them. Her breath hitched as she reached out to steady herself. She imagined a wall of bones, crowned with countless eyeless skulls staring down at her, laughing, soaking up all her secrets to throw back in her face.

Simone forced herself off the wall and caught Phillip by the collar. In the distance: another wheezing rasp, like a thousand wordless voices. The claws scraped slow, then retreated.

Simone exhaled. "All right. Keep going."

Rebeka was lagging behind. Simone whirled on her heel, searching the dark hallway. Breathing. There was breathing—

Another flicker exposed the entrance to a stairwell. This should be the radio tower, according to Phillip. But there was no telling if they'd have enough power, or if they could even figure out the Germans' equipment. She needed something faster than Morse code if they were going to get aid from the Resistance. Evangeline or not, there might not be enough aid left to spare.

They climbed the stone stairs, crooked now from the explosion. Ears strained for any more signs of the shadow beasts. The lights flickered on and off, and each time, Simone swung back to check behind them. The rifle in her grip was the only thing grounding her. Well— that and the tangled nest of memories and questions in her head.

Had Evangeline been aiding them from the start? If so, why would she lie, pretend she didn't care? Why would she let Simone scold her so, and ultimately walk away? But then there was the possibility she'd only been spurred to action after Simone left. That was no healthy exchange, either. Either way, it left Simone chilled, unsure what to trust.

Simone winced. As if she were blameless. They were both flawed, both flailing desperately to cling to a life they couldn't control. If Evangeline had decided to help, well, perhaps Simone, too, could be willing to change. Maybe even forgive.

She looked at Phillip and Rebeka. They could have easily left her to die. True, they'd needed her to some extent, but there was more to it than that. They trusted her, and in turn, she'd shown them nothing but suspicion, annoyance, aggravation. She'd been all too ready to leave them behind, despite whatever help they could offer her. How could she fault Evangeline for doing the same?

Isn't it better than being afraid alone? A shiver ran down her back. Yes, she'd tried so hard to do this alone. But she didn't have to.

"Look. It must have its own generator," Phillip said.

Sure enough, at the top of the staircase, a ribbon of light streamed out from underneath a heavy oak door. Rebeka leaned against it, but the door didn't budge. Shoved a little harder. Phillip tried to help her, until finally Simone pushed them both out of the way and slammed her shoulder into it.

"You could have been quieter," Phillip said. "If there's more of those *things*—"

"Then I'd rather draw them out now," Simone retorted. "Better that than stumble across one lurking behind a piece of equipment."

"That isn't exactly comforting," Phillip said.

Rebeka shook her head at both of them and stormed into the radio room.

The glorious, massive radio room, full of transponders, recorders, high-powered broadcasting equipment . . .

And two SS radio operators, sidearms leveled right at them.

"Drop your weapons," Simone barked in German. "I guarantee I'm a better shot than either of you."

One, a plump man with Himmler-style round glasses, started to falter, but the other brought his one hand up to steady his gun arm as he tried to aim—

Simone's shot tore straight through one hand and into his lungs, flipping him backward in his chair. The man in the glasses gasped, dropped his sidearm, and raised both hands. "I surrender!"

"I didn't ask you to." Simone fired square at his chest. She turned back toward Phillip and Rebeka, ready to have to defend her choice, but neither of them were about to shed any tears over dead Nazis. She swept the rest of the room and, finding no one else, gave the all-clear.

Phillip whistled low as he approached the operator's desk. "This is gonna do nicely." He flipped a row of switches, and the equipment hummed, ascending, at a steady pitch.

Rebeka and Simone joined him. "What do we need to do?" Simone asked.

Phillip brushed his fingertips over the equipment. "First, we'll link up these transponders. This frequency folder is gonna need some *legs*."

As Simone reached for the first set of cables, though, the earth rumbled beneath them again. Rebeka stumbled backward with a yelp, then fell eerily silent, her eyes going to that far-off place.

"What?" Simone whispered. "What is it?"

Rebeka's lips moved for a moment before she returned to herself. "Daniel," she said. "He's—he's alive. But the shadow realm—it's eating into our own, and the angry ones, Pitr's controlling them . . . I need to help him." Her voice was grim. "He can't do it alone."

Simone's throat tightened. With sudden, cold clarity, she realized she was *afraid* for this girl. She hadn't felt fear like this for someone else since . . . She couldn't even recall. But above all, she'd learned Rebeka was brave, and stronger than Simone could have ever imagined. It made Simone want to be strong for more than just herself, too.

"Please," Simone whispered. "Be careful."

Phillip hesitated, fist closing and unfurling. "Rebeka . . ."

Rebeka rushed toward him then, gripped his chin, and tugged him into a desperate kiss. Simone's stomach flipped before she made herself look away. They deserved each other—the mad, desperate American boy and the ferocious shadow girl. Simone wished she could be deserving, too.

No. That was a lie. She could be. Maybe she already was.

When she looked back, Rebeka nodded to her once, curt, and then melted into the shadow realm.

"Um. Okay." Phillip's hands shook as he fiddled with the control panels once more.

Simone rested a hand on his wrist. "Deep breaths, lover boy."

Phillip's face turned a dark plum, and Simone couldn't help it— she smirked. He drew a ragged breath, then returned to the console. "Let me work on the frequency. You see if you can hail your contact."

Simone worried at her lower lip with her teeth as she dialed into the shortwave frequency. "Carpenter hailing Magpie. Magpie, come in. Over."

She imagined her voice bouncing across Europe, against the earth covered with German forces and the sky hedged in with clouds. Imagined it worming its way through the walls of Château à Pont Allemagne. Into the narrow cubby she'd built into Evangeline's bedroom, where they used to cram inside together and tangle into a single soul. Did Evangeline keep her radio there? Was she sitting, even now, on that soft and devouring bed where Simone had left her heart?

But there was only a heavy silence, disrupted with static hiccups as two worlds crashed together.

CHAPTER THIRTY-FOUR

EVANGELINE

Though she was entering in handcuffs this time, there was something oddly comforting about 84 avenue Foch. She'd been here before. She'd walked out of it, once. But as calm as she felt as she was dragged past the secretary pool and the radio room toward the interrogation wing on the top floor, she very much doubted she'd be leaving again.

The guard shoved her into a chair in the small and grimy cell. It looked even smaller from this side of the metal grate. Hastily constructed within what must have been a lavish Beaux Arts penthouse to rival the Gaturins' château, the cell was only dull plaster walls, already badly stained and battered from the treatment its temporary residents had endured. As the guard slipped her hands around the bars of the chair to secure her further, Evangeline found herself smiling.

"What's so funny?" he asked with a scowl.

"Everything."

He blinked, unsettled, and backed hurriedly out of the cell.

At least an hour must have passed since she'd last spoken to Simone. Wewelsburg would be expecting intruders if the sorry state

Georges-Yves had been in the night before was anything to go by. Simone had seemed awfully confident about their chances of making it inside the castle, but Evangeline couldn't share her optimism. Not that she was one to talk, with this mad scheme.

Just one more hour until Simone would be waiting for her to work the kind of magic that only a Gaturin could work. She had no idea how little that name would save Evangeline. The only thing she had to guide her now was the bald-faced, aggressive certainty that she'd learned from Simone.

Three minutes passed. Eight. How long were they going to make her sweat? Hours? Surely even Stefan didn't have the patience for that. No, surely he'd be coming any minute to gloat and berate and torment, and God only knew what other tortures he had in store—

The cell door swung open, and he entered. Alone.

Evangeline's wrists tensed within their shackles.

"Hello, Magpie." He cricked his neck from side to side, took his time tugging on those leather gloves she hated so. They squeaked across his skin, too oiled, too broken in. "It is Magpie, yes? All these silly code names you cowards make up, to play at waging war."

"Yes, we're not nearly sophisticated enough for terms like Einsatzgruppen and the Torturer of Troyes."

All the kid leather in the world couldn't soften the crack of his knuckles against her jaw. Her head spun from the force of the blow, neck radiating with stabbing pain. Slowly, she twisted back to face him head-on and raised her chin, despite the blood she felt welling on her lower lip.

"Such a mouth on you," he said. "I almost forget how delicate you are. With little bird's bones."

She tucked one thumb into her palm. He was right about that.

"Ordinarily I'd let you stew in your own failure for a few days. Let you soil yourself, get hungry and thirsty and delirious. Desperate. I do so wish I could hear what kind of bargaining and pleading and begging you'd do in such a state." One finger ran down the side of her face, and she felt acid in her throat. "But I'm afraid you have us at a disadvantage, Magpie. Wewelsburg Castle is under assault, and you, it seems, were in touch with its attackers. They aren't responding to our radio calls. So I fear we must rush this."

Evangeline did her best not to sigh with relief. Probably half an hour until she was supposed to check in with Simone. Simone, who might at this very minute be waiting desperately for her to answer, to fend off countless guards—

"Understand, though, that urgency cuts both ways, little girl. If you don't give us what we need, in the time we need it, then—" His eyes slitted. "You'll be the one who's out of time."

"Tempting," Evangeline said. "But . . . I think I like my way better."

Another crack, this time on the other side of her jaw. It was so loud, so sharp, that it disguised the softer *pop* of cartilage elsewhere; it certainly lent authenticity to the agonized expression on her face.

"And what," Stefan said, "is your way?"

"I thought it was past time you took me dancing," Evangeline said.

He cocked his head, his confusion suddenly quaint, harmless somehow, like a pigeon strutting around the Tuileries. That moment of confusion was all she needed as she slipped one hand, dislocated thumb and all, free of its cuff. Then she was flying forward, good hand grasping for his waistband. Her fingers reached for the handle of his gun—

He knocked her away effortlessly, smashing her into the plaster wall. The wall rattled as she struck it—just as she'd hoped. So flimsy. They'd built their jail in a hurry, rushing about for efficiency's sake. Simone would be appalled.

Stefan pulled his sidearm free and leveled it right at her. Cocked the firing mechanism. "I'll give you one last chance to reconsider."

A trickle of sweat ran down Evangeline's back as she stared into that cavernous barrel, looming so large in her view. "My mind's already made up."

"A pity," Stefan said, and pulled the trigger.

The makeshift cell echoed with a dull *click*.

Stefan reared back, shocked. Evangeline's breath rushed out of her. It had been quite the risky bet that he wouldn't think to check his gun's ammunition between their car ride to the château, when she'd swiped the magazine, and now. But that wasn't all the Magpie had taken. Now she withdrew the letter opener from its hiding place beneath the under-wire of her bra and threw herself on Stefan. The closest she'd ever been to him. Certainly the only time she'd wanted to be.

He grappled with her, trying ineffectively to dig his nails into her face through his leather gloves. "You fucking harlot, I will destroy you!" He slammed his forehead against hers, sparking stars behind her eyes. "I will—"

But he never finished—the letter opener ground into his trachea. Enraged thrashing, crunching cartilage, and then—he was still.

A horrified sob rattled out of Evangeline's throat as Stefan collapsed beneath her, and she scrambled off him, limbs shaking furiously. Too close, far too close. Was this the game she was always destined to play to do the right thing? Victory by fractions? If they were even lucky enough to defeat evil at all.

She snapped her left thumb back into place, redoubling the agonizing pain, but it was useless. She must have torn something. She dug around in Stefan's pockets, recoiling from the sharp metal stink of his blood, until she found his torturer's tool kit. Unfurled it. Ripped free knives and kept digging, until finally she found what she sought.

The cyanide vials he'd used to torment Georges-Yves. Individually, only enough to threaten death, not bring it about . . . but here she had access to all of them. And the intimate knowledge of Beaux Arts architecture that only a carpenter's girlfriend possessed.

The interrogation cell walls were always meant to be temporary; the prisoners were never actually meant to touch them, for they'd always be cuffed. That made the plaster so easy to punch through when she hacked at it with a dead Nazi's knife for a minute or so. But she was running behind schedule; Simone was already waiting. If she'd survived. Evangeline choked back a cry—if she was still alive.

She crawled out of the back of the cell wall she'd torn through, armed with a knife, a broken thumb, and inordinate quantities of cyanide pellets. These she held loose in her good hand, a layer of fabric between her skin and the pellets; too much body heat, and perspiration could cause them to start evaporating, and then she was sure to have some serious regrets. She was within the penthouse ballroom now. To her left, she saw the backs of the cheap plaster cell walls, and to the right, the beautiful crown molding, marble colonnades, and expansive views of the Bois de Boulogne at the end of the boulevard, the park's leaves bright with violent reds and golds. There had to be something—

And she spotted it: a box hung from the wall. An air raid kit. Complete with a gas mask.

Evangeline strapped the gas mask on, then kicked at the thin metal grating that concealed a ventilation shaft. The wide shaft, necessary to ventilate such a stuffy plaster and stone monstrosity as 84 avenue Foch, was perfect for her purposes. She braced herself with her legs, not trusting her hands to the painstaking process. Down one floor. Two. This should be the radio room. She peered through the vents.

"Carpenter hailing Magpie," a voice pleaded over the static. "Magpie, come in!"

"Listen," one of the operators said, rolling their desk chair toward a new outpost. "It's from the Wewelsburg outpost."

"But who is it?"

A fist squeezed around Evangeline's heart. God, she hadn't been ready to hear her voice, both gruff and unyielding, and small and desperate. But that—that made it all worth it.

She slid the cyanide pellets from her hand and pushed them through the ventilation grate, then pulled the lever to tug the grate shut.

By the time she'd recited most of a Rilke poem in her head, Evangeline heard the gasping, flailing sounds of men suffocating to death, their own body heat and respiration hastening the poison's conversion to gas. She had to wait another minute before she dared open the grate, despite the satisfying thumps the Gestapo radio operators' bodies made as they struck the tile floors. Bless the Germans for shoving their radio misinformation team into a veritable closet. Bless them doubly for outfitting that closet with an obscene number of locking mechanisms designed to protect its inhabitants from attacks from the *outside*.

Gas mask still in place, she kicked a wheezing, bloody-eyed Nazi away from the desk and snatched up the transmitter. "This is Magpie," she shouted in French through the muffled snout. "MAGPIE IS LISTENING, COPY, PLEASE!"

A silence far too lengthy, far too heavy with uneven static. One of the dying Gestapo officers reached out for her ankle, but she stomped on his hand as hard as she could. Blood spurted from his mouth; he didn't move again.

The radio crackled with a fresh transmission. "Magpie, I read you." Simone sounded like she was in tears. "Over."

Evangeline clutched the transmitter to her chest like it was a precious gem. "I need you to use a new encryption scheme. Use—" Her heart thudded. "Use the street number of the last place we went. Over and out."

Le Monocle. A heavy gamble. But it had to work—the Gestapo was still listening, somewhere. She spun the number dial to shift her own encryption frequency to match Le Monocle's street address.

"Are you here?" Evangeline asked, tossing all protocol aside.

"Reading you. It's a bit muffled. Do I even want to know—"

"No." She laughed, manic. "My God, no. You're . . . you're alive—"

"You're on our side," Simone countered.

In the background, a man spoke in English. "This is great and all, but we really need—"

"Right." Simone shifted to English as well. "Magpie, we're inside Wewelsburg. It's a war zone right now. German forces and—and something I can't even explain. But we've been compromised. We need a way out of Wewelsburg. We need the entire Wehrmacht off our ass—"

"I'm afraid your network's been blown," Evangeline said. "Georges-Yves—he gave them everything, the encryption scheme, all of it."

There was no missing Simone's Arabic swearing.

"But right now I have something even better available to me," Evangeline said. "If you can trust me, all right?"

"Yes," Simone said in a rush. "Please, yes."

"All right. Don't go anywhere. Keep the line open. I'll update you as soon as I can. Be safe until then," Evangeline said.

"Je t'aime," Simone muttered. Or something that sounded like it. Evangeline's heart skipped a beat.

"W-what did you say?" Evangeline asked.

"I said you're stubborn and resourceful and goddamned mad, and I couldn't be more grateful," Simone said. "Now hurry the fuck up."

Evangeline did.

CHAPTER THIRTY-FIVE

He'd told Liam to stay away, so of course the idiot had come barging in, pulling down half the shadow realm around him. If Daniel weren't so damned in love, he'd be furious. But in love or not, the monsters were here, and the Nazis had more control than ever.

It was his own fault. If he hadn't gotten captured, if he hadn't been so hell-bent on killing Kreutzer and Himmler and all the rest, he could have declared his vengeance done. He'd slit plenty of throats; the bloodstains under his nails would never scrub out. He'd never forget the hot stink of fascist blood spurting across his face, cooling far quicker than seemed possible. He'd atomized enough skull and brain matter and fussy little blood vessels with a point-blank bullet from their own guns. Was this what it meant to resist? Was this enough? Surely this was as much as any one man could do.

He could have buried his stolen knife deep in the tainted ground of Germany and fled, seeking better shores in Liam's arms. Rebeka had been right, just as she always was: at some point it was no longer vengeance, but wasted breath, throwing away his perfectly good life after countless deaths. The best revenge is living well, she'd said, even though he couldn't imagine there would be any life left for them after this.

The soldiers filed into the chamber, hollow shells of men in uniform, and lined up for Pitr and Kreutzer's infusions. They merged with the shadows until they were true otherworldly demons—now demons with claws and guns and coal embers for hearts that burned hatred for fuel. The two worlds were merging further still, the shadowscape of forest and mountains and demons' warrens piling up together like a mudslide inside Wewelsburg. And in the distance, something massive was rumbling awake.

The behemoth. The one that drank his regret and sorrow and bitterness, and reforged it into something even worse.

Daniel felt its magnetic pull as it straightened from its resting place, its dozens of faces dancing with images. They played like a film reel moving at half speed:

Rebeka running to him, telling him—lying to him—about Ari and their parents' fate as she begged him to run with her.

The stink of burning bodies as their train passed Chełmno, etched like acid in his mind.

Ernst's forceful laugh, sandpaper shredding up Daniel's hope, his love, his very skin.

The way it felt to walk down a street in Berlin: not as his own person, but as an avatar, a part of a larger whole, a whole that was hated, feared, judged. To never be seen as Daniel, but as just one of the many faceless enemies.

His fear of losing Rebeka, too—

Of losing himself—

Himself, the self he'd already lost long ago when he became nothing but a number in the Łódź ghetto—

Daniel closed his eyes and choked back a sob.

The worst thing you can do is be afraid, Liam had told him the first time he'd seen the shadow world.

But there were always worse things lurking on the horizon. Things he hadn't even known to fear. The world's capacity for cruelty and horror was so much more than he could ever grasp.

REBEKA

The behemoth was awakening on the horizon, trudging down the mountainside toward their ritual platform. Its face danced with all her failures, the ones her power had thrust upon her, those impossible choices: save her brother but sacrifice the rest of her family. Embrace this darkness but become a monster for it. Seek revenge on the people who did this to her and allow her brother to pay with his life.

She was tired of being strong for him while he tore himself to shreds. She was tired of carrying all her lies. She was tired of swallowing down anger—it sat like metal shavings in her gut. Wasn't she allowed to be angry, to grieve, to hate? She'd treated her calmness as the only way to shield herself from criticism, but all along, she'd carried these monsters inside. She shared their breaths. Heard their whispers and saw the truths they saw. This path, too—it had its uses.

She moved through the ashy forest like smoke, the thick, tarry smoke of burning tires, burning leaves, burning bodies. *Set me on fire,* she thought, *and I will choke you with my fumes.*

The faceless figure stood in her path.

Stop this, it whispered. *Stop them. Spare us—whatever of us is left.*

Rebeka dropped to her knees, palms upturned at her sides. "I don't know if I can."

If you cannot stop it, then our world will corrupt yours. As surely as yours destroyed us.

It fed her images of the hungry demons who poured into her world, harnessed to the Nazis' will. They'd been whipped into a frenzy once before, when Sicarelli had torn into their world and stolen what was not his. He'd chained the hungry demons to his will and used them to tear down the faceless creatures' once-thriving cities. He'd drained their energy, used it to fuel untold works. Now the Nazis wanted to pillage it even more, tugging away everything that made the shadow world whole—stealing its energy for themselves.

It is why the Nazis hunger, why they crave. They want someone to pay.

Rebeka knew that hunger too well; it throbbed in her brother's heart, sometimes even her own. "And what do you want?"

The faceless thing shrank back into the trees, into its ruins. *We want to be left alone.*

The shadow realm stretched and contracted around her. Time and space worked differently here—she'd already learned that much. Maybe she was too late. Maybe Liam was already dead, her brother already devoured—

Then she saw him, a boy alone in the center of the forest, the shadows a hungering predator around the tight shield he'd pulled around himself. He was trying to hold it off—trying to keep himself from succumbing to the corruption—but it was a losing battle. Sparks scraped against his shield from their claws and teeth.

She thrust her hands into the dry earth and focused, all that anger inside of her spilling free at last. Distant howls of rage as the creatures were flung away from him, scrambling and twisting to right themselves.

"You have to close the rift for good," Rebeka called to Liam as he raised his head. "It's the only way to stop this. To save yourself—and the rest of our world."

"I—I can't." He tightened the darkness around him like shadowy armor. "Someone has to control it—it's me or the Nazis." His eyes flashed bright with red. "Don't you see?"

"We can still stop them." She looked up: the behemoth was nearly upon them now, and she felt its pull, as though it were sucking the air from her lungs. "We can still fight the Third Reich—but we don't have to destroy both our worlds in the process."

Liam's shoulders started to fall, the armor thinning. But then, with a roar, he swelled, darkness surrounding him once more. "I have to control it! It won't let me break free—"

"You can never control the things you fear." God, but she knew that—her terror for her brother squeezed around her throat every single day, and no matter how she tried, she couldn't dissuade him from throwing his life away. "You can only choose not to be afraid."

Liam stared at her for a long moment. The behemoth was upon them now, looming over them, mouths stretched wide as it hungered for more and more. There were too many, so many more than she'd tried to handle before. For all her familiarity with the shadows, she still felt their pull, their demand that she sacrifice everything in the name of escaping from whatever terror gripped her. She couldn't let Liam look at it. If he looked, he'd surrender for sure.

"Liam," she shouted over the gale of wind and whispers and cries. "You can be so much more than this." She thought of her brother. Of a new day dawning. Of fear, and fighting through it anyway. "You already are."

He clenched his hands into fists, and she braced herself for a blow—but none came.

Instead he lowered the shield, exposed now, vulnerable. Embracing the fear.

She took his hand.

"You'll lose your connection," he warned. "And so will I."

She set her jaw. "Good."

EVANGELINE

By the time she'd called off the reinforcements to Wewelsburg, the guards were pounding at the door to the radio room. "One bloody minute," she muttered to herself. Her fingers flew over the radio dial as her eyes scanned the map of Europe to her right. A clear path. Simone and her friends needed a clear path north, toward Drieborg in the occupied Netherlands—and they needed an RAF pickup once they got there. And all of this was assuming they survived whatever chaos they were facing right now in Wewelsburg itself. From the wild, frantic reports she'd heard on the radio—everything from explosions and fire to monsters and spies—she was sure she didn't want to know.

"STAND DOWN, COMMAND POST DRIEBORG," she ordered in her best German, across the encrypted Wehrmacht lines. "Reports from Wewelsburg are part of an Allied disinformation plot aimed at sowing chaos. They want you to fire on your own men as they head into port."

"Who is this?" the operator at Drieborg answered. "What is your operating code?"

"Great question," Evangeline muttered to herself as she prodded one of the dead Gestapo radio operators with her foot. She dug around in his breast pocket and pulled out his codebook. "K-2496, Paris Headquarters."

"And you claim the reports of an attack on Wewelsburg are fabricated?"

Evangeline growled. "We did not spend the last three days torturing the details of this plot out of Resistance members here in Paris for you to not believe us, but if you want to fire on our own Gestapo operatives as they pass through Drieborg, then I suppose that is your prerogative."

A lengthy pause. "Understood, Paris Headquarters. We will allow them to pass."

Another thump on the door. She wrenched a sidearm free from one of the bodies, checked its ammunition, then tucked it into her belt. Just in case. Just two more calls to make before it was back into the ventilation shafts with her.

She dialed the frequency in and jotted a few quick notes to remind herself of the correct encryption scheme for the next call, then pressed the transmitter button.

"Alliance House, over," a pert secretary answered. A benign enough name for the headquarters of the Free French in London.

She took a deep breath. "This is the operator known as Magpie. And I have a sizable favor to ask."

DANIEL

A gale rolled over the mountain ridge like an avalanche, too far away to hear, but its devastating power was all too apparent. The rush of wind was enough to tear his skin right off. But he was facing it: he surrendered control, surrendered the very notion that he could ever cross a final name from his list, because the list would never stop growing. He had to choose that today—today could be a start.

And what a glorious new melody the wind was.

No more rolling meadows and sighing flutes; now was the tremolo torrent of the final act. Deep, carnal notes poured from his fingertips and throat. But he felt Liam beating beside him, the rich, brassy high notes to his darker foundation. He felt Rebeka all around him, the steady bass line that grounded him, kept the beat.

"Daniel."

They came together, all three of them.

That sweet, stupid boy who never stopped striving for more. More knowledge, more power, thinking all those things could give him peace when, just like everyone else, he was at the mercy of the rest of the world. His sister, surrendering whatever had given her glimpses of their fate. One girl unafraid of what the future might bring. One man against the tide. One could never be enough.

But two, or three, or a hundred—now he was starting to like those odds.

"You can't get rid of me, you know." Liam's voice was thick in his throat as he cut the ropes that kept Daniel suspended. Dropped him down into his arms. "I'll follow you anywhere."

Daniel's limbs were so weary, he was so weak, but he was alive. Alive, and able to live on, to be held by this boy, to live the life his family couldn't. He didn't have to throw himself away, too.

Daniel pulled Liam into a kiss, and for just that moment, both universes held their breath, the moment stretching forever in time.

Liam laughed, exhausted, as his forehead came to rest against Daniel's. Daniel smiled and wiped away a smear of soot from Liam's cheek. "You were right," he said. "We both deserve to live."

Reluctantly, Liam pulled away from him and turned toward the rest of the world, where Kreutzer and Pitr were frantically conducting their ritual to imbue their soldiers with shadow. Creating more and more monsters, an unending wave of hatred to send out across the earth. Daniel tapped into that deep well of sorrow inside himself, the one he'd tried to seal up with vengeance and rage. He hadn't mourned yet. He could do so now.

He met Rebeka's gaze, and they nodded to each other. For their parents, their brother. For their memories to be a blessing. For their neighbors and classmates and millions more they'd never met.

For every yellow star, every pink triangle, every nameless soul whose voice was deemed unnecessary by a harsh and careless world. They all deserved more than his anger. They deserved better than his tears, his futile stabs.

They deserved a real revenge.

"I have to close the rift," Liam said. "For good."

Daniel nodded, throat too dry to speak.

Then, so shyly and innocently it sent Daniel's pulse racing, Liam asked, "Would you help me?"

"I'd tear down every world with you."

PHILLIP

While Rebeka twisted shadows to her will, Phillip reshaped the course of electric currents. He had way more power to draw from now than his old frequency folder could have ever handled. It would have to be enough to seal off the universes for good.

For good, Phillip thought to himself, a strange smile crossing his face. He was in control of how his device was being used. Not Mr. Connolly, not his parents, not the US Army. He got to decide.

"Come on, Evangeline," Simone muttered beside him, waiting for her honey-voiced operative to call back in. She was supposed to be clearing some kind of escape route. It all sounded nearly impossible, but hadn't everything they'd done this past week? Phillip tightened a coil of copper around the final screw and sat back.

"Monsters."

Simone dropped the receiver as they both turned. The soldier was crawling along the floor, blood smearing a trail behind him. Phillip should have known his rank from the flash cards they memorized in basic (and later used for target practice), but his mind went blank. The soldier's leg dragged, mangled, behind him. And he was pointing a Walther P38 directly at Phillip.

"Call your Allied dogs off," he snarled. "Now."

Simone dove for her rifle where she'd left it on the other counter, but the soldier was too close—he batted it away. He fired a warning shot directly at Phillip's feet.

"Your days are done," Phillip said. "You're clinging to a past that never was and a future that never will be."

"They promised me . . . They promised me"—he coughed up blood—"power beyond imagining. That we should never again suffer the humiliation at the hands of those insidious Jews and Communists. And then—then the whispers grew louder, promising more—"

The Resistance channel sparked to life behind them. "Simone?"

"Your power is gone," Phillip said, new urgency beating hard against his ribs. They needed to answer that call. "The shadow world is closing, and it'll never hurt anyone again."

The soldier glowered at him, but all Phillip felt was sudden, manic laughter. He'd fought so hard to win approval from men like Mr. Connolly, from his professors and parents and friends. He'd been fighting so long to earn his place. And for what?

He didn't need it. He knew what he was capable of. The good he'd already done. And everything he could do still.

"Simone, are you there, darling? Please . . . please be there . . . over."

The soldier's gun wavered. "Please bring it back. Bring the shadows back . . . I can't hear the whispers anymore." He choked on a sob. "Kreutzer promised us . . ."

Simone seized the transmitter and pressed the button, her glare never leaving the soldier's face. "I'm here."

"Get your friends and drive to Drieborg as quick as you can. Two hours north of your position. My friends will be waiting for you there." Evangeline's voice trembled. "I love you, you mad, idiot girl. Over."

"I love you too, you imbecile." Simone managed not to choke. "Over and out."

"I need it." Tears poured from the soldier's hollowed-out eyes. "I need the shadows. Why did you take them away?"

The soldier turned the gun on himself and fired.

Phillip yelped as blood and bits of brain sprayed the radio operator's post, but then the soldier's body slid to the floor. Simone rushed forward and kicked the pistol from his hand anyway—just to be sure. With shaking hands, she approached Phillip and leaned against the desk.

"A-are we ready?" she asked.

He snapped a casing into place. "Just waiting for Rebeka's signal."

LIAM

Pitr and Kreutzer turned together as the behemoth's shadow fell across them. The behemoth stretched closer, and in its face they saw themselves.

"Liam—" Pitr gasped. "What are you—"

Liam stood now; the shadow beasts had shied away from him. They stepped back with low growls and plaintive whines, denied their feast.

"You told me once I was afraid of real power," Liam said, voice ringing out clear in the darkness. "And maybe that's true. But I'll face it anyway."

Dark tendrils wafted around Pitr—he was trying to fight back. But he was losing his grip. He was too afraid, and the behemoth fed on it, ripping away his control.

Liam stood taller. "Because I'm no longer afraid to let it go. Even if it means losing myself." And then he raked the blade across his palm.

"Shit," Liam wheezed. The blood was immediately pulled, forcibly, out of his skin—drunk up by the shadowy air all around them. If it took a sacrifice to open it, then maybe it took a sacrifice to close. If he could—Liam blinked, his mouth suddenly dry as his head went fuzzy from blood loss. If he could just hold out a little longer—

"Stop." Pitr lunged at him, tendrils flailing desperately. "Stop! These worlds are mine!"

The tendril struck Liam across the face and raked deep into him, fishhook-sharp. Liam cried, his concentration breaking. His vision was blurring, sparking with red and pain—he couldn't see from his left eye, and his hand was burning as the shadows drank more and more—

"What are you doing?" Pitr shrieked. "Stop this! You can't close it!"

"I can." Liam dropped to his knees. Blood marred his vision as the pain crackled through him. "If it takes every last drop of blood I have to give, I will."

"You won't," Pitr seethed. "You can't surrender it. You love it too much."

"That's—that's why I have to let it go."

Liam's mouth tasted cottony. Blood loss—he felt like he was swimming, like he was teetering on the edge of sleep. If he just let go—but he couldn't, not until the rift was closed, the counterfrequency and sacrifice sealing everything—

"I've got you."

Daniel's arms wrapped around Liam from behind, dragging him away from the vortex, from Pitr. "No matter what happens," Daniel said, "I've got you."

Rebeka strode forward, her eyes burning. "You don't have to do this alone."

She stopped before Pitr, darkness like a cold fire around her. Shadows bending. Retreating. Slowly, the tendril released its hold on Liam, leaving a slick smear of blood in its wake. Surrendering under the force of Rebeka's fearlessness.

With a howl, Liam covered his left eye where the shadow had raked across it.

Pitr fell backward, sucked into the roaring vortex of darkness—

"Now!" Rebeka cried, her words amplified by shadow, ringing throughout the castle, all the way up to the radio tower.

They breathed as one. United. Solid.

And then a wave of static hit them as Phillip unleashed the counterfrequency, cutting through the opening to the other realm.

The entire castle jolted like a generator coming back online. The mountain ridge grew hazy, as if viewed on a foggy day. The worlds were beginning to sever.

"Together," Rebeka said. "It's the only way we go forward."

Liam clenched his jaw. He felt Daniel's presence to his left, even if he could no longer see him. The throbbing pain in his left eye socket fueled him for one last act. One hand in Daniel's, the other in Rebeka's, the shadows pulsing in time with his agony, with his determination, as he forced the openings closed, and closed—

And then the shadow world collapsed in a torrent of dust and howling cries. Darkness ripped out of the soldiers where they stood, leaving only empty skins that crumpled to the ground. The behemoth tottered and fell, and then everything was static and cold.

Liam's power—gone. The other world—fading. His eye—ruined. He was empty, as empty as those soldiers had been. Everything that was special about him, everything that gave him control—

Nothingness.

Daniel squeezed his hand, grounding him to their world. Reminding him.

He was more than the power he'd stolen.

His hands sturdy in Daniel's and Rebeka's, they pushed back. Together, they'd transmuted into something more, pushing against the wave of anger and fear and sorrow. The shadows melted from the beasts where they had fallen; the retreating fog revealed Kreutzer's and Pitr's bodies. With the shadow gone, all that remained of Pitr was a lump of discarded skin. He was nothing without his hate.

The dusty book sparked and smoked on its pedestal, then suddenly burst into flame. Liam held tight as the wind raked at his face, stinging the empty socket of his left eye.

And then they were standing in the wreckage of the castle tower, only a single black shadowy rift before them, dancing in the air.

Liam looked at Daniel, the strain on his face. Liam forced himself to smile through the bloody haze.

Then he teetered forward and collapsed onto the shattered stone floor.

CHAPTER THIRTY-SIX

An unseasonably warm wind gusted in off the Thames, dancing across their faces as they mingled along the roof of 1 Dorset Square, the home of the Free French in London. But nothing warmed Simone like Evangeline's hand locked in hers, like the kisses they couldn't stop stealing when the others weren't looking. Only the occasional roar of RAF bombers punctuated the perfect peace, but even that noise was all too sweet—better them than the Luftwaffe attempting another blitz.

It had started with a goodbye Simone had been all too hasty to make and ended with a pair of Allied planes sweeping over the beaches of Drieborg to extract them. It ended with a girl awaiting them on the military runway, one hand in a sling, a tremor in her chin as her gaze locked with Simone's.

It ended with the bitter ache in Simone's belly vanishing all at once, her joints loosening, her heart pushing up into her throat as she wondered if she should forgive, could forgive, if everything that had happened made up for everything that had come before.

It ended with Simone pulling Evangeline into her arms, tears dripping into her blond hair, her breath returning to normal, a normal she hadn't felt in months.

Their blow to the SS High Command had been more symbolic than they'd hoped; Heinrich Himmler had been at a secret meeting in Berlin when his castle collapsed. But Kreutzer's mad experiments and his squadron of shadow-imbued soldiers were destroyed. Evangeline and Simone were now working directly for de Gaulle's Alliance and the British Special Operations Executive, fighting to save the surviving members of Georges-Yves Sauvage's dismantled network as they forged new ones. Much to Simone's amusement, Evangeline now wore the Lorraine Cross pinned proudly to her chest.

"And you didn't even have to steal it," Simone murmured into Evangeline's shoulder.

Evangeline tipped Simone's face up with a finger under her chin. "The Torturer of Troyes might argue that point with you."

"How unfortunate for him that he cannot."

Their sextet fell silent, and for a long minute it was only brassy Glenn Miller on the radio and the sounds of London around them, autumn tickling brightly colored leaves and whispering a warning of rain. For a long minute, it was only Evangeline's body warm against hers as they swayed to "Moonlight Serenade," as Rebeka nestled in Phillip's arms nearby, as Liam settled into Daniel's. No one but themselves to see them dance this way, to care who or what they were. They were heroes, they were Free French, they were survivors.

Qadar. Simone couldn't help but wonder if there was a preordained quality to what had happened. They'd found another world only to lock it back away; they'd grasped unfathomable power only long enough to rid themselves of it for good. If this was qadar, this river that flowed back to Evangeline, to all the possibility Simone once believed in before the world had battered her down, then she would gladly put her faith in this qadar and let it lead her as it liked.

The song faded from the radio set, and a BBC news bulletin started next. With a smile, Evangeline lowered Simone's hand, kissed the very tip of her nose, and the six of them gazed into the stars once more.

"Evangeline . . ." Rebeka's voice was soft and airy, nothing like the girl she'd been. This was the girl who'd slowly emerged in place of the old Rebeka over the past few weeks, heartiness enveloping whittled-down bones and brightness returning to her face. "Evangeline, I'm very sorry about your father."

Evangeline tightened beside Simone, that reckless saint armoring herself for battle once more. Only Simone had ever seen the soft flesh in the gaps between those plates. "It's what he deserved."

Ripped out of Vichy by the Gestapo. Awaiting questioning in Paris. And then a handsome leather belt from a shop on the Champs-Élysées, a kicked-over chair, a stench rising from the forgotten cell.

"I can miss the man without losing sight of the monster he was," Evangeline said, softer this time. "I can mourn his passing without being sorry that he's gone."

"I'll drink to that," Liam said. "To shitty fathers everywhere, and a world a little less shitty without them in it."

"To having just one world to manage," Daniel added as he wrestled the flask back from Liam for a sip.

Phillip raised his own flask. "Hear, hear."

"To an after," Rebeka said, and smiled up at the stars.

Tomorrow morning, a military plane would take Liam and Phillip home to America, and Rebeka and Daniel with them, sanctuary granted by Uncle Sam. Phillip couldn't stop talking about the business he wanted to start, with the help of his friends from school: building digital machines like his frequency folder, at least, after he'd overseen the creation of a handful for the US Army's use. Rebeka seemed all too happy to help him. Liam talked, hesitantly, about returning to Princeton to finish his master's work, and Daniel had mumbled something about music—that he longed to play again.

"I wish we could go home, too," Simone said, shrinking down against the roof. She hadn't even realized how much she'd wanted it until she said it out loud. "I miss the way Paris was before." Not all of it, of course—but enough that she could call it home.

Evangeline brought their joined hands up to her mouth and placed a gentle kiss on Simone's knuckles. Then her fingertips, each in turn. "The tide is turning. The Russians are putting up a fierce fight on the Eastern front, too. When this war's over, there'll be plenty of work there for you."

Simone turned toward her and savored the way her eyes gleamed in the moonlight. "Is that so?"

"The Germans are terrible guests."

Simone cast her gaze down. "I'm not sure anyone will give me the chance."

"The crack shot of Libération-Nord, one of the Wewelsburg Five? I think you might be surprised." Evangeline arched one golden eyebrow. "And if not, I'm sure I can demand it of de Gaulle."

Simone snorted and leaned closer to her. "That sounds terrifying."

"I'm good at terrifying."

"I know. I love seeing it."

Simone caught her face in her hands and drew her in for another kiss. She wondered if Evangeline could taste the darkness on her, the forest and the demons and the blood and gunpowder. It had suited her at the time. Her time spent on the trail, the rifle in her hand. She almost hated to be dragged back into this mundane world she'd left behind.

But there was plenty else that suited her as well.

She kissed Evangeline, her honey and sunlight girl, and the world and its dark shadows fell away.

CHAPTER THIRTY-SEVEN
LIAM

Liam pulled two chairs up in front of his mother and sat down with his hands clenched tight.

"Hi, Ma." With a weak smile, he gestured toward his eye patch. "Look, we match."

A gray eye stared back at him. At least today it tried to focus on his face. He wondered what she saw when she looked at the eye patch, at the scar that stretched from either side of it, the split skin filled with a blackness like volcano glass. That he'd suffered, the same as she had? Or that, like her, he'd also survived?

He liked to think the latter. "I'm sorry I haven't checked in on you for a while. As you might have heard, there's a war. And I had to do my part."

Her throat bobbed with an involuntary swallow. An eyelash was perched on her hollow cheekbone. Liam reached forward to brush it away and let his thumb linger for just a moment. How long since he had last touched his mother, held her hand, cared for her himself? It had always been easier to pay for the nurses to do it, even if it meant eight more hours working in the boiler room or reshelving books in the stacks.

"I—I had to go away for a while. Had to get my head right. I thought if I could be strong enough, then no one could ever take anything from me."

He wasn't sure when he'd started crying; he only felt it when the first tear slid down his chin. He couldn't do this. He couldn't look her in the eye when everything he'd done—splitting worlds apart, unleashing monsters, conquering them, destroying the Third Reich's access to it all—when none of it could undo what one drunken bastard with a tire iron had wrought.

Then Daniel was leaning over him, brushing the tears from his cheek. Liam sucked in a breath and caught Daniel's hand in his own. Met his gaze, dark and heavy with everything they'd endured, everything yet to come.

Please, Liam mouthed. *Sit with me.*

Daniel gratefully sank into the other chair. Did he imagine it, or did his ma look Daniel's way?

"You were right about a lot of things, Ma, but wrong about some. It's okay, cause I was, too." Liam squeezed Daniel's knee. "But I'm going to be here for you now. We won't have to worry anymore."

Yes—she was definitely looking at Daniel now. Did he imagine it, or was the good side of her mouth trying to curl into a smile?

"Ma, this is Daniel. He's very important to me. I—I think I might be in love with him." He glanced shyly at Daniel, cheeks reddening. "He's an idiot like me sometimes, but I let him get away with it."

Daniel scoffed at that. "You're one to talk."

"The movers'll be here soon, Ma. Princeton wasn't so good for you. *I* wasn't so good for you here. The place they're putting us up, it's gonna be much better. For all of us."

He still couldn't quite believe it: the man in the suit on the army plane, the paperwork already drawn up. Special research project division, he'd said. No demons required.

A dangerous path, to be sure. He wasn't sure if he trusted the government to walk it alone, the fuzzy spaces between their universe and the rest. But maybe, if he was a part of it from the start, he could guide it. Maybe he could set things right.

"We're going back to the city," Liam said. "I know you miss its sounds." He leaned closer toward his mother. "And I'll be there with you. Every step of the way."

It was true, what Rebeka had accused him of—and accused Daniel of, too. He hadn't really believed in an after. He'd left money and instructions for her care, but those would have eventually run out. He'd left classwork unfinished, debts unpaid. He'd been looking for another world, another power source, but he hadn't stopped to think about how it fit into his life.

Well, he didn't need it to fit. He could change his life all on his own.

He squeezed his mother's good hand, and she returned it. It was enough, from her.

They stepped out onto the sunny afternoon streets of Princeton, where Rebeka and Phillip waited outside. They'd been speaking in hushed tones together, and Liam didn't miss the color that touched Rebeka's now-full cheeks beneath her hat brim as she straightened up at her brother's approach. She looped her arm in Phillip's as Liam led them to their car.

"How was she?" Rebeka asked.

Phillip kissed Rebeka's cheek, then opened the back door for her. They all climbed in, Phillip and Rebeka in the back, Daniel and Liam up front, and Daniel chugged the motor to life. Liam caught a glimpse of himself in the mirror as Daniel adjusted it, the black scar glistening with Pitr's parting gift, and he wondered, just for a moment, what lurked under it—but it was better locked away.

"She seems content. C'mon." He twisted around to grin at Phillip. "We're gonna be late. Gotta meet with our new lab rats."

"We're going to get into all kinds of trouble on the government dime, aren't we?" Phillip asked.

"Yeah. That's kind of the plan."

Liam slid his hand into Daniel's, and their fingers locked together over the clutch as he eased them down the road.

"To whatever the future brings," Daniel said gently.

Liam squeezed Daniel's hand back. Before, when he'd thought of the future, it had consisted of being better, being more. Now the future had been blown wide open; one world was quite enough.

ACKNOWLEDGMENTS

This book would not have been possible without the brilliant guidance of my agent, Thao Le; my editor, Liza Kaplan; and the rest of the Philomel/Penguin team, especially Talia Benamy and to cover designer Kristie Radwilowicz. Special thanks also goes to promotional material artist Monica Borg, and to Ammi-Joan Paquette.

My unending gratitude goes to sensitivity readers Herb Boyd, Meriam Metoui, Ellen Goodlett, and Talia Benamy, and to the staff at the Jefferson Reading Room at the Library of Congress, the Library and Archives at the United States Holocaust Memorial Museum, the University of Tulsa Special Collections (archivist Melissa Kunz especially), and the Greenwood Cultural Center.

To my relentless cheerleaders, colleagues, co-conspirators, and accountabilibuddies: Dahlia Adler, Katherine Locke, E. K. Johnston, Jessica Spotswood, Caroline Tung Richmond, Ellen Goodlett, Robin Talley, Tara Sim, Emily Duncan, Miranda Kenneally, Stephanie Kroll, Bria LaVorgna, Alex de Campi, Charisse Linsangam, and more.

To all the amazing fandom friends I've made: Saana, Meghan, Clare, Katie, Shiro, Christel, and everyone in the NWY project; V, Q, Hya, Decas, Grey, SIGF, Frog, Minty, Jano, Steph, Rache, Schu, Goop, Blue, Helen, Charlie, Zach, Star, Nox, Lois, Ruse, Donnie, and everyone in the ToFS project. Knowingly or not, you've all encouraged me to keep writing and keep finding new stories to tell.

To everyone working tirelessly to document history, fight against fascism and oppression, and shed the harsh light of truth in every dark corner, thank you. You are not alone.